MARS
UNDERGROUND

Other Books by
William K. Hartmann

The American Desert
Astronomy: The Cosmic Journey
The Cosmic Voyage
Desert Heart
Moons and Planets

With Ron Miller
Cycles of Fire
The Grand Tour
History of Earth
Out of the Cradle

Coedited by
William K. Hartmann
In the Stream of the Stars
Origin of the Moon

William K. Hartmann

MARS
UNDERGROUND

TOR®

A Tom Doherty Associates Book
New York

MARS UNDERGROUND

Copyright © 1997 by William K. Hartmann

All rights reserved, including the right to reproduce this book, or portions thereof, in any form.

This book is printed on acid-free paper.

Edited by James Frenkel

A Tor Book
Published by Tom Doherty Associates, Inc.
175 Fifth Avenue
New York, NY 10010

Tor Books on the World Wide Web:
http://www.tor.com

Tor® is a registered trademark of Tom Doherty Associates, Inc.

Design by Basha Durand

Library of Congress Cataloging-in-Publication Data

Hartmann, William K.
    Mars underground / William K. Hartmann.
        p.   cm.
    ISBN 0-312-86342-X
    I. Title.
PS3558.A7143M3   1997
813'.54—dc21   97-1398
                                                          CIP

First Edition: July 1997

Printed in the United States of America

0   9   8   7   6   5   4   3   2   1

Copyright Acknowledgments

Acknowledgments

With thanks to diverse friends
who were foolish enough to encourage me.

. . . a country and its landscapes perhaps don't fully exist until they've been written about—until poets and novelists create them.

C. J. Koch, author of
The Year of Living Dangerously,
quoting poet Vivian Smith,
from "Crossing the Gap," 1987

Prediction is always difficult,
especially of the future.

Danish proverb cited by Niels Bohr,
quoted by Walter Moore in
Schrödinger: Life and Thought, 1989

Mars in 2031

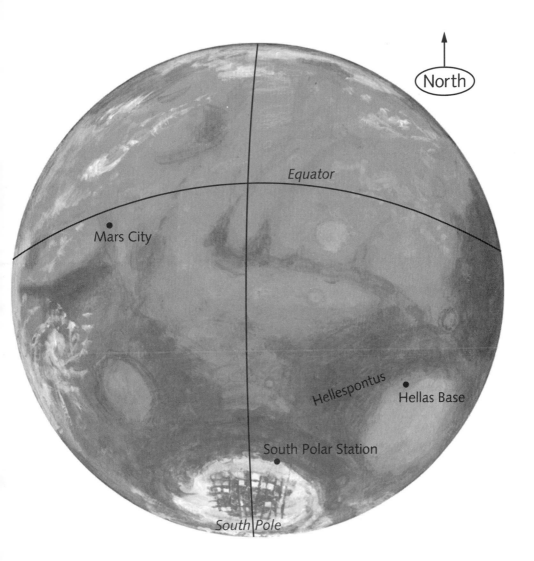

Nothing that is can pause or stay;
The moon will wax, the moon will wane,
The mist and cloud will turn to rain,
The rain to mist and cloud again,
Tomorrow be today.
—Henry Wadsworth Longfellow,
Kéramos, 1878

Prologue

The plane banks over the blue sea and the white waves, and the deep green blanket that cloaks the mountainsides.

She gets off the plane at Hilo's ancient airport, and the cool air smells of plants and humidity. Home at last.

The other end of the universe from Mars.

Upon her arrival back on Earth, during her fifteen minutes of fame, she had been called by Newsnet, "the woman who brought it all crashing down." The phrase had won her respect in Tokyo, in Moscow, and in certain hallways along the Potomac, but she knows that in the crucial hours on Mars, the actions that changed two worlds were not hers alone. Besides, respect in Earth's gray, frenzied capitals seemed no longer to matter. Here at home, amidst the perfumed greenery of the islands, people still acted as if the ancient ways of pleasure might, just possibly, be more important than the ways of power. The thought intensifies her questions about her own life.

The greenness and wetness shield her from the urgent needs of men now far away, but still in her mind. Carter. Philippe. All of them on that Oz-like red world, following their brick roads that they were laying ahead of them, one brick at a time. And here, of course, Tomas is waiting for her.

Later, she and Tomas make frantic love, Tomas betraying a hint of suspicion. But the love of Tomas is different from the love of Philippe which was different from the love of Carter. They are all different, men. Philippe had said she was sincere but not honest, and the nature of the distinction still goes around and around in her mind. Yet here, among the soft plants and the warm waters that fall from the sky like liquid caresses, she feels free.

She settles in, visits her aunt in the hundred-year-old house under the banyan tree on the hills of Ka'u. She sits on the wooden veranda and looks across the land toward the sea. Do they still have verandas anywhere else in the United States? The mainland is a teeming mess, consumed by the drought, the debt, the lottery, this year's sports scandal, the crisis *du jour*, and everyone's doomed quest to be rich, famous, a player, the winner—or at least to acquire the facade of *being something*; here, she takes time to listen to insects pursuing their business. She walks on the black beach at Ninole cove and stares at the slimy creatures in the tide pools. They have climbed over wet rocks like these for eons beyond human memory, without caring whether other species conquered the land or went still further, beyond the sky.

She is surprised that she feels no impatience in this quiet island life. She feels renewal, re-creation. Wonders if some day she will go back. Back to what? She is not sure she knows how to answer that. What was it she had sought out there?

Being on the island again makes her aware of cycles. Liquid water, for example: Earth's unique attraction. Mainlanders seem to believe that water flows in rivers because water's nature is to do so. But islanders see the whole truth before their eyes. Water babbles down from the mountains across the black lava rocks and dry grassy plains and into the sea; the only way it can get back to the mountains is for the ocean waters to be lifted through the air, to recondense, to fall on the broad summits, where it can begin the cycle again.

She feels part of a vast cycle like that, a molecule of water at one stage of its history. On this island, she sees that even the land has cycles. Twenty new acres of lava have flowed out into the sea since she left; down the coast, an old black lava cliff, where she played as a child, has fallen back into the sea. And she has been to another planet and back.

Still later, there is her tiny son and she is happy for a while, content that she has been, after all, true to herself.

One day a piece of mail arrives from Mars. It's on actual paper, with handwriting, months old. So characteristic of what Carter would dream up. Was he afraid to contact her in real time?

She sits on the veranda, and tries to think how to answer him. She gazes at the distant ocean far below, lost in haze on the humid horizon. Everything is beyond that horizon, and yet she is here and content. For now.

That evening, she checks out "Mars" on the net. Newsnet explains that Mars is reaching the point in its own orbital cycle where it is close to Earth. It is shining in the darkening east as the twilight settles in, and she goes down the road to the ancient *heiau* above Ninole cove to watch it. She sits on one of the prehistoric rock walls as waves send white foam crashing over the rocks below. Salt spray accumulates on her skin.

Mars' amber beacon is the brightest light in the part of the sky above the sea. Strange. In ancient tales of quests, the hero travels to distant empires and then escapes home, leaving the distant land far behind forever. In her case, the distant land has followed her around the sun and watches her balefully from the sky across the sea. With a shock, she realizes she will never escape it. At the right season, it will always be within direct sight. Wars and carnage, craft and madness, lust and spite; Philippe taught her Tennyson's prescient poem about Mars and Earth. *They* remain there, living their lives in that point of peaceful light: friends, lovers, enemies.

It is unbelievable to her: a glowing dot containing the whole world where she had lived, a world that already seems an amber dream. She clambers down to the tide pools in the rough lava at the edge of the sea, and looks for a reflection of Mars' red sparkle on the water. She would like to see the sea and sky, Mars and Earth, tied together by that reflection. It would make some kind of link. But the planet does not glow quite brightly enough; it is too far away and the sea is too restless.

BOOK 1

Kilroy in Hellespontus

... each tale is but a fragment of a tale
—the tale of mankind's history.
—Stephen Vizinczey,
An Innocent Millionaire, 1985

1

Morning. So, was he really going to keep driving west, after all, into the unknown Martian desert? Stafford smiled to himself.

Stafford's dune buggy churned across the ocher sands of Hellespontus. In the immense empty wasteland, the buggy looked like an insignificant blue insect crawling across a dusty parking lot. The dust kicked up by its big wheels spurted into the air and fell away slowly, sometimes twisted by uncertain gusts of wind. Along the horizon, the hazy sky was exactly the same color as Stafford's creased Anglo flesh. But high above, wasn't that a trace of blue he had been seeing in the last year or so?

They were a long way from anything, Stafford and his dune buggy. Alone. Five thousand klicks from Mars City. Three-fifty from little Hellas Base, hotbed of desert dreams. There was no road. There had been no road for more than a day.

Virgin territory, Stafford noted to himself. Well, it wasn't the first time. Old Man of the Desert, they called him. Not for nothing. He looked at the forbidding, unblemished vista. The smile was still on his lips.

The blue buggy churned on toward . . . something. Squinting, Stafford pushed his square, weathered face forward against the front window, feeling his thick white hair and even his white mustache bristle against the glass. It was as if he were trying to be out there, to be part of the landscape. The thing he was searching for would be up ahead, somewhere. He didn't know what it would turn out to be, but he knew it was there, and he had his suspicions.

When he first started out from Hellas Base on Thursday, he surprised himself by spending as much time looking out the back window as the front, watching for possible pursuers. This unexpected reaction intrigued him. Paranoia? Guilt setting in? Still, he knew that people were interested in his actions. The young engineers and scientists gossiped about him. "So where's Old Man Stafford off to this time?" It was like the Old West: when a grizzled prospector set out purposefully into the hills, the rumor-mongers said he was after some secret treasure. Well, this time they were right. Doubly so. Soon they would learn how right they were.

By virtue of nothing more than the clock's steadfast ticking, Stafford had become one of the seniors in a rusty world of young technicians.

Martians, they were pleased to call themselves. Well, Stafford had the best claim to the title. Old Man Stafford, the desert rat, the codger, who spent his retirement searching for . . . well . . . things. "Wonderful things." As a boy, back in California, Stafford read about Howard Carter's words when the archaeologist first peered into King Tut's tomb. "What do you see?" his team asked him. "Wonderful things," he said. It applied to Mars, Stafford thought.

He peered through the dust-streaked glass. Ahead, to the west, a backlit haze of dust reduced distant, eroded mesas to pale fantasy castles. They did not shimmer. The air was too thin and too cold. The castles stood, stolid and still, two-dimensional in the luminous haze. Far cry from the Berkeley cafés and the last redwood forests, old man. To a lot of the farmers, watching holeo images in their worn armchairs Earthside, Mars seemed only a landscape of desolation. Red rocks, black rocks, and dust. To Stafford, it was a new world full of Wonderful Things. Interesting oddities. Martian El Dorados. The things desert rats had sought for a thousand years.

The spartan horizon ahead was a clean, pale line that no one had ever crossed.

It's always folks from green and wet places like northern California who end up loving the desert, he mused. Lawrence out of Oxford. Van Dyke out of New Jersey or someplace.

Well let them call him what they wanted. In his twenty-one years on Mars he had had his fill of the Engineering Corps, the Agriculture Experiment Stations, the Clarke Project, the hundred other progressive projects of the clean, keen greenhorns who kept pouring into Mars City, intent on bringing it above what they called "critical mass." Critical mass for survival—that's what they were talking about. The minimum population and supporting equipment to make a self-sustaining colony. Critical mass was a shiny, polished concept from the gray halls of the universities and space agencies on Earth, but it had its dark side—a side discussed only in hushed conversations among the planners who hung out during late hours in what passed for dim bars in Mars City: they would have to reach critical mass before they could survive a catastrophic shutdown of the supply lines from Earth—a shutdown that could happen any day because of an economic collapse Earthside, a spacecraft disaster at Crystal City or Phobos, or worse. Ordinary Martians laughed it off. But some of the planners thought it might happen. Look what had happened already in Kazakhstan and Lima.

Stafford's opinion of Earth was that no disaster was too unlikely to contemplate, given the way things terrestrial were going. The farmers, as Martians called them, had a truly Ptolemaic lack of imagination: they still thought of Earth as the center of the solar system. Rich, ravaged, unheedful Earth.

Stafford was all for Martian self-sufficiency—an exciting goal—but he grew more and more disillusioned with the way the greenhorns and uncivil engineers were bent on transforming the rusty old planet not into a new Mars, but into a streamlined suburb of Earth, full of transplanted farmers and mall people.

The thing of it was, no one knew how many people and machines it would take to reach critical mass on Mars. Some experts said a population of three thousand, plus nuclear generators, soil processors. Others said five or ten thousand, plus redundant infrastructure; the whole urban mess. For every Ph.D., an equal and opposite Ph.D.

Martians hoped the present population was enough. Three thousand people—putting Mars City somewhere in limbo between a research outpost and a functioning town. Six thousand Martians in all, if you counted Phobos, Hellas, and the Polar Station. Too many for Stafford. The old days of basic, mission-driven exploration had ended. Politics was starting to rear its ugly head. You found yourself doing something because someone said so, not because it had to be done.

He glanced all around the horizon again. Nothing yet. He craned his neck to peer out the back window. Nothing behind either. The desert was empty. "Clean" was the word Lawrence had used in Arabia.

Hours later, the blue beetle was still crawling along. In the north, the summer sun had crossed the meridian and was sinking toward the west. Afternoon. It ought to be hot. Of course, it wasn't. Stafford didn't let himself think about how cold the air was outside.

He spotted something ahead projecting above the sand. It was dark-colored, not bright as he'd anticipated. He drove closer.

It turned out to be only a curious rock formation, sticking up like an African anthill. It looked to be some odd-shaped boulder, exhumed by the winds, sculpted and undercut by the blowing sand. As he drove by, he foresaw that in another thousand years it would be gone.

Once upon a time, his heart had beat fast every time he saw an odd exposure of old rock. They were windows into the past. When he first came to Mars, he had been seeking his own holy grail. He had wanted to be the one to confirm the widespread theory that life had evolved far beyond the measly microbes that had been reported—on again, off again—since the turn of the century. Given the clement conditions geologists had established for the earliest phase of Martian history, it should have been true. From the work of Krennikov and Boikova, it seemed a small step to conclude that once life got started, it had a thousand nonconvergent paths to follow—different paths in each environment, on each clement planet. Long ago, during the mysteriously moist early millennia of the planet, when the air was thick and water ran on the surface, Martian RNA and DNA should have gone off in directions never seen on Earth. He, Stafford, would be the one to find the evidence.

For years, Stafford and his cronies had hoped that they would find rich bioorganic pockets and advanced fossil forms, sealed deep in protected strata since the beginning of time, proof of their catechism, of carbon chemistry's quirky ability to adapt. They had wanted an icon, more than a rational test of a chemical theory, something they could hold in front of the cameras and proclaim, "See, it can happen anywhere in the universe. We're not alone. Copernicus and Darwin were right: we're not special."

No luck.

But he'd had his day. Dr. Alwyn Stafford—the father of a tantalizing but disappointing new consensus: ancient wet Mars had produced no more than a few stunted microbial forms, starting three, maybe three and a half billion years ago. The earliest examples seemed to be found in the ancient southern highlands. Eventually, with the atmosphere thinning, all life-forms in the surface layers had died and were buried. On the third day they had not risen from the dead, and for the rest of Martian time the arid surface soils had been sterile, while the primordial atmosphere dissipated, albeit with spasms that had left now dry riverbeds. Some of the microbes apparently hung on in buried strata, but there was little evolution because they were in static, frozen environments. And across the entire planet, the surface soil was sterile, thanks to the planet's unkind lack of an ozone layer. Seasonal dust storms churned the soil every year and exposed dust grains to the sun's ultraviolet light, sterilizing and resterilizing them, breaking up any group of carbon atoms that might have an idea of getting together for a fling . . .

That was Martian history in a nutshell, and a desiccated nutshell at that. The new dogma, which he himself had established—Stafford, biologist of the dead world as they had called him. How many hours had he spent in a spacesuit under the deceptively bright Martian sky to convince the world of that uninspiring bottom line?

Stafford regretted none of those days. His teams had dug and they had drilled. They had penetrated the permafrost. There had been that layer, deep in the south polar strata near the three-billion-year level, with its enhancement of organic molecules and microbial forms. They had labeled it just another local anomaly. Still, there had always been that next drill hole, that next spot that might be different.

Finally, Stafford's colleagues, who sat in their comfortable labs on Earth and served on review committees, had had enough. They declared him a member of several academies, and virtually shut down the BioExploration labs in Mars City. At the same time, they raised the budgets for the atmospheric experiments, which—according to the hype—were supposed to test some new theories on relieving Earth's smog. Stafford had retired in a sort of muted glory. Nice work, old chap. Send us your memoirs.

Stafford's career had left a mystery, really. Why hadn't Martian life gone further? Why hadn't it demonstrated some adaptation to Mars' increasingly arctic climate? Was life less resilient than they had thought? Was biology, after all, rarer in the universe than scientists had come to believe? Stafford was beginning to think he might see some answers to those questions, over the horizon. But for now he had to concentrate on matters at hand.

Always the next Cibola, the next El Dorado.

Stafford had never been discouraged. He had seen more of Mars than anyone. He had seen strange sunsets in the land of the Thoats, far beyond the wildest dreams of Percival Lowell and Edgar Rice Burroughs and Ray Bradbury. The new kids coming to Mars from consumerland—they had never read the Martian classics. Mars for them was just the latest hi-tech testbed, an exotic gig to put on your résumé, in the desperate gamble to establish yourself among the haves, when you returned to Earth.

For Stafford it was different. There was the desert. His desert. The empty craters; the whistling chasms whose fluted rocks sang faintly with the Martian wind, where you could get away from people. Here, you could scream as loud as you liked and no one would come running. On Earth, there was no place left like that; there was always some damned monitoring system or satellite. . . .

Truth to tell, Stafford's desert jaunts had generated some notoriety and income that allowed him a few luxuries beyond the frugal existence he had imagined for his late years in Mars City. The ice caves: he had made money selling his holeos of the peculiar crystalline formations. An Earth-side image bank had marketed his famous close-up of lightning flashing among the dust devils. And a wealthy collector in L.A. had paid well for the biggest crystal of specular hematite in the solar system. Who would have believed anyone would be crazy enough to pay for shipping that one back! Some nouveau riche MacLaine, she was, with money to burn and an idea that Martian crystals were even better than Earth crystals in terms of aura or whatever the hell it was they talked about in their sad, upscale churches.

The income was nice, but the trouble with the notoriety was that people kept an eye on him, wondering where he was off to next.

His wife, now gone, used to rail at him about the dangers. He saw it as no different from the pioneer days on Earth. His grandfather had opened up new trails in the uranium fields of the Mexican desert, traveling alone and risking death in 110-degree temperatures. He himself risked dying in −110-degree temperatures. What was the difference? The eager Reaper strikes pretty fast when the temperatures go two sigma beyond the green zone.

Anyway, he and his grandfather both had their common sense and their radios. And life always has an element of danger, he thought with grim satisfaction.

Danger or not, life had been all right since he had retired from the new Mars rat race. Not "retired," really. Detached himself. Become independent. During his official career in BioExploration, he had failed to achieve his goal, but he had failed magnificently enough to acquire clout.

Now the big balloon tires were throwing phantom minarets of powdered yellow limonite into the thin air behind him. On the left was a distant orange cliff, soft in the haze-muted sun. Its base was undercut as if dwarfs had carved out a shelter. He visualized erosion by the sting of saltating sand grains, driven by the wind. Ahead to the left the horizon was broken by a crater rim three kilometers across, looking like the scar left by an unseen hand that had punched its way out of the interior of Mars. Stafford glanced at the orbiter photo pasted to the dashboard. Crater on the left. Check.

In spite of the fact that the buggy was a tiny beetle in the empty desert, Stafford had faith in it. The redundant systems were reliable, and the cargo space between the EN-cells and the air processors was loaded with extra airpacs and water.

Stafford still hadn't played his last card. Lately he had been going around telling his friends that there were always more mysteries to discover, a little farther out in the desert. He had hinted he was on the track of something unusual, out in Hellespontus, in the rim country northwest of Hellas Base. He had arranged for his friend Carter to see him poring over the orbital photos. He had needed to plant certain ideas in their minds, so they could reconstruct it later. He had needed to set the stage for his next adventure.

It was amazing that he had ever talked his way into being allowed to take a buggy out on his own. But Stafford had his clout and Braddock, who was in charge of such things at Hellas, was an unrepentant good old boy. In the early days, Stafford had been the first to complain about good old boy networks, but now he saw no contradiction in using systems he couldn't dismantle. Operating in that strange Martian limbo between official bureaucracy and Getting Things Done, Braddock and Stafford were both willing to bend the rules in the direction of the latter.

Good thing, too. It had established the climate that allowed them to pursue what his friends—his supposed friends—had called their "special operation." He had agreed to go along with it, but he had his own motives, too. Well, don't think about that now, he told himself. Do this one step at a time. Concentrate on today's objective.

Where was the damn thing? He thought: If I'm ever going to find it, I've got to find it on this trip. In another year everything will be different, and nobody'll care about the old Mars.

Damn kids, monkeying around with a planet as if it were a toy. Spraying graphite from Phobos onto the polar ice to make it evaporate and create more air! Damnedest foolishness he had ever heard of. Still, he had to admit that the Clarke Project had driven the air pressure up to twenty millibars at Mars City. Enough to allow the geothermal sites to produce occasional puddles of liquid water instead of mere puffs of invisible vapor when deposits of permafrost occasionally melted. They had doubled the air pressure that existed when people first came to Mars—when the air had been too thin to allow liquid water anywhere but in the deepest canyons. So the engineers were making progress.

They said their work was as natural as nature. As more CO_2 snow melted at the pole, more sunlight would be absorbed by the resulting CO_2 gas in the atmosphere. The more sunlight was absorbed, the warmer it would get. The warmer it got, the more snow melted. Feedback. The greenhouse effect. Advective something or other.

If it worked, the ancient rivers would run again for as long as humans endured here. It would rain, and erosion would wipe out any relics of the previous warm period.

If it worked. Stafford took pride in a measure of cynicism. He had bet some friends back at Mars City that before they got to one hundred millibars, and before people could start going out without full pressure suits, some disaster would occur that they hadn't foreseen. He banked on Murphy's Law.

They weren't all so bad, the kids. Carter Jahns, for instance, was the best, in spite of his title. Assistant Director of Environmental Engineering for Mars City, or some such bullshit. Anyway, he worked mostly on the indoor environment, not the crazy schemes for modifying the planet itself. Besides, Carter had something that set him apart, a quiet receptiveness to new ideas. A lot of these kids, they came around to ask you about the early days, but they never listened. By the time you started an answer they were on to something else. The way most of them had grown up, the universe was ninety percent fantasy constructs, and they had trouble recognizing that reality was the real thing, the thing that was left over when the cyberspace machines were turned off.

From his vantage point of career endgame, Stafford felt he could see things about these kids that they themselves could not make out. He knew where they were in their life processes, and where they would go. Carter Jahns, he could tell, was different from the others. He had a mind like a book still being written. While molded in the assembly lines of Earth, Carter had been left mercifully incomplete, as if there were still something in him that could be shaped by Mars. Carter didn't know how good he was; he still had the potential to profit from a mentor. Well, we'd see about that. . . .

Stafford had asked him once when he was planning to go back to Earth. "Don't know." A short answer but it spoke volumes about him. He didn't say much, but you had the idea that he was thinking about things. Maybe he thought too much. Maybe that's why Stafford had adopted him as a friend. A protégé, in fact.

It took Stafford a while to accept this. Carter was his protégé, his only confidant among the younger set. In Stafford's own mind—hell, out here in the desert he could finally admit it—he had adopted Carter as the son he had never had, whether Carter recognized it or not.

For Carter's generation, the idea of ancient advanced Martian life-forms had gone up in smoke—a puff of sterile Martian dust. There were no more attempts to sterilize outdoor equipment or quarantine the outdoor environment. As the air thickened, they all wanted to get on with their cherished damned planetary engineering. There'll be litter all over the place in ten years, Stafford thought; freeways in a hundred.

He was getting carried away.

Anyway, he had come to realize that civilization is merely a process of destroying history. In the last century, civilization had "risen" to a new height: gone were the last places on Earth where you could find thousand-year-old arrowheads or fragments of pots lying where they had broken. The last ancient spots had been plowed under, paved, pulverized by bull-dozers, and picked over by mindless off-road-vehicle enthusiasts to whom no oddment was too sacred to take home, to put on their dusty mantel-pieces, to forget. The last neolithic caves in Europe had been cleaned out by sub-teenagers with robo-pacs. The last arrowhead collections in America were stored in attics of grandparents recently deceased, and were being thrown out by heirs too busy to check the contents of musty old cardboard boxes.

Of course, there was the question of whether today's crazy boondoggle trip would change everything. . . .

The cold evening was fast approaching. The low sun was sinking and the sky taking on its strange evening pallor of gray. Longer shadows made it hard to pick his way among the rocks. Soon the sun would turn into a red dot on the horizon and fade away like an old soldier.

Still nothing in sight, and it should have been around him somewhere.

Suddenly the apricot horizon tilted precariously.

"Damn."

He jerked the vehicle to a full stop as it slumped precariously to one side. He had let his musings distract him from his driving. He had let the right front wheel bog down into a pocket of soupy dust.

"Damn, damn, damn," he muttered to himself again. No matter how many times he had faced an unexpected situation out here in the desert, the familiar shot of adrenaline hit him like a kick in the stomach. Always there was that suppressed truth; you're out here alone. Death is always walking along behind you in your tire tracks.

He forced himself to pause until the adrenaline surge had passed. These little dust pockets were strange. You could hardly detect them in advance. They were betrayed only by a subtle smoothness, like the glassy-surge "footprint" of a whale on the surface of the ocean. There were stories of people hitting big ones with all four wheels and having to be pulled out. No one knew how they formed.

Cautiously he put the buggy in reverse. Holding his breath, he fed power to the other three wheels. He gave them a little nudge. The engine whined. He could feel the springy wheels turn, the balloon tread digging in. The traction held. The buggy lumbered back onto firm ground.

But the shadows were getting too long to continue his search.

Night.

Far from Mars City, far from Hellas Base, Stafford had parked to wait out the bitter hours until dawn on Sunday morning. Strange, he had "pulled off the road," into a little alcove in the lava. Habit. You didn't block the road. But in reality, there was no road. There were only his own tracks, hundreds of klicks from the nearest human.

Night on Mars was so damn dark and cold and lonely. It made you realize you were out on a limb. If only Mars had a moon as big as Earth's. Moonlight, at least, would be a comfort. How would the red landscape—those desolate orange dunes out there and the goblinlike dark rocks—look in the eerie pallor of a full moon, when everything was reduced to greenish-gray?

Night was the most frightening time in the deserts of Mars. Only the thin walls of the buggy between him and the black coldness, which must surely be populated by unimaginable ghosts from the ancient past of the dying planet. Or worse yet, he often thought, a night in a desert so foreign and sterile that it offered no wandering souls to keep sad or menacing vigil; a night impassive and uncaring, with no ghosts at all.

He rolled his head over against the cold, curved window and looked up at the stars. Alpha and Beta Centauri. Dim patches of the Magellanic Clouds almost obscured by reflections of the softly glowing dashboard lights. The night sky in the Martian south always disoriented him. Try as he might, he could not get used to a sky that did not feature the Big Dipper, pivoting around Polaris. Down here, the constellations pivoted around God-knew-where and were mostly unfamiliar anyway. He tried to learn them, but they made even less sense than the three-thousand-year-old asterisms of the north. Telescopum and Sextans and Microscopum and whatever other damn fool things the seventeenth-century navigators had stuck in the sky. Cultural continuity. He thought he remembered that the south celestial pole of Mars was somewhere just off the Milky Way toward the Large Magellanic Cloud, but he could never find it. It was disorienting to fall asleep noticing Orion upside down at a crazy angle, and then wake up later to find that it had moved in the wrong direction from hour to hour. Skies don't transfer well from one planet to another.

Later, in the darkness, he awoke with a start. Some strange dream had startled him. From his bedroll, laid out across the back of the buggy, he looked out the windows, half expecting to see lights on the horizon—the lights of . . . what? There was nothing. Perhaps unexpected night winds had jostled the vehicle.

His mind had been racing with half dreams, half rationalizations. It was past midnight. Today a lot of shit would hit the fan. Fully awake now, he tried to recover what had been bothering him. It was the whole enterprise; the plans he had allowed himself to be caught up in, the plans behind the plans. What would Carter think of him? Strangely, he realized that if things went too wrong, he could live with the ensuing mess, but he would feel guilty in front of Carter.

2

"It was, how would you say, merely by chance I found out they were coming up here to the equator. They were laying out a new seismic net. Ten days' stay. So I talked them into letting me come along. Of course, in my heart I know it was not by chance at all. I always wanted to build something exactly on the equator. It was destined to happen, Carter."

"Get serious."

Two figures, alone in the desert, examined the strange circle of rocks, whose shadows stretched across uneven ground. Sunday morning, dawn. The equator of Mars. Far to the southeast, Stafford had already resumed his explorations, churning across Hellespontus in what was late morning at his longitude, moving toward his hidden goal.

The two figures at the equator were suited in puffy blue. They were on the plateau at the west rim of Hydraotes Chaos, the valley badlands north of Mars City. The high sky was the unearthly gray-violet of Martian dawn. The puffiness of the figures' outer insulation suits made them look like blue snowmen. One was of average height with a white stripe on the crest of his blue helmet. The other was tall; his helmet boasted a fleur-de-lis design. He waved his arms around the landscape, enthusing earnestly.

"It is magnificent, yes?"

"Calm down, Philippe. Just let me look."

The sun was rising in the southeast over the distant canyon. The hazy badlands below were filled with brilliant morning fog. Golden sunlight flickered through wisps of mist that whisked like Martian sprites across the gullies, up the slopes, and out of the Chaos, only to lose themselves on the sandy plain.

"Too bad we did not get out here before dawn," the taller figure continued. "Earth is coming around into the morning star position. Did you know Tennyson wrote a poem about Earth seen from Mars? It has great lines:

Would we dream of wars and carnage
Craft and madness, lust and spite,

Roaring London, raving Paris,
In that point of peaceful light?

Tennyson, he was ahead of his time."

The two figures were surrounded by a ghostly ring of man-sized, russet stones that stood erect and caught the morning sun like sentinels who had been standing guard all night. The ring of stones was surrounded by a broad circular ditch and adjacent bank of brown soil a hundred meters in diameter. Two broad flat avenues, like wide paths cleared of stones, broke through the circle, one running northeast and the other southeast. Centered in each avenue in the distance was a huge, solitary boulder standing as erect and quiet as a Buckingham Palace guard.

The shorter figure turned toward the taller. "You built this all yourself?"

"Of course."

"It doesn't look right."

The tall figure began moving in long, low-gravity hops around the circle, from stone to stone, patting each one in turn. "You see, Stonehenge marks the sunrise at summer solstice in England. But since my Stonehenge is exactly on the equator, I decided to give my Stonehenge two avenues: one for summer solstice in the northern hemisphere and one for summer solstice in the southern hemisphere."

The two friends moved to the center of the circle. The radio voices cut back and forth invisibly and inaudibly in the thin air, sounding only inside the helmets. "I studied it, the original Stonehenge." The taller figure continued, sweeping a puffy and awkward arm toward the northeast avenue, "The builders, they were very sophisticated about astronomy." He had a European accent, French but with a touch of British, like a French speaker who had learned English in London. "Of course," he added parenthetically, "we Europeans always were more sophisticated than you Americans. You did not even have pottery by that time, if I recall. . . ."

"Mornings are damn cold out here, Philippe, and I've got to be getting back. So just cut the BS."

The tall figure ignored him and pointed directly toward the outlying stone, partway down the northeastern avenue. "You stand in the center of Stonehenge on the day when summer begins, and you look down the avenue, and the sun will rise over that outlying stone. In England it was called the Heel Stone. No one knew why before they discovered it was a calendar observatory. Finally, people realized the word came from 'Helios.' Greek for sun. Somehow that name had carried down through the ages."

"So you . . ."

"I always liked the design of Stonehenge. I saw it first in winter. It was covered with snow. So simple and quiet, as if it had its own secret purpose. I liked it so much. That is why I copied it here. We will come back in June. You'll see. . . ."

"Where are the big stone gates in the middle? I thought you were going to build the whole thing."

"I re-created the original design, which they started in 2500 B.C. The big stones that impress everybody, with cross pieces on top, they were added later, perhaps for some ceremonial function. Trilithons. They had nothing to do with the original astronomical purpose." He emphasized the last words, as if they were part of a sacred formula. "By 1800 B.C., the people had forgotten the original purpose. They took a beautiful observatory and converted it to a temple of superstition. It's always that way, I think. Knowledge gets discovered, then degraded. The original design was just this simple ring, with the solstice avenue. Very elegant, yes?"

"How could you build this by yourself?" The smaller figure had a broad, Midwest American accent, with a hint of something else.

"It was easy. I came out with the seismic crew every morning. I told them I just wanted to observe what they were doing. We got friendly. Soon they let me start driving the equipment. It was a game, you know? The French artist, driving a tractor. They were waiting for me to have some disaster so that they could have a laugh. You Americans are transparent, you know, even when you think you are being devious. Finally I convinced them to let me take the caterpillar out here on my own. It was just a few kilometers from their base camp."

The shorter figure sat down on one of the smallest stones, as if pondering the whole enterprise. "Damn irregular, Philippe. First it's Old Man Stafford soloing in his dune buggy, now it's you driving a caterpillar like some cowboy construction worker. The rules are going to hell."

"Stafford would like this place. He is interested in everything."

"Yeah. His strength and his weakness."

"He is—how do you say it—an okay guy."

"Of course. I love the guy. There's no one like Stafford. Somehow, he's taken a shine to me. Tells me about the old days, his adventures . . . Still . . ."

"What?"

"It's dangerous for him to go out alone. It's a goddamn bad precedent is what it is."

"They say he goes everywhere, Hellas, the desert. They say he knows of secret treasures. . . ."

"It's just talk, because Stafford has been out alone, and other people haven't." He picked up a pebble and threw it in a very long arc. "Anyway, it's all Braddock's fault, down at Hellas. Lets Stafford do whatever he wants. He shouldn't let him go out alone like that. Something goes wrong, there'll be hell to pay."

"It must be incredible to be out there alone in a vehicle. Did you never want to feel what it is like to drive one of the vehicles alone? In my caterpillar, it was fantastic. The power! You know what you can do with it? How it feels? A flick of the wrist and you are moving one-tonne boulders around like the building blocks of children. Fantastic. I dug the ditch and bank in three days. I can imagine how Stafford must feel, master of the desert. You know what I think, Carter? I think it is valuable for all of us to let an older, proven person like him have free rein, to be free of the procedures and the committees. It is a good idea of our Mars society. We ought to export this idea back to Earth. It is like the Aztecs. The young warriors were not supposed to drink, but old people could drink as much as they liked. It was their reward."

———————————————●———————————————

In the hazy light, Philippe stood by the door of the dune buggy, waiting for Carter to take one last walk around the New Stonehenge circle.

The wind was beginning to come up. He could hear the rustle of sand grains hitting his suit. Carter should hurry up. Carter always spent too much time poking around, thinking about things, instead of absorbing . . . what? Philippe could not find a word for it. He gazed to the north, across the unexplored desert.

A memory came to him. Once his parents had taken him to Algeria. They showed him an estate and told him that his great-grandfather had once owned it. The estate bordered on kilometers of trackless desert. It had been abandoned years before, and the desert was reclaiming it. Philippe could still see the dead trees like black sticks, with sand lapping at their roots. Peculiar lineations in the sand had once been irrigation canals, sparkling in the Saharan sun. On that day, the concept of "owning" land became very strange to him. The estate in the boundless desert was not like a farm that had been tended for generations. It was just a vast, empty space, a piece of weathering landscape that had been there for eons before his great-grandfather or any of the French had come from Europe, and would be there for eons to come. How could anyone say such a thing was owned? It would be like saying you owned the bubble of air that surrounds you.

As a youth, then, he began to think of himself as a visitor everywhere he went. He would pass through, and perhaps leave something that some child of the future would enjoy. But he was not an owner or a competitor for things that other men seemed driven to seek. . . .

The empty Martian desert stretched like a dream beyond the circle he had built: more land than all the continents of Earth. Unknown. Unused. Winds blew dust to lord knew where, piling it in little dunes and sweeping them away ten years later. And to what purpose, if there was no one out there to see it? It was hard to imagine a universe full of events, which no one witnessed. . . . A planet on which no one had lived. Till now. Purpose? Through what perverse history had Western culture transmitted this fixation with "purpose," down through the centuries? Well, the Martian desert, it was just there. Empty.

He had built something in it. He had been seized by the vision of building this structure, here, in this four-thousand-million-year-old desert. Well, so, it was something he had to do.

He hoped Carter would not ask him why. He could not explain why.

High above the equator of Mars, as Carter Jahns and Philippe Brach departed the New Stonehenge, Annie Pohaku sat under the glass-roofed promenade of Phobos University. She watched the red globe sliding overhead, moving ponderously beyond the branches of the potted Xylosma trees. They were passing over the night side of the planet, black against the stars. It was very different from the night side of Earth, which she had seen from the shuttle as she left home. Earth's night side twinkled like a jewel box with the lights of a thousand cities. Here, no lights at all. Just a black bulk blocking the stars, vaguely menacing.

Now Phobos crossed the terminator and came into sunlight. There, on Mars, was the Lake of the Sun, Solis Lacus, a fractured dry plain, emerging into dawn to meet its namesake. During the last months, on the long voyage to Mars, she had been studying her maps and holeos.

The amber light of Mars revealed hidden warm highlights in her long, glistening black hair as Mars passed overhead, languorously, once every ninety seconds, in response to the rotation of the Phobos wheel-shaped colony itself. The warm light caressed the planes of her face, her high brown cheekbones, her wide jaw. Her smooth Eurasian features betrayed fascination as she watched the red, broken landscapes swing by, one famous landmark after another.

Mars overhead and no one else along the promenade paying any attention. She ought to write something about that.

There were lots of journalistic opportunities here and not many journalists to cover them. A few stringers were in place here and there, she knew, but she felt like the only journalist here who was alive. She looked forward to an interesting assignment. Phobos University was an amazing place, but she couldn't wait to get back to Mars City and out on the surface. In the few weeks since her arrival, she had been to Mars City once, to claim the room the net had provided, and to establish a beachhead. She had returned on the shuttle to Phobos, exploring the University. She had made videos, interviewed researchers, run hours of satellite imagery from the archives in the big library. Now she looked forward to exploring the planet itself, and its people.

Chance of a lifetime, she thought. Coming to Mars, not having to live here, but just to drop in for a matter of weeks and skim the cream off a world the other nets were ignoring. Being here long enough to experience the place, without getting out of touch with the real news back on Earth. Almost anything she chose to do could contribute to her assignment as the one-woman advance team to scout out an IPN special: "Mars—The Next World." The network did something like that every year or so. While she was here she should get some imagery and write a few pieces for the network's E-mags.

"Mars—The Next World." There were people back in the network offices in New York and Tokyo who laughed cynically about the corny title. It was easy for them to laugh at people who departed Earth full of enthusiasm and came back with wide tourist eyes and earnest tales of amazing sights. Journalistic dogma said that any assignment off Earth was a career dead end. Mars, some of her friends had told her, was the farthest outback in the solar system. Big mistake, they said. Maybe so. To network execs, who thought an office was a natural habitat for humans, anyone who would begin to like provincial Mars seemed naive, out of touch with The Latest.

In the beginning, when she was a kid, Mars had been news. Scientists and engineers, carving out a human presence. But what did they have to show for it now? Two decades of dead, dry rocks and a struggle to keep things going. . . . The viewers had lost interest pretty fast. Tokyo had lost interest. Maybe her career was on the line, but try as she might, she didn't really worry much about it. Being here was too much fun. Anyway, here she was. Chance of a lifetime. She'd show them.

Once you were here, the phrases began to take on real meaning: new world; frontier. To her surprise, a story was starting to come together. With luck, the net might extend it into a series. Four, maybe five parts. Takemitsu had said he would consider it if she could come up with enough interesting stuff.

Two students from the University walked by her bench, arm in arm, not much younger than herself. They were speaking Russian. Interesting place, Phobos. Strange in its own way. It was true what returning off-worlders said. Phobos was like nothing in the Earth-moon system. The difference was not so much the physical place, but something about people's attitude toward what they were doing. . . .

She shifted her weight on the cast glass bench, leaning back to watch Mars slide by overhead.

Maybe it *would* turn out to be a dead end. . . . Sometimes she thought about chucking her whole hectic career and returning to her native Hawaii, where the tempo was still slow and she knew she could be happy. Back to Tomas, who would always be waiting. . . .

She closed her eyes.

Memories. Scenes, like invisible perfumes, wafting into the windows of her mind like a sea breeze. The sun bright as a bomb shining in the window of that other shuttle, taking her away from Earth for the first time, lifting off from South Point . . . Looking down; looking back. The planet curving away blue and white; and on the planet an ocean blue and green; and on the ocean as far from anyplace as someplace could be, an archipelago; and on the island curling ferns and streets with pink flowers and trees with broad green leaves; and on the leaves drops of fresh rain, beaded like little spherical lenses, waiting for something; and in each lens a sparkle of the sun, and a dozen motes circling like planets . . .

The eyes of Tomas saying good-bye . . .

Memories popped into mindspace like subatomic particles popping into existence after the big bang, and what if whole planets, including dusty red ones, could spring into being as easily as that?

She opened her eyes and looked through the graceful arch of glass. Sun, Mars, Sun, Mars, swinging by. There were still adventures to be had in her life, before going home.

Suddenly she caught sight of the shuttle drifting against the curved hazy horizon of Mars. It was getting bigger. The shuttle from Mars City. She could see the antennae, and the protruding landing legs, as useless here as legs on a fish. It was majestic. She ought to get a shot of that with Mars in the background. Viewers were used to seeing the slow-motion dance of spacecraft, but not with a red backdrop. With a little image processing, they could create a 3-D effect. Shuttle hanging in front of Mars, like a model. Fakey as hell, but Takemitsu and the viewers loved it. It looked more like what they saw in the action-sensies.

The same shuttle would take her down to Mars.

The most interesting part of the planet was coming into view. The gashlike rift, Valles Marineris, was carpeted with a deposit of gray-brown dust, forming a dark streak visible from Earth and mapped in the 1800s as the thickest of the mythical "canals." It was given the name Coprates, curiously derived from the Greek root for dung. Shit canyon. An ironic name for the biggest canyon in the solar system.

She ought to write something about that, too, a little piece with photos of the canyon as seen overhead through the roof of Phobos's famous promenade. She pondered a title, smiling mischievously.

The empty hills and river channels, passing below, made her think of Earth. She remembered a flight down the California coast, not long before she left. Masses of houses, the ragged coast with its decaying luxury hotels, the ribbon roads with their scattered crawling ants. That green and tan land was pressed down by an enormous accumulated mass of history, the people who had lived there and disappeared. The first unknown hunters pouring onto the continent through Alaska; Ulloa and Sir Francis Drake probing the coast, Junípero Serra and his missions, young Richard Dana on his whaling ship visiting an empty peninsula, and old Richard Dana coming back twenty-five years later to find the massive city of San Francisco with its bustling American enthusiasm. And the masses of faceless construction workers, businessmen, farmers, and dream merchants who had built the land—all lost in history. The tangled invisible mass of events and personages, piling up year after year, seemed to weigh down that land, becoming denser and heavier each year.

Now, as she looked down on this empty red land of Mars, where no history had accumulated, it seemed light and airy by comparison, an empty slate.

A thought flashed in her mind: She'd be writing this history. She'd be adding density to the landscape below.

Yes, she could get a story out of Shit Canyon if she wanted to. A

California geologist she had flirted with a few days before arrival at Phobos said that the canyon was long enough to stretch across the U.S. Said it formed because of uplifting just before the big volcanoes erupted in Tharsis. Or some such. He seemed to think this was exciting, and quoted some meaninglessly long time ago in the past—she couldn't remember. Two billion years? Why did they even bother to talk about time periods so long?

Still, he might make a good interview. When he described his esoteric knowledge, he radiated pure joy, the way scientists do. How the canyon's formation had exposed underground ice deposits that turned to water. Cascades of water, gushing out of the faults, rushing down the valley to the east, carving out the river channels around Mars City. She gazed up at Mars, where she could see them now, ancient dusty traceries of the twin dusty riverbeds, Eos Chasma and Capri Chasma. The Californian had loved trying to impress her with this story of diluvian drama. His big hands moved a lot and his eyebrows went up and down when he talked about what they were learning from ancient strata. He had been kind of cute, in a boyishly confident haole way. Yes, Takemitsu would love him, describing giant floods and waving his hands in a low-gravity dance, superimposed on some huge holeo of the canyon.

She ought to find him. He said he had to go directly on to Mars—no time for an interview. He hinted at dark, important, masculine projects, but she forgave him. When she got back to Mars City, she should find him again. What was his . . . She leaned over the 'corder strapped to her wrist and spoke slowly.

"What is the name of the California geologist we met on the flight from Earth?"

"Tubin. Peter Tubin." A quiet female voice from the 'corder.

Tubin, that was it. He'd said he and his crew were doing some kind of research out in the field; that he might be hard to find. Surely he'd show up sooner or later. Somebody would know how to contact him.

If all went well, Takemitsu would also love the other interview she had already arranged in Mars City, with the current holder of the artist-in-residence grant, a European named Philippe Brach. Rumor had it, he had erected some big Stonehenge-like monument out in the desert. It was a crazy idea but there had to be some good visuals there.

She glanced back at the east end of the Martian canyonlands passing by. Somewhere in those badlands the aliens from Earth had erected the soil-banked domes and tunnels of Mars City. Three thousand souls in the wildest maze of Mars, she thought to herself.

All those scientists toiling away, hoping people back on Earth would not lose interest. She tried to pick out some sign of it but there was nothing. Three thousand people, tinier than ants, invisible, huddled in their domes and tubes and towers at 6° south latitude and 35° west longitude. For no good reason, the coordinates had stuck in her mind like magic numbers. They had managed to build Mars City at the east end of Shit Canyon. It'd make an interesting dateline.

She had studied Mars City, gone through a dozen holeos.

She rehearsed her lessons. The location had been chosen according to three factors. First, it had to be near the equator, under the orbit of Phobos's bustling port, to allow a minimum energy transfer orbit.

Second, the scientists clamored to have it located where the rivers had run. They wanted to study the great mystery: Why the climate had changed and reduced Mars from a river-running, lake-dotted, pleasant planet to the kind of place that could elicit the line "my warmest day in Hellas was a cold day in Hell." It was the celebrated phrase of the wild-eyed, bearded poet, Deckard McKinnon, who had been artist-in-residence in '30, but who had left in disgust halfway through his term, disappeared into the pubs of London, and never written another word about Mars. She recorded a note to herself under "story ideas": see if Takemitsu's people could find McKinnon and put him on the show, two years later, reflecting back on his unhappy view of Mars. The disgruntled poet was gone; Mars was still here. What would he say to that?

There was a third reason for the city's location: everyone wanted Mars City to be at low elevation. If the experiments to increase the air pressure continued to succeed—it amazed her to think about it—Mars might once again see summer lakes at the low-lying sites where air pressure is highest. The once-flooded basin near Mars City was one of the lowest spots near the equator, three thousand meters below the zero level. The extra three thousand meters gave Mars City 20 percent more air pressure than most of the planet. Already, people told her, it was enough to make a suit noticeably more comfortable outside Mars City than up in the highlands; and enough to make the dust fall differently.

There was so much for her to set down about this place. She wanted to start recording striking word pictures from which she would assemble a marvelous story like a jigsaw puzzle, but it was always hard to get started.

Hoping for inspiration, she gazed at the spot five hundred kilometers north of Mars City, where the now-dry river channels emptied into a tangled mass of gullies called Hydraotes Chaos.

Coming into view were the low, broad lava plains of Chryse Planitia, from which the American lander—was it *Vanguard I?*—transmitted the first clear photos from the surface of Mars, back in 1976, when the mainland haoles were celebrating their two hundredth anniversary. After the era of water, the Chryse plains were covered by lava flows from Tharsis, which slithered across the desert, fuming and rumbling, 1.4 billion years ago. Today the lava was covered by windblown dust and tumble-down rocky debris, and the first lander was still sitting out there somewhere, alone, never seen by human eyes since it had come to Mars. She peered hard, as if concentration would enable her to find it.

Far below, Carter and Philippe in their buggy had joined a convoy heading back to Mars City from the seismic base camp.

"One thing I don't get about your Stonehenge. Why didn't you put it out in front of the city, by the landing pads, where everyone will see it?"

"When I found out I could get to the equator, I knew that would be perfect. It gives a planetary scope, the equator. The work becomes part of the planet itself, turning in space, going through its cycles. The equator runs literally through the circle. That is what they tell me. They have triangulated it, the seismic crew."

"Triangulated."

"Something. Imagine. Someday the tourists, they will come up from Mars City just to see this. Take a day off for sightseeing outside. Stonehenge on Mars. It makes a continuity of culture, if I may say so. Of course, it is only my own little effort. . . ."

"Don't give me that false humility, Philippe. I'm onto it."

Philippe brushed his long, sandy hair back from his forehead. "What a relief to get rid of the helmet. I tell you, someday people will drive the 360 klicks every June and December, just to witness sunrise over the Heel Stones. It will be an historic spot, Carter. I am very happy with it."

"This calls for a celebration, Philippe. Tell you what. I'll buy you a red back at the Nix Olympica."

"No time, my friend. Already my little project has had its greatest success."

"And what would that be?"

"Why do you think men build things and make artworks? It is to attract women. We have no tail feathers to spread, no big air sac on the throat to inflate like a frog . . ."

"You should know."

"Be quiet, please. So we have to build things. And it works. You won't believe it, but I am supposed to meet some woman who wants to come out here. A journalist. She came all the way from Earth to talk to me."

Carter snorted.

"Oh, I am sure of it." Philippe's voice dropped to a conspiratorial whisper. "I am at liberty to tell you she is beautiful. Well, I assume she is beautiful because she has a beautiful voice. Sometimes it is enough, a beautiful voice. A beautiful voice in the dark."

3

Late afternoon already as Carter Jahns hurried down the hall toward his office in the old core of Mars City. For the hundredth time, he noticed that the new flooring in the hallway was not holding up as well as promised. It wasn't supposed to show wear for six years, they had said. The afternoon meeting with the architecture committee was over, thank God. He entered his cramped white office and glared at the do-screen on his desk.

The screen glared back. Every day for a week it had grown more offensive. Now his URGENT list ran off the bottom of the screen. Intolerable.

The time said 5:10. Good; after five, he wasn't obliged to sit down.

One three-day weekend in the field with his friend Philippe, and already things were out of control. Even during the committee meeting, the screen had acquired three new flashing URGENT messages. The pulsating red letters were the only thing that marred the clean efficiency of his office.

He had discovered after leaving school that adult lives were devoted to achieving clean screens. Once he had had a dream of coming into his office and finding the screen blank. The dream turned into a nightmare when he realized that this goal would never be reached until he died. He had awakened in a sweat, still half dreaming: a few weeks after he died, the messages, one by one, would wink out until the screen was empty and there would be no letters, no paper trail, and no longer any trace of him in the intercourse of the worlds.

He paused ruefully by his open doorway, considering what to do. The door carried a discreet title on a blue plaque:

ASSISTANT DIRECTOR
ENVIRONMENTAL ENGINEERING

A certain amount of jargon inflation in that, considering the number of hours of politics relative to the hours of actual engineering. He had arrived in Mars City in 2028 with a staff position, and had been quickly noticed for his diligence. His thick, dark hair was cut short. His Slavic square face, clear blue eyes, and chunky athletic build fit what he was: a sample from the new American melting pot. He had risen suddenly to his present rank when his boss, Stefansdottir, had died of a heart attack eight months after he arrived. (In the heat of an argument, Philippe had said he could understand why she died soon after Carter joined her staff.) Philippe had also remarked that the memorial service for the former Assistant Director seemed tempered with relief that people were beginning to die on Mars of prosaic natural causes, rather than accidents. Carter was appointed to the post, youngest of four who had held the position.

How had Stefansdottir put up with all the crap when she held the job? he wondered. Or had Mars been simpler then, only two years ago? Nowadays he spent half his time dealing with the latest staff arrivals and their new VR fetish, "personalizing," tripping that left personalities warped for hours. They'd show up for work, acting like strangers. He couldn't stand them like that. It took days to find the real person.

Stefansdottir's death had been a loss for Mars. Those Icelanders—tough as the meteoritic iron Philippe had been using in his sculptures. Mars Council should have populated the whole planet with them. Probably wouldn't have needed spacesuits.

Carter was still in the doorway; 5:15 and the three new URGENTs still flashed. One message he might have checked and answered but three . . . He'd be there all night. Hell with it. Quitting time was quitting time. He had already shut off the 'corder on his wrist during the committee meeting, and he had left it off, in case someone tried to call him direct with some other damn URGENT message.

He ran his square-tipped fingers through his dark hair. It was more a gesture of despair than anything else. Why couldn't every division do its own "paperwork" without demanding his input? Of course, if he ever verbalized that idea, he'd be out in a year. Not a team player, eh, Jahns?

That was the trouble with Mars these days: the bureaucracy was expanding into some inflated realm where "urgent" meant "routine." It made him cling desperately to his private fiction that he was somehow outside the bureaucracy, a free player, a free thinker, taking bold initiatives. Building the new Mars and all that. The new module at the east end of town. The lab facilities at Hellas. South pole's incessant equipment needs for climatic research or whatever it was they were doing.

Yes, definitely, the hell with it all. It was time for his traditional Monday night drink with Philippe at the Nix-O. All right. He admitted it. Nix-O was the real reason he wanted to get out of here.

He snapped off the room light, and the red pulsations from the screen made weird reflections and shadows on the sculpture Philippe had given him. It sat atop the data file by the door. It was one thing in his office he was proud of—a fractured, strangely textured sphere Philippe had cast from one of several meteoritic chunks found during the early days of the city's construction. Most of the original iron had gone into a larger sculpture Philippe had made for the Mars Council chambers. Since Carter's sculpture was made from the leftovers, it gave him a feeling that he had a secret link with the Council. It looked like a weird alien egg, or perhaps an undiscovered asteroid. It was the one completely irrational thing in the antiseptic office, and therefore the one he could care about.

He gave the egg a pat, stepped out, and started to close the door.

The desk phone pipped.

Too late, pal. Nobody had any business expecting to find him here at 5:20. He paused at the door to listen for the message recorder to cut in. A soft female voice came on at the other end. "Mr. Jahns. This is Driscoll in the Security Office. I guess you've heard we've got an 03 situation at Hellas Base. We just got a special assignment for you, direct from the Council. They say you're the one for the job. Guess everybody knows you've got what it takes. (A snicker.) They say you can turn over the Architecture proposal to the Espositos for the rest of the week. You better call as soon as you get this message. We'll try your apartment and . . ."

Angrily he locked the door. The voice rattled on inside as Carter stomped off down the hall, seething with indignation.

God, another special assignment! Why didn't they just create a full-time emergency staff or police force and be done with it, instead of pulling people from one job to another every time something comes up. Mars City was getting too big to handle problems this way.

And what was with Driscoll anyway? Every time she called with some problem she managed to make it sound like a come-on. And what the hell was an 03 . . . ? Missing equipment or something? He could never remember the code that security insisted on using. Why couldn't they just say what they meant? Hellas, eh? Why drag him into their problem? Probably wanted another outside review of procedures. Well, there'd be time enough tomorrow morning; maybe even later tonight if his conscience acted up.

Those soft voices trying to control everyone's life from machine-space . . . Soft voices throughout the solar system. Always polite, always informed, always bringing trouble.

Carter strode down the hall looking forward to the evening. Philippe, ever cultivating his air of mystery, had called in the morning to say that Carter should be sure to come, there was a special surprise in store.

Carter walked faster. The truth of the matter was, the weekend in the desert had put him in a strange mood. Usually, on his excursions outside, he saw Mars as full of promise. He remembered growing up, his screen at home blazing with images of people settling into the new bases on Mars, and his mother telling him that they did not know it yet, but they were building a new society. At twelve he had a map of Mars on his wall, and he would recite the mystical names: Tharsis, Elysium, Sirenum, and Syrtis Major, the great dark splotch that had first been charted in the 1600s. He had built a telescope a few years later. In certain years of astrological import Mars came close enough that he could see the polar ice and Syrtis Major itself. He had grown up imagining himself severing the constraints of Earth, standing on the red sands, helping to build this new world. Usually he could recapture that feeling when he looked at the endless empty plains. But this time, it was the emptiness that lingered in his mind, along with the endless budget fights with Mars Council. Here he was, part of the mating dance of humanity and nature, locked in their yin-yang embrace, and he was beginning to wonder, as Felicia back on Earth used to say, where the relationship was going. Felicia, who had left him for some rich lawyer type who ran around in a gasoline-powered car.

High above the equator of Mars, the Phobos shuttle made its normally scheduled departure from Phobos University. With its small steering jets puffing like a dragon out of breath, it backed away from the colony's giant rotating wheel. The wheel was pegged through its heart to the north pole of the potato-shaped moon. The ship turned slowly, aligning itself for the main engine burn. Its shadow slithered silently over the dark craters of Phobos's soot-black surface.

Suddenly the sun slipped behind Mars. The ship glowed in a brief blaze of deep red, and then disappeared into blackness. It was as if the whole ship had ceased to exist.

Aboard, Annie Pohaku, tall, dark, and uncomfortable in the cramped cocoon seats, tried to slip off her jacket. With annoyance she noticed a worn LIKELEATHER commercial tag protruding from the seat lining in front of her. She tore it off, cramming it into the little seat pouch. Her long black hair began its billowy zero-G dance, a crown of softness, more luxurious than it could ever be on a pillow. A halo. She started gather it into a knot, then decided to let it float free.

She was startled when the ship slipped into blackness. It was as if *she* had ceased to exist. Other passengers began turning on their individual lights. She peered out her window, holding up her jacket to block the reflections from the nearby lights. Mars hid the stars.

"Planets have a way of blotting out the universe." She recorded the thought quietly. She'd use all these pithy phrases someday. Right. Another triumph of optimism over experience.

The ship's maneuvering took forever. Finally, the requisite prerecorded voice came on. "For your comfort and convenience, please"—she always finished the sentence for herself—"remain tightly strapped into your cramped cocoon and pray while we go slamming into the Mars atmosphere at five kilometers per second."

The main ascent/descent engines (the pilots called them AC/DC) fired on schedule. The great dragon had regained his pale, luminous breath. From the middle of night, the ship began its forty-five-minute arc down toward the surface, toward early evening in Mars City.

The engines made a minute-long, visceral, low-frequency shudder, and then ceased. Now she floated again in her cocoon. She thought about atmosphere entry, coming in a few moments, but her main emotion was anticipation of a real bath in Mars City, where water was an abundant luxury after the stingy showers of Phobos.

It would have to be a short bath. Damn. Well, luxury would be sacrificed in a good cause. In a couple of hours she was scheduled to meet the guy who had created the Martian Stonehenge. Art on Mars; it would be a great little segment. She could see Takemitsu smiling. Brach, the artist, had already offered to take her out there to see it for herself. After all, what man could resist showing off his latest project?

Brach sounded interesting. Euro artist on Mars. She liked his accent. She had vaguely fantasized about going out into the desert with him Wednesday, bringing him into her orbit, seducing him with her radioed voice as they walked in their suits among the stones he had erected, as she encouraged him to brag how the sun would rise over some particular stone. Business-wise, they had something to offer to each other. They'd have a great time together. If his installation was really impressive, and if the shooting schedule worked out right, she could maybe get the camera crew out there on the day when the sun came over . . . what had he said about a special stone? She'd get him to explain it during the dinner interview she had cunningly got him to suggest.

Business aside, she had discovered that it was always interesting to meet people here. Some of the people—she was not yet comfortable calling them Martians—seemed to pulse with the newness of the place, a pulsation missing in the crowded cities back home.

The shuttle floated into dawn. The topography, now definitely "below," took shape in a tangle of pale, long shadows, hazy with dawn fogs. After her childhood in the green-blue-white contours of Hawaii and the angular urban geometries of Earth, the pastel apricot dawns and red afternoons of Mars excited her in some way she had not expected. Mars offered some possibility of surprise.

Weightless in her cocoon, she stretched like a cat.

By the time Carter got to the main arcade he was calming down at last. Anyway, there was this clerk at Music N Books; in the last few days she smiled at him when he went by. No doubt about it. Tomorrow he'd have to go in and start talking to her. A great thing, women smiling. Besides, against all odds, maybe she actually liked music and books.

He liked having women on his mind.

He had avoided wasting energy psycho-profiling himself, but Philippe did it for him. Philippe would ask questions about his childhood, and then analyze the answers, whether Carter asked for analysis or not. When Carter was ten years old, back in Illinois, his American father had separated from his Russian mother. It was amicable, but he never saw his father much after that. Carter had convinced himself that this had not affected him. He had always liked his father, and his father's middle-American pragmatism, which he had inherited. His mother, with her Russian romanticism, had always been different from other people he knew, a loving mystery.

Philippe said that this parentage made Carter the perfect citizen of Mars, with its Council set up through Russian-American collaboration in the second decade of the century.

Carter's mother had been a beautiful woman with enormous eyes, which always seemed wide open in private amazement. Even now, when he saw the old videos of her, laughing as a young woman, there was a shock in recognizing her extraordinary beauty. What bit of genetics, he wondered, makes it so difficult to see our mothers as beautiful women?

Early one day in Illinois, with the morning fog hanging in the fields beyond the screen of trees at the edge of town, his mother had taken him for a walk. She had talked about Russia, ruined and reborn every century.

While the whirlwind of technology was stagnating in the rest of the world after 2010, Russia was booming and blasting its way through its resources. Using technologies and ideas of the twentieth century, it had become the America of the twenty-first century. The two countries were amazingly alike, she said: shaped by frontiers. But she said that they would never fully understand each other, that the Americans were too set in their ways to try. "And it's important for you to understand this," she said. "Soon you'll be out in the world and you'll always have a foot in both camps."

Like a parent revealing the facts of life, she had explained the twentieth century to him—as much as anyone could explain chaos and chance. She owed her own existence to an accident in 1942, she told him. Her grandmother, as a little girl, had been sent out for a bottle of milk at a chance moment when Hitler's men—or was it Stalin's men—had come to the house. When she returned there was no one there. . . . It was a century of chance survivals and narrow escapes and the luck of being born in the right country, or finding your way there. It was the century, his mother remarked gravely, that turned existentialism from a dry philosophy into reality.

She had been one of the lucky ones, she said. At least that's what she thought when she arrived in America during the collapse of the seventy-year Soviet experiment. But she found America to be a strange world. The Americans crowed of their success and exported their ideas around the planet, but it was the streets of the most Americanized cities of Earth that were haunted by the most tragic derelicts.

She told him an old Russian joke to explain the difference between the Russian and American social systems. In America, if a man struck it rich, his neighbor said, "What a success! I hope I can be rich like my neighbor." In Russia, if a man got rich, his neighbor said, "I hope a disaster strikes him so he becomes an ordinary guy again, like me."

The problem of wealth concentration, she taught him, had been the key to the last two centuries—the widening gulf between the haves and have-nots. Her country had at least recognized it in the 1900s and tried to solve it in a grand, terrible, failed experiment. The Americans had never admitted the problem. Their upper classes produced complacent sons and daughters who cheerfully burned through most of Earth's riches. Now, as the Russian upper classes became the richest on Earth, the problem had returned. Earth's last chance at sustainability was being squandered.

Carter had absorbed a sense of irony from his mother, who had met his father in Moscow during his tour of engineering facilities of the old USSR. She had arrived in America just in time to witness its slow downward slide. She had left Russia just before its fortunes ascended on the double tide of resources and climate change. Carter was lucky, she said, to have a foot in both camps.

Now, on Mars, he seemed to be carrying out some dream that she had prepared him to dream, trying to build a new world. She had given him a picture of history as something dense, having a gravity that held events down, fitting into some dialectic that only her generation had seen. He came to see that his father's people had believed that anyone could change history, while his mother's side believed that it had a large and random component of fate. The more he saw of the world, the more it became a marvel to him that he had been born in Moscow. "Our beautiful Moscow," she had called it sadly. Ever since, whether he was on the Earth, moon, or Mars, he could feel each world's ponderous, silent turning as it churned out the history of the ants crawling across its back.

It frightened Carter, now, to look back at his mother's ideas and realize that one's experience of life pivoted entirely on the random spot where he was born into the four-dimensional *yü-chou* of spacetime. His own great-grandmother, shaped by an era of war, saved by a one-minute quirk of fate. And what if you were born a middle-class, educated Jew, in Munich in 1905? What sense could you make out of a life that rode a monotonic tide from comfort to catastrophe, a train ride toward the abyss with a free ticket provided by the state bureaucracy?

Carter couldn't help but feel that Philippe viewed all this through a different filter. His was such a long, European view of history that history was relegated to the background; not up front as in his mother's consciousness. If history was a series of random waves and tides, it was not something in which you wanted to be immersed, but something that you tried to ignore because immersion led to drowning. You tried to stay afloat on the stormy surface of history.

Carter and Philippe had formed their friendship as soon as Philippe arrived in '29, the year after Carter came. They felt brotherly similarities. Both had experienced a variety of cultures. Both were, in effect, citizens of the solar system and of no single country, except on paper. Both were born in the magic year of 2000. (How did other people remember their age, Carter mused.)

Almost with a start, Carter came back to the present to find he was still striding through the garden area that Philippe called the Tuileries. A pair of lovers were immersed in the world of their bench among the palms and the flowers. The garden was one of Carter's favorite spots. It was like a gift from the designers to the inhabitants, a place that worked wonders for people's psyches. Even the plants looked happy. Martians loved plants, the companions they had brought with them from Earth because they couldn't bring animals. Plants had evolved the perfect means of transporting life through space—seeds. The arrivals at Mars City, the only Martians, had brought seeds of philodendrons and potted rubber trees and blazing ginger flowers.

The hallways of Mars City were nothing if not horticulturally exuberant. An article in the *English Garden Society Journal* applauded the Martians for their interest, but said that they lacked a sense of taste. A gardener who was a Japanese National Treasure, sent to Mars for a visit by a Japanese television network, gave up in bewilderment and went home. Gardeners, flitting from plant to plant, reminded Carter that the debate about whether to introduce certain species of insects on Mars had not been settled in Council. Carter himself had argued that the "insect-free Mars" experiment was working so far; "besides," he said, "which would you rather have, gardeners or bugs?"

Carter hurried on through the garden, feeling better.

●

Having become a cynic about urgent messages, Carter had cut himself off from the news that pulsed back and forth on invisible pathways through the nonexistent ether. For an hour the news had been flashing from dusty Hellas Base. Silently it sped back and forth, through comsats to Mars City and dark Phobos, and southward to the Polar Station, and outward through the surging solar wind toward Earth, and even to the tiny Phobos shuttle.

Aboard the shuttle, Annie Pohaku's 'corder pipped to get her attention. She had programmed it to alert her to any new Martian postings on Newsnet. She had not expected much, but she always wanted to be on top of anything that developed in her vicinity. Career and all that. She fished uncomfortably for the screen in her bag, and turned it on. She read the full announcement with growing horror . . . and excitement. This could be big. Takemitsu had defined for her the quality that made the top journalists. Luck. The right place at the right time. . . .

●

Carter found Philippe in the Nix Olympica Bar, in his usual corner table, spread out like an octopus. He wiped his unkempt hair from his brow as

Carter approached. "I was reading this novel," Philippe said. "Czech. Last century. The author describes the Russian tanks rumbling into the heart of Prague, because he and other writers were publishing things that were too . . . frank. You know? For the government. So your Russians sent in the tanks. Right in the heart of Europe!"

"Times have changed."

"Perhaps yes; perhaps no. We never know, do we? Anyway, he talks about a lover who returns from a trip and has lost six kilograms. He wants to know what happened to those six kilos. Did they just dissipate into thin air? He was attached to those kilograms. But my question is different. My question is: If I have a lover and she comes back from a trip minus six kilograms, perhaps only ninety percent of her is left. As her lover, have I lost something? Is she the same person? Scientists would never accept this—to have something come back with only ninety percent of its mass, and say casually, 'Oh, well, we will just ignore the fact that ten percent of the mass is missing.' "

"Yes, but you're not a scientist." It wasn't quite true. Philippe had studied physics, along with everything else. A couple of years, then gave it up. Said he wasn't interested in picturing the universe as if it were uninhabited.

"Ahh, you are wrong. We are all scientists. You understand nothing, as this writer would say. Kundera, you know him?" Philippe did not wait for an answer. "We are all scientists because we have to figure out how to live in the universe. You, especially, you are a scientist because you have a theory of how we will live on Mars. You try to force other people to live according to your theory, like the Communists did in your mother's country. This time you had better be right."

"You going to be like this all night?"

"People expect me to be this way."

It was true. Philippe was stimulated by the fact that people wanted him to be unusual. He was their visiting French artist. He used their expectations to advantage. His youth in Paris, with seasons in London and points global, lent him a cosmopolitan air. He had learned English mannerisms that he could turn on and off at will. "Right. Won't be a moment, thank you very much," he could rattle off in perfect BBC. Americans, who dominated Mars City, wanted Philippe to be French, because he was an artist. When they were in the company of others, Carter teasingly called him "The Artiste." He had olive Mediterranean skin, which emphasized the incongruity of his longish fair hair. Though he was Carter's age, his thinness and extra height made him look younger and more awkward. He had won the annual Mars Residency Prize, which gave him two years on Mars to produce work for Mars City, with the option to renew for a third year by vote of the Mars Council.

Carter Jahns and Philippe Brach were happy to sit under an arching giant fern in the Nix Olympica Bar and recycle their old arguments. The pulsing blue neon lights around the door reflected off the chrome fittings around the room. Fans overhead added a *noir* atmosphere, though Carter could not see them without remembering a flap over their impact on the larger air circulation filtration system.

A sign over the door was rendered in green self-glo, in the latest sideways-turned Martian lettering that the previous artist-in-residence thought would be a cute design innovation to export from Mars back to Earth:

2020 VISION

The subtitle referred to the year of the establishment's birth—one night after a Russian team had pulled an American team out of an emergency hut on its last night of air. This according to apocryphal tradition.

Carter mused about the sign, with its faintly pulsing bright color. It reminded him of his screen, flashing in the darkness of his office. . . . The current fad for signs that consumed little energy was a sort of reverse ostentation. With the fusion generators, there was plenty of power on Mars, yet energetic sign illumination was viewed as being in poor taste. The attitude was a remnant of social tradition from polluted Earth.

The barkeep sent over a waitress with their customary drinks, Martian blues. The waitress was a new face to them. It was wonderful how new women kept coming to Mars for adventure. She had long legs and a lingering smile. "Do you like her? I will give her to you," Philippe said after she departed.

"Stow it, Brach." Carter leaned back against the wall, studying the bluish glints off the ice in his glass.

Philippe Brach leaned back as well, hands behind his head, ruffling his sandy brown hair and giving more prominence to his large ears. His arms and legs seemed to have a life of their own, independent of his lanky body. In the shadowy light of their corner, the light from behind the fern he looked slightly sinister. Now he folded his hands in front of him in a prayerful attitude. "Well," he said at last, "it will not be so interesting if you spend the night staring around the room like a tourist. Are you going to tell Brother Philippe your problems?"

Carter sipped happily at his blue, and began to explain his theory of office life. He could never decide if the Martian blue tide felt warm or cool, but its calming waves washed over him like a tide.

"You should be glad you don't have to work in an office," he told Philippe.

"Oh, but I am."

"There's this infatuation with the latest tidbit of news or rumor. Drives me nuts. Whoever has the latest item is at the top of the pecking order. But these tidbits have a half-day half-life. By the next day, everything has become obsolete. Why don't people realize this? They always view the time they wasted on yesterday's rumors as keeping up-to-date. Then they start in again on today's 'news.'"

"There's another Eastern European writer who says that in every office there's someone who hasn't produced anything in years. But, he says, the funny thing is, that's the person who is always the most feverishly busy. *The Compromise*. Amusing book. You ought to read it sometime."

"Mmmm. It keeps getting worse, the office politics. Stafford says things are going to hell on Mars. Sometimes I think he's right."

"This does not sound like you. This attitude, it could be fatal to your job, you know? You have to play this game if you want to be an American big shot. You had better keep these ideas to yourself!"

Philippe was right about that.

"The trouble is," Philippe continued, "you cannot expect Mars City to keep growing as it has. Today, in your profession . . . Well, the crises will multiply as the budget goes down. You could become like one little fish, who is trying to stop a tide from going out. Your problem is you are still enthusiastic about building Mars."

"You're not?"

"I am an observer. I watch tides come and go."

The waitress, legs and all, passed by. They watched her.

"Maybe I ought to order a red. Wake myself up," Philippe muttered. "We're the only ones who care about history, you know. Mars is mostly American, in spite of what they say. Today is the only day that counts. Everything is now. Now, now, now."

Outside, it was February on Mars. More significantly, it was summer in the southern hemisphere, the season of dust storms, triggered by the summer "warming." "Warming" in quotes, since these were still temperatures that would make a polar bear stop wanting to go fishing. Still, the sun beat as hard as it could. Invisible parcels of air, perhaps stagnating over a dark basalt flow during a momentary lapse of wind, grew warmer than usual and ascended like a hot air balloon without a bag.

During this silent summer shuffling and reshuffling of air, during these invisible ascents and descents, the light dust of the Martian surface stirred uneasily. In the afternoons, if you could hover above the unexplored mesas and secret valleys of Hellespontus, you would see the first stirrings of the dust. A formless cloud here, a twisting, typhoonlike column there. The first spindly dust devils. Then bigger ones, rising like fat Minoan columns, gathering themselves up to their full height of a kilometer or more, and then wandering off on aimless journeys like beheaded giant warriors who staggered for hours before realizing that they had to die: mindless ghosts of Edgar Rice Burroughs's Martian monsters.

On the outskirts of Mars City, as Carter and Philippe argued like Buddhist monks about how to create good karma on Mars, dust clouds swirled also across the landing pad on the outskirts of the town. But these were not summer dust devils. They were clouds kicked up by the beetlelike buses that crawled around the Phobos shuttle that had just landed.

Soon, two buses lumbered from the landing pad toward the soil-banked mounds and gleaming towers of Hellas Base. Inside the second bus, IPN correspondent Annie Pohaku watched the twisted tufts of dust picked up by the wheels of the first. They looked like little question marks, floating in the air.

The woman who had piloted the ship down from Phobos was riding in the same bus. She sat a couple of seats forward of Annie, but turned as they rumbled along toward the city's main terminal airlock. She eyed Annie carefully and identified in her shining eyes an undisguised intensity, the signs of a relative newcomer. "And how do you find Mars?" she asked.

Annie was always excited by an arrival, and excitement brought out her feistiness. "I just follow signs through airlock doors."

The pilot flashed a smile of appreciation, a smile that established a fleeting bond between two strangers—a jaded pilot and a tired reporter with enough humanness to make a joke at the end of a day.

It set Annie ruminating. Easier to get a smile from a stranger than from a lover.

As soon as they got inside and the pilot left the airlock, Annie hunched down in a peculiar posture she had developed to keep her voice private, and began speaking to the 'corder.

"Impression upon entering Mars City. Humidity, and a faint smell of humanity. A nice smell, as if friendship could have an aroma."

She gave up. She didn't know where to go with the thought. Her 'corder was getting so full of disconnected fragments that it was getting heavy.

She sighed. Philippe Brach's name was staring at her from the little screen in her lap. Nix Olympica Bar, eight o'clock, it said.

In the Nix Olympica Bar, by eight o'clock, Philippe was smiling broadly and waving a pen. "You are about to see artistic inspiration, in the modest person of myself." He took out a reusable pad and began sketching. The aimless sketch began to take the form of a tree branch with leaves hanging down. "God, by the way, is the entity in the universe with which artists and scientists conduct dialogues."

"Are you drunk, Philippe?"

Philippe added a touch of pencil to the sketch and then shook his head. Presently he noticed a flicker of change on Carter's face. Carter was looking toward the door.

Philippe followed his gaze.

When Annie Pohaku appeared on the blue carpet in the fluted chrome art nouveau doorway at the end of the Nix Olympica Bar, she was framed unself-consciously for an instant in the vertical beam of the entrance ceiling lights. The intense lights excited her clean black hair into a resonant glow, both cool and warm at the same time.

She paused inside the door, and spoke to a waiter, the light still framing her. The waiter nodded in their direction.

"She's coming this way," Carter was whispering.

"Of course she is," Philippe whispered mischievously. He drew a line through the sketch. "I told you there was a surprise. Ah, she is as beautiful as I predicted, based on her voice. Look at her hair. Look at her mouth. And so, you will be a good boy and run along after a few minutes. After all, she has come to interview me. Of course, I would have let you stay if she had not been so . . ."

She strode confidently to their table. "You're the artist-in-residence, Philippe Brach?"

Philippe nodded.

"Annie Pohaku: journalist for IPN." She said it with—was it an air of sadness?—and yet some trace of a smile that seemed to encourage friendship. "You said we could talk about your work, but now . . ." She turned and appraised Carter, with her grave smile.

Philippe introduced Carter. "Assistant Director of Environmental Engineering. He's the one who decides how we're going to live."

She extended her hand to Carter, and then to Philippe, who stood and took it with a slight bow.

"Can I join you?" she continued.

"Why?" said Carter. "Do you think we're coming apart?"

He is trying to be cute, Philippe thought. He likes her.

She sat with her inhibited smile. A rapport had been established, but her expression still had a hint of gravity.

"Madame," Philippe continued his playful flourish, "welcome to our private table. And more importantly, may I buy you a drink?"

The waitress, antennae at the alert for new customers, was already approaching.

"May *we* buy you a drink," Carter corrected. The waitress hurried away with an order for three reds.

In Annie's mind, some rudimentary attraction, directed toward both Carter and Philippe, skittered along the undersurface of her consciousness, like a bubble in water, hitting the underside of a restless surface. The thoughts did not surprise her, but she could not focus on them because of the news she carried.

"I'd like to talk about your work, too, Carter. Sometime. I'm supposed to be gathering contacts for yet another Mars special. But now, with this news from Hellas . . ." She paused.

"What news from Hellas?" Carter said, suddenly recalling his office screen, with a chill in his spine.

"You haven't heard? Alwyn Stafford took a dune buggy out from Hellas Base and he hasn't come back," she said. "He's disappeared."

B O O K 2

Cold Days in Hellas

[Through the media,] moments break loose of the gravity of history, which means that history . . . is reduced to surrealism.

—Steve Erickson,
Leap Year, 1989

4

East of Stafford's parked buggy, the cold sky was finally growing lighter. High, thin clouds began to catch the rays of incipient sunrise. And here he was, half-awake, sitting alone in the middle of the desert in his buggy. Crazy, crazy, crazy. He was at the point in his life where things that seemed valid and attractive by day seemed crazy and pointless in the hours before dawn.

Outside, brown rocks seemed scattered on the sand like seashells on a foreign beach. Each rock seemed to have its own personality. He remembered a phrase from John Nichols, who pictured electrons spinning inside rocks. Stones, Nichols said, have heartbeats. Hell, did any of these kids read Nichols anymore? Who would be the poets of the Martian deserts? . . . Maybe Carter's French friend, Philippe Brach; he seemed to take time to feel the pulse of the place.

Elena Trevina had been in his half dreams. Lena. She cared about Mars. She had moved heaven and Earth—literally—to get the go-ahead for her polar research base. Bent a few rules in the process, out of love and curiosity. Capacities for love and curiosity were the dangerous, essential qualities that led to infatuation with flush-faced Mars. That much he admired in her. But he hoped she knew what she was doing.

Suddenly he thought of her sex life, down there at the South Polar Station. She was attractive, in a remote sort of way. As if she wanted you to crack the shell . . . Who among the males there . . . He, of course, was too old for her. Still, he sensed a real connection between them. She was divorced long before Mars, obviously knew a few things. A woman had once given him a rule of thumb: If you think you're getting a conversational come-on, you probably are. But Lena and himself?

The question made him think of the place in his life where time had brought him. This filled him with unease. For most of the people on Mars, like his friend Carter, there was a clear role in life. Biological. Sexual. Unconsciously—he could see it now—they were all trying to lay up status points, trying to impress a potential sexual partner. Biologic programming—wasn't it great? After his own wife died, his own programming had waned; mortality had begun to loom in his own mind, tied to the question of his own sexual role. What was it? No longer procreation, thank God.

No longer power or establishing status in either a male or general social pecking order; he had enough of that. Still, the relation to a woman like Lena took on some unfinished quality, like a problem to be solved.

There he was, intellectualizing again. If sex was no longer instinctive, it was not really sex, and a vacuum had been created in his life. It needed to be filled, and the paradox was to fill it with something that fertilized life—like sex itself—and not something that fertilized death.

And what about the rest of them; the tangled web they were weaving with their programs . . . ? Maybe it didn't matter, as long as it gave him a chance to follow his dream. At his age, that's what he cared about.

Still, he wondered how they were handling things, Trevina at the pole and Braddock back at Hellas Base. Braddock he had never figured out. The man was inscrutable, always citing some regulation that turned out to be in his own favor. They always seemed to have the rules on their side, Trevina and Braddock and the rest of them. Lately, Braddock had been invoking guarantees that went all the way back to the Russo-American accords that had fostered Mars exploration in the first place.

The rules here had always seemed chaotic. Chaos was a sign of a dynamic society, Carter Jahns had said once. Or was it his artsy friend, Philippe, in one of those tongue-in-cheek, swaggering monologues of his? It helped that there were many bureaus back on Earth that wanted Mars City to grow in spite of unpredictable budget cuts: Live long and prosper. Be fruitful and multiply. As long as those rules applied, a lot of infelicities could be swept under the rug.

The bureaus applied those rules to themselves, too, like ancient desert tribes.

The confused international lines of political, governmental, military, scientific, and industrial connection between Mars City, Phobos University, and Earth grew more tangled every day. Mars Council issued policy edicts and did its best to pretend that the old accords still mattered; and at the same time it had to respond to the pressures of Russian-American, European, and East-Asian corporate conglomerates that held the Mars franchises. And there were the U.N. "directives" from Rio, to which all the companies paid lip service with condescending geopolitical correctness.

Occasionally the Martians mutinied and said "no." And an unspoken idea ran like silent electricity through the back halls of Mars City: Who was to stop them from running their world as they liked, once they reached critical mass?

Stafford yawned and stretched and put the seat upright. Back to reality. The sun was up now. He grabbed a breakfast bar and brewed up a little tea, scanning the landscape outside by habit. No sign of his objective. According to his calculations, the thing was supposed to be just ahead. Maybe it would be visible from the top of that highest ridge on the right.

He fired up the buggy and headed that way, remembering how the rumor started, many weeks back, when he had been in Mars City. One night in the Nix Olympica Bar, a seismic crew member named Ivanov said he had seen something the previous winter when he was flying a hopper out from Hellas Base to one of the geophysics sites. Of course, he couldn't do anything about it; hoppers traveled ballistic trajectories, and the landing point was more than a hundred kilometers away. Something bright, flickering maybe, down in the red desert. He didn't even record the exact coordinates, except to note that it was somewhere along the rugged Hellas Rim at the edge of the Noachis desert. At the time, Ivanov had said nothing. He had not even been sure of seeing anything, so quickly had he passed over the area. Had it been some speck, a reflection in his window?

Everyone at the bar laughed at Ivanov's story. Next time, they teased, he would tell them he had seen a Russian bear. Nix-O was a place to swap yarns. The Martian frontier had given the tall tale a new lease on life. Stafford remembered the time they got a greenhorn believing that a dust storm near Mars City had grown so thick they didn't have to turn on the retro engines in the shuttle coming down from Phobos.

Stafford didn't laugh off Ivanov's story. He had the advantage of being an old-timer. Old-timers had heard a lifetime of stories. Every once in a while, two different stories fitted like pieces of a jigsaw puzzle.

There had been a fellow years before—a little bushy-haired fellow, Stafford couldn't remember the name—Castillo?—who had lived out at the Hellas Base for a year when it was little more than a single geodesic dome for the first geophysicists. One day, when Stafford had been promoting more polar drilling, he had talked to this fellow. How did it feel, living out there with unmitigated Mars only a meter outside the walls in any direction? What were the snowfalls like? How did the tractors hold up? That sort of thing. After the interview, the fellow had gone to a drawer and pulled out a scrap that looked at first like an old hankie. It was a piece of light-colored material with an odd sheen. Perhaps it had been metallized originally, and the metallic luster had worn off. "Ever see anything like this before?"

Stafford said he hadn't.

The bushy-haired fellow told Stafford how he had found the piece of material when he was out with some visiting geologists studying the Hellas rim structure. Out among the great stepped cliffs, between two ridges, caught on the projecting hard crystals of a wind-sculpted rock, was this bit of something that didn't belong.

What had the geologists thought of it? Stafford asked.

They thought it was a piece of junk, some scrap from a shuttle that had landed at the camp, or something that had blown into the desert from the Hellas Base.

Maybe so, Stafford had said.

But the geologists hadn't taken into account the wind. They hadn't lived there and seen the wind, blowing and blowing out of the desert of the Hellespontus rim country. This scrap must have come with the wind out of the Hellespontus desert, where no one had ever been. The bushy-haired fellow had said he couldn't prove it was anything special. It had looked like a bit of man-made debris, all right. He had put it in his drawer and told Stafford he always had thought it was the darndest thing.

Years later, when Stafford heard Ivanov's story in the Nix-O Bar, he said nothing about the scrap. He just smiled. Went home, lay awake most of the night. Went down to the Image Processing Lab the next morning, and started poring over orbiter photos of Hellespontus and the Hellas rim. He plotted Ivanov's flight path, and drew prevailing wind lines paralleling the dust streaks east across the rim of Hellas, from the place the bushy-haired man had been.

Given the uncertainties, the intersection of the flight path and the wind vectors corresponded to an area maybe fifty kilometers on a side. He accessed the high-resolution photos and sat there for hours, looking at one after another. There had been two high-res photo surveys covering the area in '12 and in '21. He compared the images.

On the second day he found something. A triangular object, maybe ten, fifteen meters across—only a tiny white spot on the photos, a few pixels across at best. It couldn't be snow; the photos were taken in summer. It appeared in both photos. In the second, it had shifted position by twenty meters.

There had been no Hellas Base in '12. Whatever it was, it wasn't litter from the Hellas Base.

Stafford went home and brooded over enlargements of the photos, and sent through a request for a dune buggy out of Hellas Base. It would be a two- or three-hundred-kilometer run out to the site, but he had made jaunts that far before. . . .

By coincidence that was the same week when he received the strange note from Lena Trevina, hand-carried by the pilot of the monthly shuttle from the Polar Station. It was handwritten, in a carefully sealed envelope, marked PERSONAL. She had risked no electronic trail. . . . Maybe he should have tossed the damn thing.

Stafford's dune buggy crawled to the crest of the ridge. If he had triangulated right . . .

At first he didn't see it. According to the orbiter photos it should have been somewhere in the broad hollow stretching before him. There were only a few rocks. Then he did see it, as if it had suddenly materialized. It had snagged on a corner where a rock had been etched sharp by a thousand dust storms. From this distance it looked like a sheet of plastic tarp. But then he caught the dull silver gleam of an object lying beyond, in the distance. He knew what it was. By God, he was going to succeed! Today would be a historic occasion!

He drove on past the tattered parachute fragment, toward the silvery object. He mumbled a little prayer of thanks to the long-lost, patient Martian gods. He parked the buggy, and turned on its short-range transmitter.

He started to reach for his cavernous helmet, but then he remembered the medallion. He pulled it out of his pocket. It was a little brass medallion, inscribed on the front and back, and hinged on the side like a Victorian locket, or an old pocket watch. Medallion number 216, it was. Jesus, the places he had been, the sights he had seen. He popped it open. Inside was a piece of foil, which he placed carefully on his knee. Using a fine-tipped screwdriver from the tool kit pocket on his puffy legging, he incised carefully on the foil:

2031, FEB. 43

With more dexterity than patience, he laboriously inscribed his signature on the foil. He replaced the foil in the locket and snapped it shut with a smile. He put the screwdriver, which had always served him as an all-purpose tool, back in its kit, and looped the medallion on its nylon cord through one of the velcroed loops on his suit. He put on the helmet. He heard the comforting hiss of air around his face. The auto-elasticized inner suit tightened around him as he depressurized the buggy.

Everything was working fine.

He stepped out, tingling with anticipation. Through the suit he could hear his muffled footsteps crunching—a sound he loved. It sounded like his feet were in another room—in a toolshed with a crunchy dirt floor.

The metal apparatus was resting in a little hollow.

He walked up to the object and put his hand on it. It had waited sixty years for him. It was pretty beat up. He could feel little nicks or dents—pebbles blown into it during previous storms? He patted it. "Stout fellow," he whispered. "It wasn't your fault."

There was a bent, broken rod protruding from one side of the device. He fished up the medallion and looped its cord securely around the rod, being careful not to disturb the device itself. The little brass disk gleamed as the sun grew stronger in the dusty sky. On the outside was engraved:

Alwyn Bryan Stafford explored here.
This is the 216th disk left by him at
noteworthy sites on Mars. Date inside.

On the reverse it said:

Alwyn Bryan Stafford came to Mars one
Mars-year after the first Martian landing.
He landed in year 2010 by the Christian
calendar. He was the 237th human being on Mars,
and godfather of the first child born on Mars.

Egocentric, for sure. But what the hell. A hundred years from now when people were finding his disks here and there, no one would criticize him for leaving this record of the first explorations.

He stepped back and admired the scene. He backed off farther and sat on a rock, memorizing the whole landscape. What a thing to remember.

Stafford had always been interested in history. Often he had mused over the irony that Earth's park rangers and environmentalists—anyone with decent style—decried modern litter, but would give an arm for the litter of early explorers and colonists. Castoffs and inscriptions more than two hundred years old were priceless, recapturing early travels and adventures. He recalled his visit as a teenager to El Morro National Monument, the historic inscribed rock of the Southwest, in a landscape not too different from this one, except for the bushes. Weary travelers, resting in its shade under the vast New Mexican sky, had carved their names and dates and proud messages. From Oñate in the 1600s to American fur trappers in the 1800s, they had left a record that clarified movements of the pioneers, both famous and faceless—important if you had a sense of place and time. El Morro: that is where the idea of medallions was born in the adolescent Alwyn Stafford.

That night, under El Morro's looming presence, young Stafford's eyes had glowed like the distant stars in the space-black skies of New Mexico's Indian reservations. He lay in their camp at El Morro reading a book on Coronado's expedition, the Mars Project of its day. A thousand men with the latest sixteenth-century technology, setting forth with their banners into the unknown on a months-long journey of discovery. They had published the first written eyewitness accounts of native American villages now destroyed by malls; of burbling rivers, now sucked dry by cities. But historians were still arguing over their exact route. Which villages? Which rivers? They had neglected to sign in on the great white rock of El Morro. If only *they* had left some carvings, some bronze plaques, or some inscribed medallions for someone to find someday along their route. Under the stars, visions of ancient relics burned in young Stafford's eyes.

On Mars, old Stafford, pioneer of a new desert, had a chance to carry out his boyhood dream: to leave a record of the pioneers. How to do it? Social niceties forbade that he should go around carving his kilroy on every cliff. He could hardly leave ostentatious brass plaques; aside from the weight problem that would allow him to transport only a small number of them to Mars, they would be quickly removed. When he had hit on the idea of his little disks, he told no one. He simply salted them away in a crevice here, under a rock there, at sites he thought noteworthy. The sequential numbers established the record of continuity. Slowly they would come to light, one at a time, in random order, decades later. They would show there had been someone with enough gumption and courage and craziness to get out and find these places, but also with enough respect for nature and history to leave them undisturbed.

They would give the next generation of fourteen-year-olds—the first real Martians—something to dream about, in the same way that he had once dreamed of finding Coronado's relic. Mothers would tell them, "Maybe one day you can find one of Stafford's medallions." Perhaps some of his markers would last centuries before being found. And then people would know: within twenty years of landing on Mars, they got as far as *here.*

There would be legends of the conquistadors of Mars.

He looked at the little medallion gleaming in front of him. No telling how long it would take them to find this one. Maybe a decade. Maybe a week. Who would they send out looking for him?

In the midst of his elation, he realized that this discovery would make his next goal all the more achievable.

He climbed back into the bus and sat at the wheel, glancing repeatedly at the device outside among the rocks, feeling good about his discovery. It was time to move on.

He knew he should sit and think it through one more time. He needed to plan how he wanted things to look.

He began driving in long, leisurely loops around the site. Finally, a half hour later, he turned the nose of the buggy westward across a rocky outcrop and took a deep breath. He began driving, away from Hellas Base, deeper into unexplored desert. Suddenly he wondered: When the time came, would Carter Jahns ever remember the conversations he had choreographed, about Percival Lowell and the canals of Mars?

5

For Carter, it was as if the light level in Nix-O had suddenly dimmed. Stafford? Gone? In a fatal instant, amid the ordinary clinking of glasses and the everyday chatter and laughter of the Nix Olympica Bar after a hard day's work, everything had changed.

The air itself seemed suddenly to gel into a dark fluid, as if it had been supercooled all along, as if disaster had been lurking in the background of everything they had done on Mars. The lights and glinting chrome of the Nix Olympica now suddenly seemed to shine only in darkness, like stars with no planet to illuminate.

The background chatter of the room transformed itself into sounds of—what?—prisoners, locked in a weird outpost of humanity. Carter had prided himself on his awareness that outside the thin walls of aluminum and glass and brick the air was thinner and dryer and colder and far less oxygen-rich than the air on an Earthly mountain twice as high as Everest. And that it was a deadly world of risk. Deaths had occurred since he had been here, but they had been statistical accidents, part of Mars City's equation that they all bought into, with that first step onto the rusty soil. Now his old views seemed theoretical and sterile, replaced by a personal element of horror. Could callous Death really reach out of the desert and penalize his friend for a single mistake? Someone he knew, someone who had looked him in the eye, smiled, breathed the same air, shaken his hand . . . ? Besides, Stafford didn't make mistakes.

For that instant he was transported outside the walls of Mars City, and he was surprised to see that the whole mighty city, the safe fortress he had been building, was only a fragile intruder. Sunset. Mars City, unfinished tubeworks covered with freshly turned Martian dirt, bathed in the last moments of brick-dust light. The hundred-meter layer of ground haze beginning to take on the color of blood along the horizon.

Suddenly Carter felt older—the first time this sensation had crept into his spine. "God," he heard himself say, involuntarily. His heart was pounding.

Philippe had said nothing. He sat stony-faced, holding his drink as if it had frozen in his hand.

"I . . . I thought you knew," Annie said. "I'm sorry to be the bearer . . .

sorry about the news. Of course, they don't know what happened. Maybe Stafford's still out there. There'll be a search. . . ." She studied them, quietly, watching their reactions.

Carter and Philippe were still silent, staring into their drinks.

"I understand both of you are friends of his," she prompted.

Carter nodded slowly, coming back to reality, looking up across the table at her. She was watching him, as if probing him. She had been defined by that moment of light, framed in the doorway like someone arriving from some other dimension. Now, just as quickly, the illusion had been snatched away, smashed . . .

Carter felt a chill in his spine. "What happened . . . ?"

"He set out from Hellas Base Thursday. Didn't come back. Supposed to check in yesterday."

Philippe muttered, "It had to happen sometime. You know how he was . . ."

"Shit." Carter's head was down again, as if he were trying to find something in his empty glass. He banged the glass down on the table.

Annie touched Carter's arm, a gentle, brief gesture. "Really, I thought you had already heard." She smiled slightly, sympathetically. It was more of a look than a smile. "It's only been five days. I understand the dune buggies have air and water for as much as . . ."

"Eight days. He always took extra airpacs. He'd have enough air until Friday at the latest, depending on his level of physical activity."

Philippe looked at his watch. "The forty-eighth." He drew three more lines through his sketch, deliberately.

Carter caught Annie studying him, as if still appraising something. "I know you'll have to . . . Listen, could I just ask you . . . ? You know him well . . . ?"

"Yeah," Carter said, numbly.

"Could you tell me about him?"

"Interesting guy. Unique. We're friends. But he has a core that's hard to reach. I never knew what he was thinking, inside. But he's like an uncle. He helped me; helped me get started here."

Suddenly the waitress arrived with the three reds they had ordered. She was all smiles until she saw in a moment of confusion that the jolly familiarity of the table had disappeared. She hurried away from the pall of gloom.

"Well, we've got to do something," Carter said, finally. He took a big drink.

Annie studied him. "Carter, there's more. They're running the search out of Hellas Base but you've been named by Mars Council to report on what happened."

"Jeez." Carter remembered the urgent message he had left unheeded in his office. He glanced guiltily at his 'corder, which was still turned off.

"It's the first flat-out disappearance in the history of Mars, right?" She was still probing. "Fatal accidents, yes, but this is the first time anyone's gone out alone and not come back. Do you have any ideas . . . I mean about what happened? Why he would go out alone?"

"Stafford was a special case. He had arranged some special deal. They'd let him go out alone. . . . Now, we'll have to . . ."

"Carter's the man for the job," Philippe said unexpectedly.

She turned to him. "What do you think of Stafford?"

"I admire him." She and Philippe talked, while Carter sank into silence. He would have to turn on his 'corder, of course; link himself again into the world of electronic anxieties. He would be catapulted into the thick of it. First, though, he had to take a moment to collect himself, to prepare. After taking himself out of circulation earlier that night, one more minute wouldn't make any difference.

Why me? he thought. Mars Council must have picked him because of his friendship with Stafford. Everyone knew of his friendship with the famous recluse. If anyone knew what made the old man tick, it would be Carter. That's what they would be thinking.

And now, he realized with a shock, he already had the damn press on his heels.

His reaction was an instinct bred by a semipublic professional life. Be careful, the press is the enemy of the public official. Yet when he examined the instinct he couldn't see why it should be so, at least on struggling Mars. They were all in the same boat.

"Look," she was saying. She had turned to face him again. "I'll level with you. I came here to interview Mr. Brach, here, Monsieur Brach, about his Stonehenge in the desert. That's something I still want to do. But now I've stumbled on you at the same time, in the middle of this. . . ." She waved her hand. "I know this will be a tough time for you. But I want to cover this story. There aren't many reporters here, none with the connections I have. I need to cover this story. It's important for everybody. Will you let me talk to you about it? If not now, then at least when you get the investigation under way?"

It was as if he could no longer concentrate on what she was saying. He gave her no answer. He turned on his 'corder screen. She watched him in silence. The lines of tiny, precise, black words scrolled across the screen, the little machine blurting out its news like an excited child who couldn't wait. She was right. They had temporarily reassigned him from his office. The search was already under way, out of Hellas; his own job was to investigate the causes and outcome of the accident. One strange thing. Stafford, apparently invoking his usual privileged bending of the rules, had filed only the vaguest of itineraries. "Going out into Helles-pontus desert for purpose of historic explorations." Whatever that meant. Then he had typed one more thing. "If problems, Carter Jahns may be able to find me." What the hell was that supposed to mean?

Tomorrow he'd have to go down to Hellas Base, monitor what was going on. Even if Stafford was found alive, they wanted a report on what had happened. And recommendations. Always recommendations. . . .

"Look," he said. "I better go log in."

Annie held up a finger. "Before you go, can I just ask you one more . . ."

"Jesus. Listen, let me go check in with them. I'll come back. You guys wait here? I need somebody to talk to."

They nodded, like conspirators.

In his office, Carter ended the conversation with Hellas Base and logged off. He sat at his desk in the darkness of his office, illuminated only by the blue-green glow of the screen. He had acknowledged the assignment, then reserved a spot on the Hellas shuttle. Then he just sat there, in the faint glow. Where the hell had Stafford gone? What had happened to him? Nobody knew. Tomorrow it would be his problem. Why would Stafford think Carter could find him?

He turned off the machine.

"Have a good night, Mr. Jahns," it said.

Right.

He headed back to Nix-O. Maybe Philippe would have some good ideas. Maybe this lady from the press would know something. The press always knew more than anybody else about what was going on.

She was full of questions when he got there. Hellas Base. What's it like? He'd been there a lot? Were their dune buggies just like the ones she had seen here? What were they like to drive, the buggies? How far could they go? How fast? Were they dangerous? Why was Stafford allowed to go out on his own?

Carter explained Stafford's position as Grand Old Man and Professor Emeritus of Mars. Some time ago he had wrung informal permission from the new Hellas Director, Braddock, to go out on his own.

"Can Braddock do that?"

"At the research stations, they still make their own rules. Besides, Stafford convinced them. What they risked in losing one old codger out in the desert, they gained in a faster flow of new information about the wilderness around them." Carter tried to explain to them what Stafford had said to him once. "Hell's bells," he had said, "I've made my contribution to Mars. I'm old enough now. I want to take some risks. Go for the big discovery. Braddock understands, thank God. It's in his interest if I find something. I like nosing around. Between you and me, I'd like to die with my boots on, instead of sitting in my little steel box of a room."

Secretly, Carter had liked the agreement for Stafford to go out "nosing around"; he thought it meant they were coming to terms with the planet.

The agreement was not widely publicized at first. Management wanted to see how it worked out. Perhaps a precedent had been set—after retirement, maybe Martians would be allowed to break the stultifying rules. Carter thought there was some merit in Philippe's idea about the Aztecs, letting their elders flout the taboos as a reward.

Eventually, of course, word got out. Whenever Stafford made a trip on Mars, everyone waited with interest. Rumors would fly in the bars among the construction workers. "He's seen stuff out there. Stuff they never tell you about . . ."

Stafford was the classic desert rat. The more interested the public grew, the more secretive he became.

"Did he ever get in trouble before?" Annie asked.

"All the time, but nothing serious. Stafford knew every part of a dune buggy inside out. When he goes out alone he can carry enough spare parts to make a new one."

"When Stafford gets enough canned air to go out for a week, he is happy as a clam," Philippe said. "I know. I talked to him about these trips." Philippe had been nursing his drink, watching them, watching Annie.

Annie's Red sat on the table, hardly touched. "Do you think he had some sort of death wish? Did he develop an urge to . . . you know, cash in his chips out there in his beloved desert somewhere?"

"No. No. The guy was . . . the guy is vibrant. Besides, he wouldn't waste everyone's time making them track down his dune buggy."

"How hard is it going to be to track him down?" Annie asked.

"There's something weird there. . . ." Carter hesitated. Was there some reason to use discretion? No, he thought. This is Mars. We—humanity—we're all in this together. Something in the back of his mind laughed at his own naiveté. He plowed on. He needed someone to talk to. "Stafford, as usual, didn't file much of a trip plan. Just said he was going out in the desert, in effect. But the weird thing is, he said I might know where to find him. They tell me they used to complain about the vague trip plans he'd file, and he'd get mad, tell them he didn't know which way he'd go till he'd seen the country. But a few trips ago he started adding this note that I'd know where to find him."

Annie perked up. "Do you?"

"I don't have the foggiest idea what he's talking about. I don't know where to find him."

"But he said that? He said you'd know where he was?"

"I guess the wording was that I might know how to find him."

Philippe grumbled, "That's different."

With a start, Carter found himself wondering if Stafford really *had* been his friend. Did he really know Stafford? Or just admire his reputation and independence?

The conversation lagged. Little Japanese bean cakes, products of experiments between the greenhouse and the Nix-O chef, lay ignored on the table.

"We've got to go after him," Philippe said at last.

"We?"

"I liked him. He would tell me stories about the desert. A natural arch he discovered once. A hundred meters long, he claimed. And the time he saw a pond of liquid water form in the bottom of Valles Marineris when he uncovered a bare ice layer there. He told me it lasted twenty minutes. Of course, I could never tell if he was, how do you say it, pulling my leg. I think he liked to pretend this is the Old West and we were all the new boys in the town, and his duty was to spin yarns to see how gullible we were."

Carter reflected. "I think a lot of those stories were true . . . the guy had such a reverence for what Mars is *really* like. . . ."

"Anyway, I want to come with you on the search," Philippe repeated. "More assistance. It cannot hurt. Besides, the more places I experience on Mars, the better for my work."

Carter decided he was grateful for this left-handed offer of help. "I'm not in charge of the search itself, you understand. The search crews are already out there. I don't know if I'll go out in the field. Far as I can tell, I'm just supposed to monitor what's going on, lend a hand, ideas . . . write it all up so they have some sort of record to analyze. I'll go down to Hellas, of course. Had a trip budgeted down there next week, anyway, to look at our monitors. I moved it up. Of course you can come, Philippe, if you want to spend the time."

"The important thing is, I want to help."

"Why didn't he just radio in?" Annie Pohaku asked. "Couldn't it still happen, a radio message from him?"

"If he were in his buggy, and conscious, he'd radio in. It's hard to imagine all his backup radios, everything, failed."

"So . . . ?" She paused, running out of questions.

"Tomorrow I'll know something," Carter said.

Philippe remained quiet, for once.

Annie looked around as if searching for a brighter subject. "In a happier moment, I would like the colors in here. . . ."

"Everyone on Mars likes blue," Philippe said without enthusiasm. "Their optical nerves are starved for it."

Carter woke before dawn. The lights hadn't come up yet. He looked around the dark room, almost in a daze.

No it hadn't been a dream. Stafford was missing.

Tuesday morning. Three days left for Stafford's air supply. A couple hours till the Hellas shuttle.

In a stupor, he got up and took a bath. Water was one thing Mars City had plenty of, in spite of its being a desert. Water of hydration abounded in the minerals. The oxygen processors produced more than the city could use. As he was drawing the water and stripping off his sweater, he caught sight of a black spot in the tub, and for a moment thought it was a beetle. It shocked him, like hearing about Stafford. It was only a ball of black lint, of course. The great spaceships that floated like feathers around the sun from Earth to Mars were perfumed with deadly efficiency. The only bugs on Mars were in the computers.

Remembering that Hellas Base was spartan by comparison to Mars City, he gave himself a long soak. A chance to think. He thought about Stafford, old Stafford who had been here like a fixture ever since Carter arrived. Stafford radiated crusty competence and his face seemed to hide a thousand secrets of the desert. Stafford, who always knew what he was doing, to whom nothing could happen. Carter soaked, waiting for some stroke of genius.

What had Stafford been up to? That's what they had to find out. Maybe he should interview some people, ask Annie to come along. She could poke around while he was gone, ask questions in her guise as journalist, report back to him in exchange for giving her interviews. Make her work for it. It bothered him, the way she had shown up in Nix-O. He had been conscious of attraction in those initial moments. Had the ensuing conversation been fully natural? Or had she taken advantage of his moments of loss? The questions had been hovering all along, at some subliminal level. Even now, he had trouble focusing on it.

The water was cold. Well, show time.

He toweled himself off.

He was frightened for Stafford. But at the same time, he felt strangely alive. It surprised him. On an ordinary day, people would meet him in the hall, "How ya doin?" And he'd say, "Fine." But how long had it been since he had felt like this? After the office gloom yesterday, he felt reborn. Was it just the sense of challenge? Pride? Annie? He had always loved the way the mere presence of a woman—a woman who attracted him— could make him come alive. As if the life force had emerged from its cocoon. In a way he hated it, too, as if he had no control over his own feelings.

On and on they went, Carter and Philippe, through the halls and plazas of Mars City. On the way to Hellas. In the blue-tiled concourse to the airlock, Carter preferred the walk to the little humming electric go-carts. With a flight time of less than an hour, the shuttle would arrive at 5:00 P.M. Hellas time, taking into account the time zone shift.

It was a strange walk, this morning. The threat of death in the air made Carter see everything as if in a dream, as if he were some detached television monitor, floating high on some ceiling robot. They passed the fat cylindrical ornamented concrete pillars that supported the high roof, the upper floor, the mezzanines, the floating green lobbies. Past the trees, looking out of place like travelers in a new land. Some were forlorn and homesick, missing their friends, feeling transplanted, while others smiled behind their leaves, shouting in silent tree language for joy at their existence in a whole new landscape. Secretly, they seemed to await the day when they would burst out of Mars City and go marching, as trees will do, across the soil and carbon dioxide of the hills. ("If only there were a little more air, a little more ozone, a little more moisture . . . then see what we'd do! We could make over the place so fast it would make your human heads spin!")

Past children running from shop to office to salon—children who, in tedious fourth grades, would learn about the Ptolemaic, blue, central planet, which was still the central planet. The Washington Monument, the Bolshoi Ballet, Big Ben, the New Brooklyn Dodgers. They would learn it all from flickering holograms and ancient movies; rarely from precious books brought in spaceships, and read now by a first and then a second generation, in private, quiet corners. Books—whose pages, if taken outside, would dry up and break off and blow away, clattering like dry leaves back in Illinois in the fall.

In one curious moment they found themselves trailing a couple of Earthside college boys parading loudly down the arcade. "I spent a whole semester up at Phobos University. Can't believe that place. What a rock! Alcatraz. Come all this way and they've got nothing to do. So I quit and came down here. God, it's even worse! Don't tell my parents. They'll go berserk."

The kids turned off toward a sugar bar.

Carter gave Philippe a disgusted look.

"Forget it," Philippe said. "Earthside kids are a different species. The end of childhood is discovering the world beyond childhood. Most people, they never discover it at all. They remain unsatisfied kids. I'm not going to have any, you know."

"Have any what?"

"Kids. I'm happy the way I am in life."

"That's what a caterpillar thinks before it turns into a butterfly."

They passed a young Catholic priest, who Carter had seen off and on in the malls and avenues: he always looked lost, Carter thought, as if Jesus never really had a plan for Mars. Religions, perhaps, were only spawned one planet at a time, nontransferable.

He was beginning to think that although he was raised an American, his Russian heritage was catching up with him, like a genetic disease. According to his mother, the Russians were always philosophizing and trying to build new systems: Marxism to achieve fairness from social structure, rampant capitalism to develop the country's resources. He was as caught up in trying to build a new Mars as a Soviet bureaucrat trying to build a new order. His American friends, by contrast, never seemed to be building anything, just going off in their own directions, pursuing one personal scheme or another. That's what Safford had done, and now he, Carter, was going to have to set aside the abstract rules of community and come to grips with real life.

The chips are down. Your bet.

In the suiting room they found Annie Pohaku, struggling with a helmet and fittings. She looked up and smiled at them, enjoying their surprise.

Carter felt an unexpected rush of irritation. "What's going on?" Part of his irritation was toward his own unpreparedness for this; it wasn't part of the plan.

"I'm coming along." Judging his expression, she added, "You said you can use all the help you can get. And I know there's a story there."

"But nobody said . . ."

"Oh, Carter, don't be such a tightass." She was smiling at him. "You don't have to hate me because I'm a reporter." Was she teasing him?

Oh, hell, Carter thought. He wasn't sure why he reacted this way. Reporting was supposed to wait until later, when they knew answers. Well, he had better decide something, fast. The press tagging along? Not that there was much press on Mars. Annie and her network from Earth had stumbled into the right place at the right time; it was a bombshell of a story and she knew it.

"What . . . what would you do there?" he stammered lamely. He knew his eyes betrayed irritation.

"Get a story." She flashed in anger. "You got a problem with that? Look, I'm as free as anybody to go to Hellas. There were still empty seats on this shuttle. Besides, Network has a lot of clout when it comes to tickets. I don't exactly need a permission slip from you or the Council." She softened. "Besides, I could help."

"Help?" He remembered his daydream of trying to enlist her.

"Why not?"

"You're a reporter. That's why not." It sounded stupid as soon as he said it.

She smiled a wry smile. "Does that really make any sense to you? It's very traditional and all that, very . . . Earthy. Know what I mean? But does it really make any sense to turn down help when your best friend is missing? When you're supposed to find out what happened, and you have only Philippe to help in the investigation?"

It made no sense.

"Besides, there's the reporter's golden rule: The more you learn, the more you earn. Is that crass enough for you? But I *would* help you," she added.

"Welcome to our expedition," Philippe said. "I am sure we can use you." He smiled. "And no doubt you can use us."

Carter fumed.

Their attention was diverted when a Hellas-bound field construction team came in for the same flight. Five men and a woman, they talked jovially about Stafford as they broke their suits out of their lockers. "Never shoulda let him out on his own anyway."

"Aw, the old guy's got a right. Wouldn't you like to go out there poking around someday when you got nothin' better to do? Nobody telling you where to go?"

"Not bloody likely. I'm just on this rustball for the pay. You won't catch me outside when the old timeclock ain't tickin'. Gonna retire Earthside, soon as I save up for another coupla years. 'Swhat Stafford shoulda done if you ask me."

"Too late now," the woman said. "He's a goner."

"Martians got him, if you ask me."

They laughed.

"I say he got on a slope and flipped, just like those boys that flipped their buggy in the polar tunnel. You get careless, you pay."

"It wasn't in the tunnel. Nobody's ever been killed in the tunnel. It was on their way back, on East Road, way I heard. They'd always get to going too fast out there. They were desert-crazy. Hit a boulder and tipped the tractor right over!" The man spoke with a drawl and affected a blue baseball cap emblazoned with absurd gold scrambled eggs on the visor. He tossed the cap in the locker. He spoke with enthused animation, as if describing football instead of death. "Decompressed. Killed all six of 'em right away. Everybody except the driver. He had his helmet right there."

"But you know," another man replied, "it's a wonder they didn't lose a dozen people in those tunnels. Excavating all that volume. Huge, you know, in those damn soft sediments. Stuff would just as soon crumble and collapse on you as hold its shape. They were always shoring it up. . . ." Two other construction men with beefy faces were nodding expressionlessly.

"Hey," the first speaker turned to Carter. "Ain't you the guy heading the search for old Stafford?"

"The search is already under way," Carter said brusquely.

"Hey, sorry I asked, man."

"I'm supposed to write it up. An accident report."

"Well, tell them to keep dune buggies away from slopes and boulders."
The workers turned back to their suits in silence.

Clad in their puffy garments, Carter, Philippe, and Annie passed through the pressure check and left the suiting room. They headed down the main exit tunnel past the gray warehouses with the yellow flowers painted on their doors, where supplies entered Mars City after long flights from the orbiting ports of a white-clouded Earth. Toward the airlocks.

"Hey, they say he's a tough old guy," the woman called after them. "Maybe it'll turn out okay."

6

FEBRUARY 45, TUESDAY

The Hellas shuttle, a glorified hopper, was a metal biscuit on stilts, bristling with antennae, reaction jets, external cargo flanges. The main engine hung underneath: tubing and testicles of tanks containing liquid oxygen derived from the Martian air. Inside, ten removable seats with their worn webbing were dotted around the central cargo area. A sealed pilot compartment protruded on one side like a bay window, giving a view fore and aft.

They had scarcely webbed themselves in when the pilot told them to hang on. As the shuttle rose from the Mars City pad in a storm of dust and pale flame, Carter caught a glimpse through his little window of the loading dock workers in the distance, going on about their incessant business: cartons and yellow tractors. The ground outside the window dropped away, pivoting like a trapdoor on an axis through the horizon. Normal launch. No one down there paying any attention.

Now the engines stopped. The craft sailed silently in the sun above ruddy Mars, climbing east and south. The passenger and cargo area was pressurized, but the pilot ordered the occupants—Carter Jahns, Annie Pohaku, and Philippe Brach—to keep their helmets handy just in case. "Regulations," he said.

A hundred kilometers below, the lost, broken valleys on the eastern outskirts of Valles Marineris slid by as if in a slow-motion silent movie. The land was not the rumpled bedspreads of mountainous Earthscapes, but rather a cracked tile floor, splintered into irregular blocks. Veins of faint dry arroyos laced the ocher desert. The scene reminded Carter of aerial photos of the California desert, after the ridges and arroyos had been smashed and twisted by the Big One in '14.

Carter sat alone, webbed into his own cocoon seat against the tiny window, brooding. The cocoons were arranged around the wall of the cylindrical payload bay; cargo was stored in the middle. Human occupants here were an afterthought, which added to his sense of frustrated anticipation. He could not swing into action until they arrived at Hellas. Now, there was nothing he could do but listen to his own heartbeat counting out Stafford's last minutes.

Annie and Philippe were cozy in the side-by-side seats two rows behind him.

So . . . Carter thought to himself, Philippe was already chatting up Annie, talking about where she grew up. As if they had somehow accepted that this trip was an isolated fragment of time, when they could do nothing to save Stafford, and were permitted to . . . Why should he begrudge them their talk? He was the one who had to figure out what to do next, while they rested. He was the one in charge. He could hear bits of their conversation. Her soft voice.

". . . Hawaii. I've been here only a few weeks and I miss it already."

"You are an ocean person, then."

"The ocean . . . it's always a presence . . . flowers and rain . . . petals on the sidewalks and moss on the rocks. The rocks here look naked."

"You should come with me to the greenhouse sometime."

"I'd like that. But this thing with Stafford . . ."

Jeez, can't they take this seriously? Flirting while Stafford is . . . Compulsively, Carter looked at his watch and checked his 'corder. Stafford was still missing, according to the latest updates.

He tried to think ahead. When the shuttle arrived at Hellas, he would talk to the buggy maintenance crew, find out what he could about the condition of Stafford's vehicle when it went out. He also wanted to review orbital imagery of the area. Satellite images had been one of Stafford's favorite sources of inspiration; maybe they would be his salvation. Everybody knew that the orbiters couldn't resolve anything as small as a single buggy, and that the imagery covered any given region only every few days. Still, the images might give some clue. . . .

Carter tried to concentrate, but his mind fought back. Flowers and rain. How had she talked her way into this? Well, his other voice answered, what was wrong with it? The more help we have, the more chance of finding Stafford. But she's a reporter, the first voice said. Second voice: So? First voice: Who ever heard of bringing reporters along while an investigation is in progress? Second voice: This is Mars. We do things differently here. Besides, it's not really an investigation. It's a rescue. First voice: You're rationalizing everything. Second voice: Yeah, I know.

Carter turned and faced them directly. "Philippe was right. This search needs all the help we can give it."

Annie and Philippe broke off their conversation with a start.

"We need to do whatever we can to find Stafford. We need a plan."

"Plan away," Philippe said, still disgustingly jovial.

Annie looked concerned. "Can we talk to the search-and-rescue teams when they come back?"

"We'll talk to everybody. We'll start with Braddock. He's the manager at Hellas Base, so technically he's in charge of the search. But we're not gonna sit on the sidelines. The only way to carry out this assignment is to get directly involved, as much as Braddock lets us."

"Tell me about Braddock," Annie said.

"Crusty. I only met him once when he came through Mars City. Took the job, oh, a month or so back, when they expanded the research program. Administrator type. Everybody was talking him up. They say he's a tough hombre. They hired him directly from Earth. Headed some government lab there, I think."

"Did he know Stafford?" Annie asked. "I mean before coming here?"

"Who knows? They might have had some professional contact."

"Did Stafford have close friends?"

"He had a wife here. Kept to himself after she died."

"And there was you."

"Yes."

"So he was a loner?"

Carter paused. "There's a kind of person that can be a good friend and is still a loner inside."

Philippe said, "What do you want us to do?"

"Work with me. Keep your eyes open."

"Whatever happens, we'll be with you," Annie said. She stretched forward and touched his shoulder.

———————————————●———————————————

Mars slid by underneath holding on to its secrets. The shuttle coasted silently. It had passed far beyond the broken canyonlands, drifting over three thousand kilometers of cratered wilderness. Now they were coming in over Hellespontus, a tangle of eroded craters superimposed on ridges that defined the vast basin rim. Somewhere down there was his friend. . . . Carter strained to look through the little window, as if careful enough peering would reveal Stafford, standing by his stranded vehicle, waving up to them. But the smallest details he could see were craters the size of football stadiums. . . .

When Carter looked up, he saw that the others were also straining to peer at the ground. In their faces, he could read the same thoughts.

They drifted quietly over a vast hazy circle, a crater whose width must have equaled their altitude. Inside it was another little, sharp-rimmed crater. Inside that, a landslide had tumbled parts of the wall into a rubbly apron that had slithered halfway across the crater floor. Details within details; you could never escape it.

"Look." Philippe pointed out his tiny window. Annie leaned across him to look and Carter turned to his own window.

Ahead, the crater-peppered landscape ended in a band of whitish haze that stretched along the horizon. They were sliding toward it. As they approached, they could see that the cratered terrain ended at the summit of a line of broken cliffs, which descended onto a bright foggy plain. The edge of ancient, mighty Hellas, largest impact basin on Mars. The huge, bright circular patch had been mapped and named two centuries earlier by the nocturnal eccentrics who found cold pleasure in squinting at distant red Mars through antique telescopes.

They were flying now above the haze, and they could see through it as if it were gauze. At the foot of the cliffs only a few broken ridges protruded from the sea of sandy sediments that had filled the vast basin. Somewhere down there was Hellas Base, offspring of Mars City.

Finally Carter spotted it below them, tiny in the distance, growing. Eight half-cylinder Quonsetlike modules radiating from a geodesic-domed center, like spokes on a wheel. Brave little Hellas Base.

It was a seed from which some larger settlement, like Mars City, might grow someday. Whereas Mars City was a complex accumulation of modules, levels, additions, towers, repairs, and retrofits, Hellas Base still showed its rough simplicity. A long circular hall, like the tire on a wheel, had been added to surround the Quonset mods in a ring, with entries into the outer end of each. Additions of new mods into the outer edge of this ring had begun in one sector so that the city was fanning out to the northwest. In plan, it looked like a textbook illustration of an organic molecule. Or a spiderweb abuilding . . .

While Mars City had been sited among billion-year-old lava fields and puzzling dry riverbeds, Hellas Base dealt with mysteries much older. It lay near the edge of the giant 3.8-billion-year-old impact basin, and below the hulking upland hills, pocked and scarred with four-billion-year-old craters, rim upon rim. The stark and violent reality of the craters was softened only by the cosmetic of powder—hundreds of meters of dust dropped in the crater floors by capricious winds. What celestial rain of stones crashed onto Mars in its first days to make these craters that the shuttle coasted across so effortlessly? Were seas, lakes, and rivers present throughout that first billion years, or just sporadic? Whence the bacterial life that had eventually emerged by three or three and a half billion years ago? These were the questions that drove scientists into the southern hills, into those tiny buildings below.

Suddenly the telltale whine of airflow could be heard. Reentry. They were no longer drifting lazily above Mars. They were screaming through the pink air toward Hellas Base at more than a kilometer per second. Newtonian science incarnate and triumphant. Startling bumps along the way: What invisible violences did the shearing Martian winds commit at this altitude? All in all, it was an ordinary landing on an extraordinary day.

One of the Quonset spokes of Hellas Base contained a series of little studio apartments for visiting staff: a fold-out bed, desk and chair, closet, lamp, tiny bathroom. Carter was assigned one down the hall from the two given to Annie and Philippe. In Hellas, these simple little nests seemed homey, private, away from everything. If only there were time to enjoy isolation.

By the time they were checked in, it was Tuesday afternoon. Midday by Mars City time; they felt disoriented by jet lag. Their clocks had advanced six hours during the short flight.

Stafford had three more days left.

Carter sent Philippe and Annie to scout the lay of the land, talk to people. Carter himself headed up to Braddock's office. He encountered a grim-faced aide. A little pin she wore said BECKY. She seemed nervous. "I'm so sorry about everything, Mr. Jahns. We really liked Mr. Stafford when he came around here. A great old guy. He used to tell us about the old days."

"He was here a lot, then?"

"Oh, yes, he'd come and go. Said he was working on several projects."

"Out in the desert?"

"I think so, out in the desert, yes. And back and forth to Mars City. His visits here were usually only a few days. But I got to meet him when he'd come around Mr. Braddock's office."

"Well. It's Braddock I need to see now."

"Sorry, Mr. Jahns," she said. "He's out in the field to coordinate the search. He told me to tell you how terrible everybody feels. They're out there now. He took the hopper out to the end of Hellespontus Road this morning. He knew you were coming, and he said I should set up a meeting tomorrow just after lunch, when he comes back. He wants to help you with your report, but, you understand, the search comes first."

"I'm here to help."

"He left this for you. What we've got so far." She handed him a data button. "You can check it out at your leisure."

There was not much to learn when he slotted the button into his screen. On February 40, Stafford had checked out a dune buggy, as usual. "As usual" for him meant filing that minimum travel plan, reporting that he was heading northwest into the Hellas rim country of Hellespontus and Noachis, where he had been prospecting off and on for the last few months. "Prospecting" for Stafford was a euphemism for poking around. Looking for mineral specimens, enjoying sunsets, photographing dust dev-ils, turning over rocks to see what was under them (no scorpions), and brewing tea with Martian ice when he could find it (no germs).

One of the recommendations Carter would have to make was already clear. Carter didn't look forward to telling Stafford there would be no more sketchy travel plans, no more solo wandering. If he ever saw Stafford again.

The mention of Carter's own name came not under the travel plan but under "People to notify in case of emergency." There it was: "Carter Jahns might be able to find me."

What was that supposed to mean? It made no sense. Stafford had said nothing to him about this trip or where he might go. Had he written it just to satisfy the rules?

Becky volunteered to show him the pictures he wanted to see. She had arranged a status report and briefing session for early evening. As they headed down endless halls, Carter tried to sense the mood of the place.

Hellas Base wasn't so bad, in its own spartan way. It was the provincial outpost of Mars City. Unlike Mars City, its cluttered hallways looked like any research station's hallways. Instruments bereft of adequate storage space; boxes of data cubes. None of the malls or decor panels of Mars City; no clumps of vegetation. Only a solitary potted plant here and there, looking like a guilty afterthought. Metal walls with notes held by magnets. Dense, old plastic office furniture with the vinyl peeling off the seats; castoffs from Tycho and Mars City. Some of them even looked as if they had come on the first ships from Earth. No one here had put through any purchase orders to replace them. When it came to precious cargo, the Hellas staff would rather import new seismometers than new seats.

In the hallways, he also passed subdued men and women, the scientists, with their furtive manner. It must have been the loss of Stafford that threw a pall over everything. Their gazes never seemed to focus on a visitor. They could be seen through doorways, hunched over screens in little cubicles, perusing the kaleidoscope glow of geologic maps, talking about magnetic contours and consulting charts on their walls. A screen that Carter saw through a doorway blinked and glowed with a new map, ragged swaths of green and purple spiraling out from the south pole, cut by the bull's-eye of Hellas and its concentric rings. The abstract expressionism of a newly mapped planet.

The staff at Hellas Base had quirks that seemed to get worse, month by month. An iconoclastic and linear-minded lot, they were famous for the perverse pride they took in keeping humans in the data analysis loop. They'd hold out to the last that robotic exploration might be okay for Earth, but not for Mars. Machines could only deal with what you already knew was there. They *wanted* to believe there were undiscovered wonders out there. And that wasn't all. Crusty veterans of the frontier, they looked on Mars City like the Israelites looked on mighty Babylon. Mars City, gleaming jewel of the red desert, with its towers and minarets, center of easy living and decadent kitsch.

The staff at Hellas gloried in their toughness. Sometimes their talk had biblical overtones. They shepherded their myths of God's fiery destruction raining down from the sky to make the craters, and the Great Flood: the mythic forty days and forty nights, long gone, when the icy Martian soil warmed, and water gushed forth, engulfing the desert, swirling rocks and molecules before it. The Great Flood, which had been not a destroyer of life, but perhaps a builder. Even after Stafford's work, they were sure there was more to say about ancient water and ancient life. At Hellas Base they had strange dreams, these ragged-faced pioneers. The scuttlebutt in Mars City was that they were all crazy. Too much desert.

Late Tuesday evening. Becky had arranged for Carter to use a conference room in the imaging center, the "war room," as Philippe called it. Two huge screens dominated the wall. Twenty thousand pixels on a side. Only one screen was lit; it displayed a rust-colored image of the region of Stafford's disappearance. "It was taken on Saturday," Becky said. "He was out there somewhere."

Her briefing did not tell him much new. She reviewed the arrangement with Stafford, how Stafford had been seen on the Hellespontus Road, et cetera, et cetera. The last radio fix had placed him at the geophysics array at the end of the Hellespontus Road . . . where the desert was scarred by a hundred dune buggy tracks going off in different directions into the hills—testimony to a hundred expeditions, VIP tours, and unauthorized joyrides by researchers and adventurers (only in the best cases were they the same, Stafford had told Carter once). They all wanted to say they had been out in the virgin Martian desert.

Becky marked the spot on the wall screen with a yellow circle. The image had nowhere near enough resolution to show the road or the tracks.

When Stafford had not radioed in on Sunday, February 43, and had not returned on schedule that night, the rescue had been organized at once. Crews who were already out in the desert, tending the seismometer at the end of the road, set out into Stafford's unknown country to the west. A hopper had flown from Hellas to the end of the road this morning, carrying Braddock himself and backup equipment. Braddock was out on the trail, now, in one of the buggies trying to find Stafford's tracks.

If only they hadn't cut out the funding for the Mars Airplane, Philippe had interrupted. What they needed was the ability to cruise over the terrain, back and forth, thin air or not. The stupid ballistic hoppers could fly only on a single arc to a safe site that had been prepared in advance.

More news had come in from Braddock. One of his crew thought he had found Stafford's fresher tracks among the hydralike maze at the end of the Hellespontus Road. They had followed the tracks twenty kilometers, but lost them in the rocky terraces and ridges that led up the empty cratered highlands. The hillocks of fossilized dunes, and the outcrops of ancient, Arizona-colored strata, were covered with only thin layers of track-holding dust. Storms of recent years had swept the region, cleaning off the sheetlike surfaces. It was hard for the desperate search teams, surrounded by empty pink horizons, to be sure anyone had ever come this way, ever. Teams that ventured farther in hope came back in silence.

Braddock would be coming back to Hellas Base tomorrow, midday, as planned.

In short, nothing new.

After the briefing he sent Annie and Philippe to socialize with the workers from the airlock, who had come to the briefing to report old news about Stafford's checkout with his buggy a few days before.

"Find out if they know anything else," he whispered to Annie.

"Right, chief," she whispered back. Was she making fun of him?

Later, Carter bent over the desk Becky had told him was his. On the screen, the blowup of Hellespontus still glowed. The yellow circle, where Becky marked Stafford's last known whereabouts, looked lonely and morbid.

Photos.

Becky had assured him that new satellite mapping photos had already been obtained, emergency priority. In recent days, three sets of images had been made. The first two were routine weather and mapping images—resolution, thirty meters. Discouraging. One set had been made on the thirty-fifth, five days before Stafford set out; additional coverage crossed the area by chance on Saturday, the forty-second, two days after he had left—while he was out there. By luck, both days were relatively clear.

On Monday at dawn a third set had been made—high-resolution blanket coverage, ordered on an emergency basis when Stafford had failed to show up. The geometry was not ideal; the satellite orbit required that the photos be made at an oblique angle, and there had been some very thin cirrus as well as a dust pall. But routine image enhancement should beat the low contrast and they should have four- or five-meter resolution of much of the area—not good enough to show an individual dune buggy, but better than the earlier views. At four meters, Stafford could have marked out some distress signal in the desert that might be visible. . . .

"Braddock looked at these photos?" Carter asked Becky.

"Before he went out."

"See anything?"

She gave him a shrug. "They didn't find Stafford, if that's what you mean. Braddock took a set of blowups with him to the end of the Hellespontus Road."

"I may want to have new photos made."

"You might have to wait to get them back."

"Wait?"

"We were lucky. We could get the pictures back in a few hours. Doesn't always work that way. Satellite orbits . . . Reprogramming . . . They relay through Phobos. The orbits have to be lined up . . . When it comes to images, you take what you get. That's my field, meteorology imagery, when I'm not gophering for Mr. Braddock."

Annie and Philippe came back from the transport bay. They looked tired.

"What did you learn?" Carter asked them.

"Nothing," Annie said. "They saw him go out. Perfectly routine. One buggy. Packed with his stuff. No manifest. Just the sketchy travel plan saying he was going out toward Hellespontus. That's it."

"Couldn't you . . . Did you get a sense of what was going on with him? Between the lines?"

Annie was shaking her head. "We talked to them for an hour. Talked to the guy that outfitted Stafford. Said there was nothing unusual. He took along his usual extra airpacs. They say its not enough to last beyond Friday. We already knew that. We talked to everybody we could find."

Philippe: "We even separated them. Engaged them in separate conversations. How do you call it? We grilled them. Third degree. Nothing."

Annie: "Everybody was friendly, of course. But nobody seemed to know anything specific about his plans. We did the best we could."

Carter: "Okay. Look, Becky, tomorrow I want everything you've got here. All the images. We'll go over it all with a fine-tooth comb."

"I'll have it all here, but you won't see much."

7

Dawn over Hellas. Carter, Philippe, and Annie were up early. They met in the war room. Jet lag still enshrouded them like fog. It was midnight back in Mars City.

Becky had ordered in coffee and rolls. "I've got the high-res photos from Monday, and the early photos," she said. "Let me show you." She seemed most at ease when talking about the new images.

She took them through the long hallway around Hellas Base, to the war room. This time, Carter noticed a sign on the door that said CARTOGRAPHIC, and there was evidence that a second word, once mounted below this, had fallen off.

Philippe nosed around in the corners behind equipment, as if looking for something hidden. "You analyze satellite photos?" he asked Becky.

"When I'm not fetching things for Mr. Stafford, I study cloud formation patterns and motions."

"Okay," Carter told her. "Let's review the situation. On Saturday the thirty-fifth, you got photos of the whole Hellespontus region. Let's see those."

"What are you looking for?" Annie asked.

"I don't know yet. I'm just looking."

"You've only got thirty meters resolution," Becky said. "You're not going to find anything."

"You already said that, last night."

At the console in front of the screen Becky shrugged with irritation and punched in some coordinates and file numbers. A mosaic of photos came up in oranges and ochers, a near-vertical view of old, worn ridges and a field of secondary impacts caused by debris thrown from some major impact site, offstage. Low sunlight slanted in from the left. The mosaic was almost seamless. Here and there a blank, brickish-tan trapezoid, matched to the color of the adjacent background, indicated a gap in the coverage. Carter had a fleeting thought: What if the solution to the whole mystery fell into one of those bland little holes?

"Hey, craters!" Philippe said. It was supposed to be a joke. Nobody laughed.

"Zoom in and scan," Carter asked. "I just want to get the feel of the place."

Becky fiddled and the image blew up, the montage growing into a single frame, a random area fifteen kilometers across. There were some wind-swept hillocks, rounded by the wind into streamlined forms like inverted boats set out on a vast beach. Becky leaned back with her head tipped to one side. The scene slowly slid to the right, like a view from an airplane. The bowllike hills grew more densely crowded. A few kilometers farther on, they merged into a desiccated low plateau, which eventually gave way to featureless desert.

Carter stirred. "Whoa!"

Becky stopped the scan.

Now they were seeing an expanse of open desert with faint dunelike ripples, loose dust on ancient, hard sediments. The field was peppered with half a dozen hundred-meter craters. Among the craters and dunes were amorphous lighter patches bordered on their right sides by long, dark patches: long shadows. The shadows were often triangular, narrow at the contact with the light patch and fanning out from there.

"Look at that," Carter breathed. "Dust devils."

Philippe: "How do you know? They just look like blobs."

Carter turned to Annie. "Sorry. We have to put up with these green-horns, you know what I mean?"

"I was going to ask the same question myself," she said.

Carter pointed out how the hills had much stubbier shadows, and de-scribed how each light patch was a cloud of dust stretching a column up from the surface, and how the long shadow revealed the form; funnel-shaped in many cases; sometimes straight vertical or slanting columns, like typhoon waterspouts. "From the shape and direction of the shadow you can sense the relief: this one is maybe six hundred meters high and a hundred meters wide. That's no hill! Second: they move. Becky, can you punch these coordinates from a photo on another day, maybe the February forty-second set? Do you have a blink routine?"

Becky's fingers conversed with the keyboard. In a moment the picture was blinking back and forth between the original and a new view, per-fectly registered with each other. In the new view, the craters and dunes were in the same places, with slightly longer shadows caused by a lower sun angle. But the light blobs and their shadows had vanished. Two new ones had appeared in the east. "Voilà!" said Carter. "Here today, gone tomorrow."

"*Magnifique,*" said Philippe, clapping Carter on the back.

"Hmmm," said Annie.

"So," said Carter, "we know there were big dust devils in the area on

February thirty-fifth. Stafford set out on the fortieth for four days. We know there were more devils on February forty-second. Also, we know devils are nothing unusual for this time of year. Stafford liked to photograph them. He even chased them sometimes!"

Annie: "So you're saying . . ."

"I'm just thinking out loud. Devils aren't considered dangerous. Usually. But Stafford was always waiting for that big one. The perfect dust devil . . ."

Annie's eyes widened.

Philippe frowned. "How does a big dust devil destroy a buggy? Flip it? What?"

Carter pushed back from the table. He ran his hand through his dark hair. He stared at the ceiling for a moment. "Hypothesis: Stafford goes out on February fortieth. Runs his dune buggy up into those hills, infested with dust devils. Tries to chase one down. Gets hung up on a rock or something. The dust devil turns on him. Comes along and flips him . . . or somehow disables his vehicle and transmitter both."

He turned to Becky. "Okay. What I want to do is look at the high-res set from Monday. You have stereo pairs from that pass?"

"Most of it. The stereo didn't cover everything."

"Set me up for stereo. Start with the end of the Hellespontus Road. You have coverage there?"

She punched the console. The screen jumped into a holographic 3-D image, faintly flickering. Becky adjusted Carter's chair position directly in front of the screen and swung an optical stereo mask over Carter's face. "It's sharper if you use the mask."

The rest of them watched the screen from the side. Craters and furrowed hills glowed at them, from a slightly oblique angle, with traces of haze here and there, hovering above the landscape.

Carter exclaimed, "Jeez!" as the stereo came into focus in his mask. "Can you give me exaggerated relief?" he added.

"You've already got two times exaggeration."

"Give me four times. I might as well be sensitive to the slightest . . . No, that's too much. How about three times? There, that's great." Tiny depressions in the terrain loomed as deep hollows, and gentle swells of dunes rose as sharp, domed hills.

"Now, Becky," Carter said from behind the mask, "give me a blowup of the Hellespontus Road where it comes to an end. The highest resolution pair you've got. Monday's. February 44th. That's a resolution of . . ."

"Five meters give or take. You're still not going to see a buggy."

After some keypunching and screen flickering, the image shifted to some broken ridges, running north-south across the screen. Winding through them toward the west was a clear thread—the Hellespontus Road. The rest of them could see it even without the stereo mask. The thread weakened and the country grew more rugged toward the west.

"The end of the road is here"—Becky pointed—"where the seismometer installation is." The thread turned into a jumbled patch, where random spidery lines trailed off in all directions, like a hydra's tentacles. They promptly faded into the desert. "The road goes beyond that a ways, but the country gets pretty wild. You can see where groups of people go joyriding off the end of the road, like I told you yesterday. It's really torn up out there. Every year it gets a little farther."

"Like lemmings," Philippe butted in. "You say it's five-meter resolution . . ." he continued, as if pondering some fine point of logic.

"Maybe four, three in the very best pictures," Becky said. "The distance between pixels. You never know the size of the smallest craters and rock shadows you can actually see. Depends on the lighting, the clarity of the atmosphere. But you're never going to see a buggy, that resolution."

"What about the trail?"

"Certainly not a single buggy's trail." Becky looked annoyed at Philippe's density. "If you can't see the buggy with its shadow, you're certainly not going to see its tracks."

"You know, Stafford said something to me about that," Carter spoke up from his mask. "We had this conversation once about seeing small things on orbiter photos, like the Viking landers and the old rovers from the turn of the century. He said everyone believes the resolution in the routine satellite imagery isn't good enough. Then he started talking about rovers leaving trails, and he said . . ." Carter sifted through his memory. "He said they ought to read their Percival Lowell."

"Ha," Becky snorted. "What did Lowell ever get right about Mars?"

"Lots of things," Philippe shot back. "A dying planet, escape of the atmosphere because of low gravity."

"Four meters is four meters," Becky insisted. "A whole buggy and its shadow covers one pixel. You can see a road but you're not going to see any tracks from a single buggy."

Philippe hunkered down on a desk in the corner, speaking into his 'corder.

Carter was still studying the hydralike image of the end of the Hellespontus Road. "Blow it up." The hydra head expanded. You could see individual house-sized boulders casting stubby shadows on the hillsides, but the picture was breaking up into tiny squares. "Listen, did Braddock and his people actually *look* for buggy tracks on any of these images?" Carter asked her.

"He was in here Monday morning before he went out. Braddock and a couple of the other guys. Had me run through the images. I'm not sure he actually looked for individual tracks. I keep telling you, they're so small . . . Besides, he was in a hurry to get going. He studied the area farther out to the west, looking for signs of something unusual. You know, like a distress sign. Something Stafford might have traced out if his radio quit. They made a big point of the fact that there was no distress signal out there."

"Don't you think he should have looked for fresh tracks heading out from the Hellespontus Road?"

"Not if you can't resolve them. . . . Look, my job is normally to look at big fuzzy cloud masses, not tiny details. . . ."

Carter was still hidden behind his mask a few moments later when Philippe, bent over the little screen on his wrist, interjected "Ah!" He held up his wrist and 'corder in triumph. "I've been reading Lowell. Lowell's books. Let me teach you something that good old Percival figured out over a hundred years ago in the days of Martian canals. You can see a line even when you can't resolve the width of the line. You can see a power cable at a distance when you wouldn't be able to see a piece of the wire itself, because the line covers many adjacent cells in your eye. In the same way, you pick up a three-meter-wide trail even if you can't see a three-meter-wide spot because it stretches along many pixels."

Carter broke away from his machine to listen.

"And there's more to it than that. Lowell popularized the canals, but he claimed what astronomers were seeing were not the canals themselves, but the vegetation strips along both sides of the canals. In the same way, the disturbance of dust along the sides of tracks is wider than the tracks themselves. With the right enhancement techniques . . ."

What Philippe was saying matched Carter's intuition: somehow, you ought to be able to see some trace, with a picture this sharp.

"Carter," Annie broke in excitedly, "that's what Stafford was trying to tell you about Lowell! That if he ever got lost, his track might be detectable, if you use all the tricks. . . ."

Carter went back to his mask. "Give me more contrast. Let's see how much you can get out of this thing. . . . Give me a spiral search pattern, outward from the end of the road."

They stared as the image snapped into masses of dark gray and white.

"Aha," Carter breathed from behind his goggles. Was there a thin tentacle there, winding its way toward the west?

Annie: "It looks like a mess, Carter. Can you see anything?"

"I've got something."

———————————————————●———————————————————

Becky brought them lunch, what passed for ham salad sandwiches. They stayed glued to the machines.

At two o'clock there was a commotion at the door of the lab. Four people barged into the room together. A barrel-chested older man, balding, with steely blue eyes; a striking woman, about thirty-five or forty, with short dark auburn hair and a wide, smooth face; and two younger men still in the process of shucking their down-stuffed suit liners, suggesting they had just come in from outside.

"Once you get cold out there, it's like you can't warm up," one of the younger men muttered, as if by way of introduction.

"Carter Jahns?" the older man said.

"Yeah."

"Braddock. I'm director around here. Don't get up." He shook Carter's hand with a quick gesture.

"I remember. We met when you were coming through Mars City. Glad to see you again, Braddock. I've been meaning to come and see how things are going."

"Not so well."

Everyone used Braddock's last name. Carter couldn't even remember the man's first name.

Braddock glanced gravely at Annie and Philippe.

Carter introduced them. "We wanted to help," Annie said.

Braddock's baldness lent him a stern, commanding look, but he had laugh lines around his eyes. He looked like a man who laughed under other circumstances, but not on this particular day, not with these particular people.

"I heard you were coming." He turned back to Carter. "The search is already under way, such as it is. I'm not optimistic. Hard to identify new tracks out there. I should have put a stop to that stupidity of Stafford going out on his own."

"I thought you were the one who approved it."

"I've got my share of the blame."

One of the two young staffers, who had finished removing his suit liner, piped up, "I still say the Martians got him."

Braddock scowled. "Ain't funny. And don't go starting stupid rumors. Oh"—he gestured to the woman at his side—"this here is Elena Trevina. You've probably met." He turned grudgingly toward Philippe and Annie. "Brach, and Ms. Pohaku, have you met Lena? Well, you know of her. Director of the Polar Station. She was s'posed to come up here next week—came early to see if she could help out."

Carter had met her only once before on a quick trip to Hellas Base a year before, out in the field. They had spoken only briefly. They had been wearing suits. He felt he had never really met her. She was an elusive figure of the south. She monitored the Clarke Project's black carbon dust coating of the polar ice cap, but her own interests lay with those of the planetary ecologists in her shop. She was known for her team of geologists and their work on the permanent water-ice deposits at the core of the south polar cap. Something to do with the interwoven strata of ice and dust that seemed to be involved with the wild climate fluctuations of ancient Mars. Carter had been meaning to visit her little research station to see the installation and the polar ice fields for himself. Someday . . .

On that day a year before, when they had met, he had visualized that behind that filtered helmet lurked some sort of austere Valkyrie. He was surprised to find her intriguing, if formidable. Her no-nonsense demeanor and square Eastern European face contrasted with her slight smile and smooth . . . She started to say something but Braddock, nodding gruffly at the displays on the screens, cut her off.

"We've been over all this, ya know," Braddock said. He walked over and glowered at the largest blowup. "Nothing there. Vehicle's too small to see on orbiter photos."

"Tell it to Percival Lowell," Philippe said.

"What?"

"Never mind."

"I'm looking for tracks," Carter said. "Not the vehicle."

"Find anything?" Lena asked.

"Yeah."

Braddock looked surprised. "Yeah? What? What ya got?"

"Look here," Carter replied. He disappeared behind the stereo mask and began moving the cursor on the big screen. "Maybe you can't see it unless you use the stereo viewer, but there's at least one trail running off a long way west into . . . what's west of the end of the Hellespontus Road?"

"Dust devils," Braddock said grumpily. "The summer dust storms come out of there. If you'll look farther west, you'll find a lot of dust devils out there. He musta got hit by one."

"Yeah, yeah. We found those."

"You found the dust devils already?" Braddock looked surprised again.

Carter turned away from the screen and studied him. "Yeah. What do you see when you're out there on the ground?"

"Nothing. A lotta dust in Hellespontus country . . . lotta craters. Not much else."

"I think you'd better mobilize all your people out there to follow this." He pointed to the screen.

"What? I don't see anything."

Carter drew his finger along the screen. "Tracks. The only ones this far from the end of the Hellespontus Road. It's got to be him. Even with the mask, you can only see segments of tracks. Just here and there. I have to use stereo and a lot of blinking with the earlier images, but I can project it and follow it from one segment to another. Listen. You get in touch with your people in the field, I'll follow this damn thing as far as I can and tell you the coordinates of each fragment I find. They can head out there on the ground and see what they can see." Braddock glanced at Trevina in surprise.

Late Wednesday afternoon. Only two days left for Stafford to survive. If he was alive at all.

Braddock and his party had gone grumpily back to Braddock's office to manage the search, promising to relay any track positions from Carter to the field crew.

Carter continued studying the images on the screen. Behind the stereo mask, he was immersed in the machine. "Look," he would say from time to time, "I've got something."

There was a moment when Annie and Carter were in the lab alone together. She was silent at first.

"What's eating you?" Carter asked her from behind the mask.

"I'm getting hungry and I've got a story to write. . . ." She stepped close to Carter and looked intently at one of the images on the screen. Low ridges and boulders casting shadows. She put her hand on the back of Carter's chair and peered intently at the screen, not at him. "Carter, I want to ask you something. I don't know why I'm saying this. A journalist isn't supposed to ask this question. It's supposed to come from you, but I want to ask you this because I want to keep . . . a good relationship with you. Look at it as my own cynical investment in the future of my news source, if you want. Anyway, we may need each other before this is done. I think I know how you feel about me tagging along. Anyway, here's the question. Is there anything so far that you want off the record?"

Behind his mask, Carter felt a million thoughts, running from anger to pleasure. He had to do all the work and she got to write . . . Still, she was trying to be helpful. . . . "No. Use what you want. There's no secrets on Mars as far as I'm concerned. We're all in this together." Why did it feel like he kept forcing himself to say that?

"You're an interesting man. Do you ever have any serious doubts? I mean, about what you are doing?"

"Doubt?"

"Maybe that's what I can help you with. Doubt."

"What do you mean?"

"Reporters have to be more skeptical than builders."

He wanted to ask her what she was talking about, but Philippe returned.

She stepped back, away from Carter.

Carter kept his eyes on the screen, afraid that if he looked away, the thread of the trail and the thread of the conversation would both vanish. But he called: "Hey, Annie, thanks for asking. If we get into . . . an uncomfortable situation, I'll let you know." It could all be so simple, Carter thought, if I just accepted her for what she says. How do I distinguish a person's reality from what they say and do . . . ?

He heard Annie leaving.

Philippe followed her out like a puppy. "See you later, my pal," he said. Carter could see that eager little smile on his face without looking away from the screen.

8

DATELINE HELLAS

Evening. There was no sense of time in the war room. Carter had been poring over the pictures for hours.

After Philippe and Annie had left, he had begun to brood about what he had said. Hell, he thought, if we do find anything I don't want her to report yet, I can always . . . He couldn't quite complete the thought. Besides, the story wasn't over yet. Stafford would be tracked. Stafford would be found.

Annie . . . It bothered Carter that she was cast in an old-fashioned parody of a woman's role, hanging around, saying little. All the scene needed now was for her to stand in a doorway as Carter set out: "Oh, Carter, be careful. . . ."

As she promised, she had genuinely tried to encourage them. But of course, thought Carter, the more she hung around, the better the story she got. "The more you learn, the more you earn," she had said to them. Why was he being so uptight as to let this needle him? The trouble was, part of him wanted her there, and he couldn't afford to think about that now. He didn't even want to admit it.

Now Becky had come back to help him. He had wrenched his mind back toward the pixilated screen, back toward Hellespontus, where a tiny thread like a faint pencil line could be glimpsed here and there among the hillocks, at least with the mask. There it was, crossing a dune crest, or coursing across an otherwise bare patch of dust between two boulder fields. Blue crosshairs were projected onto the stereo image, floating in space, shadowless, just above the surface. Each time he found a trail segment he moved them to the end points of the gossamer track. "Send them these positions, Becky. Make sure Braddock gets them."

He could hear Becky punching buttons.

Sometimes, he could pick up the next faint trace in a few minutes, a few hundred meters farther west. Other times, he had to scan for half an hour or more, until he found the next bit of track, a faint hairline, kilometers farther west.

Finally he called Braddock. "You getting all this? Have your people found anything?"

Braddock sounded moody, like someone who had not had enough sleep.

"Don't worry. We've already got one crew a hundred klicks west of the road. They've been to the first three positions you gave me. Found some tracks there. I s'pose we have to assume it's Stafford. They're just moving down the line from one of your positions to the next. In between, Stafford was on rocky ground. The places you're seeing tracks, that's where he was crossing softer dust." Braddock got a hopeful note in his voice at last. "Maybe we're finally getting somewhere."

Carter felt exhilaration.

He looked at his watch. Eight o'clock Wednesday night. A day and a half to go. Two days max.

Suddenly he realized he was exhausted. Becky brought him a sandwich and coffee. He spent another hour plotting positions, tracking Stafford a little farther, now a bit northwest. And at last something strange. Under the highest resolution, the highest contrast, the track seemed to break up, or dissolve into a confused tangle an area only a few hundred meters across, with a spider pattern of—could it be?—tracks heading out into the desert, but disappearing.

Some sort of disturbance.

Excitedly, he called the coordinates in to Braddock. "Get your people there. Fast. Call me when they've got something."

Now he was hours ahead of the field crew, who were racing along behind him, from position to position. He recorded the index numbers of the best photos on his 'corder. He told Becky to take a break. He wanted to be alone.

He raced to his room for a quick shower and change of clothes. He was running on adrenaline now, but he felt better, charged with the energy of discovery. There was no doubt in his mind. They were on the trail of Stafford. And it had been his doing. Not Braddock's. He had a strange feeling that he had triumphed over an adversary, although, God knew, he had no bone to pick with the hard-boiled head of Hellas Base. In fact, as he had looked around, he was impressed with the efficiency of the place . . . the tight-lipped scientists scurrying around with great intensity, like ants, doing whatever it was that scientists do.

Even this short break to eat and shower made him feel guilty, as if he had abandoned Stafford, whose air was running out. He dressed quickly— his sweater and the comfortable jeans he had thrown in the bag—and headed around the corner to Philippe's room. He knocked hurriedly. No one answered his knock. At Annie's room he knocked twice, louder the second time. No one home there, either.

"Oh, hell," he breathed. He headed back toward the image processing lab.

———————————————●———————————————

Had she dozed off? Lying in the narrow bed, she was disoriented. Her tiny room had no window. God, what time was it? Who had been knocking? She had wanted to see no one. Her body did not know what it wanted. More sleep? A walk? The sound of rain?

Her screen glowed dully on the table beside the bed. Philippe had insisted on going to dinner with her. Then she had broken away to come back here to finish and file her story. Great reporter, waiting this long. Well, there was no competition and she had put together a good report. Then she had crashed after filing.

Time to face reality again. What was she going to do about Philippe? And Carter?

She looked at her watch! Eleven P.M. local time. Maybe a day and a half left. God.

She threw back the covers, trying to blot out ghostly imprints of the night before. The bed, with no headboard, butted against the wall. She propped herself up against it with two pillows and reached for her 'corder and screen. She fired up the screen to see if her story had made it onto Newsnet. The story, as she had written it, was there:

SEARCH CONTINUES FOR LOST SCIENTIST

(IPN) Hellas Base, Mars, Wednesday, Feb. 46 (Marsdate).
Well-known scientist Dr. Alwyn Stafford, famed "biologist of a dead world," is still missing in the Martian desert. Following his initial failure to return from a solo outing, as reported two days ago, search parties have been sent out. Today, satellite photos revealed apparent segments of his trail in uncharted desert west of this remote research station.

Background: Stafford set out from Hellas Base on Feb. 40 and was due to return on Feb. 43, according to the Martian calendar, with day lengths virtually the same as Earth's. Search parties have turned up no trace of him or his vehicle, a standard Martian "dune buggy" equipped with supplies to last eight Martian days. Searchers from Hellas Base hold out fading hope that Stafford may still be found alive before his air runs out two days from now.

In the 23-year history of exploration on Mars, there have

been a number of fatalities, but this is the first disappearance, in which a vehicle and occupant simply did not return from a mission.

Alwyn Stafford grew up in California and studied biology at Berkeley. He is known for his research on the history of life on Mars. Although technicians here make black quips about Stafford being spirited away by hidden Martians, Stafford's research is widely regarded as proving that after life evolved here, it never went beyond the simple microbial level.

Search parties were sent out from Hellas Base along "Hellespontus Road," a bulldozed dirt trail known to have been traveled by Stafford. This road leads to an installation of robotic scientific instruments. Initially, the searchers on the ground were unable to distinguish Stafford's tracks from other tangled tracks in the area where the road ends. Stafford apparently left the road to travel into the deserts of Hellespontus, an area of ancient craters west of here.

A break in the case may have come from satellite images that reveal faint evidence of what may be Stafford's tracks across the desert. Steven E. Braddock, Director of Hellas Base, stated that navigation in that terrain is difficult, but that satellite photos may lead ground parties to Stafford's westward track.

Satellite photos have shown dust devils in the vicinity where Stafford was believed to have gone. These dust-bearing whirlwinds reach giant proportions on Mars. Mr. Braddock speculated here that his vehicle and its communications system might have been disabled by one of these storms.

Carter Jahns, Assistant Director of Environmental Engineering in Mars City, has been appointed to head an investigation of the entire incident. Jahns arrived at Hellas Base yesterday. Although satellite photographs were initially deemed too poor to show objects as small as a dune buggy on the surface, Jahns used special processing of satellite photography to detect hints of the buggy tracks many kilometers west of the position where Stafford was believed to have left the "Hellespontus Road." Searchers are now racing to the westernmost sites of those tracks, in hopes of following Stafford's trail into the desert.

More background: Jahns is being assisted by Philippe Brach,

the well-known artist-in-residence on Mars, who used his graphic skills to aid in the image analysis necessary to conduct the search.

The search now faces a desperate time deadline only two days off, when Stafford's buggy will run out of air. Mr. Braddock and Mr. Jahns say they will carry the search directly to the area indicated by the tracks revealed in the photos by Jahns and Brach.

Aerial search is not possible, because the shuttles and lighter "hoppers," used for point-to-point travel on Mars, follow ballistic trajectories and do not have the ability to make repeated passes over areas or to land at unprepared sites in rough areas. Airplanes have not been developed here due to lack of funding. Dr. Natalia Petrova, who works with the cartographic survey program here, told this reporter that "We might have had a viable piloted aircraft by now if the developmental funding on the 'Marsplane' project had not been cut off in '25."

A question hanging over this incident is that irregular procedures have been allowed in the past when Stafford ventured out on his own. Normally, vehicles are allowed into the Martian outback only two or more at a time. Mr. Braddock stated that Dr. Stafford has made a number of solo forays, approved by Mr. Braddock himself. "Stafford knew more about the desert and desert vehicles than all the rest of us put together," Mr. Braddock told this reporter. Dr. Stafford had reached retirement status but continued his own unofficial research and collecting expeditions. Mr. Braddock stated that Stafford had gone out on short solo trips even before Mr. Braddock took over management of the Hellas Base. "Most people believed that after all the years he put in here, and with all the knowledge he had, he had the right to pursue his ideas," Mr. Braddock said. "It would have been impossible to take people off other projects to send along with him. We all felt that Mars would gain tremendous benefit from the discoveries he could make out there on his own time. Obviously, we are reevaluating that policy at this time."

Nervously, Annie wondered if the story had made it into the wider Earth media. She accessed the New York Timesnet, where she found it buried in a sublist under science. She mistakenly punched up an op-ad piece titled "Now you can own one of the last fur coats." Then she got her own piece on the screen, somewhat edited:

SCIENTIST DISAPPEARS ON MARS
Procedures at Mars Base Criticized

(IPN) Well-known scientist Dr. Alwyn Stafford, christened the "biologist of a dead world" by Timesnet in 2025, has been reported missing in the Martian desert. Stafford was reported several days overdue on a solo jaunt, with only two days of air remaining in his vehicle.

Under questionable circumstances, Stafford was apparently given a unique privilege of taking equipment into the desert by himself. Mr. Steven E. Braddock, recently appointed Director of the Hellas Base research station, from which Stafford departed, justified Stafford's trips on the basis of his years of experience and the lack of manpower to send support for Stafford's missions. However, Professor Guido McIntosh, of Cornell's Institute of Scientific Sociology, stated, "I find it incredible that they would let someone out on Mars alone. It adds one more doubt to the many questions that have been raised about the efficacy of the whole program on Mars."

Dr. Robert Washington, chief scientist on UNSA's Newton Pluto Mission project, echoed these feelings. "When you think of the billions we are spending to keep people on Mars, and then find out we're losing them . . . it's crazy. Why risk people on Mars when we could do so much more with robotic instruments?"

The Times version had been picked up around the U.S. She found it in the Arizona Starnet, buried after a lead story headlined TUCSON DEVELOPERS SAY DRY RESERVOIR IS NO PROBLEM.

SCIENTIST OVERDUE ON MARS
Procedures Questioned

(IPN) Well-known scientist Dr. Alwyn Stafford, famed "biologist of a dead world," has been reported missing in the Martian desert. Stafford set out from the remote research station Hell

Base, and was due to return several days ago. Scientists have
called for an overhaul of procedures at the controversial base.

Annie snorted at the typo and the muckraking slant. No telling what
they had done in other markets. She punched up the Planetary Inquirer
Net and found it as a lead.

ALIENS KIDNAP BIOLOGIST!
Officials at Mars City Cover Up Mystery Disappearance!
Proof of a lost civilization on Mars was one step closer last week
when officials admitted that Alwyn Stafford, the famous biologist, disappeared on the mysterious red planet, leaving no
trace. Staff sources at Mars City have been overheard admitting
that the mysterious Martians, who have remained hidden in
the Martian desert, may have kidnapped Stafford while he was
on a secret mission.

This journal has been telling you for years about the scientific
cover-up of alien life on Mars. Mars is the next planet beyond
the moon, and the one most like the Earth, according to astronomers contacted by our reporters.

The fact that the Martians, like Bigfoot, have continued to
escape clear detection in photographs confirms how clever they
are at keeping their civilization hidden. California astrophysi-
cist Prof. Alan Adamski, descended from a long line of famous
space scientists, in an interview at the Barstow Cosmic Institute, stated that he believes Mars is laced by a network of underground volcanic tunnels, and that the Martians moved their
civilization into underground hiding during the last century,
when space probes first were sent to Mars.

"The Martians had canals that were visible until the 1950s,"
says Adamski. "Many famous astronomers, including Percival
Lowell, recorded them. It's in all the books, but there's a conspiracy to cover up what was known about Mars in the last
century. The canals disappeared in the 1960s. The first space
probe, *Mariner 4* in 1965, took only a few fuzzy pictures that
could not show the Martian cities and canals. But that alerted
the Martians to our interest, and they went into hiding. They
destroyed everything they had built on the surface."

Adamski also noted that early space probes revealed mysterious giant sculptures of faces and pyramids on Mars, carved

into hillsides. But later probes showed the same hills had been changed to look natural! "It's just one more proof that the Martians have been disguising the huge edifices that they built centuries ago," says Adamski. "It's criminal that our activities are forcing them to destroy these great monuments to civilization." In support of Adamski's theories, scientists on Mars admit that Mars is sterile today, in spite of hundreds of direct observations of the canal system only one hundred years ago. "The astounding thing is that they could have destroyed all detectable traces of their global civilization so fast, even the organic residue," says California psychiatrist Dr. April Crystal-Luna. "This alone shows how far advanced their technology is!"

In the face of this overwhelming evidence, officials at Mars City continue their cover-up, denying that there have ever been any Martians. Asked how Stafford *and* his vehicle could have disappeared without a radio SOS, the officials claim he may have been a victim of a giant dust devil, a theory that Dr. Adamski brands as preposterous. Search parties have been sent out to look for him, Officials once again denied any evidence of Martians, but their story is wearing thin. The fact that even Stafford's vehicle has disappeared shows that the Martians may have begun a more aggressive approach to the human presence on their planet.

In an exclusive to this journal, one technician on Mars says that Stafford has been known to make several solo trips into the mysterious Martian desert during the last few years—a privilege granted only to him because of his senior status. "No telling what he does out there; he's kind of eccentric. Everyone says he's discovered incredible treasures." Others speculate that Stafford had already made contact with the Martians, and may be negotiating with them on behalf of the human race.

This possibility is supported by Stafford's status. He is one of the oldest and most respected scientists on Mars, having come there in 2010. Does our future in space hinge on the delicate negotiations that this famous scientist is carrying out on our behalf? Be sure to read our forthcoming issues, as we follow this amazing story.

Annie disconnected in disgust.

9

Thursday. One day left. Carter had gone to sleep at two A.M. and set his 'corder for dawn. Its morning message said that the field team was still following the tracks he had found. They were progressing only slowly, but they were confident that they were on Stafford's route, since no one else had been known to venture this far into the desert. The search party was now heading toward the westernmost disturbance that Carter had identified.

One bit of news. Experienced field hands said that the pattern of the claw marks, and the fall of dust along the road, proved they were following Stafford's outbound leg—not an inbound path. More news: there was no inbound path, no evidence that Stafford had ever returned along this route.

The waiting was impossible. Carter could not stand it. Even his dreams were contaminated. He realized he had been dreaming about Stafford, about the air running out. What do you do if you know the air is running out? Sit at the controls of your buggy until the last breath comes, until the air becomes fetid carbon dioxide and your mine reels and your lungs scream? Or do you end it all at once? Crack the seal on the buggy and listen to the deadly hiss, and become the first to hear the real music of Mars with your own ears; the last music you'll ever hear . . . ? Or do you dress for death? Dress formally in your suit, step outside into the impassive desert, and then crack the helmet seal? The Martian desert has hungered for organic material for a billion years. . . .

He had a nightmare vision of the story his mother had told him of the three Russian space pioneers who had died on their way home when the valve of their capsule stuck open, and all the air hissed out into the stratosphere even as they were parachuting back into the loving arms of Earth's atmosphere. She had told Carter that he was distantly related to one of them, through one of her cousins. . . . There is always danger in exploration, she told him. That was the moral to the story. There was always the unexpected circumstance just when you thought you were safe. . . .

Part of Carter was desperate to be out there in the desert, looking. He was like a parent whose child is lost in the mountains, and the county sheriff says "wait at home, wait for a call." Part of him couldn't stand to wait at home; the other part recognized that he had to stay, otherwise there would be no directions for the searchers in the desert. Strange, how he was the only one who seemed to be able to locate or follow Stafford's tracks, though he had to admit it had been with Philippe's help.

He tried not to think about the feelings he had bottled up about Philippe and Annie. And where had they gone? Off to dinner together according to Becky. At a time like this.

Well, hell, this was no time to start a fight or give in to . . . He didn't like the word "jealousy." Fighting violent impulses, Carter prepared to go back to the cartographic lab for another attempt to track Stafford even farther west.

When Philippe woke early from his own fitful sleep, he thought about calling Annie but abandoned the idea. Better to let it lie, he thought. There was Stafford to think about. Philippe had no guilt over his attraction to her, the things he had said to her during their time together at dinner, that island of time away from all this tension. She was a beautiful woman. But there was a limit of decency, considering the circumstances. He owed Carter some help, whatever that might be.

Of the three of them, he thought, his role was least clear. What was his real reason for being here, Philippe asked himself. Carter's right-hand man, sure. Eyes and ears. Well, he had tried, not that he had turned up very much. It was part of his theory of himself that he was just as much a reporter as Annie. His medium and timescale were different, and whether he was "a good artist" was for other people to judge, but he was certainly a reporter of what he had experienced. He could not be the artist—the person—he wanted to be without seeking interesting events and new sights.

Well, it was time to seek a few more, explore the place, find breakfast, to find Carter, and no doubt to find Annie.

An hour later, Annie called Philippe's room and found no one home. She wandered down to the war room and found Carter seated at the console with his back to her. Becky was standing to one side, fussing over him. He looked tired. His broad shoulders in a gray and tan flecked sweater looked . . . warm was the word that came to her. She watched him for a minute without saying anything. When Annie said "Carter," softly, he twisted quickly with a forced smile that disoriented her.

"Have you learned anything new?" she asked.

As Carter started to answer, Philippe appeared at the door behind Annie, and put his hand on her shoulder. She felt Philippe's presence, and at the same instant saw a fleeting grimace flit across Carter's face and disappear. It was a reaction, she saw, that he tried to reject. Things were more complicated than she had realized. . . . And in the middle of all this . . .

The extended answer Carter had been about to give suddenly faded away. "Not much . . ." He collected himself so quickly that only she could have seen what had happened, as if his reaction had been a message meant just for her. He was cool, she thought, she had to hand him that. He added, "I spent a lot of the night here. There's a disturbed area out there. I don't know what was going on, but I can tell you it wasn't there on the photos from February 42. It means Stafford was there after the forty-second. I sent the coordinates of the spot to Braddock."

"How could Braddock have missed this stuff?" Annie asked.

"It seems like they believed they couldn't see anything like this, so they just didn't."

"Like the old expression," Philippe said, " 'I'd never have seen it if I hadn't believed it.' "

"Braddock's people should be there by now," Carter finished, ignoring Philippe. "They can probably land a hopper. If Stafford's there, they'll find him. If he's alive, they'll get him out."

"There's no tracks beyond there?"

"That's the problem. I found multiple tracks in the area, going different directions. Like a big spiderweb. I haven't been able to project and search in every direction. Last night, and this morning, I looked and looked and still I can't trace him beyond that spot. There's various trail segments, but they don't seem to link up with anything. It's a big mess. Braddock's crew's probably there by now, and I don't know where to send them next. There's only a day left, and I feel helpless."

"You've done more than anyone could have expected," Annie said.

"I feel like we ought to be out there," Carter said, suddenly realizing with a shock that he had included Annie in the "we."

They spent much of the rest of the morning dancing around each other, an ever-changing constellation of three stars, going over the images. They were exhausted by late afternoon when Becky told them that a call had come in. It was Braddock on the other end. He wanted them up in his office.

"He says there's been a new development."

When they arrived in Braddock's office he was standing with Elena Trevina beside his desk and two other young men, one muscular and the other beefy and red-haired. Both were wearing suit undergarments. They looked hot. The office was spartan, with bits of equipment lying around. It reminded Carter of the office in a hundred cycle repair shops where he had taken his bike *in extremis*, Earthside. The beat-up desk lacked only a couple of wrenches and an oily rag and a couple of holograms of near-nude women on the wall.

"This here's Kevin and Red"—he gestured toward the men—"just came in from outside. They were in the search party out in Hellespontus. They found that disturbed area you sent us to last night. We sent a hopper out there this morning. They found something." He turned back to the two men and nodded. He didn't seem to think any other introduction was necessary. "Go ahead and tell them."

Their story unfolded. They had worked their way to the point where Carter had detected the last of Stafford's track. They had come out of some dark, hilly country onto a broad plain, in the direction in which Stafford had been heading. They had spotted something unnatural. They thought they had found Stafford. Instead it turned out to be . . .

"We don't know what the hell the damned thing is," Braddock interrupted fretfully. Braddock seemed not to like the thought that there was anything in or near Hellas he did not have under control. "Some damned big metal ball with, like, wings and rods sticking out." The existence of something unknown threatened him. "They brought the thing back on the hopper."

"It's some piece of space junk," Red added.

"But the important thing," Braddock added, "is that Stafford had been there on his little jaunt. They found one of Stafford's cutsie medallions." He tossed the disk on the table where it made a ring like a nineteenth-century coin on the hard acrylic. It promptly rolled off onto the floor.

Philippe picked it up and appraised it critically, turning it this way and that.

"Cutsie?" Annie asked. "Have you got something against Stafford?"

"Naw. It's just that, well, he got to be a little much sometimes, with his bending the rules and all. You never knew what he was going to do next. We couldn't very well cross him. Had too much reputation. Thought Hellas revolved around him."

"I thought you were the one who bent the rules to let him go out."

"Yeah, well. He leaned on me pretty hard. Had a lot of clout with Mars Council. Sometimes it's more trouble to turn down someone like him than to change the rules. Know what I mean?"

Carter took the disk from Philippe. " 'Alwyn Bryan Stafford explored here.' "

Philippe: "I think those disks are a good idea. Humanity in the desert."

"Yeah, yeah," Braddock said. He fished around on the table. "This was with it," he added, slapping a little piece of imprinted foil in front of Carter.

Carter picked it up. "2031, February 43," he read.

"The point is," Braddock harrumphed, "what are you going to do about it, Jahns? You've tracked him this far. Everybody seems to think you know how to find him."

"No sign of his buggy?"

"Hell, no."

"Dust activity?"

"Oh, yeah. It's been blowing out there. We saw dust devils in the distance. Spooky damn things."

"Couldn't tell where he went, though." Red spoke up. "His tracks were all over, like he drove all round the site. But we couldn't follow anything very far away. We kept thinking we were onto him, you know. Then we'd lose him in the rocks, or where some dust devil had crossed the track and messed it up. We had three tractors, couldn't tell where he went next. And the more we drove around, the more confusing it got."

Carter: "Between the Hellespontus Road and that site, did it look like he knew where he was going, like he headed straight out there?"

"Whoever made the track we were following—well, I guess it had to be Stafford—went right to where we found this machine. Oh, yeah, he was looking for that thing. I think he knew it was out there. He knew roughly where it was."

Braddock: "He should have come straight back before he ran out of air."

"Wouldn't he have wanted to tell everybody if he found something interesting?" Annie asked.

"Yeah. You'd think so," Red said.

"Not necessarily," Carter said. "That wasn't his way. He liked to leave those medallions where people'd find them a hundred years from now. He had a quirky sense of history."

"Eccentric old coot," Braddock said.

"And you saw no sign of a return track between there and here?" Carter said.

"If he had come back anywhere near that route, we'd have seen it. Our vehicles were pretty spread out sometimes."

Carter spread his hands palm down on top of Braddock's desk. He tapped his fingertips, nervously, like a medium summoning a spirit. "So . . . to sum up . . . we know he went out on Thursday, the fortieth. We know he reached this old probe or whatever it is on the forty-third. Then he disappeared."

"And now it's the forty-seventh," Braddock added, "and what are we going to do about it?"

Braddock's phone pipped.

"Yeah? Braddock here. . . . What? . . . Oh, hell." He hung up.

They all looked at him expectantly.

"Seems this metal beach ball of yours was pretty dented up and sand-blasted; but they found another plaque on it. Some sort of design. Sounds Russian, from the way they describe it. Soviet. As if things weren't complicated enough already. That means it's last century."

Philippe: "So what's the matter with that?"

"Probably means there's some historic regulations we'll have to hunt up. Probably have to turn it over to their delegation officially. There's some treaty about that."

Philippe: "There is also some treaty about leaving historic space vehicles in place. The Russians landed the first devices on this planet back in the 1900s. This thing is historic. You got a problem as soon as you moved it."

"It'll be months before some do-gooder decides to raise a flap about that. Hell, that's the least of my problems."

"It was partly buried in the dust," Red said. "Looked like it had been there a long time. The way the dust was banked up against it . . ."

"You say you brought it back?" Carter asked.

"Off-loaded it at the dock," Red said. "Heavy sucker. Four hundred kilograms or so. Damn thing must be a meter across. Some of the guys put it on a dolly and took it to the shop to clean it up and have a look at it."

"Clean it up?" Philippe repeated.

"Oh, hell," Braddock wailed again.

"The rest of your people are still out there looking?" Carter asked him.

"Oh, yeah," Braddock said. "They're not going to find anything. He must have wandered off and run into a dust devil. Lotta dust devils out there. That's my theory."

"There ought to be a vehicle."

"Maybe he hit a sand sink or something."

"You're not giving up?"

"What do you want me to do?"

"Fly us out there tomorrow morning."

"Oh, hell, Carter."

"What's the matter with that?"

"Tomorrow's the critical day. Tomorrow he runs out of goddamn air. I don't want to be out flying around the goddamn planet. I want to be here, ready to respond to anything."

"It's not all over the planet. It's his last known position. He could be out there. Somewhere. I want to be looking, damn it."

"Yeah, well, I don't want my hoppers tied up flying out there when he could turn up anywhere."

"Look. I'm supposed to be in charge of the investigation of this accident and I want to be out there."

"Well, I'm supposed to be in charge of the goddamn search itself."

"Braddock, I've got Mars Council backing me up. Who do you have backing you up?"

Braddock stared at him incredulously. "I'll tell you what I'll do. I'll fly you out there Saturday. We'll look around all you want. Tomorrow, we'll wait it out here, ready to fly out anywhere at a moment's notice if we have to. I'd even risk landing at an unprepared site if we get word from Stafford."

Carter looked around the room. Annie and Philippe were watching him expectantly. Lena Trevina was staring at the floor.

"Shit," he said.

Braddock started angrily shuffling papers on his desk. "I'm not giving you a hopper and I'm not giving you a choice. I'm in charge and I'll fly you out there Saturday. For now I want you in the photo lab, and I want the hoppers ready to go if anything turns up."

Carter's instinct to fight was muted by the small voice that told him he was the only one who was likely to turn up any evidence of Stafford's tracks on the pix. It didn't make sense, but it seemed to be true. So he'd wait it out in the lab, but at least he could try to do something. . . . "One more thing," Carter said, finally.

"What's that?" Braddock looked up angrily.

"Could we take a look at that . . . thing they brought back."

"Take them down there and show them, Kevin."

———————————————— ● ————————————————

Kevin had taken them down to the receiving dock at the freight airlock. Carter noted that the room had seen a lot of wear. Some of the ceiling tiles were missing, exposing arteries and veins of pipes and ducts. The paint was chipped on the railings of the platform where the object sat. It was silvery, old-looking, more than a meter across, full of old-fashioned wiring and archaic-looking instruments as worn as the room itself. Pay dirt, Carter thought to himself.

"Takes up a lot of space," Kevin was telling them. "See, this is the way it was sitting when we found it. These big petals are hinged. Spring-loaded. They were sticking out on three sides, like they deploy on landing to turn the thing upright. Clever design. This one over here, see, it's missing. Like it broke off. Maybe a bad landing or something. Stafford's medallion was attached over on this side. And, see, over here is the little medallion that Braddock says is Russian."

Carter examined it closely. On the little pentagonal plaque a hammer and sickle were inscribed in a wreath of leaves or wheat sheaves. "Soviet," Carter said. "Definitely last century. My mom used to show me this stuff. Soviet coat of arms. They used to inscribe it everywhere. This baby is old."

Philippe and Annie circled the strange object. Philippe was waxing ecstatic. "Recovering one of the old probes! Finally—archaeology on Mars! Annie, you must report this."

"Don't know about archaeology or whatever," Kevin said laconically. "But I'll tell you, it was hard to move." He tapped one side of the object. "It was pretty beat-up, but not all of these dents were here when we found it. We added a few."

Kevin went on describing their adventures in trying to hook the old probe to the crane on the hopper, and Philippe talked excitedly. Annie pulled out her minicam and started dictating notes as she shot the device from several angles. But Carter wasn't listening. Their voices faded. Pay dirt, he kept thinking. He was interrogating his own 'corder.

"Encyclopedia," he said.

"Encyclopedia," the tiny screen displayed.

"Space probes. Mars. 1900s. Early robotic probes. Landings on planet Mars."

The screen logged the key phrases. "One moment, please."

Finally the machine started chattering back to him in its tiny letters. "Encyclopædia Britannica service. Seventeen artificial robotic probes hit the surface of Mars before the first human landings. First device to reach the surface of Mars was *Mars-2*. Launched from the Soviet Union. An earlier probe in the Soviet program failed on launch. *Mars-2* parachuted into Hellespontus at a reported position of 44.2 south and 313.2 west. Date: 1971, November 27. It failed before it could send back any data. Cause of failure: unknown. There was a heavy global dust storm raging at the time. Experts stated that the winds may have twisted the parachute, or . . ."

"Jeez," Carter exclaimed. "Do you know what this thing is? It's the first human artifact to land on Mars! The very first contact." He repeated the story that his 'corder had related.

Kevin, Philippe, and Annie fell silent. "My God," Philippe breathed. It was as if the receiving dock had been transformed into a church, and this was the silver chalice.

"Is this the first thing to reach any other planet?" Annie asked. The gleam in her eye betrayed the story beginning to take shape.

Carter consulted the 'corder and found that the Soviets had landed probes on Venus a few years earlier. Venus comes closer to Earth and was easier to reach. Mars was the second planet to be reached by robotic probes. "But this machine in front of us is the honest-to-God first man-made object on Mars."

Annie consulted her own 'corder for a few minutes, and eventually began speaking softly into her minicam as she scanned the object again. "Today we are witnessing a tremendous discovery. The object you see before you is the first human-made device to reach the surface of Mars. Its name is *Mars-2*. Sixty years ago, humans were reaching out with the first tentative steps across the seas of space. A few years before humans first walked on the moon, scientists in the Soviet Union had already built and launched robotic probes to Venus. Then they built and launched this device to make the first explorations of the surface of Mars. It was called *Mars-2*, *Mars-1* having failed during launch. The device you see here sailed across space for months. In 1971, only two years after the first footsteps on the moon, it entered the atmosphere of Mars and parachuted toward the surface. But something went wrong. Transmissions stopped before its instruments could relay any useful surface data. However, that event marked the first time that an emissary from Earth touched this distant planet, Mars. Its calculated landing position was only a few tens of kilometers from the site where this artifact was discovered today in the desert.

"The identification as *Mars-2* seems certain. This battered machine is as important as the first boat that carried humans across the seas to an unknown island or continents. It is the *Niña, Pinta, Santa María* of Mars, all rolled into one. Imagine the sense of victory and frustration in that control room in Russia in 1971 when those men and women—or perhaps it was just men in those days—realized they had reached Mars, but then at the last minute lost contact with this, their robotic ambassador. They lived the rest of their lives and died without ever knowing what happened to the craft you see before you. Today we have contacted it again, and now we know what took Stafford out into the desert. . . . Somehow, Stafford must have realized there was a chance of finding this historic object. . . ."

Philippe came to stand beside Carter. "Can you imagine that?" Philippe whispered. "Sending a machine all the way to Mars . . . before we came. You know, some of them still thought there was life on Mars in those days. Look. It has a lens. Probably they expected to see pictures of strange plants and creatures. . . . *Mars-2*. First probe on Mars. Why hasn't everyone heard this name? Every child in school should know about this machine, and yet I never heard of it. This is a historic relic! It must go into a museum!"

"Yeah. So now we know what took Stafford out there . . . but why didn't he come back?"

1 0

Friday. Zero days left, even if Stafford had conserved his last air. Carter spent the day pouring over the pictures.

The previous evening, in the presence of the *Mars-2* probe, he had experienced a moment of hope. *Mars-2* seemed to provide a glimmer of rationality at last. It revealed a goal, a destination, an explanation of Stafford's purposeful trek west from Hellespontus Road. Bits of a plausible story began to fit together. Perhaps *Mars-2* had been an obsession of Stafford's for years. He could have looked up the twentieth-century tracking data that placed it somewhere in Hellespontus. Somehow, Stafford must have had some additional clue, since the tracks in the desert made a beeline to the general area of the artifact's landing site. Could he have spotted something on some earlier orbital photo? The craft itself was too small to show up, of course, but perhaps a lucky reflection when the sun was at a certain angle? Or the large parachute that had brought *Mars-2* to the surface . . . ? The idea that Stafford could spend years chasing such a dream, risking his life even, made sense. It fit his personality.

But this morning the sense of rationality had faded. In truth, *Mars-2* had explained nothing. Why had Stafford disappeared from there into the desert? Why his maze of tracks around the *Mars-2* site? The situation was seeming increasingly surreal.

Carter had begun to question his own involvement. Why had he been dragged into it in the first place? To help find Stafford, which he didn't know how to do, and to write a damn accident report, which was useless? What was his real role? (Why did the word "real" come into his mind?) Now, no matter what he wanted, it would not help. . . .

He jarred himself out of his paranoid musings. Stafford's chances were flatlining. Why hadn't Braddock's people been smart enough to find those thin traces a day earlier? One day might have made all the difference. . . .

He ordered up new hi-res orbital photography of the *Mars-2* site. Maybe there would be something . . . The message back from someone named Romero, at the Phobos Imagery Lab, said there would be no satellite in position until later in the day. Too late of course. But he wanted to see the images anyway.

Philippe and Annie came by in the morning, looking glum, wanting to empathize. Carter shooed them away, said he wanted to wait alone for the hi-res photos to come in. They said they'd go off to the library work-station to research the history of the *Mars-2* probe. Carter stared forlornly at the pictures. Every cell in his body felt like lead.

They had all tried to avoid talking about Stafford's air running out, little by little.

Nothing heard from Stafford.

Afternoon came. Annie had come by to speak to him, and had burst into tears and left without saying a word. What had she wanted to say? There was a look in her eye. . . . Ever since she left he had been trying to put it out of his mind. But it left gloom that seemed to hang in the air like a cloud. Later in the afternoon, Annie and Philippe had come by to say they were going off to dinner again. "A wake," Philippe had called it. "We need to be together. We need to be human beings. You should come with us." Carter had told them he preferred to be alone, that he wanted to look at the images one more time.

It was true, but the whole truth was that he didn't want to have to watch Philippe with Annie together again. At least he could admit that to himself, he thought with black satisfaction.

Evening. Stafford's air had run out.

B O O K 3

Desert Secrets

Three may keep a secret, if two of them are dead.
—Benjamin Franklin,
Poor Richard's Almanac, July 1735

11

Evening. Stafford's dune buggy sat parked against the crude wall of boulders under its protective shroud.

The sun was just touching the far wall of the shallow volcanic crater. The warmth of the golden glow belied the coldness of the empty place. The empty buggy had been powered down, though Stafford had left the full charge of air, just in case.

The sun sank below the crater rim. Inside the buggy, where there was air, you could hear the creaks and groans of the vehicle cooling down rapidly. A thin film of frost condensed on the windows and then all the interior surfaces. Outside, where there was not enough air, you could hear nothing.

Beyond the crater rim the sun was setting and the sky overhead was beginning to take on its unfamiliar, violet-blue glow as the upper atmosphere scattered the last traces of sunlight. The violet hour was approaching. Stars were beginning to come out, moving slowly in the sky.

The vehicle was waiting, but Stafford did not return.

12

Annie had spent most of the afternoon walking and walking and stifling her tears. She was no stranger to tears. But her tears today surprised her. The tension and involvement had been building inside her. She had come to know Alwyn Stafford through Philippe and Carter. He was a real person, a friend almost, even though she had never met the famous man face-to-face. She had seen Carter suffering, even though he struggled not to show it. When she stopped to see Carter that afternoon, she had made everything worse. Now, with the fatal hours passing, and all of them impotent, the dam had burst. She had returned to her room and had a final purging through tears.

Philippe had come for her and when Carter turned down their invitation to spend the evening together, he had asked her to spend the evening with him. It was time to move on with life, to see what the future would bring. As Philippe had said, they needed to be human beings again. She had said yes.

Philippe's brain was always active. Sometimes he worried about himself. Other people seemed to be able to shut down for hours at a time. During a moment of pregnant silence, as they walked down the hall toward the Oasis, Hellas's gathering place, he found himself thinking: What did he really want? To understand how Annie felt. About Mars, Stafford, what she was doing here. About everything that she was thinking.

They came to the Oasis Café. It was better than he had hoped; they found a table in the corner. Not bad, considering that the "Café" was a spartan dining room with a hand-lettered sign. Like attempting a romantic engagement in a college cafeteria. Is that what he was after? On a day like this? The place was as sterile as a military station. The music that usually played was turned down, in deference to the pall that had settled over all of Hellas Base. He should have waited to talk to her until they were back amid the comforts of Mars City. They ordered sangria.

When they sat down, Philippe said, "Your piece on Newsnet, I read it. It was good."

Annie smiled sadly. "Let's avoid talking about Stafford. So much has happened, I just want to get away from it for a bit."

Philippe shrugged agreeably. "There is not much we can do now, anyway. And Carter will tell me when he needs help. . . ."

"Will Carter be all right? He looked so . . . hurt."

"Carter, he will be all right."

"What does he think about, on ordinary days?"

"In his job, he has to think about mechanical systems. In his own life, he thinks about people. Societies, I mean. How our Mars will evolve. Mars Council versus the technocrats who actually understand the infrastructure. Maybe he will be, you know, the Thomas Jefferson of Mars."

"I thought Jefferson was a racist."

"That's what they teach you in your schools while they try to keep the lid on the American melting pot. The reality was more complicated."

She didn't want to talk politics. "You know what I was thinking when Carter was talking about the dates, and the number of days left?"

"What?"

"I've never *really* understood the Martian calendar."

"Do you want to?"

"If I say yes, do I get a lecture?"

"Is there any way to explain something without a lecture?"

"Just don't make it condescending. You get five minutes."

"I have studied it. I need only three minutes." Philippe cleared his throat ceremoniously. "We are very lucky on Mars. By chance, one rotation of the planet, which is called a sol, is only half an hour longer than on the Earth. So, our body clocks hardly notice the difference. But of course, if you keep your watch running on Earth time, you will get hopelessly out of phase with local time on Mars. Pretty soon your watch will read noon when it is really sunrise outside.

"So, to keep your watch in synch with the sun, we make a new watch, a Mars watch. It runs about three percent slower than normal. So, we keep twenty-four hours in a sol, to keep it familiar, and we keep sixty minutes in an hour, but they are all three percent longer than hours and minutes on Earth. Voilà. We are running on Mars time."

"What's that have to do with a weird date like February 43?" She looked at her watch. "You've got two Mars-minutes left."

"Ah. Now we have to decide what to do about the months. We have twelve of them just as on Earth. That way we can keep the same names. But it is a problem. Mars takes 670 sols, or Mars-days, to go around the sun. Nearly two Earth-years. So if we were going to have twelve months they've got to be nearly twice as long as on Earth."

"But why not have nice thirty-day months like on Earth? I hate it being February for week after week."

"Then you have to invent new names for all the extra months, January, February, Bacillus, Ambrosia, it would get confusing. Besides, the months are actually functional. They divide the year into twelve parts and these twelve parts, they tell us what the seasons are. Mars has, how would you say, stronger seasons than Earth. Earth, it stays about the same distance from the sun all year. Southern summer comes when Mars is closest to the sun, so the southern summer heating is quite pronounced." He drew an exaggerated ellipse, stretching his hand beyond the edge of the table and bumping a passing patron. "Anyway," he said sheepishly, "the extra heat in the atmosphere is why the dust devils are strong here in the south."

"And the seasons . . ."

"Same as on Earth. Summer comes in June in the northern hemisphere, and so on. Here in the southern hemisphere, we have summer starting in late December on the day of solstice, like Australia."

"How did you learn all this? I mean, you're an artist, not a timekeeper."

"Madame, in my youth I was a student of physics. Before art, physics. But the real reason is, when I started my Stonehenge project, I accessed all the information I could get. My Stonehenge works as a calendar, the same as the original. It is why you wanted to see me in the first place, yes? When this business with Stafford is all over, we will go there. I will show it to you. I love the place now more than when I started. It is like a ruin left by the ancient Martians."

"It's a wonderful idea. I want to see it."

"Someday, if they zero out our budget and we discover we have not reached critical mass, we will have to abandon Mars. But someone will come back centuries later and find my Stonehenge. . . . Maybe they will get a shock. . . ." He took a sip of the sangria. "The fruits from the greenhouse, they are perfect. But they do not belong in wine. It is a Spanish abomination. Only grapes belong in wine."

"Sorry, but I think it's wonderful."

He stared into the liquid. Suddenly he felt morose. "I am between projects. To be more precise, I am not between projects. I have been working on a second project, but I am not sure about it."

"What is it? Tell me."

Philippe recoiled in mock horror. "But it is secret! Maybe it will fail."

She wrinkled her nose at him.

"I hope that someday they will make a committee and give a special

interplanetary award for artists whose careers showed extraordinary promise at the start, and then collapsed into a sea of uncompleted projects. I
am, how do you say, a shoo-in for this award."

Annie laughed and held up her watch. "Back to the subject. When it's
February here, it's not February on Earth, right?"

It heartened him to see her smile. Conversation with a woman like
Annie was like cultivating a garden . . . She was one of the women who
understood this, too, he was convinced. One could always tell . . . One of
the great mysteries . . . "Of course not," he said. "The two calendars are
totally independent. A calendar is for the convenience of the people on
the planet using it. A calendar is tailored to a planet. But we keep the
number of the year the same as it is on Earth. 2031."

"Very educational."

"But you couldn't repeat it."

She laughed and held up her finger in an obscene gesture. "I told you,
no condescending! Besides"—she tapped her watch—"you're ten seconds
over the limit."

"Ah, but we didn't agree on a penalty."

"I could see what I can dream up."

They smiled at each other conspiratorially over their glasses. "When I
studied it all for my Stonehenge design, I thought: Those old English,
four thousand years ago, they knew what they were doing. Solstices. Calendars. Everything. One last interesting thing. We want to keep the
seven-day week—yes? So we can all sleep in on Sunday. And so the
religious people . . . you're not religious?"

She gave her head a noncommittal tilt sideways. "Maybe I believe in
the old Hawaiian gods. I think Madam Pele and Madame Poliahu visited
Mars, you know."

". . . so the religious people get their sabbath once every seven days.
With a seven-day week, we can have a perpetual calender if each month
has eight weeks. Every month starts on a Sunday. Twelve 56-day months
make 672 days—two days too much for a year. So we knock two days out
of the middle of the last week of December—a bonus of a short work
week. Holidays are celebrated according to the schedule on Earth, where
they originated. So we have Christmas when it's December twenty-fifth
on Earth, which falls at various times here. That way we get to share all
our holidays with Earth."

"Except Founder's Day—or Mars Day as they're trying to call it now.
I hope I can stay long enough to celebrate it."

"You will stay. You are hooked."

"No, I'll have to return to Earth. I am thinking of going back to the islands."

"Then someday you will come back to Mars. Once you are hooked, once you have made love on Mars, you will always come back. Have you made love on Mars?"

"That's rather personal, don't you think." She laughed. "Besides, it's superstition. You say you studied physics. You should know better."

"It's not superstition. It's my own personal irrational belief. There's nothing wrong with a little irrationality. Peasants around the world know that if you intellectualize too much, it's bad for your mental health."

"I never know what you're talking about and now I know you don't either. . . ." She laughed again and took another drink, smiling at him with her eyes over the rim of her cup. She tossed her dark hair. "Do you think we should go back and find Carter? Maybe we could do something to help."

"What can we do with him plugged into that machine? With that machine he has to work alone."

She had told herself she would start work on a new report immediately after dinner. In the end, when he said he wanted to be with her that night, it did not really surprise her. It did surprise her that she said yes.

Later, she played it over in her mind.

They had made love that left her feeling, as usual, released, but at some level unsatisfied. Philippe had been ardent, full of cheerful enthusiasm. She tried to describe him to herself—obviously he adored the excitement of a new lover, a new place, a responsive woman whose shudders were, as with all women, different, new, and yet the same, old. When they had entered her room and closed her door, she had started to her bathroom to take her pill, but he said, "Wait." And he took her hands and put them on his shoulders and grasped the back of her neck and kissed her. When they started to make love, he insisted on undressing her, a little at a time.

For her that night, there was something more than enthusiasm. Her hunger had surprised her; it was something she had been burying since she had arrived here. Philippe had reveled in himself as a lover; covered her with kisses, exploring her as if turning her inside out for her to feel herself. "We must forget everything now," he whispered to her. "What has happened has happened. We must re-create ourselves. For everything there is a season." He didn't have to say the rest. A time for death and a time for love and a time for beginning again.

They made love as if they were two souls hiding in a bomb shelter with bombs falling all around; the visit from Death, beyond their control, seemed to necessitate an expression of life.

He shared her body with her. She forgot everything. He almost preened with satisfaction at what he imagined to be his ability to excite her, excite himself, enter her, and feel her respond.

And yet . . . Happy as she was, something in her mind, the hunger, told her that it had been only a doing with; he had smiled the whole time, as if it were a children's game. He had wanted her to smile the whole time. As if it was an exercise for him to assure her happy cooperation. Hence she had not fully opened to him. She did not feel owned by him, a thought that made no sense to her. Her subconscious whispered to her: There had not been a doing to.

They lay together, sometimes resting, sometimes with his finger stirring, sliding to her breasts. They lay and listened to Ravel's *Le Tombeau de Couperin*—the Peruvian recording by Emilio Sanchez, which she had put on the music button she had brought with her. It went on for a long time, like rain pattering into a lake. After it was over, they still lay, resting, for a time more.

Annie lay looking at Philippe. He looked sad. "What's the matter?" she asked him.

"Nothing."

"Memories?" A look like that always meant memories.

"The music reminded me of something."

"Some*one*?"

"Are you my friend?"

"Always."

He kissed her nipple tenderly now, and then lay his head sadly on the pillow. She turned and studied him closely for a moment. Yes, his face was sad.

He looked back at her.

She prompted. "There was this woman. . . ."

"Yes. Of course. There was this woman. She was like the ocean."

"You're being Philippe again," she teased him. "Grandiose." Suddenly she felt his longing and was touched. "You're serious? This is the secret of Philippe? This is why Philippe pretends he can't be touched?" She kissed his lips softly. "Your devil-may-care facade is calculatedly charming, of course, but you're a terrible actor."

"And you are always radiating . . . something. You are like a stream in the mountains, full of energy and laughter, even when you are quiet." She liked that. "I could live with you, easily." She thought he was being presumptuous, but it was nice to hear. "But this other woman . . . I never knew how deep the currents went. . . . Many women are just out there collecting experiences, you know? Perhaps even you. Which is wonderful, of course." He kissed her and touched her again, a kiss and touch that made her breath begin to come hard. But he was still floating in his own world, she realized, and they lay quiet for another minute. . . . She waited for the rest of his story.

"She was, I think, discovering herself, not collecting experiences. When I made love to her, I was making love to an entire being, a psyche, not just a body. There was no end to her. . . . After she left, I came all the way to Mars and now I know I can't run away from what she planted in me. I won't be the same, and it frightens me, sometimes. . . ."

"What was her name?" As soon as she asked it, Annie knew it was a silly question, not addressing the reality of his feelings, and his face was like a readout, which displayed the thought: Why do women always want to know the other woman's name . . . ?

"It doesn't matter," he said after a pause, after his face changed.

"But you were hurt? I'm sorry . . ." She was stroking his hair now, looking at its richness, its slight curl, the brush strokes of gray that she had not noticed before.

"Not hurt so much as changed. It was aborted, the relationship."

"So now you have this playboy facade—that nothing can hurt you?"

He said nothing.

"I've never even told Carter," he said sadly. He said it like a request. "Some things, you can discuss only with a woman. . . . Is it like that for you, with men?"

"Sometimes." She didn't want to go into it. Not her own life. Not her own problem. Not Tomas and her hungers . . .

"I go on with my work," he said, accepting her silence. "Sometimes it is as if a sea breeze comes in off her ocean, which is beyond the hills. I can't see the ocean, but I can feel that it is there." He still lay with his head against one breast, running his fingers over the other and down her side. His fingers moved like absentminded wanderers.

"Is it hard for you?" she asked.

"Hard to talk about. Not because of pain, anymore, but because I don't know what I want to say."

"Will you tell me more about it? Sometime?"

"Only if you'll tell me about the life of the sex-starved journalist."

She wanted to know his secret. What was below Philippe's carefree surface? But they had begun to lose mind contact. He began to get restless. She could be only his friend, again.

They lay quietly, touching each other softly. She rubbed his back.

Philippe rolled over, listlessly.

"Had enough? It's 'thank you, ma'am' time, now?" She teased with a gentle smile.

He turned to her again, raising himself to study her bare shoulders, his fingers coming alive again and now tracing her cheeks, her nose, her lips. "There is never 'enough.' " He brushed her hair gently with a forefinger, and then propped himself up on one arm. "Ahem. I will tell you my theory. Sex is like sledding. You have this wonderful ride down the hill. Then you spend a lot of energy getting everything organized back up on the top of the hill, so you can do it again."

"The sledding theory of life," she said. She felt a mixture of warmth, intensity, and teasing, stirring together inside her.

"The sledding theory of sex. I think art is like that, and science, for all these researchers that I see in these labs. You must go out there all by yourself, and slog up that hill with your sled, slipping and sliding every step of the way, for days, weeks, months. All for those few climactic days when you have a sense of completion or wholeness. You sit, you enjoy the doneness of it. It even feels like sex, sometimes, painting. Then you get restless and start over."

"Are work and play all mixed up for you? You give that impression, you know. I think you try to give that impression."

He shrugged. "It is a good thing, if work and play are mixed up."

"You're being Philippe again."

"Of course." He sat up on the edge of the bed, dressing.

He left her.

She lay still for a long time. Another one had entered her and entered her life. She had never determined for herself whether these two were synonymous, and if so, whether it was a good thing. It had all been so easy. The music, the same music she had not played for a long time, was full of new chords.

13

Late Friday afternoon in Hellas Base. Carter Jahns had returned to his war room in the old Cartographic Lab, discouraged and lonely. So, Stafford was gone. Annie was probably off with Philippe somewhere.

Life would have to go on. He'd have to think about the future. All that crap.

The screens in the lab flickered with a blue, melancholy glow. Tiny lights glinted at him: red, yellow, and green eyes of the machines, watching him, waiting to see what he would do next. He felt like the fluid in his cells was jelling, pulling him down.

Braddock called from his office. "I guess it's over. His air couldn't have lasted this long."

Carter said nothing.

"I'm sorry. I know he was your friend."

"Yeah."

"You gonna file your report or what?"

"I'm supposed to figure out what happened. That's what we still don't know. I'm looking at the photos. Looking for trail segments."

"Find anything yet?"

"No. I'm searching in different directions from the *Mars-2* site. Stafford had to leave there in some direction. But I haven't found anything . . . yet."

"I think we're going to have to call off further searching, you know. In a place like this, there's a limit to the resources we can devote, I mean, after the air runs out."

"You've got a missing vehicle out there."

"Yeah, but we don't know where to look for it and we don't know that it's in working order. It probably isn't. Otherwise Alwyn would have called in. I don't want to risk other personnel looking for a broken down . . ."

"I need to know what happened to Stafford."

There was a pause at the other end. "Well, fine. Let me know if you find anything. We'll take it from there." Braddock clicked off.

Fine? Fine? What kind of reaction was that?

He was feeling more than lonely. He was feeling frustrated and angry.

How could he write a report on someone who just vanished without a trace? Something else had to happen; some new development. Trouble was, it looked as if the new development would have to come from him.

He had been waiting for inspiration. Often, in the past, his ideas just seemed to pop up from someplace else, like telephone calls. This time, the muse seemed to be avoiding him. If she did call, it would probably be collect. He had a premonition that some kind of bill was going to come due when this was all over.

He still had an ace up his sleeve. The image he had requested of the *Mars-2* site was on its way downlink. A message from Phobos had said there was a processing problem, but finally the image arrived. Why, he thought, did everything have to be delayed during the week when time was most critical?

Then he had to remind himself: Time was no longer a factor.

As he worked, he seemed to sense Stafford's shade hovering over him. Smiling. "Get that picture," it whispered. "Don't give up. Keep looking . . ." It was creepy.

The new hi-res image showed the confused tracks of Braddock's teams' vehicles at the *Mars-2* site. Multi-wavelength. Thermal infrared. Cloverleaf patterns of trails looped out into the desert and returned; probably Braddock's people looking for clues.

Finally, he made a spiral search pattern with the new thermal data folded in. And at last he saw them: broken traces of a soil disturbance—tracks—leading to the west. He felt excitement rising, but felt his own anger at the same time. Too late, too late, too late.

The trail was not continuous. He could not even pick it up within the first few kilometers near the *Mars-2* site. Maybe there was rocky ground, with no dust to show the tracks. Here and there, farther west, he could just see a trace. . . . The trail seemed to zigzag one way and then another. Detours around obstacles?

Hours later he had traced the trail to a point beyond which he could find nothing. He was not sure he could find any unusual end point; the last segment faded out of resolution just as the other segments had. There was nothing unusual in the area: an eroded flow, a well-formed but non-descript cinder cone, some poorly developed dunes. But projecting the trail farther west, search as he might, he could find no further segments.

He grabbed the phone and told Braddock he was tracing Stafford's trail west.

"I've got to get out there. We can reach the *Mars-2* site in hoppers and take buses west from there. You've got to back me on this. I'll go to the Council if you don't."

"Okay." Braddock sounded defeated. "One thing, though. I want to go out there with you. I'll arrange it. Two buses. And listen: You better not be wasting my time."

●

It was late. Carter hadn't even eaten. He had tried to find traces of the trail extending beyond the last region. Nothing. They would have to go that far and then see what they could find. He felt tired, excited, alone.

He was pondering this when suddenly he knew he was no longer alone. He turned. It was Elena Trevina, standing just inside the door watching him. He still found her disturbing. It wasn't sexual; he was sure he couldn't feel anything sexual now. But there was something . . . She wore her auburn hair very short. It illuminated a face that had grown not simply older, but more interesting, in the mysterious manner that most American women, in their eternally frustrated quest for youth, had not mastered. She was, perhaps, in her early forties, maybe a decade older than Carter. She created the impression that these years had let her in on some secret knowledge that Carter had yet to discover. The secret gave her an air of authority, yet there was also a perfume of empathy.

"It's been a bad day," she said. "They told me you were here." She didn't say who "they" might be. "Still working, I see. I guess now it's too late. . . ." She radiated an air of we-have-to-move-on.

"Ummm."

"Well?"

"Well what?"

"How are you? What have you been doing?"

"I've been here most of the day."

"With what result?"

"I've been thinking . . ." Carter paused.

"That's a result?"

Carter shrugged.

"Maybe we won't find out what happened to Stafford right away," she pressed. "Maybe it will be fifty years from now, when his . . . his body turns up?" She stepped into the room. "I think you have to face that. Accidents can happen to anybody."

"He knew the country. He told me once that any other direction from here just took you out into the basin—just a big bowl of dust. But Hellespontus, up on the rim, he said it was full of ghosts. That's actually what he called them. Ghosts. Now that we've found this *Mars-2* thing, I know what he meant. Talking to him was like talking to a Zen master. He'd say something crazy. A year later, you'd realize it made perfect sense. Anyway, he liked the country up there. My job is to find out what happened, and I haven't. . . ."

"He checks out a buggy. He gets into an accident. End of story. What more can you do? Do you want to expose others to danger, to go after him now? I knew him, too, you know. If he died with his boots on, he'd rather be left out there. . . ."

"He knew dust devils. Chased them. So I don't understand . . . I can't see him getting into danger. Anyway, I don't know what happened. I don't plan to speculate."

"Our ace reporter doesn't seem to think you're so uncertain about what happened."

"What?"

"Look at this." Lena went over to the big screen console, put Carter's picture on hold, and punched voice control. "Call . . . up . . . Newsnet. Find . . . the . . . story . . . about . . . Stafford," she said very slowly and distinctly. The screen flickered and displayed a page of print.

HELLESPONTUS CASUALTY THE WORK OF DUST DEVILS? the headline said. Lena was pointing to the byline. "Filed by Ann Pohaku." It was Annie's story with a new headline and a bulletin added at the end.

> Update. Feb. 48; 3 P.M. Hellas Base time. According to records of the supplies checked out by Dr. Stafford, the staff here estimate that his air would have run out by midday today. Stafford was born in 1968 and was a pioneer of Mars. No sign has been found of his vehicle, but new high-res satellite photos have been ordered. Officials believe he has died as a result of an accident, possibly involving dust devils known to have been active in the area. Stafford was famous for his research on ancient Martian microbes and his unsuccessful search for evidence of more evolved ancient life forms. As reported previously, Stafford's last triumph, and perhaps his most dramatic, was his discovery of the *Mars-2* probe, the first human artifact to reach the red planet.

The article went on. Carter feigned coolness. Lamely he said, "She's got it pretty much right, hasn't she?"

"New satellite photos? Where did she get all this? From you?"

"No. Well, I mean, not directly. She's been helping out." Carter glanced at the headline again. "What's the problem? Or is there a problem?"

"She's the press, Carter. The press doesn't just 'help out.' She's a reporter, for God's sake."

"Well, jeez, Lena. Why are you so paranoid? She reported the story, yes, that's her job. But this is Mars. It's an emergency. There's a man missing and we don't know what happened. When we came down here, we expected we could use more people in the search. She's available to get involved—that's her job, too, in a sense. Besides, I couldn't stop her from coming. And it hadn't occurred to me to stand in the way," he lied. "And the discovery of *Mars-2*," he tried to change the subject. "That thing really is historic . . . that was a great story for her. I wish they had left it in place. I mean, it's a sacred spot."

Lena wore an exasperated-by-naiveté expression. "They didn't know. They were just a construction crew from the reactor, not historians."

Carter studied the screen.

> . . . investigators close to the scene think Stafford may have encountered a giant dust devil that could have damaged his vehicle. Recent photos have shown dust devil activity in the area . . . search continuing . . .

"That's another thing I can't figure," Carter said. "As far as we know, no one's ever been tipped over by a dust devil, or sandblasted, or whatever the hell's supposed to have happened."

"What *was* supposed to have happened?"

"You heard Braddock as well as I did. I don't know if he's right."

"And your theory?"

Carter remained silent. He had tried to avoid having a theory. If you stood around and tried to explain what happened, it meant you're no longer actively involved in finding out.

Carter studied her. She was smiling at him expectantly. A curious smile. A Cheshire cat smile. Carter took a deep breath as if to say something, but ended in a sigh. It felt like he was expelling something evil that had been building up inside. It felt strange to begin to talk about an explanation.

"Well?" Lena repeated. She was trying to help him get it out. He had wanted to try to work all this out with Annie, but with Annie he never felt free to talk. No telling what would end up in print. Maybe he could work through it with Lena.

Out loud, his thoughts sounded like bullshit. . . . "Suppose Stafford is excited after finding Mars-2. He forgets to be careful. He gets in a dust storm and maybe can't see and drives off the edge of a ravine. Or something. Wind speeds and particle velocities are higher in a dust devil core than in your run-of-the-mill dust storm, right?"

"Oh, yeah." She smiled. "You got that right."

"Do you think a dust devil could pit the windshield of a buggy so he couldn't see?"

"Ummm. Maybe, yeah . . . I don't know if anybody really knows."

"Anything like that I come up with, I can't figure out why he didn't just radio back that he was in trouble. Unless it was a sudden accident." Carter sighed again.

"Maybe it did something to the antenna, too. Something he couldn't fix. Then there's always the dust sinks."

"Dust sinks."

"Drivers occasionally run into mushy spots. Vehicles sink in. Nobody knows how they form. Nobody's ever hit one big enough to sink a whole vehicle, but there's a sort of mythical belief that it's bound to happen. People have this idea of whole buggies just sinking out of sight and never being found. I think that's one reason Braddock doesn't want to spend more time looking for the vehicle."

"He told you?"

"Yeah. Besides, Alwyn was his friend, too. I think Braddock thinks Alwyn would be happier this way. Out there . . . Anyway, maybe a dust devil, maybe a dust sink. It could have been a dozen different things."

Carter considered. "Maybe maybe maybe."

She looked at him expectantly. "You may never find him."

"We ought to try."

"But don't you think, ummm . . ."

Carter took the plunge. "Look, Lena, I've got something else here. The new pictures came in." He returned the screen to the images he had been studying. "Look, you can see tracks leading west from the Mars-2 area. Away from Hellas. Into the desert. When he was done, why would he go farther into the desert?"

She was silent for a moment as he showed her. "That could be anything."

"No, it's tracks. Look. Here, still farther west!"

"And you think . . ."

"Now we have something to follow."

"Carter . . ."

"I'm onto something," he said. "I'm on his trail. Tomorrow we can find out."

"You need to take a break. I'll stand you a drink at the Oasis. You need to talk, to unwind."

It was true, he was exhausted. Better to start the search again when he had rested.

He headed toward the Oasis with her. He was confident now about Stafford's trail. What he needed to know more about was—what was going on here. Maybe he could learn something from Lena. Okay, so he was rationalizing again.

———————————————————●———————————————————

He walked with Lena, mostly in silence. She was saying. "It's been hard on all of us. It'll do you good to get away for a few minutes. You've got to, you know, pick up the pieces."

They were coming out of a corridor. He suddenly caught sight of Philippe and Annie striding away from the Oasis, in the distance, heads together, his arm at her waist. They were talking earnestly. They disappeared around a corner. They did not see him. Lena did not see them.

Suddenly, he felt, somehow, abandoned. So, they *were* together. Now he could feel almost relieved. Pretenses were gone. Time for a new beginning? He had traced Stafford in the pictures as far as he could; maybe Lena was right, it was time to become normal again. Thoughts and feelings collided in chaos. "Come on," Lena said. "A red will cheer you up."

———————————————————●———————————————————

In the Oasis, there was music. Indonesian gamelon orchestras and little wind ensembles, very quiet, very sad. The inhabitants of Hellas Base had tried to make the Oasis into a poor man's Nix Olympica. It had a blue ceiling. The insistent rhythms, the hollow sounds of flutes, and the tinkling of bells seemed to fit the spirit of weirdness that, in Carter's mind, pervaded everything here. Outside was the desert, always the desert, always the presence of Mars itself, like a giant monster outside the cave door, breathing quietly, probably asleep.

Unknowingly they sat at the same table where Annie and Philippe had sat earlier during the previous hour. They both ordered blues, not reds. They ordered it served hot, which made it taste like mulled wine from a different dimension.

Carter, feeling lousy, finally tried to force himself back into the stream of life, as Lena kept telling him to. For now, he had done as much as he could. It hadn't been enough. "What do you all do, down there at the Polar Station?"

Lena smiled. "Subsist."

"No, I mean really."

"Never been there?"

"No. Wanted to."

Lena's eyes drifted to a spot somewhere high on the wall behind Carter. "It's different down there. . . ." Suddenly she looked directly at Carter. "Do you spend most of your time at Mars City? Yes, I guess so." She said it as if she had performed a brain scan on him. Then her eyes drifted back to the spot on the wall. "The pole is very different from Mars City."

"Tell me about it."

"At Mars City, you've got a lotta people. And a different landscape. Not very many clouds. At our station, we're at the edge of the permanent ice deposits. Lotta fog. Dunes. The whole place, it feels lonely. Cold, as if the cold seeps through the walls. We wear heavy clothes. Cold and dark as Novosibirsk in winter. The dunes to the north of us, they're the biggest dune fields in the solar system. They make you feel like you're cut off from everything. Just a few kilometers to the south of us, the ice fields. They're kind of pink when the sun is up in the summer. It's pretty then. The sun burns the frost off, and the orange colors come out from under the white. If you go far enough south during the summer, on the permanent ice, you see the soot the Clarke people are spreading on the ice cap. Someday you can come and see it."

"Yeah." He forced a smile. "Tell me about the research. We ship a lot of stuff down there to you guys."

"We want a record of the planet's climate history. The pole is the place to look. The geology is ancient sediments, not like Mars City. The summer winds blow in deposits of dust, on top of the winter ice. So the layers pile up. Flat strata. They go way back in time . . . clues to the past and all that. We do a lot of drilling and tunneling to expose the lowest layers. Summer's the best time to work; February is our best month. But the fogs will be coming in soon. We're under the polar hood in fall and winter, you know." She was warming to her subject, the ice and the cold. "The winds come whipping off the ice. In early winter when the sun comes up for a few hours at midday, it'll be all gray and misty, with the hills lost in the haze—like orange sorbet made out of dry ice, somebody said. And the CO_2 snow. It just appears out of the air and pretty soon it covers the ground."

The drinks arrived, steaming. She held hers up and looked at him through the vapor. "It looks like this. Fog. On the first days after the snow, the rocks that stick up stay warm. You have all these red and brown rocks sticking up out of little holes in the ice. After a few weeks, the CO_2 snow covers everything and we're in the midst of the transient winter ice cap. It's a good time to stay indoors. It's dark outside. We all get a little bit crazy. Summer will be ending down there soon."

She said all this almost wistfully, and Carter was intrigued by the strange warmth she exuded as she described the cold scene. On one level, she seemed unprepossessing, a scientist-administrator patterned on some no-nonsense stereotype. At first, she had seemed to radiate no power of attraction. And at first, there seemed to be little laughter in her. Surprised, Carter realized he was measuring her against Annie. And yet, with her sense of assuredness and maturity, Lena radiated . . . something. A sort of confident femininity? She seemed too used to being responsible. As if she would have to relax entire sets of undreamed-of muscles in order to enjoy a holiday. Yet, if there was little laughter, there were still smiles: sometimes a forced smile, less often an unconscious smile of empathy, and sometimes the Cheshire cat smile. Always, a certain intensity, as if she were watching for something. Her face, her intelligent eyes, and wide, smooth East European jaw were really quite beautiful. Seen in this light, her short hair had a boyish sexy charm, as if challenging his own sexuality. He found he wanted to touch it. But there seemed to be some puzzle beneath the surface of her personality. He couldn't figure her out. What was she really saying? What was her angle?

For some moments she had lost her self-consciousness, but now, suddenly, it returned and she seemed almost embarrassed by her outburst of enthusiasm.

"It's okay at the pole," she said, as if to make up for her lyricism. "It changes with the seasons and the winds. It's better than the moon, for instance. God, I'd hate to live at Tycho. Nothing ever happens on the moon, you know what I mean?"

"But what do you do, day to day? I mean scientifically."

"Oh . . . there's lots of core sampling and drilling. How the water ice layers and CO_2 ice layers and soil layers relate to the climate shifts."

"How many people down there now?"

"Oh, it varies. A hundred will winter over. Winters are our low season. We call summer the tourist season. People come and go. Come and work for a few months, and go back to Hellas or Mars City."

"Do you live with anybody there?"

"I was coming to that." She smiled her most intriguing smile yet. "The short answer is 'no.' You?"

"No."

She was looking at him intently. "How do you feel about that?"

"Usually okay. Sometimes too alone. I think the social picture on Mars . . ."

She was smiling again. "You interested in doing something about that? Tonight, I mean? You intrigue me. Let's go to your room."

"Tonight? You and me?" Carter was surprised at his own words. He sounded stupid. He knew this thought had been there all along, lurking out of sight like a spy in the back of his mind. He had wanted no involvement with this woman. More accurately, on cross-examination, his brain revealed to him that while he didn't want an involvement with this woman, he wanted an involvement with *a* woman. Especially since an hour ago.

———————————————●———————————————

They went to Carter's room and stayed until she rose at midnight from the semisleep they had fallen into. After their lovemaking, Carter had found himself thinking again of Philippe and Annie. He imagined himself with Annie, and in his imagination, Annie was entirely different from Lena. With Lena, Carter felt . . . what? Not in control? Not out-of-control frenzied, but out-of-control cast-in-a-role. There was no doubt Lena Trevina wanted . . . wanted something for herself and perhaps for both of them. Almost as soon as they closed the door, she started to undress silently, leading him slowly around the room in a peculiar slow-motion striptease walk, as if she wanted to look at everything in the room from every angle . . . as if putting on a show. Carter said, "Wait." He wanted to do it. She acquiesced verbally but her hands kept helping, slipping things off.

She had adopted a role of her own. She guided, always guided Carter, as if she felt it was her duty because she was the older of the two. Carter played with her, but she guided him onward, as if the only thing that mattered was to have him slide into her, and more significantly, as if she thought that was the only thing that would matter to Carter, and that once done, it would establish something between them. There was little playfulness in her, and suddenly she breathed heavily, shuddered, and lay still. Carter tried to continue the game, using his fingers and lips, but she grasped his hand. Carter felt he had made love using only his penis, not his imagination.

They lay together, wordlessly. She played with his dark hair. "What will you do?" she said at last.

"Do?"

"About Stafford. Whether it's really worth more searching."

"Stafford? You're asking about Stafford? Now?"

"I was thinking about the search crews."

"I just want to know what happened." He rolled over, on his back, with his hands behind his head. "Tomorrow. Braddock's already agreed. We'll take hoppers out there and follow the tracks. . . ."

"I know. Braddock told me. He's not very happy about it." She lay still.

"So, you're his shill?"

She smiled pensively. "I wanted to hear about it from you." She looked like she was dreaming. "Carter, I want to go, too."

"Sure. The more people we have out there, the better, way I figure it."

"Yeah."

She sat up and listlessly began dressing. Suddenly she stopped and ran her hand slowly across his chest toward his heart. She studied his face with strange care. He had not seen her look at him this way. In spite of their lovemaking, it was only now, at this final moment, that he felt he could see beyond a hardness in her eyes. After a peculiar pause, she said, "You are a good man, Carter Jahns. Keep being a good man." And then as if excusing something that needed to be excused, she kissed him and smiled, "I don't get to do this much at the Polar Station." Her eyes still aimed at him, but the moment of contact had stopped.

He lay there and watched her finish dressing. She did it with grace and an occasional smile, which evolved from the empathic smile to the Cheshire cat smile, with each new piece of clothing. She seemed to enjoy his gaze, and he was grateful for that. She came over and stroked his cheek once with the back of her hand. "I liked that," she said. "I'll see you tomorrow." She cracked the door, peeked cautiously outside. Then she was gone.

All the time they had been at each other, she had never blocked his hands from her body, but as the door closed, he felt as if she had. And he felt that she was sorry about it.

14

In his room after Lena left, Carter felt exhausted. Strange how you never knew what life would bring. . . . Stafford would have granted him dispensation. Naked, he pulled the covers over him. He tried to put everything that had happened out of his mind, to lie still at last. The room was cool and pleasant. Quiet as a tomb.

Stafford's dune buggy was parked far to the west of the crashed *Mars-2* probe and Stafford was sitting at the controls. No, Stafford was outside. In his suit. He heard strange sounds. They were hissing sounds. Stafford looked down. They were the sounds of his own shadow sliding across the stones.

Carter's dream was vivid. He seemed half-awake, wanting to believe that the dream could tell him something about what had happened. His half-conscious mind rejected this wish as superstition, but he was surprised by his strong desire to believe it.

In his dream, he could follow Stafford's every thought. He could follow Stafford's growing panic. The hissing sound was back.

It was not his shadow. Fitful wisps of brown, air-dropped dust blew off the tops of scattered boulders like first wisps of smoke from a fire. After his fantastic luck in discovering *Mars-2*, Stafford had decided to explore more of the vicinity. Could he find some other detached parts of the probe or the entry package? Far out in the desert he had seen . . . something. Objects. A lot of them scattered across the flat sands. In Carter's dream, they were formless somethings, white like bleached cow bones scattered on the prairie. . . . Stafford got in the vehicle and started driving.

The way was easy. But the beckoning objects were always farther ahead, plunked here and there across the plain, like sirens on their little islands. He drove on and on, crossing little ravines . . . Up ahead, one of the bone-white objects, embedded in the dusty soil. Part of the descent mechanism? Incredible. Two priceless finds in one day. The first thing to do, Stafford thought as he sat at the controls marveling at the ancient relic, was documentation. Get out on foot and photograph the site. In his excitement he forgot his years of accumulated caution, forgot his own rules about checking and double-checking and having a fallback option if something went wrong.

Hurriedly he sealed his faceplate and clambered out onto the sunlit orange soil. The huge sky arched overhead, bright and clear. He would leave the vehicle here in this little gully so as not to disturb the immediate site. He walked the distance to the object, photographing it from this side and that. He was almost close enough to touch the sandblasted metal, lying on crusty soil with loose dust banked around it. Suddenly he perceived flickering shadows falling across him and noticed the wisps of dust being sucked into the air. The ground itself heaved as he turned to face the horror wandering mindlessly toward him. He had told himself that it was too early in the season for the big Hellespontus dust devils to spawn. But here it was, spinning capriciously across the desert, as if the Martian gods had lost a toy made of nothing more substantial than winds and pale vapors. People had joked about this threat but nobody took it seriously. The statistics . . . Now he was actually in danger. The giant Martian dust devil bearing down on him. Surely it would turn aside . . . dust devils don't keep coming in straight lines.

It was even bigger than the one he had photographed years earlier. A huge, ghostly brown column of ever-changing profile, it reached two hundred meters width and rose several kilometers in a strong curve. The dust at the top sheared off into the dusky sky. As it moved relentlessly closer, it seemed more like a hurricane on an old weather map, bearing down on Florida. . . .

At first, Stafford's reaction had not been fear. Carter admired him too much to let him be afraid at the beginning of the dream. In fact, Stafford reached instinctively for the camera. But even as he turned to face the monster, he realized it filled more than the frame of his camera even if he zoomed to the widest angle. He could not get a meaningful image. It was still moving directly, aimlessly, toward him. A random universe could bring fortune or malevolence. . . . The winds began to whip furiously at him, sucking, and he heard a sound like salt being poured onto a table: dust grains hitting his helmet and faceplate. That was when the fear began. Oh, God, he thought, help me out of this one. Now he tried to retain his footing, and then he crouched. His instinct was to throw himself down, but he had an experienced explorer's distaste for getting on the ground and letting the insidious Martian dust twitch its way into his suit fittings, hoses, valves. The wind was too powerful; he went down anyway. In the last instant, he looked up and saw a skyful of dust, a tan fog in the shape of a giant beast. He made it into an image that he hadn't known he remembered, a childhood memory from some Edgar Rice Burroughs story, of an enormous Martian animal galloping across an empty, ancient dry sea floor. The salt sizzle sound intensified. He realized he was being immersed in dust.

Old Man Stafford was huddling for his life. He had to present the minimum cross section to the wind. No one knew how big an object a Martian dust devil could loft, but there were stories about car-sized boulders showing skid marks out in the salt flats west of Mars City. He doubted them. The calculations said the air was too thin. Mostly, the dust devil was composed only of tiny grains, moving at, what, a hundred, two hundred kilometers per hour? A man could be killed by ants as well as tigers.

God, how stupid, he thought. How did I get into this?

Carter was sweating. He hated the dream, now. Some part of his head wanted to wake up. He couldn't. It was the kind of dream where all you had to do was open a door to get out, but you couldn't get the door open. You had to stay and watch the drama play itself out.

The wind shrieked. Tiny grains of dust and pellets of sand drove into Stafford, seeming to sting, even through the suit. Could Stafford really feel them through his suit, or were they just stinging Carter's mind? He felt the sand slipping out from under him, and had a memory of himself as a kid on the beaches of Earth, a beach in California—yes, that was it, Stafford was from California—a specific beach with the surf swishing around him and sucking the sand out from under him, leaving him in a little hollow with his swimming suit and tennis shoes full of sand. Why these memories? Flashbacks of a drowning man? The noise waned. The ground finally stopped vibrating.

Stafford sat up and tried to look around. The entire landscape was a pearly tan haze. He shook his head, as if to clear his eyes. Why couldn't he see?

My God, he thought, it's sandblasted my faceplate. He turned his head, as if that would help. I can't see anything. My God. Two hundred kilos from anywhere and I can't see!

He knew from his orientation courses years ago, from the experiment they made every recruit perform in the name of confidence-building, that you could not shatter a faceplate with the strongest blow of rock or hammer. At most, you could make only a nick. But now, unwillingly, he had made another discovery: the facemask could be frosted in Mars' worst moments. He had become one of the long line of unsung pioneers whose fatal discovery could add to the survival lore that would allow other humans to persist in a new environment.

Don't panic, Stafford urged himself. He felt at the mask. When he touched the misted glass he could see the gray fabric of his glove, but as soon as he moved his hand away, it vanished in a blur of suffused, pink Martian light.

I've got to sit still, he said to himself. A tiny thought flitted through his mind: Over the last hundred thousand years, how many lonely men had sat still in the woods, in the mountains, in ocean storms, on the arctic ice caps, in the lunar lava tubes, wondering how to get back home, how to transmit the survival information they had just learned by some life-threatening accident? And what tiny fraction had made it? How many deaths did it take for each new bit of survival lore to be learned?

This is no time for philosophy, he thought. Think this out. Don't lose orientation. The sun is over there, in the glare. I turned around, saw the devil. Did I turn away before I threw myself down? It doesn't matter; the sun is over there. That puts the buggy back to the right. How far was the buggy? A hundred meters, two hundred? God, I'll never find it blind.

He wanted to rip the pearly mask away, to get an instantaneous glimpse of the buggy and run for it. It would be fatal, of course. Asphyxiation in the thin carbon dioxide. The young planetary engineers had not yet been successful enough that you could hold your breath and make a dash.

He had maybe forty-five minutes of air left on his back. Plenty of time. He just had to think it out.

He had to fight a compulsion to start walking. Somewhere. But if he did, he'd just get more hopelessly confused. Sit still and think.

He reached out and felt around. He could feel the hollow that the whirling wind had scooped out around him. Little rock fragments had collected in the hollow and nestled against his body. With a shock he realized he had already decided he was going to die here.

Carter tossed and turned. Part of his mind was trying to figure out how to save Stafford in the dream. Stafford would think of some clever solution, à la Jules Verne or one of the adventure holeos. If he could coat his frosted faceplate with liquid, perhaps, it would be clear and he could see through it. He would think of his urine bag, rip it off the suit, splash some of it on the faceplate, smear it around. It would evaporate immediately, of course, but if he could just catch a glimpse of the buggy. Only three or four applications . . . That would be enough to get back . . .

But Stafford had not come back. . . .

Carter woke up, drenched with sweat. The clock on the wall of the windowless room told him it was two in the morning. Saturday.

What were those white bones in the desert? It was a stupid question—it was a dream, after all. But they had seemed so realistic and mysterious in the dream.

Two A.M. craziness.

Suddenly he felt an unexpected wave of relief. At first, he could not explain it to himself. More craziness. Then, he realized that for the first time, he no longer felt a captive of the desperate race to save Stafford. Gruesome uncertainty had ended; a morbid weight had lifted.

He came more fully awake. He felt as if he were coming alive for the first time all week. Things would fall into place. In his calls of yesterday he had used all of the clout of his appointment by Mars Council to organize a ground search. He realized he divided time into two halves. Yesterday was before Lena.

Anyway, by now, Braddock's field crew would have expanded the landing pad at the *Mars-2* site. In a few hours, after dawn, they would take four hoppers out to the site, carrying two buses. With his new photos he would be able to direct them much farther west than Braddock's crew had penetrated. . . .

The feeling of desperation, which had compounded during the last few days, was being replaced by a sense of positive challenge: find out what had happened. The new feeling seemed to emanate from Stafford himself, still a ghostly presence lurking after the dream: he sensed the unblinking practicality of the old coot. Now, he could use his head without everything else getting in the way. His assignment was to solve a mystery.

He got up.

At five in the morning he was back at the war room, in some weird, fresh and alert postsexual state. He had almost forgotten about Philippe and Annie. When the thought of them became conscious, he was surprised that, for the first time, there was no jealousy. How long would *that* last? The little lights glowing all around him in the dim lab were comforting friends, like lights at Christmas. They seemed brighter than last night.

He called up the pictures he had abandoned the night before when Lena had lured him away. Lured him away? Don't think about that; look at the pix, a hidden voice said. Find Stafford. The voice seemed like Stafford's, urging him on.

Even the faint tracks in the images looked different to him now. They crossed the desert purposefully, west and then southwest. They led Carter's mind on, further and further, into new terrain . . . What if there had been no dust devils, no accident . . . ?

●

Philippe and Annie went to breakfast at the Oasis.

Odd, Philippe felt, that after they awoke and held each other and made morning love, after they got up, there was little acknowledgment of their time together. Annie was cheerful; she made enthusiastic small talk over their breakfast. Beneath the talk was comfortable affirmation of their bond. She seemed relaxed.

Philippe had looked forward to the morning, expecting to be aroused by her closeness. Instead, he was surprised to find himself . . . contented. He laughed as they put down their napkins.

"What?" she said.

"I was thinking; this is the moment in a relationship when there are no problems."

"Oh?"

"I mean, we talked. We established a common . . . um . . ."

"The technical medical term is fucking."

"Right. And if we moved apart now, there would never be any problems between us. The total of contact between us would have been joy. Two people who have made love could separate at this point; they would have had only the happy part. No pain. The world would be so much simpler."

"And so much less populated."

". . . But if they keep seeing each other, there is so much trouble. He is late. She loses her keys. He gets angry. . . ."

"Don't worry."

"Of course, on the other hand, we could keep seeing each other."

Annie smiled at him, a long, quiet smile, her response to many things. "Let's go," she said. She got up from the table.

●

Four hoppers, carrying the search team and two buses, made the flight out to the *Mars-2* site.

As they descended from the sky, they could see the maze of tracks that surrounded the site. Carter squinted through the window, looking down for the thin line he had seen heading off to the west. For a moment, the craft pitched over and he got a good look, but he could pick out nothing. . . . The hopper righted itself and the engine kicked in and jarred him too violently for him to see any details. Below was the large cleared area that Braddock's men had prepared for the vehicles.

They bumped to the ground.

"Woooo," Annie whooped. She sat with Philippe. The whole trip had lasted only twenty minutes and they felt cramped among the scuffed cargo packs.

Annie loved getting out of the hopper. It was her first time outside, this far from habitation. She felt at last that she was seeing parts of Mars that were not familiar to her companions. Even Lena said she had never seen country quite like this, and Lena had been everywhere: the moon, even Antarctica.

Annie would have only a few minutes outside here. Carter had made a point of coming over to talk to her, short range, after they stepped out of the hopper. He explained that when the buses were assembled and ready to go, they would head off to the southwest.

"Why drive? Why don't we fly off to the last position where you saw Stafford's tracks?"

"The safety rules, for one thing. You know they don't like taking hoppers to unprepared sites. But there's a more basic reason. All I can see on the photos is that someone has traveled on this route. I can't tell if Stafford went out to some end point, turned around, and started back. So we want to cover his route on the ground, see if we see the buggy anywhere along the way. For that matter, I'm not sure that the last point I can trace on the photos is really the final end point on his route."

Carter went off to look at the *Mars-2* touchdown site, but Annie walked quickly in the other direction, away from the hopper toward the edge of the maze of tracks. Here the desert was undisturbed. She simply stood, looking around at the vast plain. It looked as if you could walk and walk forever.

She did walk, tentatively at first, beyond the edge of the maze of buggy tracks. Now she was where no human had ever been; this was the real Mars. Exposed in the soil were eroded lava surfaces, weathering into gravel. The scene reminded her of the empty eroded lava expanses of the

Ka'u Desert, south of the dense green fern forests of Kilauea. Masses of twisted lava broke through the dust and gravel here and there, betraying the processes of its own formation from flowing, viscous, molten rock. She wished she could open her faceplate and smell the lava baking in the sun. She was sure it would smell like the flows in Hawaii—like baked cardboard, faintly resinous: the smell, somehow, of newborn rocks. It was as much a presence as an aroma.

She set up a holeo recording rig and shot a panorama of the scene. The four hoppers glinted in the sun, seeming much more in their own element out here in the desert, and more elegant than when parked in front of the cargo-littered trash mound site of Hellas Base, where they seemed merely additional pieces of construction equipment or castoff debris from some project not quite finished. Philippe and Carter were over there, small figures through the viewfinder, talking to Braddock's crew. Annie finished the pan and clicked off the cameras but still stood quietly, savoring the strangeness of the vista. She gazed up at the bright sky and tried to imagine the alien parachute from planet Earth, opening high on a lazy afternoon—first contact with humanity after four billion years of loneliness. Sixty years ago.

She made another slow pan with the cameras, this time vertically, from the violet-tinted zenith down across the nearly featureless apricot sky toward the brightening pink horizon, following the floating path that the emissary from Earth had taken so many years ago. . . . And finally down, across the horizon, to the machines and suited figures.

Actually, the site was a mess, as Carter had complained. She could see how Braddock's crew had torn up the place with wheel marks and footprints. Someone had even thrown down a videotape wrapper. Work crews were the same everywhere.

She felt disgust at the desecration of the historic site. Part of her wanted everything on Mars to be preserved in some pristine, "historic" state. But history, the other part of her whispered, never stands still. Health, her grandmother had told her, lies in looking into the future, not into the past.

She walked forward, across the historic ground, into the future, to find Carter and Philippe.

●

They spent too many hours poking around. Carter wanted to understand the broad pattern of disturbance he had seen in the orbital photos. Which of the looping tracks was Stafford's and which had been added by Braddock's crew? Why had Stafford driven so much around the site? Braddock was emphasizing how his men had looked everywhere for more footprints or tire tracks.

"But you let your people destroy the evidence of Stafford's movements," Carter told him. "It's a mess."

"Aw, quit your bitching," Braddock responded. "It was an emergency. You'd have done the same thing, circle around looking for exit tracks."

"Anyway," one of the men said, "seems like Stafford had driven out, curved around, and come back—lots of times. We could see his tracks all over when we got here."

"Maybe he was photographing it from different angles," Annie said.

Carter had no answer to that. He herded them into the buses so he could push the search on to the southwest, where he had made out buggy tracks in the satellite photos. "Let's get as far as we can before night," he told them.

The buses were ridiculous-looking beasts, like giant bright blue crustaceans. Evolution gone wrong. Their antennae gave them an alert appearance. Their puffy tires of enormous radius kept their bodies a meter off the ground, so they could clear scattered boulders, traverse dunes without bogging down, and even clatter over the rugged lava flows. For safety and redundancy, the driver occupied a separately pressurized forward compartment. Each half of the vehicle thus offered a refuge if the pressure seal failed. As they rocked and rolled over the gravel and hummocks, Carter marveled that the pressure seals didn't continually spring slow leaks.

There was more room in the buses than in the hoppers. Again, Carter, Lena, Philippe, and Annie were in the lead bus with one of Braddock's drivers up front. Braddock himself, with four of his crew, rode in the second bus, following them like a shadow. The second bus gave them the security that Stafford had lacked. If they lost pressure throughout one bus through some weird accident, they could clear a landing site for a hopper, huddle in the other bus, and wait to be rescued.

Carter rode up front with the driver, an enlargement of yesterday's orbiter photo spread in front of him. For the first hour, he triangulated among the hills and largest boulders, trying to put them in the area where he had glimpsed Stafford's supposed tracks.

They were in a sandy area three kilometers from the *Mars-2* site when Carter and the driver finally picked up the tracks. As the bus came off a rocky flat, they saw the indisputable tire marks where Stafford had crossed featureless drifts of fine red soil. They pulled up alongside so that they could study the tread marks recorded in the dust. The marks revealed an outbound vehicle, heading off to the southwest.

We're on the way, Carter thought. He gave the driver the coordinates for the next point, and crept carefully through the door to the passenger compartment of the bus, where he had more space to spread out the photos.

There were four single seats, two on each side separated by an aisle wide enough for a person in a full spacesuit. The seats were spaced well apart, so that they could fold back for sleeping, and giving room for each person's equipment storage including the oxy tanks. Lena sat in the front right seat. There was a three-person bench across the back, shared by Annie and Philippe, each by a window with a space between them. The back bench made a fifth bed, two more could sleep on the aisle floor if necessary.

Carter started to take the left seat in front of Annie, thought better of it, and sat behind Lena where he could talk to her or turn back toward Annie. The others remained uncharacteristically quiet when he entered, as if acknowledging his need to concentrate on guiding the expedition. He spread out his photos on the seat across the aisle.

They rode on to the southwest. The air inside the vehicles seemed to take on the smell of the fine dust, in spite of the pressure seal. The dust clung to the windows, in vertical rivulets, sliding down the windows like little streams of opaque fluid.

It was the first time Carter had been in unexplored territory—unexplored, that is, except by Stafford. Once in a while Carter glanced back. Philippe was utterly relaxed, half dozing in his corner by the window. Annie looked slightly bored as Philippe nodded. Why wasn't he talking to her? Carter thought. He's here with her and he isn't even talking to her.

The lava flows they encountered in the late afternoon made a new type of landscape: smooth swelling expanses and knobbed ripples like twisted glass or coils of rope. The lavas were like poorly laid asphalt parking lots, broken here and there by tilted slabs.

"Pahoehoe!" Annie called loudly. She elbowed Philippe. "Pahoehoe, just like home."

"Huh?"

"It's a Hawaiian word," she said proudly. "It means a kind of lava that flows out all smooth like molasses."

The landscape around them now could indeed have involved frozen molasses. The Martian lavas had tended to be very fluid, and had flowed long distances from ancient cones and vents. In the area around them, there was no volcanic cone in sight, only a sea of undulating bare rock surfaces, gentle swells, little slopes where the lava had begun to harden and then backed up in semicircular coils. He saw Annie smiling curiously as they passed the formations.

Moments later he felt a tap on his shoulder from behind. Annie leaned forward across the aisle. "It reminds me of landscapes around Kilauea," she said, as if she wanted him to know where she had come from.

Then she sat back before he could say anything.

Later they came to a different terrain, where squeeze-ups of lava loomed like ruins of ancient fortresses in the haze. A line came into Carter's head, distilled perhaps from old fairy tales of quests and knights-errant: "Then one day they came to a new and different kingdom."

The lava flow made a broad, frozen sea. Carter had never seen so much lava. The lava fortresses were part of a flow that lay atop a smoother, older lava surface, which Stafford had driven onto. It fit the idea that was emerging in Carter's mind: Stafford had deliberately driven over the longest stretches of rock, where he would leave minimal tracks. Carter turned that idea over and over, but it led nowhere.

He turned to the photos spread beside him. He had to stay one jump ahead of the driver. On the rocky surface, the bus bumped along more slowly.

A million thoughts were racing through his head like rabbits. He had led everyone down this rocky road. Or was it a garden path? They would have to spend the night out here. Would they be able to trace both the trail and the story to some sort of ending tomorrow? Or would the tracks just peter out and leave them knowing no more than they did tonight, out here in the cold dark? If so, Braddock might do more than complain. Braddock had said little civil to him all day, and had remained out of radio contact in the bus behind them. Did Braddock have something against him? He could imagine Braddock agitating for his dismissal if the expedition was disastrous. Perhaps Lena would intercede for him if he needed her. But the farther they traveled, the colder even Lena seemed.

The bus was jostling over more rocks, and Carter retrieved the puffy down overjacket from his outside suit and rolled it into a cushion between him and the hard wall of the vehicle. They were all wearing jumpsuits that formed the inner layer of the pressure suits. Deflated, they were like multilayer sweaters or thin down garments. The rigid collar was the only uncomfortable feature of the suit; a helmet could be added in a second and the suit pressurized to give a layer of protection in case of an emergency. The heavier down jacket with its heater coils, that Carter was using as a cushion, was part of the outer layer, added for protection against the bitter Martian cold of the thin air and surface soils.

Their progress across the landscape must have been slower than Stafford's, Carter surmised. They made stops to pore over the photos and choose the route, and stops to check the tracks outside wherever patches of soil recorded them. Judging from the purposeful tracks, Stafford had known where he was going.

Finally, the sun was sinking in the west, producing an ominous red glow in the haze layer along the horizon.

"This whole trip could be just a wild goose chase," Lena said, turning back to Carter. Then, seeing him engrossed in the photos, she abandoned him as Annie had.

The driver told them he was afraid they'd lose the trail in the lengthening shadows. They stopped for the night. The bus was soon filled with the smell of warming food.

In the gathering dark they could see the other bus, windows cheerfully aglow, a little island of warmth, a mobile camp in a night that seemed as cold and vast as space itself.

They tried to make small talk. What a big day it would be tomorrow. As if everyone were trying to cheer up everyone else. Were they all secretly worrying about what they would find?

Philippe hit his head trying to extract his bag of personal belongings, which was jammed in the cramped storage space in the back. Then it came loose and he swung it easily over the back seat. "You know what the song says," he called cheerfully. He sang it, waving his long arms.

"All is hard on Mars above,
"but lifting things and making love."

Then he looked uncomfortable. He looked around the bus and joked that Mars didn't know the first thing about hotels. "Concierge! I need some more hot towels, *s'il vous plaît!*"

The small talk died a natural death as they settled down. In the stillness, they could hear the bus making an occasional gurgle or creak as it cooled, and then it, too, grew still, as if defeated.

The darkness seeped into the bus. It seemed to create an atmosphere not of gloom, but of apprehension. Something had happened to Stafford out here.

Midnight. In the daytime, you could marvel at Mars going by outside the windows of the bus. Everything was strange, new, real, as if it were the sun that gave physical reality to the hills and the eroded rock formations. But now, at night . . .

Carter could not concentrate on the stars.

Carter was surprised at his own emotions, here in the night. Darkness hid the hills and rocks, which had changed little since before the days of the trilobites. The Martians could come out from their hidden crevices and stalk the land unseen. It seemed that any minute after midnight, you might hear footsteps outside in the darkness. There might be a rap on the window, and when you turned on the outside lights in a panic, no one would be there. . . .

The beds were neatly separated. Annie had made a show, it seemed to Carter, of selecting her own, on the left side, forward of the back bench. "This will be mine," she had said, almost too loudly. She was across the aisle from him. Philippe made his bed across the back bench, bustling to unfold it and smooth its pads. Everyone in his own little nest. But in the absolute quiet Carter imagined he could sense Philippe reaching forward, touching her quietly in the dark.

Did the Martian spirits in the darkness outside the window care about human feelings? Safe in the peacefulness beyond existence, didn't they laugh to themselves at humans who could dream of love while sleeping in a little glass and metal coffin, in the middle of a nearly empty planet?

Hours later, Carter awoke. Something was different. Where it had been black outside, now there was a faint pallor. The landscape seemed faintly illuminated, but the color was morbid, as if life had drained out of the lava hills. Rocks gleamed dully, like skulls. He craned to look upward.

High in the enormous sky a mass of noctilucent clouds had formed, catching the sun's glow from beyond the northeast horizon. It was their flat, pearly glow that lit the landscape. And in their midst blazed a dazzling star with a faint companion.

He reached across the aisle and touched Annie's hand. He could see her eyes flash open. He pointed upward out the window. "Look," he whispered.

Quietly she leaned across to look out his window and her long hair brushed his arm.

"Earth," he whispered to her, brushing against her. "This month it's the morning star."

The bright star stared back at them, unwavering as a streetlight.

"And the moon," he added. "See? Just above and to the right."

Carter tried to see the blue color of home, but the bright light seemed as pale and white as a ghost. Nine billion people, he thought. A third of them asleep, a third of them hungry, and one percent of them rich.

"It's beautiful," she whispered, one syllable at a time. She leaned close to him and kissed him lightly on the cheek. "Thanks."

They watched together in silence, neither making a move, until the light of the clouds began to fade.

15

In the morning the buses started rolling across the open desert, pausing now and then to spy out the faint tracks. Progress was slow. Carter directed them to areas where segments of tracks were visible in the orbital images. In other places, Stafford's tracks climbed purposefully onto the rocky outcrops or onto gravel fields, where they could scarcely be traced.

In these areas, Carter manned the seat next to the driver in the front of the bus and studied his photos, looking for the next elusive spot, a kilometer or so ahead, where he could glimpse the next faint segment of tracks. Annie, Philippe, and sometimes Lena peered through the glass door between the compartments, until he would finally point off in some forward direction. "It looks like the next possible segment on the photo is at 44.4732 south and 313.6885 west," he would tell the driver, who would punch in the coordinates and study the glowing map on the console in front of him.

It was hard talking with the driver, who, like an old-fashioned aircraft pilot wore 'phones and a mike, and seemed immersed in his tasks. He seemed to be conversing at frequent intervals with Braddock in the vehicle behind them.

Carter, returning to his seat in the main part of the bus, alerted all of them to keep looking for any sign of Stafford's buggy, since Stafford might have reached his end point to the west of them, turned around, and headed back along this path. But whatever tracks they found always appeared to be outbound.

When they were on the rocky areas, the two buses would move ahead slowly in tandem, until they picked up the trail again. Braddock's bus would then fall in dutifully behind them as they bumped along. Each success in identifying Stafford's track gave Carter more confidence.

Several times, they parked, donned suits, and clambered out of the vehicles, scouting around until they found Stafford's lonely pair of furrows heading off along a shallow gully or a terrace of outcropping lava. Trickles of windblown dust were already obscuring the tire tread prints in several areas. The stops, they barely acknowledged, broke the tedium of long hours in the bus.

Once, as they returned to their vehicles, they realized Philippe had not joined them. Carter spotted him crouched some distance off, kneeling beside a rock. What now? Carter and Annie went over.

Philippe was scooping loose dust in his glove, holding it at eye level, watching it sift through his fingers. The air was still and the dust fell like a little waterfall in the vacuum. It had a beautiful burnt adobe color. "Mars," Philippe was whispering to himself, unaware his short-range transmitter carried his voice to the rest of them.

"Philippe, you're always off in a world of your own," Annie chided him.

"Hey, Philippe, let's go," Carter added.

Philippe was startled. He jumped and the motion was visible even through the suit.

"Why, Philippe," Annie teased him. "You're embarrassed."

"It's different when you know you are the first human being ever to touch something," he mumbled.

───────────────────────●───────────────────────

Mars rolled by outside, one hour, two hours. The sun arced upward into the northern sky.

"You know," Philippe piped up in a deadpan voice, "I've been thinking that we ought to plant one of every kind of cactus we can get our hands on, just to see what happens. I bet if you came back in a year, one of them would be prospering. This just looks like the right kind of country."

It set Carter to musing. In a land devoid of vegetation, he realized, the scattered rocks themselves took on the role of plants. In the verdant landscapes of Earth, rocks had historically been faintly repulsive to the puritans who wanted to believe in a Garden of Eden or a Gaia. Fair Earth's rocky rocks seemed like protruding bare bones that should have been clothed with flesh. Exposure of the rocky bones of England or Massachusetts came down through the language as faintly obscene—"naked rock," "strip mines," "a wound," "a sore upon the earth."

But in the ancient hills, the rocks filled the landscape with variety. The rocks and soils of Mars had as many textures as trees and flowers. There were dark rocks with gleaming crystals and bubbly rocks like sponges on the sea floor. They passed a dense basalt sculpted with conchoidal fractures like the sides of elephants' skulls. They saw vistas studded with rough boulders and hillsides of patterned fine soil, blown by the wind, smooth as a woman's thigh. Rocks dislodged by Stafford's wheels protruded from freshly disturbed ground along the road like newly planted bushes along a country lane. There were mosses of gravel. Once they passed a meadowlike patch of faintly greenish olivine cinders, a striking color contrast with the rusty vistas.

Watching out the bus windows, Philippe pointed out the rocks' facets taking on the colors around them: upward facets catching the lavender of the high morning sky; shaded groundward facets reflecting and concentrating the red of the sunlit soil.

They entered a country of stratified sediments. Distant hills showed banding, slightly tipped. Closer to them, house-sized slabs of tilted sandstone jutted out of the ground, as if the long-departed gods of Mars had built houses of playing cards, and then left them in a half-demolished state.

Down into a little hollow they rode, along the front of a thick flow, whose twisted rocks loomed above them. Here, the horizon closed in upon them, claustrophobic after the grand vistas they had been seeing.

They crossed one more stubby lava flow, where Stafford had deliberately turned up a cobbly ramp onto the rocky surface. As the driver cursed the rough country, they threaded their way across the flow, aiming for high dunes on the horizon to the southwest, where Carter had found the next faint line on the orbital photos.

No doubt, now, Carter thought to himself; the old guy was trying to hide his tracks. Stafford hadn't had to pick his way across this rocky plain. He could have driven around the south side of this flow where the dusty dunes allowed slow but steady going, but the photos showed that he had picked the widest part of the flow to cross. The only rationale was that Stafford didn't want to be tracked. Since Stafford had used orbital images in his earlier rambles, he must have known the potential for image processing to find buggy tracks. He had tried to hide his tracks but hadn't he known it would be impossible? It didn't make sense.

And why the hell hadn't Braddock put someone serious on the orbital photos right away? Carter felt like calling Braddock again on the radio, but it would just produce another argument. What was the use? Better to bide his time. The end of the trail should reveal more answers than any half-baked argument with Braddock.

Later in the morning they came down a slope onto one of those unsung marvels of Mars, a vast, flat plain of sullen black basalt boulders, scattered like toadstools, weathered out of some partly buried lava flow. Black rocks. Flat-lit by the high sun, the plain looked like a giant's sheet of music, with rocks scattered like notes that would play some strange music if only you knew how to read it.

Suddenly Carter noticed that beyond the boulder field, lined up along the horizon like smoke stacks in the distance, pale columns of midday dust had begun to rise. He sat watching them. Were they the answer to the Stafford mystery? He began to want to see one at close range.

Annie was in the seat behind him. She leaned forward. Her smile was nearly against his shoulder. "Dust devils?" she said. Carter nodded.

"I've never seen anything like that before," Annie said in wonderment as the bus chugged along. "You know, everything is new to me on this trip. "Dust devils seem alive, the way they come into being, grow, move around."

"And ultimately vanish. To me they seem like phantoms. Look at the way that one comes and goes. See? It gets thick for a moment . . ."

". . . and then twists around and thins out, as if it turned sideways and vanished . . ."

". . . but in the next minute it's back again, dense as ever." They laughed at their complicity in the thought.

She leaned over the seat, closer to him. "Thanks again for letting me come along," she whispered. "It's wonderful." He liked the way she pronounced the word, accenting the first syllable and rolling it off her tongue like a waterfall spilling over rocks. "I could be sitting back at Hellas earning my keep by writing about Stafford and everything that's happened. But this is so much more—visceral—being out here."

Carter shifted uneasily in his seat. This seemed almost too much, like a come-on. He turned to her with a grin. "Try as I might, I couldn't find a valid reason to keep you from coming. You're . . . involved."

"Because you allowed it to happen." She paused. "It's interesting, watching you with people, watching you take charge of things."

"What do you want, this time?" He said, still smiling.

"No, no. I don't mean it that way." She seemed genuinely distressed. "I think you're doing a good job," she added, as if explaining something.

Lena had turned back to listen to the conversation. She gave Carter an I-told-you-so raise of the eyebrows.

They watched silently out their own windows as the bus maneuvered down a bank into the remains of an ancient riverbed. The soil here was as dry and dusty as that on the plain. "Downstream" they could see the pointed end of what once had been a streamlined island in the channel.

Philippe gestured at the expanse of river bottom. "Water level's right low this year."

"Yup," said Annie. She leaned forward again and whispered in Carter's ear. "Well, here I go. Time to interview the ice queen." She got up and moved to the seat across from Lena.

Ice queen? Ice queen? Carter watched as she approached Lena's seat with a body language of deference. In a moment, to Carter's relief, they seemed to be talking peacefully enough. Occasionally over the noisy lurching of the bus, he could hear phrases.

"These rocks remind me of . . ." Lena muttered something that Carter couldn't hear.

"You must have taken a lot of field geology, preparing for your work," Annie persisted.

"Yes."

Carter watched the two of them, Annie's long black hair brushing the back of the seat as she sat across from Lena. "What causes the varieties of rocks," he heard Annie ask. Lena launched into an answer. Lena's not buying it, he thought, but Annie plowed ahead with little harmless questions. Carter caught snatches of Lena's answers. ". . . deep polar strata . . . reconstruct the cycles of climatic history . . . volunteered to come along on the search . . . Yes, of course I knew Stafford personally . . . we're all concerned." Some of it covered the same ground Lena had covered with him the other night, but her voice sounded more tense. And finally, Lena's voice, testily, "Look, I'm really not here to be interviewed."

Annie shrugged. "Sorry." And now it was Annie who nodded at Carter with an I-told-you-so expression as she moved back to her own seat and watched the landscape silently.

———————————————— ● ————————————————

By noon Carter could see their objective, a volcanic cinder cone breached on one side, forming a distinctive horseshoe-shaped amphitheater about two kilometers across at the base. The photos indicated an unusually red coloration in the formation, but it was too far away in the horizon haze to show much color.

Stafford's tracks had disappeared. The last definite tracks, visible on the photos or on the ground, were in the hills a kilometer back. There were none beyond that on any of the photos. Both Lena and Philippe had voiced doubts about whether they could possibly pick up any new tracks by driving around on the ground, this far from the last set. "If you can't see any more tracks, and we can't see his vehicle, then it's been a wild goose chase," Lena told him. "Stafford's buggy could be out of sight in any of these hollows, anywhere out there. We can't keep driving around forever looking for it. Face it, Carter, we're done."

But Carter had noted that the tracks lined up purposefully in the direction of the crater ahead of them. The only landmark in this area. "Keep going," he told the driver. "If we've come this far, we're going to go check out that cone."

To the south, the low butte of the cinder cone, lit softly by the midday sun, seemed to take on the color of brick dust. In that same direction, three cloud-topped dust columns hung uncertainly, like lost poplars that had wandered by mistake out of their forest grove.

Approaching the crater, they encountered a shallow arroyo Carter had spotted on the photos. It led out of the crater, and had all the earmarks of an ancient lava flow channel, perhaps modified later by water flow. It had a broad sandy bottom a hundred meters wide. Crumbling gravel formed the banks on both sides. Here and there in the silty sand were faint but unmistakable remnants of dune buggy tracks. Stafford had driven down the riverbed. They could all see his tracks.

"Voilà," called Philippe, clapping Carter heartily on the back.

The drainage led toward the cone that now loomed ahead of them. It was bright red, even by Martian standards.

"Stay around on the right side of the cone," Carter told the driver. "Toward the opening."

They continued up the drainage on the crater's flank. The cone was surrounded by a smooth apron of ejected ash, consolidated into a firm smooth surface, like a field of dried mud. The faint gully led toward a breach in the north crater wall. Here they could faintly see Stafford's tracks again, following this course toward the narrow opening. Passage through the low, eroded gap led to a broad floor of hummocky lava, broken into cracks and hollows by the final stages of the cinder cone's collapse. Scattered boulders had rolled down from the walls. Tracks would be hard to find on that surface, Carter thought. Surrounding the floor, the steep interior rim walls of the crater rose sharply, cresting in ragged outcrops and tumbled architectures of stone.

There was expectant silence in the bus.

Carter's eye followed Stafford's faint tracks through the gap in the wall. If Stafford had entered the horseshoe crater . . . It was like a box canyon. "Hold it a minute," Carter told the driver.

Lena studied Carter and said, "What do you think?"

Carter said, "Stafford went into this crater this gap seems like the only way in and out. I don't see any tracks coming back out of the crater. I think this may be the end of the road."

Annie had pulled out her minicam and started panning around the inside of the bus and then the landscape, aiming it through the windows first on one side and then on the other.

"Braddock wants to know what's up," the driver said.

Carter answered, "Stafford drove into this crater. I don't think he came out. We've got a kilo or so of rough floor there. Lotta boulders and land-slide deposits from the rim . . . they could hide anything. We could drive in there but it would be hard to check everything. So I say we should stop here, and climb up the wall to the rim. Survey the floor from above. See if we can see anything."

Carter reached for his helmet.

They climbed the slope on the right side of the gap, at one end of the horseshoe. It was a low rise to the crater rim, perhaps fifty meters above the crater floor. It was not a hard walk; time and dust storms had worn down the rim's profile. While the inner crater wall dropped steeply toward the crater floor, the outer wall of ash sloped gently away, broken only by contorted exposures of brown rock.

The climb felt good; it freed Carter from inaction. It was a strange feeling, as if freedom and the possibility of death were a two-horse team, drawing them onward. Halfway up the hill, the radio resounded with their heavy breathing, loud enough to activate the audio circuits.

Carter turned to watch the others scrambling up behind him. Philippe paused below. "Look at this color." Philippe's voice was tinny and panting on the radio. Carter could see him stooping, picking up a handful of the fine red cinders, coarser than the usual Martian dust.

Carter called, "Come on."

Philippe stood and waved his arm around the panorama of the crater floor, which was opening out below them. "Look. You can see the shape of the eruption from the vent. Look at the symmetry of the bedding. Craters, they are wonderful. Everything in the landscape follows so di-rectly from a single initial event."

"Come on," Carter called again. "We've got to get to the top."

As if he had suddenly got a second wind, Philippe made a low-gravity bound up the slope.

Where was Lena? Carter searched for her white helmet with its black stripe. There she was, climbing easily, with Braddock, off to one side of the group. Anxiously he pushed himself on to see what they could see from the top of the rim.

They reached the crest.

Below them, and stretching to either side, was a panorama of the horseshoe as seen from atop one of its tips. Their two buses, topped by white finder-flags on tall masts, were toys parked a few hundred meters away in the mouth of the horseshoe.

The crater floor spread before them, red as a wound. At the foot of one wall was a striking deposit of dark gray dunes, looking almost black against the fiery ash. The prevailing winds had burbled across the rim and through the arcane workings that only winds know, dropped a load of gray dust. "Anybody see anything?" Carter asked.

No answer. They scanned the panorama. Carter took out three pairs of high-relief binoculars, designed for use while wearing a helmet. He handed the second pair to Braddock and the third to Philippe.

Carter noticed that Annie had taken up a position behind him with her camera, and was shooting over his shoulder, with him in the foreground. "You don't mind, do you? It's what I do. . . ." Carter tried to ignore the feeling of being further into her story at every turn. It was as if their efforts and discomforts for the sake of Stafford were more and more a drama just for the benefit of Annie's future audience and present career—a thought he didn't want to pursue, even if it were true. He glanced at Lena. Annie seemed careful not to be obtrusive or shoot near Lena; not risking a blowup? Lena seemed uncomfortable in any case, even through her suit. She stood rigidly, near Braddock.

Carter scanned with his binoculars, straining forward in his helmet to get his eyes near the faceplate and the lenses. Here and there, the dark dunes appeared, molded under the guiding hand of the Great Martian Sculptor, the wind. Swelling and falling, the dunes lapped against the inner crater walls, where boulders the size of houses had clattered down and lined the edge of the floor.

Against the southeast wall, movement. Instinctively, his heart leaped: a column of smoke, like the campfire you seek when a hiker is lost. No, ridiculous. It had to be dust. It had to be the wind.

"There's something!" Philippe said from behind his glasses.

Carter tried to follow the direction Philippe's glasses were pointing. At first, he thought Philippe had picked up the same dust. No; he was pointed more toward the south or southwest.

"Across the crater, on the dunes—about one o'clock. Now come forward from the wall itself. That high dune. The right side. It looks like more buggy tracks across the near face of it, sloping to the right. See?"

Carter saw.

The tracks rose across the lower slopes of the dune and disappeared, tantalizingly, over the top. Well, Carter thought, this is it. There was no way Stafford could have climbed the far wall of the crater. His dune buggy had to be on the other side of that dune, somewhere near the base of the far wall.

"Let's go!"

It took them a twenty minutes to return to the buses and another hour to reach the dune, where they followed the dust-blown tracks slantwise up the face of the dune. At the top they got out again.

They stood on the dune top, sliding into the sand, and followed the tracks with their eyes. They did not even need binoculars to see their destination.

In the distance the tracks led toward a hollow at the base of the crater wall. There, next to tumbled boulders the size of a house was a pile of rock that wasn't right. Not just a jumble. Artificial. A low wall, about five meters long, higher than a man, obviously piled up, piece by piece.

They all stood looking at the pile. No one wanted to speak. It was as if each disbelieved, and each wanted to hear it from someone else's lips.

"Let's walk it," Carter said. "Walk single file. I don't want to disturb this with vehicle tracks, like they did at the *Mars-2* site."

Annie was at work with her camera again, the lens zooming in and out. Dancing around them, shooting Carter as he pointed, then shooting the whole group from a distance. Carter felt glad for the anonymity of his suit and helmet.

"C'mon," he said again. "Let's see what this is all about."

They trooped down the dune, toward the base of the crater wall. All around, the crater rim rose above them, an enclosing cliff. It gave the crater interior a sheltered feel, like a giant nest.

The crude rock wall was in front of them now. And behind it, was Stafford's dune buggy, neatly parked and wrapped tightly in a faded, dusty tarp. Sand-colored. Like camouflage. They tore the tarp away in minutes.

The buggy was empty.

The radio, engine, everything seemed functional. The white-flagged mast was neatly folded down and tucked in, so as not to protrude above the rocks that Stafford had piled up. There were no dust pits on the windshield, no dust damage.

Carter could see at once that the whole theory about dust devil damage, or a crash, was nonsense. The strange thing was, it came as no surprise. He felt like he had known it all along.

There were a few footprints around the vehicle, but they disappeared among the outcrops and tumbled slabs at the base of the crater wall. Carter could imagine Stafford, leaping lightly from rock to rock, leaving no prints. He could have gone in any direction, could have traveled miles, even on foot. How would they ever track him? There he was, in Carter's mind, hopping from one bare rock to another like a squirrel, chirping derisively at them as he disappeared.

And why did no one say anything? Braddock, Trevina, Pohaku, Brach—they all stood staring, mute as the stones.

"There must be a body somewhere," Philippe said finally. "Somewhere among these rocks. Perhaps he fell . . ."

Don't you see, Philippe? Carter wanted to say. *Don't you see? We'll find nothing here. Stafford wanted to disappear. He planned this from the start and hid his tracks so we almost couldn't follow him. And now he's hidden his footsteps. We won't find a thing.* But Carter said nothing. Annie's camera was recording everything. He had no desire to speculate, not on camera. Why show his cards? What was going on here anyway? He had to figure it out. He had to think instead of talk.

So he had them fan out. They searched the crater for the whole afternoon in near silence. Up, down, crossways. It was a thorough search. There was no trace of Stafford. There was definitely no body lying in the crater. Anywhere. They clambered around the crater floor until they had left tracks everywhere. The tracks were much to Carter's disgust, as if they were destroying evidence. But you couldn't look without covering all the ground, and you couldn't cover all the ground without leaving tracks in the dustier areas. Well, if Stafford had left tracks in the crater, the searchers had missed them and the tracks were gone now. It had been a gamble.

Carter directed the party to climb the crater rim above Stafford's buggy. They clambered up the cliff, which was stepped and broken on this side of the crater. They stood panting on top. They turned their back on the crater and peered across the broad smooth plains to the south. Nothing.

The sun would be getting low, soon. Carter announced that he would hike around the entire rim. "I just want to be able to look for tracks on the rim, and look around. Outside the crater, as well as inside."

"It doesn't make sense that he would drive into the crater if he were going to leave it," Lena said.

"Stafford could be anywhere," Braddock said. He waved at the vast horizon. "If he isn't inside the crater, we'll never find him out there."

"I'm just going to look. I need to get away from everything for an hour. I need to think."

Caught by surprise, they watched him trudge off around the rim alone.

The walk revealed nothing. The floor of the crater was empty as a clean mixing bowl, except for the antlike figures, returning to the vehicles, still searching fruitlessly. Outside, he peered to south, east, north, and west as he walked around the rim. The desert spread off to the horizon in all directions, featureless flat spots interspersed with dunes and boulders.

When he returned, the group had reassembled on the rim from different directions to meet him. Annie waved and called to him as he approached. "Well?"

Suddenly Philippe was shouting, "Look, look." He waved wildly toward the sky. A silvery hopper was descending on its pedestal of pale bluish flame. "I called it in," Braddock's voice said over their headphones. "I had the boys clear a spot out in the plain to the southwest while you were off on your little hike. It'll land out there. Then we can go home. We'll make some aerial survey images during takeoff. Maybe locate something. I'll send another crew out by hopper later."

Sure, Carter thought to himself. Braddock and his unilateral plans. Just go along with them for now. . . . "Make sure they cover the whole area with images during takeoff. High resolution. And make sure I get copies."

B O O K 4
Phobos

Haven't you heard of Einstein's Law? Pleasure turns
into energy.

—Stephen Vizinczey,
In Praise of Older Women, 1965

16

Afternoon. Stafford drove on toward the little cinder cone, where he planned to park the buggy. In his mirrors, Stafford could see a little dust devil listlessly crossing his path far behind him, whipping dust across his tracks.

"That's okay," he muttered to himself.

For the hundredth time, he found himself thinking it through. At the *Mars-2* site, he had made a dozen false trails, turning far out across the sand, then crawling onto the dustless flat rock outcrops, where the buggy left no tracks, then looping back again. Sometimes he would backtrack along his own original trail. He made many loops, paralleling and crossing his own tracks until the pattern was a confused mess with many false start tracks, ranging a couple of kilometers into the desert.

Assuming that a rescue party tracked him as far as the *Mars-2* site, he had the problem of keeping Sturgis happy. Sturgis, the smart-ass from Washington who had masterminded this scheme, would be pleased at his efforts, when his rescuers tried to figure out where he had gone next.

It was prudent to replay everything once again: the scenario he wanted them to construct if they made it this far in pursuit of him. In fact, it was more than prudent, now that he was nearing his final position, because his little inner voice was chiding to him again: This whole thing is a dumb idea. Dumb, dumb, dumb.

Well, the hell with it. The temptation had been too much. He had bought their idea and he was committed now. Anyway, it would all be over in five or six weeks.

Chances were, Council would send a crew out after him. If he had played his cards right, it would be headed by Carter Jahns. If only his sponsors had brought Council in on the plan, then Council could have kept a lid on things, and there would be no need for these games. But Council was made up of international corporate types and political appointees who would smell publicity and profit. Sturgis had probably been right: Council would blow the cover of the whole project if they found out what was really going on. So Sturgis, who had got him into this in the first place, insisted that they would have to lie low; let the Council pick an investigation team on their own. Let them spin their wheels in consternation about Stafford's disappearance, while the project went on about its business. "Just make sure they can't track you, Stafford." That's the last thing Sturgis had said to him. "Just make sure they can't track you. And if they do track you, just don't leave them any clues about what happened."

Now he could see the little cinder cone up ahead. He smiled to himself about the double game he was about to play. If Council put Jahns in charge of the search, Stafford thought to himself, things should get interesting.

Well, sure, he would fix it so no one could easily trace his movements. But Jahns was clever. He had experience with using surveillance monitors in his job. If he just had the doggedness to push the orbital imagery to the limit . . . Anyway, the main thing now was to get to work on what Sturgis was offering him. . . .

To Stafford, the whole scheme seemed a risky gamble. He had stuck to the rocky outcrops and tried not to leave tracks, but he would have to be especially careful from now on. If they did track him as far as the *Mars-2* site, his trip could be explained as a successful attempt to locate the historic object. But as soon as Carter tracked him going southwest from here . . . the shit would hit the fan. He smiled again.

As he approached the worn cinder cone, his body felt like lead. It was a pang of conscience. Tempted as he was by Sturgis's offer, how could he feel good about what he was doing? Jahns was more than a clever young buck. He was also a friend. You don't manipulate your friends.

Well, why develop guilt toward either Sturgis or Jahns? Certainly he owed Sturgis nothing, the smug bastard. He had agreed to Sturgis's plan servilely enough, but if it failed there was nothing to lose. All Stafford wanted was a chance to be in on the ground floor, to have the extra two months that he needed to start his analysis. What happened after that was of little concern except to the narrowest minds in the solar system—the lawyers from Earth. And what did they matter when science was at stake? Make the discoveries first. Then let them adjust their laws and programs and bureaucracies to the realities of the universe. Otherwise, they would begin to try to make the universe fit their ideologies, as philosophers and bureaucrats had tried to do for centuries. Science's ultimate discovery was that you don't try to fit the universe to your ideology; success in life is making sure your ideology fits the universe.

And as for Carter Jahns, Stafford would probably see him soon enough. There'd be time enough for apologies. With beer and champagne at Nix-

O, they'd all laugh together and celebrate what a fine adventure it had been. Just give me these last few weeks without distraction, he prayed to himself.

He piled the last rocks up around the buggy.

Even if they tracked him this far, they wouldn't be able to do it in a single afternoon, stopping here and there as they figured out his path. He smiled. Now he was getting into the spirit of the game, crazy as it was. Maybe that was it: life really was a game and history was the summation of all the little games and big games people had played. . . .

He still had an hour. That was cutting it almost too close.

Now he stood beside the buggy, puffy in his blue suit. He patted the fender. "Faithful steed . . ." He sealed everything, carefully threw the brown tarp over her, and tied it down with patient attention. Good. Completely wrapped. In a few weeks they would have to come and fetch her. He didn't give a damn about disciplinary procedures—what could they do, take him out and shoot him? With no guns on Mars? He wanted to be able to say the buggy was in good condition.

He had to hurry. He piled some rocks in front of the buggy, on the side facing the entrance to the crater. No use making it too easy for them. To keep Sturgis happy, he had to make at least a pretense of slowing them down at every turn.

At last he picked up the transmitter beacon and clambered carefully uphill, choosing the least dusted rock tops, leaving no footprints. Up the crater wall he climbed, enjoying the exercise and the view of the circular expanse below him. Curious, how nature occasionally produced symmetry in a random universe. In a few minutes, he gained the rim. The buggy, covered by its dusty tarp, was an inconspicuous dot among the crags.

After a last look into the crater, he turned on the rim crest and peered away from the crater, to the southwest. There it was—the smooth expanse that Sturgis had selected from the orbital photos. An unusual expanse of smooth, firm bedrock, with only the thinnest dust cover. Good. Just what they needed. All he had to do was make a surface inspection, pick the best spot, do a little clearing, and send them the coordinates.

He bounced lightly down the rim, selecting a path among the clusters of ejected boulders. Soon he was out on the flats, checking the broad expanse of featureless ground. He examined the area on foot. Good. Firm ground, no boulders, no sinkholes. He unfolded the transmitter beacon.

In the red glow of the slowly sinking sun he climbed atop a massive, fractured rock back on the cinder cone slope. It was a good viewpoint. He laughed to himself, suddenly, as he realized he was posed atop a jutting prominence like some conquering hero.

He didn't feel like a hero. This is the craziest thing you've ever done, said the little voice of his conscience. Still . . . The high rock offered a magnificent view as dusk settled in. Long rosy shadows crossed the landscape, and the sky took on the unearthly pearly glow of the high, illuminated dust. It reminded him of the sunsets on Earth the year after the Owens Valley eruption.

He turned slowly, admiring the panorama. Suddenly he caught a glimpse of something moving. He turned quickly, frightened as much by his own surge of adrenaline as by the object itself. It was an object moving low across the northwestern sky. That's not right, he thought. They shouldn't be over there.

As the object exceeded twenty degrees above the horizon and assumed a tiny, lumpy shape, he smiled to himself. It was Phobos, of course. Now he could see two little stars alongside it like satellites of a satellite. Ships. The Phobos shuttle, and perhaps a cargo ship from Earth.

Phobos and its attendants faded in the east as silently as they had come.

Well, it was a nice view, and a nice way to cap a great day, for that matter. But it was not what he came here for. He scanned again toward the south.

Finally he caught sight of another moving light in the sky. High in the sky, this time, and getting brighter. He began to relax.

17

BLACK MOON IN SIX SCENES

Scene One: Somewhere in the Milky Way Galaxy. Time: 4600 million years ago.

Stardust swirled in the dark, spawning a star. It was an average star, yet destined for peculiarity. It was born in one of the ragged spiral arms of an undistinguished galaxy, ten thousand million years after the universe flashed itself into existence.

The star took shape in one of ten thousand black, interstellar clouds— each ten thousand times as big as the present solar system. Like Newton's apple falling to Earth, each grain of grit in this cloud, each psi-wave singing atom of hydrogen and helium, felt itself tugged toward the cloud's ethereal center. So the cloud shrank, spun, and broke into smaller, shrinking clouds, each becoming denser and hotter. Each became a star. A prehistoric Pleiades had formed, one of a thousand star clusters illuminating the arms of the galaxy. The stars orbited lazily around each other like slow-motion bees in a swarm. Eventually, with each star trying to pursue its own trajectory, the stars drifted apart, each to follow its own galactic destiny, sibling birds leaving the nest. They were lost to one another forever. The sun was on its own.

Scene Two: Inside the disk-shaped cloud of debris surrounding the early sun, two astronomical units away from the sun. Time: Fifty million years later.

The solar system aborning was all sky, a sky full of rubble, a sky full of surprises. Like snowflakes clumping together, bits of drifting dust collided and aggregated into clumsy fluff balls. In the earlier days, the fluff balls drifted slowly like snowflakes, and gravity held them together once they hit. They grew to the size of snowballs, breadbaskets, mastodons, houses, skyscrapers, mountains, worldlets.

Now they were bigger and had stronger gravity. They fell together faster. Gentle collisions evolved to explosive crashes. Impacts excavated craters, blasted silent sprays of debris, and gave each object a case of the pox.

Gravel-pile mountains and worldlets grew toward something more significant. The bigger they grew, the faster they grew, so that the largest ones ran away from the pack, emerging suddenly big and important from the swarm of lesser debris, like presidential candidates from a field of anonymous politicians, when their time had come. The bigger the world, the greater its gravitational appetite. The few biggest worlds eventually snared most of the rest, sucking them in, digesting them into mantle and crust. A system of a million worldlets transformed itself to a system of a few genuine planets.

One was Mars, a modest world, not yet red. It had pleasantly gray-tan rocks, a dense atmosphere of carbon dioxide and water vapor, with thick white fogs. New craters were blasted out every day as the remaining meteoroidal debris streaked through the high blue sky, punched through the fog, and exploded on the ground. At Mars' distance from the sun, many of the bodies hitting it contained ice. Molecule by molecule, the iceborne primordial water floated in the air, froze into polar snowfields, or condensed into Nature's rare blessing, rain. When conditions were right—a rarity in the universe—the water gurgled its way down valleys in glittering, frothing, laughing rivers, forming deep Martian lakes with only limited patience.

Scene Three: The orbit of Jupiter, five astronomical units from the sun. Time: Forty million years later.

Jupiter was growing to the largest size of any of the planets. By the time it reached a mass fifteen times that of Earth, its voracious gravity began to trap the very gas from the surrounding nebula. Jupiter became no solid planet with a reliable surface, but a murky, lightning-laced gas giant three hundred times as massive as Earth. It had a malevolent disposition and a potential for violence.

Gestating Jove's neighboring worldlets, those that had not yet been swept up or flung aside were different from the worldlets of the inner solar system. Not for them the inviting warm gray colors of the rocky planets formed in the inner solar system, but velvet black of sooty carbon compounds condensed in the dusty darkness. Though black, they were full of ice and tinted with flecks of red and orange, organic compounds condensed also in the carbon-rich coldness. Tinted or not, they were blacker than the ash-black snow pushed off winter roads in Jersey City. The planet-spawning process of devil-may-care collisions in the night had produced a distant sky full of icy soot balls.

Gravitationally, each planet now reached out for the last remaining worldlets in its own orbital domain. Mighty Jupiter, winner of the gravity sweepstakes, was the master. Millions of black icy worldlets, passing nearby, were deflected from their original, comfortable circular orbits around the sun onto new, out-of-kilter orbits. Jupiter's long gravitational broom reached from the asteroid belt halfway to Saturn, and swept black planetesimals skittering across the solar system, like the countless spaceships that would, four thousand million years later, swing by Jupiter, giving happy space engineers a free "gravity assisted" midcourse maneuver.

Many of these icy soot balls were thrown nearly out of the solar system where they wandered for aeons in the exile of the Oort cloud, waiting to return toward the sun one day, when their ices would be warmed and turned to gas, creating diaphanous streamer-tails, and they would be enshrined as comets in the tapestries and equations of the transient creatures of the third planet. Others of them collided with planets and made craters. Still others were swept by Jupiter onto new orbits that took them inward toward the sun, across the orbit of Mars.

Scene Four: Near Mars. Time: A million years later; 4509 million years ago.

Of the millions of black, flying mountains scattered around the solar system by Jupiter, thousands approached Mars. Of those thousands, most escaped Mars' weak gravitational grasp, and sailed on. But a very few were targeted by chance at a critical distance from the planet. Had the miss-distance been a little farther, each would have sailed on to join its errant brothers. Had it been a little less, each would have been dragged down by the friction of Mars' thick primordial atmosphere toward Skylab doom, to break up in the atmosphere or crash on the surface of the new planet— one more crater among the millions. But at the Goldilocks distance, just the right distance from Mars, an asteroid could be slowed just enough by the atmosphere to swing into an orbit around Mars.

Chance giveth and chance taketh away. Of the objects that established themselves in miraculous orbits, most kept feeling the drag of the Martian atmosphere. They spiraled closer and closer to the planet, eventually crashing. But . . .

This was a critical era in the history of the planets. Radiant winds from the newly formed sun were blowing away the rest of the interplanetary gas. Suddenly (from a cosmic point of view) the infant planets were no longer bathed in a nurturing, nebular placenta of gas. Space around them grew empty. Their own natal atmospheres began to leak away, molecule by molecule, into this surrounding void. Small planets like Mars suffered the greatest indignity; they lacked adequate gravity to slow the rapid escape of their original dense atmospheres.

At this magic moment at the end of planetary formation, one black asteroid found itself destined for a special history. It plunged into the extended but thinning Martian atmospheric envelope. Like many of its brothers who had come this way, it was laced with cracks, having already suffered countless meteorite collisions in the asteroid belt. Like many of them, it broke into pieces due to tidal forces and the stresses of deceleration as it encountered Mars' atmosphere. The smaller pieces were the most affected by drag: they spiraled inward and crashed in a celestial fireworks display. But the two largest fragments had a different fate. Like their siblings, they had begun the inexorable inward spiral, but the thin air around them was dissipating too fast. After some centuries their rate of inward spiraling came to a halt. They were hung up, as it were, in orbit. Mars now had two moons. They were scrappy tiny moons, as moons go; flying islands. Deimos, which ended up in a relatively distant orbit, was a lumpy potato only eleven by fifteen kilometers across. Phobos, stranded in a closer orbit, was a larger potato of nineteen by twenty-seven kilometers.

No more moons could be captured. Mars' outer atmosphere was now too thin.

Scene Five: Earth. Time: 4509 million years later, in the golden age when all things seemed possible, before World War I.

On Earth, more or less as induced in the gospel according to Darwin, life had evolved to the level of intelligence where people could settle arguments with guns instead of stones. On Mars, microbial life remained more peaceful but less interesting. Long ago, Mars' atmosphere had lost most of its water, and the day of the last rains had come and gone. Like iron garden tools left to dry in the sun, the iron-bearing rocks had rusted; Mars had become the Red Planet.

In the late 1800s, the American astronomer Percival Lowell concluded that life *had* evolved on Mars and had produced civilizations even greater than that of France. France had tried and failed to construct the Panama Canal, whereas the Martians had constructed a whole system of desert-spanning canals to irrigate their otherwise dry and barren planet. Fine, cobwebby lines crisscrossed the whole planet, according to Lowell and many astronomers. Single-minded as a spider, Lowell built his own observatory to map them and spun a whole theory from the web of lines that he created. Mars was drying up, don't you see, turning into the desert that would shame the Sahara; and the Martians built their canals to bring water from the melting polar ice caps to cities of the warm, habitable, but dry equator.

Unfortunately, Lowell's pen was mightier than his telescope. His eye/brain equipment was peculiarly inclined to perceive fine straight lines where Nature had placed only streaky splotches. His canals turned out to be the streaky, dusty deposits that prevailing winds left in the Martian desert, only a bit less illusory than other beckoning chimeras of the desert.

Fired by Victorian Mars enthusiasms, another American astronomer, Asaph Hall, set out with less poetic vision but a more mundane mind to search for moons around the Red Planet. During the same golden age, when astronomy could still be done from observatories in cities, Asaph Hall sought Martian moons at the U.S. Naval Observatory in Washington, D.C. The two mini-moons of Mars were so small and so black that Asaph Hall failed to see them, even though he searched night after night with a great telescope, during Mars' close approach to Earth in the summer of 1877. Discouraged, he was about to give up. His wife encouraged him to press on. He went back to the dome and found them. He named them after the two mythological horses that drew the chariot of the war god Mars, Phobos and Deimos: Fear and Terror.

A century later, when a spindly, human-built, camera-bearing probe, Mariner 9, first mapped these moons, the largest crater on Phobos was given, during an academic's scramble to respond to feminist philosophies, Mrs. Hall's maiden name: Stickney.

Mars' two demonic moons, errant carbonaceous asteroids, were destined to attract both men and women. Chock-full of water, vitamins, and minerals, they became prime bits of attractive real estate on the path to Mars. The Viking orbiters and the Phobos-2 orbiter, sent from Earth during the era when America and the Soviet Union were working to resolve their mutual testosterone complexes seeing who had the biggest rocket booster, hung around for a while, courting both Phobos and Deimos with their cameras, but never got up the nerve to touch them. Later robotic probes landed on them, danced on their mini-gravity surfaces, and pursued ecstatic intercourse by means of various obscene probes. The first manned expeditions began to coax forth buried moisture and used Phobos as a supply cache outside the gravity well. Eventually they emplaced their own permanent orbital station. With the giant international Phobos/Mars expedition of 2010, scholars and scientists arrived en masse to stay for many months, and Phobos University was born: the first permanent habitation outside the Earth-moon system.

Scene Six: The shuttle to Phobos University. Time: 2031, February 55, Friday.

What struck Annie Pohaku was that everyone here treated the flight as routine, these people who lived far from Earth. How could such a thing be routine, flying between worlds where humans had lived for only a generation? Had it been like this when her ancestors, the first Polynesians—there was Hawaiian blood on her grandmother's side—arrived in the Hawaiian archipelago two thousand years ago, and shuttled from one island to another in their tough double-hulled boats? She imagined the terror with which she would face a canoe crossing from Maui to the Big Island, not to mention sailing all the way from Hawaii to Tahiti on an ocean as empty as space.

And now she was getting used to flying at five kilometers per second in an aluminum can. What's worse, everyone was getting used to it.

As a writer, Annie liked to watch the people on the flight. She noticed that of the few who carried old-fashioned books, no one opened to the middle of a story in progress. They strapped into their cocoons, and opened their books to page one. Books were not part of their lives, but merely entertainments for flights. And most of the passengers from Mars City were not reading at all. They were young—the engineers who ran things and even a few students from the University. She watched them punch up the credit numbers on their screens, and call up the latest action VRs. With blank and passive expressions, they disappeared into VR cyberspace.

It depressed her. That's something she liked about both Carter and Philippe. They seemed to have lives that reached beyond electronics.

She had debated catching the Phobos shuttle. But something had to be done. The thread she had been following into the desert had ended. It had been cut, and she needed to find the matching end, lying somewhere in the future. The next part of the story, she was sure, would begin with Carter. Carter, she found out, had flown off to Phobos the day before, without saying anything to Philippe or herself. Why hadn't he talked to her first? That's the way he is, Philippe said. He doesn't tell you much. Just goes off to work.

He intrigued her. She knew she had hurt him, being with Philippe. Philippe, supposedly sensitive, yet who had seemed at some level oblivious to what was happening among the three of them.

They'll find Stafford's body someday, Philippe had said. That was the theory that everyone seemed primed to accept: that Stafford had wandered off and gotten into trouble, somewhere in that landscape. Yet no one—not even Braddock's subsequent search party that had brought back the buggy—had been able to find a trace of him. So Philippe had gone back to his own work. Until Carter needs me again, he said. "It's not that I don't care," he had added sadly; "sometimes you just have to work, to let your good karma begin to build again." She smiled to herself: Philippe and his ceaseless internal life.

Why had the thread of the story come to such an abrupt halt? It was absurd that they had tracked Stafford all the way to the crater, and then returned empty-handed. Was there really a body out there, somewhere, that they had missed? Had Stafford fallen into some unseen crack? Carter had been acting strangely since they left the crater. He had clammed up. Hardly talked to anyone on the way back. She could sense his mind churning. She found herself wanting to get into that mind.

It was strange, what had happened with Philippe. She had been attracted to both of them since the beginning, entertaining the possibility of becoming lovers as well as friends. Passing lovers they would be, in the sort of way that happens in far-off places and leaves you with pleasant memories. On that point, Philippe had quoted Yevtushenko, whom he called Carter's countryman: There are no rights and wrongs, only good memories and bad memories.

She had to confess, if she thought about it, which she was not ready to do, that something had happened. She felt she could see through Philippe, while Carter maintained a mysterious air of peculiar attraction. "See through" was too caustic a term for Philippe. She could see through a translucent outer layer, down to a core where he kept his motivations, artistic and otherwise. But the core seemed so immutable and permanently inscrutable that she no longer wanted to fight to penetrate it, any more than she wanted to see what was inside a piece of granite. Meanwhile, Carter . . .

She didn't want to think about it too much.

When she did think about it, she recognized her own dilemma: she wanted a story from Carter, and she had never let herself be attracted— well, involved—with men from whom she wanted a story. Except for Philippe and that was different. She had learned it was too easy to get what you wanted from a man. There were ethical limits, after all. . . . She definitely didn't want to think about it. She retained an image of herself as an ethical woman. Whatever that meant.

Still, there had been no more leads in Mars City. The next part of the story had to start with Carter himself. It was logical, she told herself, to fly to Phobos.

If you started from Mars City, Philippe said, Phobos was halfway to Earth. In terms of fuel and society, he was right, she realized now. It was more sophisticated than Mars City, at least in the view of those who lived there. Oh, she had read all about Phobos. The University. The hum of commerce. It was the poor man's Crystal City, Mars' equivalent of the great rock docks orbiting Earth, except that they didn't have to bring in an asteroid from somewhere. . . . Phobos, the moon, had been Nature's gift: a crumbly black rock from which Phobos, the city, drew its suste- nance: water in the buried hydrated minerals, and peculiar organic compounds, a valuable resource as long as Earth's agencies were willing to pay for R and D.

Floating as effortlessly as the shuttle itself, Annie daydreamed about what she had seen so far. While Hellas Base, at least under Braddock's reign, would never be more than a research station, Mars City and Phobos University pretended they were real urban centers. Two cities in the ex- tended desert of Martian space, far from the life of Earth. While Phobos claimed to be more ultra, Mars City claimed to be more connected to gritty reality. Mars City saw no disgrace in its dust-blown domes; Mars City proudly viewed its uncluttered life as beyond reach of the bureau- cracies of Earth. But Phobos University wanted to imitate Earth, to imi- tate Crystal City orbiting in haute majesty, high above Earth's teeming urbanscapes.

For all its attempted sophistication, Phobos had developed a curious quality of stasis, in contrast to the freewheeling growth of Mars City. Phobos was haunted by time and change. In the teens and twenties, Pho- bos had been the center of the Martian universe. The Mars Council es- tablished its chambers there. Mars had orbited around Phobos. The great ships arrived, pregnant with girders and masses of raw plastic, computer clips and cartridges, and prefab housing mods. It was the time of the feverish rush to create the first sustainable colony outside the Earth-moon system. Phobos University grew and grew.

But now, Phobos was like a bucket with water flowing out a hole in the bottom as fast as it entered the top. Commerce from Earth flowed through Phobos on the way down to Mars, but the water level never rose. The giant ships docked for a few days, unloaded their cargoes onto the shuttles and onto the spidery, unmanned freighters, and flew away again with new crews. The cargoes went on to Mars City.

Phobos had reached its limits, Annie speculated to herself. Its inhabitants lived the good life high above the dust of Mars, reveling in their mastery of Mars and their hipness to the latest events on Earth, not realizing that history was passing them by. With a moment of surprise, Annie realized that the woman in the cocoon next to her was intently studying a page of screenzine from Earth, blazing a title "Horoscopes." Annie sneered to herself. She knew the 'zines. The horoscopes were calculated by computer months in advance, distributed electronically across a hundred million kilometers. And purchased. The unimaginative merchants of cultural sleaze in New York City still lived. Marketing genius and adaptability had triumphed again.

But Annie gawked: didn't this lady know she *lived* on one of the "celestial" bodies that, according to astrologers of Babylon and New York, radiated strange influences across the now well-traveled spaceways? Mars could hardly be in Gemini for her. She walked on it. What did she make of that blue morning star, casting its occasional gleam across the timeless sands but absent from her astrological charts? What cosmic influence did it cast for a child born on Mars where no red martial god rose in the sky, but only blue Earth, ascendant in the sign of the fishes?

Farther back in the shuttle she noticed two young men, clones almost, in their anachronistic white crisp shirts, dark ties, and last-century-style jackets. So, the solemn folks from the desert in Utah were still sending their boys to hype their unique interpretations of old manuscripts from other deserts, distant in space and time. From the first desert in Israel/ Arabia to the second desert in Utah to the third desert, Mars . . . Deserts, religion, missionary zeal . . . Some strange correlation . . . She hoped perversely that tweedledum and tweedledee were going home empty-handed, after striking out in sinful Mars City. She wondered what Carter would think of them, proselytizing on his turf, as it were. She expected that one of the few subjects that might drive Carter to outspoken ire was superstition living in the midst of exuberant reality. Especially here, in the still-untrammeled house of God, Mars.

She was falling asleep.

Awakened from cocoon slumber by tinny announcements of imminent docking, Annie turned to the tiny window. Outside, in the glaring sun, Phobos loomed in the distance, above the bright horizon of Mars. The tiny wheel-shaped city, slowly turning once every ninety seconds, provided the shock of scale.

The Phobos shuttle approached the black moon cautiously. Now she could see the one new project proceeding at Phobos University: construction of the tether. It ran like a hairline into the distance toward and away from Mars. Dotted along it like nodes were little ships and work crews, dots moving and glinting in the light. In a year, the tether would be operational, and the shuttles and cargo ships would save energy by docking at the lower end of it. Passengers and cargo would ride up or down to Phobos in so-called elevator cars, powered by the sun. In its initial phase, it would be five hundred kilometers long.

A dull thud reverberated through the ship. The shuttle had docked at a central tower erected at the north pole of the satellite. Waiting to debark, Annie studied the scene outside. Surrounding this tower was the amazing structure: the enormous wheel-shaped University. The central tower protruded through the center of the wheel. Cables and four connecting tunnels ran from the tower to the rim of the wheel.

At the base of the tower, airlocks opened onto the black surface. Like a separate city built around these airlocks by ants of Phobos, a maze of storage bins and cases lay tethered to the surface, scattered in rough alignments. Figures in spacesuits and jet packs drifted lazily above them hopping from one to another like insects among flowers.

The station turned around them lazily, at a rate to provide eight tenths of Martian gravity—a compromise between those who worked on the surface of Mars and those who had to go back and forth from long periods in zero G, working outside in the Phobos environment. She remembered Philippe claiming that Phobos University, not Mars City, was the best city in the solar system for sex. The gentle pressures of sub-Martian gravity . . . the most bearable lightness of being, Philippe had called it. Strange, she thought, with sexual plagues coming and going, how some generations were blessed with sexual paradises, and others were cursed with sexual dangers and uncertainties—

through no fault of their own. It seemed yet another of the cosmic jokes.

The great bicycle wheel of steel rigging hardly looked erotic. How many women had Philippe had in the cloistered apartments along its rim of the great wheel, rotating slowly outside Annie's tiny window as the ship approached the docking port? Come on, Pohaku, she urged herself, pay attention to the job at hand. And she remembered Philippe's joking voice: "I have learned that one cannot live on sex alone, except for the first fifty years." She could not forget that Philippe had made her laugh.

An hour later she was striding lightly down the halls of Phobos University, where people bustled with focused, if unidentifiable, purpose. She enjoyed watching them. Her journalistic skills were challenged by the thought of trying to define the something in the air here that was different from Mars City.

Write one true sentence, Hemingway had said. Mars City had the builders, rough and tumble. Phobos had the people who made the builders dance like puppets below, by pulling on the purse strings.

She walked the glittering arcades of Phobos, the great shoplined promenade, with its view of Mars spinning dizzily overhead. Banks; university bookstores with 3-D posters of St. Basil's, the latest from Earth; a week more hip than the stores at Mars City . . . all built by global corporations so vast and rapidly anastomosing that they hardly seemed to have names or logos or fixed identities anymore. The corporate entities, like the ancient gods, seemed like powerful celestial spirits, angels who had arrived from somewhere far away, and who hovered permanently but unseen in some economic exosphere around each planet. They permeated the very air of Earth and Mars, like smog, miraging throughout cyberspace, which pulsed with their lifeblood, secret electronic plans for the next stage of the great global shopping center. Now, they were probing out into space with delicate, invisible tentacles, and making cities on Phobos and Mars, through unsteady alliances that changed too fast to be tracked by politicians or networks.

Phobos also had the University. Phobos University, like university towns everywhere, had citizens who looked detached from anything concrete or steel. There were brash young professors, men and women, who talked fast and were the first to latch on to new ideas and words. They were on the make. Being on the make, for them, centered first on careers: getting that grant from Mars Council or, better yet, direct from some

Earth agency; making a splash at the next conference. You could tell they were thinking of themselves when you interviewed them, much as they tried to dissemble in strained academic modesty. When you asked them about their research, their real subject was always the same: their place in the scheme of things academic. They were generous with left-handed compliments and veiled put-downs of rival colleagues. The viciousness of academic politics was matched only by the inconsequentiality of its victories.

During her initial weeks here, the men on Phobos had seemed an odd lot. The corporate men were impossible, of course, like ladder climbers on the mainland. The university men . . . well, being on the make extended to the opposite sex, naturally, but in a weird way, because they were mostly physical scientists: geologists, atmospheric chemists, seers of the invisible magnetosphere; a secretary she had befriended once at a research institute had told her: There is no such thing as a *physical* scientist. Anthropologists, maybe, you didn't know what to expect from them. But not physicists or chemists or, worse yet, left-brained mathematical theorists, God help us . . . Still, she thought, every once in a while comes along someone whose technical vigor spilled over into a general vitality that embraced all of life. What set them apart was hard to put into words.

Academic women . . . something unfamiliar to her there. Mainland academe fostered some attitudes she had heard about from her mother, but which were outside her experience after her upbringing in Hawaii: in academia, her friends told her, a woman could not flirt and still be a serious researcher. Urban and university women, who wanted to be taken as serious beings, were distinguished by a mode of dress at the opposite end of the spectrum from the loose, provocative styles that had evolved for leisure in space cities or in the hedonistic Pacific pleasure grounds of Hawaii, where men and women consciously dressed to please each other. She had been amused by this urban primness when she first went to work in mainland city newsrooms. Philippe had claimed that the unspoken dress code's mandatory vestigial retro-bow was left over from twentieth-century office culture, and was in turn a relic of eighteenth-century lacy propriety, when impractical clothes were a sign that you belonged to the upper class, i.e. you did not have to work. "Hence the word 'classy,' " Philippe had said. "Everything, it has an origin in the past."

Yeah, well, she told herself. The business at hand was to find Carter. And then . . . There was the question of how to interact with him. She still didn't want to think about that.

18

Carter Jahns stared at the screen in his cubicle at the Phobos Library. Glowing back at him was an orbital image of a red volcanic cone, isolated in the desert like an anthill in a sandbox. He replayed his mental tape of the trip to the cone: time spent outside in the Martian desert had a disconnected quality, like dreamtime. He remembered climbing the cone, finding Stafford's buggy, walking around the crater rim alone. And then what? Then his world had changed.

He had debated with himself about coming up here on the Phobos shuttle. Not debated. Rationalized. It was as if he couldn't think anymore at Mars City. He had a budget of three Phobos trips per year and he hadn't made the trip for six months, and the data archives in the Phobos Library were rumored to have a much fuller set of satellite imagery than was down-linked to Mars City. Intuition had whispered to him: Don't put in requests for pictures. Go to Phobos; you want something done right, do it yourself.

Intuition. There had been a time, when he was a student technocrat, that he would not have admitted the word "intuition" into his internal vocabulary. Too mystical. Now . . . No apology needed. Experience had changed his definitions. Intuition was no longer some magic sixth sense. It was simply the knowledge squirreled away in the back of your brain, subliminal knowledge, the knowledge you didn't know you had, gained from cumulative experience—the churning reservoir stored below the surface of frozen pack ice of consciousness. Strange, that he used to deny its existence. Now, he counted himself rare among the Martian scientists and technicians because he could recognize it instead of denying it. Was that Philippe's influence?

He knew that a personal search through the Phobos files, even if it didn't drop an answer in his lap, would lead him to thoughts he would not have had if he had sent some earnest assistant. You can't send someone to fetch the answer to a question you aren't sure how to ask. Great line, he mused. You should go back to Earth and produce one of those holeos for insecure administrators.

The cinder cone stared back at him from the screen, an eye with no expression.

Carter's intuition told him Stafford's disappearance was no accident.

Rationality said he still ought to keep the accident theory open, especially since everyone else seemed to want to keep it open. But what was rational here?

To believe the accident theory, his intuition needled him, you have to explain the hidden tracks, and the tarp, and the wall. Suppose Braddock was right that Stafford, like any good prospector, tended to hide his tracks out of sheer habit, to protect what he found. And that the tarp was just protection when Stafford had set out for a long walk. But the wall? It was obviously to keep the vehicle from being spotted—the opposite of normal practice. And what about the lack of footprints? Carter himself had left footprints. But Stafford had tiptoed around on dustless rock. Why? Answer me that one, Carter, my lad.

So he had crossed some watershed, some Martian Great Divide. There had been ordinary life, before Stafford disappeared. Now there was this life: Mars was not what it had seemed to him before. Stafford had engineered his own disappearance, and had tried to hide his tracks.

This new life was only five days old. It excited him. The suspense of the seeming accident had ended in something stranger. He had tried to deal with it at Mars City, but he had been paralyzed by the conflict between his intuition and his frontal lobes. If Stafford had been hiding something from him, who else was hiding secrets? Here, he felt more mental space to explore the paranoid territory where his new ideas were taking him.

There was the little matter of the report that was due. Around Mars City, the weirdness was compounded by the feeling that people were watching him, waiting to see what he would do about the report. One option was to do what people seemed to want him to do: tie it up in a neat package and get out of the situation. He could send in some routine report that Stafford had driven off into the desert to explore, parked and protected his vehicle, walked away, found himself in a tight spot that he couldn't escape. His body might be hidden in some crevice or lava tube. A report like that would get him off the hook. More importantly, it could buy him time. Maybe then he could pursue matters quietly on his own.

But such a report would be nonsense, he believed, and he refused to sign his name to nonsense. Besides, as long as he had submitted no report, he had a certain amount of clout from Mars Council; useful clout. He could string things along for at least another few weeks, tell them he was working on it. Project emotional distress over Stafford's death. In the meantime, solve the mystery. If he could figure out how.

This whole thing was very murky, and Carter was uncomfortable with anything being murky on Mars. In fact, he was paid to abhor murkiness. Like nature with a vacuum. Meaning? He had to rush in.

On the flight up to the little moon, he had tried to steer his consciousness away from these ideas. They were ideas that needed to simmer, unexamined.

Maybe here on Phobos he could finally open Pandora's Box. Since the days of the first climatology programs, photos of Mars had been beamed directly from the various satellites to monitors on Phobos. In the Phobos processors, raw numbers from the unthinking sensors assembled themselves into pictures. Millions of pix were stored in the data banks of Phobos. From the ethereal cyberspace files of Phobos the pix found their way to various scientists and technicians who had ordered them: meteorologists in Mars City, geologists at Hellas Base, geophysics grad students writing theses in the cubicles of the spinning University of the black moon. Sometimes there was even an order from Earth for the Martian images. Usually it came from a god-awful crackpot organization, trying to prove something about conspiracies to hide discoveries of vast deposits of oil, the ancient elixir, fountain of civilization's youth. Still, it was refreshing to know that someone in the terrestrial gravity well occasionally wanted a product from Mars, instead of the other way around.

Perhaps, he thought, returning to the business at hand, among all the pix stored away on Phobos, there were images that could tell him something. Images that no librarian had thought to suggest to him: damaged images, or images from specialized sensors. So far, satellite images had been the key to this whole thing. They were his allies. They could reveal some secret truth. As a social engineer, he was trained to use whatever surveillance data he could get his hands on, as a tool for solving problems. He was aware, however, of whole organizations on Earth who argued that social surveillance should be stopped; that the orbital surveillance of farm field production, the automated imagery of every traffic intersection, the routine analysis of garbage, and all the other data-gathering techniques—in spite of the cleaner society it had built—left everyone with too little privacy and spontaneity.

Carter stared back at the impartial eye that glowed on the screen. The juices were starting to flow. If he could just sit in the archives for a day or two, surrounded by the original data and the best image-processing equipment, he might come up with some unnoticed fact about 44.2° south and 313.2° west, the site of the little crater from which Braddock had flown them out of the desert, empty-handed, with Stafford's dune buggy dwindling to a point below them.

There was a hidden ostinato in Carter's thinking. As Carter's ship was docking the day before, he had found himself thinking of Annie. With a shock he realized he was visualizing himself coming back from Phobos with some new discovery, a solution to the mystery—not to show to Mars Council or Philippe, but to show to Annie. So it was Annie he would be returning to when he took the ride back down to Mars City?

As Philippe used to say, the human male was conspicuously bereft of bright plumage. Philippe, of course, had his art to show off. Perhaps if Carter could solve the mystery of Stafford's disappearance . . . A distortion of his thinking, he realized; perhaps it had been touched off by the sight of a particularly attractive young woman—a graduate student at the University—bouncing from wall to wall out of the airlock, with gleaming red hair that exploded in low-G profusion around her shoulders.

What made it much worse was that all thoughts of Annie were darkened by a cloud that he could not disperse. He was beginning to see it more clearly. It materialized from what Elena had said: What about Annie's role? Fact: Annie appeared on the scene as soon as Stafford disappeared. True fact: She insinuated herself into the search effort. Or was that a fact? "Insinuated" was a biased word. Still, she cozied up to Philippe and there also certainly seemed to be something going on between Annie and Carter himself, even though nothing had happened. . . . Anyway, if he wanted to be suspicious—which he needed to be—Annie's role in the case could be questioned. And the deeper he got into this mess, the more suspicious he became. Was she using them for some deeper agenda beyond her obvious purpose of getting her story? Were her actions part of the larger story, or a chance sideshow? He realized that it was this very sense of mystery that attracted him to her. What was going on in her mind, behind the veil of her actions? He wanted to learn more about the tapestry of her life.

What had started out as logic had dissolved into a branching chain. If Stafford had simply been lost, then there was one set of inferences. But if the disappearance was part of a plan, the list fanned out in a new direction. And if Annie had some hidden plan of her own, there were still new branches. New facts became relevant at every turn. . . .

On Phobos, the clocks ran on Mars City time. Carter had arrived in the afternoon the day before, on Thursday, February 54. The month was running out of days as fast as Stafford had run out of air. If that's what had happened. In the afternoon, he had rushed directly down to the Mars Reconnaissance Lab, the library division that stockpiled Mars orbital imagery. MRL occupied a large suite, quiet in the midst of its loud colors, on the lowest floor of the wheel. At the front desk an attractive lady of dictatorial air presided as if MRL were her private domain. He found himself faltering as he tried to explain what he wanted, knowing secretly that he wasn't sure. The conversation started with ambiguity, in which they had danced around the issue of which of them had the authority. He was the visiting official, with a mandate from Mars Council; wasn't it he who was in charge? Or was it she who was in charge of the institution to which he had come, hat in hand, so to speak, requesting her assistance?

It was an unpleasant start, but it ended with Carter being given a cubicle, a console, and instructional data cubes. In principle, he had access to all orbital picture files starting a week before Stafford's journey, and to the staff, who knew the system and could answer his questions.

His cubicle was painted hot pink. The neighboring booths were peach and vibrant purple. Environmental designers in the teens had gone into a period of brilliant hues—a rebellion against the earth tones and pastels that had marked public and corporate design of the previous decade. They called it the Hispanic influence. Vibrant colors for a new millennium, they said. But there was no psychological theory behind it, Carter felt; just chic decorator talk.

The plastic laminates that surfaced his cubicle were beginning to chip here and there, exposing low-density honeycomb structural sheets beneath. Someone with knife or nail file had scratched "Trish '27" on the back of the booth. Smooth bright cubicles all in a row: decorator sterility of the early twenties. The Phobos facility was going to need significant refurbishing one day.

As soon as he was settled in the cubicle, he had checked the screen for the entries under STAFFORD. He hadn't checked Newsnet for days. Annie had been at it again.

STAFFORD'S BUGGY FOUND IN DESERT
*Widely Known Researcher Located First Human Artifact
on Mars Before Disappearing*

The mystery over Alwyn Stafford's disappearance took a new turn on Sunday when a search party under the direction of Carter Jahns, Assistant Director of Environmental Engineering at Mars City, and Steven E. Braddock, Director of Hellas Base, located the lost buggy of the famed Martian biologist. Using highly processed orbital images, Jahns was able to trace Stafford's faint tracks, and to direct a search to the remote desert site 300 kilometers west of Hellas, where Stafford had apparently located the damaged remains of the first artifact on Mars, the *Mars-2* lander launched by the Soviet Union in 1971. One of Stafford's famed medallions was found on the lander wreckage, but Stafford's tracks indicate he left that site, traveling for unknown reasons farther into the desert, where his buggy was found in a small volcanic crater.

Mr. Jahns was assigned by the Mars Council to the search project. He stated that . . .

Carter erased the screen. For reasons he could not articulate, he felt he had to stay one step ahead of Annie. Life was crazy.

Eventually it was closing time and he had accomplished nothing. No inspiration had come, after all. Angrily he locked the cubicle with the key card he had been given and wandered off to find the tiny quarters he had been assigned. He was disgusted he hadn't accomplished more.

Maybe he needed to assemble a list of the facts in the case. Had he really examined all the facts? Maybe he knew them and maybe he didn't. When you examined anything closely enough, facts broke up into indistinct assertions, like subatomic particles. Fully clothed, he ended up crashing on his bed with his little screen, glowing an empty page titled FACTS, on the nightstand beside him.

●

The muse who had asked him to search through the images on Phobos toyed with his subconscious, like a cat playing with a mouse. During that first night on the black moon, Carter had had another of his dreams. This one was set in the far future. It was Mars, but with more air. There was a little boy—was it a great-grandson of Carter's, or Philippe's? Or Annie's? Or some pairing of them? Playing in a dune, the boy had found a sand-battered holeo cube. Carter knew, but the boy did not know, that the cube contained all the orbital images of Mars ever made. They were images of higher resolution than Carter had ever seen; you could enlarge them as much as you wanted, and the details stayed sharp. Like reality. It contained all the information needed to track Stafford to his fate.

More than that. The cube contained all the images from all the explorations through the outermost solar system. Moons and rings beyond measure. It was a precious repository, this cube; humanity's knowledge of the solar system.

But something was wrong. The boy took the cube to his father, in their dusty hovel by the dunes. Red windblown sand grains pecked at the frosted windows and shimmered in amorphous clouds that made the rest of the town hazy, as if seen through a veil.

The boy held out the cube to his father. There was no sound in this dream. Carter saw it, as if trapped in a camera. The father was shaking his head. Then Carter realized what was wrong. Inside the dimly lit house there were no screens. On the shelves were a few old magazines—scavenged from the final shuttle arrival? There were no contrails in the milky sky above the house. In the corner of the room was a radio, silent. Broken. There were no other tronix in the room at all. The father had a worn face, a face that radiated fatigue. Their supply lines from Earth had broken down. They had their nuclear and geothermal generators, their farms. The basics. But no way to read cubes. The last of the sophisticated tronix had broken long ago. The father shook his head. There were trillions of bytes of data and no way to read them.

The sun was setting. The boy went outside. He set up a telescope his father had helped him make. He was looking at Jupiter and its moons— four tiny pinheads. It was all he would ever know of them because there was no way to access what the previous generation had learned.

Friday, Carter had been the first one at the MRL door. He started the day forcing himself to play his new theories out to the end. If Stafford had arranged his own disappearance, he must have been picked up. That meant a conspiracy theory.

How could he have been picked up? The only buggies within range of Stafford's crater would have been from Hellas Base, and there seemed no chance any of them had done so. There were only five vehicles out from Hellas on Feb 43: Stafford and some members of the seismic party. All the seismic vehicles returned and were accounted for, and none of them had left tracks on Stafford's trail to the *Mars-2* area or beyond.

The other alternative was to have airlifted Stafford out with a hopper, but you didn't take hoppers into virgin desert. Well, it wasn't virgin. Stafford himself would have been there and could have cleared a landing site. But the photos they made as they left with Braddock's team showed no other marks of a hopper landing anywhere in the vicinity. Carter had gone over and over them in detail; there was no disturbance in the vicinity of the crater.

So the conspiracy idea didn't hold together any better than any of the other theories, but at least they couldn't say he hadn't considered all the possibilities.

He wondered whom he meant by "they."

That confused mass of thought had brought him to this moment in his cubicle in the Phobos Library, looking for some previously unnoticed fact about the little cone at 44.2° south and 313.2° west. Hoping, in other words, that inspiration would finally hit if he immersed himself far enough in the facts.

He glanced out the door at all the other workers working purposefully over their clean, colored desks. *They* seemed to know what they were doing. The lab seemed to vibrate with the sub-audible hum of intercourse between machines and human beings. Philippe would say they were turning into each other.

He had accumulated the relevant files on all sorts of images: wide-angle synoptic weather images; telephoto views targeted by various researchers, showing specific geologic formations and experimental instrument arrays; multispectral images made for obscure mapping programs, in wavelengths that not even the strangest Earth animals could see. He had seen geologists poring over images like these. "Carbonotite," they would say to each other. "Scapolite and montmorillonite. Charge transfer bands." Then they would nod with smiles or fly into arguments. Apparently the words meant something to them and they would go home happy.

Carter had compiled an inventory of all the wavelengths in which Stafford's little crater had been imaged in the last few weeks. At this point he didn't care how full of static, how low the signal-to-noise ratio, if there was some image or some data that contained a new clue. He was grasping at straws.

He sat staring at one of the images he had called up. It glowed in multiple, surrealistic colors, greens and purples; colors assigned to the different, exotic infrared wavelengths of the original image. Images spun in his head. Pictures at full scale; pictures at expanded scale breaking up into pixels; pictures in false colors; pictures with grossly enhanced contrast. Pictures until his retinas accepted only scenes made out of dots.

The breakthrough came, ultimately, because he had asked for *all* the imagery at *all* the wavelengths. He was looking at thermal infrared images, used by the meteorologists for studying seasonal weather patterns. The inventory included thermal images on February 39 and February 44 that covered the region of the small crater where Stafford's buggy had been parked.

The thermal infrared images were made with the radiation given off by objects due to their own greater or lesser heat. Dark areas on the images were cooler than their surroundings; bright areas, warmer. The images took the thermal pulse of the living landscape.

According to the data block on the February 44 frame, the picture had been taken at 23:08 L.M.T. Well after sunset. The landscape of night gave off its own dull infrared light, as the daytime-accumulated heat radiated into space. Brighter dots and smears marked individual house-sized boulders and rock outcrops that had deeply absorbed the sun's daytime warmth. Being warmed by that deep heat, they were now still radiating that warmth into the cold darkness. The north and east crater walls were bright and spotty, marking the rocky outcrops warmed in the day by the low polar sun. He had climbed those very outcrops. Outside the crater walls, an apron around the crater was dotted with boulders thrown out by the ancient explosion. Beyond the ejecta apron, the dune country was dark and cold because the dust made an insulating surface layer that stored little heat during the day. Everything was as it should be.

Carter played with the console controls. The resolution on the thermal infrared pictures was not very good.

If only he could bring out some kind of detail that would give a clue . . . He began to play with the contrast, blowing up first one part of the scene and then another. With contrast enhancement, and false color, he could separate various temperatures. Chartreuse equaled everything warmer than ten degrees above the average of the pictures; dull brown equaled everything else. Nothing. Then a step up. Chartreuse equaling everything more than five degrees above average. Still nothing. An active buggy, warmed by its heaters, would have been a blazing beacon with high enough resolution, but at this scale it was too small to be seen, a candle floating in the ocean at night, viewed from ten kilometers up.

Carter's arsenal of techniques went beyond analysis of single images. As a long shot, he looked at differences between images preceding Stafford's trip and following it. The method was simple enough. Registering the pixels at four corners of a latitude-longitude grid around the crater, he could subtract one rectified picture from another. This produced an image that registered strong tones only in areas that had changed between the date of the first image and the second. If nothing had changed, the result was a featureless gray. There was a correction for sun angle, but if the sun was at substantially different angles, the resulting image would show a pattern corresponding to changing shadows. He had already used this technique on the high-res visible-light photos that bracketed Stafford's trip. It simply revealed spidery traces of the buggy tracks that he'd discovered at Mars City and used to track Stafford on the ground. Carter didn't know what this technique might yield in the thermal infrared, but he needed all the ploys he could get.

The difference picture, 44 Feb minus 39 Feb, two kilometers on a side flashed quietly onto the screen. False color thermal infrared of a square, two kilometers on a side, centered on the crater. There was nothing. The image was frustratingly gray. Both pictures had been taken at night. The temperatures must have been similar everywhere.

He called up a contrast stretch and the screen obediently created a revised version of the picture that broke up into a garish chartreuse-and-brown pattern that appeared to be random noise. And yet . . . Southwest of the crater, a few hundred meters out on the plain, was a patch of light. Was it more noise? No. It persisted even when he changed the temperature limits and reduced the stretch coefficient. It stood out from the noise. There had been warmth there on the forty-fourth that was not there on the thirty-ninth.

What the hell did *that* mean?

A warm patch that had not been there a few days earlier. He expanded the scale. The picture broke up into a grid of pixels. The warm spot had structure. The central pixel was the brightest pixel in the frame. It was surrounded by a target ring of slightly less bright pixels, and an outer ring of still fainter ones that nearly blended with the background. The whole thing was perhaps thirty meters across, relatively circular. A round spot warmest at the center; at night. There was nothing else like it in the frame.

Fumbling with the disks, trying to beat the library's closing hour, he went back to the high-resolution visual at visible wavelengths. Here, the dark rocks and light dunes appeared in their ordinary sunlit colors. The region of the warm spot was unusually smooth, free of rocks, but there was nothing extraordinary in the picture—possibly a darker smudge in the questionable spot in the views made after Feb 43, but nothing to fecundate a theory.

Carter sat, staring at the picture and at the cluttered desk.

"I'm sorry, it's closing time." It was the librarian, standing in the cubicle entrance behind him. "Have you found what you're looking for?"

"I don't know. Maybe I'm on the track of something."

"Good." A professional smile. She left.

Carter regretted the awkwardness with her the day before, when he had checked in. He could have liked her, he thought. Librarian on Phobos. Interesting lady. Lots to talk about. Reluctantly he began clearing up the disks.

The subconscious mental cauldron was simmering. Bits of ideas bubbled to the surface where the inner eye of his semiconsciousness could catch fleeting glimpses of them. Suddenly the pieces bubbling up at random meshed into a pattern. His mind clicked.

The librarian was back. "There's somebody to see you," she said, coolly. Annie Pohaku was standing behind her with an unprofessional smile.

19

Carter's first reaction to Annie was mixed, though he quickly discovered that pleasure outweighed distress. Pleasure from her smile, the sheen of her black hair that made his own dark hair seem somehow dull by comparison. Her movements as she leaned against the cubicle door . . . Her carriage seemed to go beyond any self-consciousness to some sort of universal awareness. The distress—oh, yes it was there—was an odd feeling that his moment of discovery was being interrupted. By what?

A small part of his brain said: If only she had come an hour later, when I'd had a chance to digest things. Am I supposed to work this out in her presence? And then is her role codiscoverer, reporter, or what?

It was as if her presence might revoke his discovery.

"I heard you were here." She smiled. "I decided to come up on the next shuttle. I hope it's okay. Have you found anything?"

"Yeah. Something. Thermal images late on February 44. I could show you."

"I'm sorry," the MRL librarian broke in testily. She was still standing behind Annie. "The library is closing. You'll have to wait till tomorrow." The librarian was even cooler than before.

They decided to walk the promenade. The full circle was almost four kilometers. Carter and Annie, a spin around the neighborhood on Friday night. So, he had reached the stage where he liked their names together in the same sentence; it was worse than he thought.

The promenade at Phobos University was billed as the greatest walk in the solar system. All the brochures about Phobos used the cliché. It wasn't entirely local boosterism.

The design of the city went back to sketches by crazy visionaries, Nordung and Von Braun, and to the reality they never lived to see: space cities orbiting Earth. The living space inside the wheel was divided into four decks. If the wheel were compared to a bicycle tire, the floor of the lowest deck would be the inside of the tread. The promenade deck was the inside rim of the tire, where the spokes attached. Like spokes, cables and four large tunnels ran from this roof surface to the central axle of the wheel. The axle was a massive tower erected vertically on the north pole of Phobos. The city was a giant wheel, pinned through its heart to Phobos.

The roof, the spoke-supporting rim of the tire, was constructed not of the pale aluminum of the rest of the station, but rather of laminated glass panels fused at the lunar glassworks. What a fleet these panels had made, shipped from Tycho via solar sail, glittering through space all the way to Mars. Now they arched overhead, linked into a spectacular space-window roof over the promenade deck. Triply laminated, they were as resistant to meteorite impact as the rest of the station skin. They offered a topsy-turvy view of the Martian system.

Carter and Annie stood, looking out at the scene, intermittently bathed in a palpable russet glow. Arching directly overhead was the rest of Phobos University—the other side of the great, wide wheel. Carter enjoyed thinking about the fact that they were turning; but as they looked up, it seemed that they themselves were standing still, while the universe turned lazily around them: the Ptolemy effect.

Carter and Annie started walking in silence. They had shared only strained pleasantries since leaving MRL.

Above them, through the glass, the far side of the wheel filled part of the view. To the right of it loomed the dark mass of Phobos, standing on its side. Like a wall, the horizon of Phobos rose toward the zenith beyond the glass, parallel to the far side of the wheel and to the edge of the window. Soft-shouldered craters pocked its sooty surface. It rolled away from them like an Ohio hillside. As the station turned, the panorama swung by a little at a time, but faster than the change of scene in the rotating restaurants of L.A. New land slid above the window and climbed vertically into their glassy sky. Always the slow turning of the station brought some changing vista into view. Now came vast Mars, rising and passing overhead, harboring some quiet secret. In the opposite direction, brought around into their view by the wheel's rotation, was the sun. It hung over a shadow-filled crater, swinging now to shine like a searchlight into their eyes. The kaleidoscopic effect filled their senses with constantly changing impressions.

Carter and Annie continued in silence. Sharing the view was enough for them, a form of communication in itself.

Shadows changed around them as the sun swung through the 90-second mini-day of Phobos University. Every minute and a half the Phobos panorama repeated on the right, carrying the sun overhead in the narrow gap between the Phobos horizon and the far side of the wheel. Then the sun would set and Mars would loom up, casting its ruddy glow, as if a fire were crackling outside. Below Mars, ordinary life. Trees in planters, couples strolling, shops and booths along the side.

"Behold," Carter said, sweeping his arm around. "Humanity breaking free of gravity."

Annie walked in silence, glancing in the windows of the little shops along the arcade. It didn't look like humanity breaking free. It looked like a flying mall.

"You act like you're waiting for something," Carter said.

"As you like."

"Well? What might you be waiting for?"

"I'd like to hear about what you found."

The very idea of journalism touched off something in him. He stopped and faced her. "Annie, dammit, I've got a problem here."

"?" A gesture. She waited quietly.

Music drifted from a shop, something angular, with a compelling, un-syncopated rhythm, played on soft instruments. A guitar and tubular bells? The rhythms of bells and Mars-glow propelled him forward. Her patient smile filled the universe.

"I've found something . . . I think. Something in the image archives. I'm excited about it. I'd like to talk about it with someone. Well, I'd like to talk about it with you. I haven't worked it all out yet. But . . ."

"But?"

"I want to talk to *you*, but I'm not sure I want to talk to a reporter. . . ."

"To me, as a friend?"

"Yeah. How do I do that?"

"You say it's off the record."

"And you go out and write: 'Highly placed sources close to the investigation say . . .' " He paused, trying to find the words he wanted, when he wasn't even sure what he wanted to say. "Look, maybe I'm wrong about this. But you see my problem."

"?" That gesture of hers again. "Tell Mother your problem."

"It doesn't look right, for one thing, having my own private reporter in my pocket."

"Am I in your pocket?"

"It looks like I'm playing for publicity. I don't want to get ahead that way, and I don't want people to *think* I get ahead that way. Media success . . . it's just a flash in the pan. . . . Does any of this make sense to you?"

"Yeah . . . you're hardly dragging me along, you know. Look, I'll buy my own dinner if you like." She had laughter in her eyes, as if she enjoyed watching him squirm.

"Come on, I'm being serious. Besides, you know I'm attracted to you. I mean, who wouldn't be? But it makes it all the more difficult. I mean . . ."

"Thank you." She made a little curtsy, enjoying his suffering more than ever.

He plunged on. "So what I really should say is, it's not for publication at all. If we talk, you've got to sit on it till I'm ready." He felt as if he were asking for all of her.

"Look, you're making too big a deal out of it. The story's over for the networks, until Stafford is found . . . one way or the other. It's old news. I'm the only journalist on it right now, and that's just by luck, 'cause I happened to be here to do 'What's Happening on Mars.' Everybody else, they think Stafford's dead. Meanwhile, I watch you work; I think something interesting is going on here. But I'm cool. I'm sure as hell not breaking any of my own rules if I sit on this awhile and watch it unfold."

"If you sit on it."

"I've only filed four stories. I'm done for a while. Now, I'm following the reporter's golden rule: 'The more you file, the more you earn; but the more you file the less you learn.' George Fenton."

"Who's George Fenton?"

"Journalist, of course. A hero of mine. Forty, fifty years ago. Pacific rim. Did this book, *All the Wrong Places*. By chance, he kept turning up in places where big stories were breaking. Maybe that's what's happening to me right now." She stepped under a tree and touched its branch, caressing the leaves. "Of course, you can kick me out of here if you want. Then you won't have to talk to me. Course, I'll trail you, dog you around, watch your travel schedule, and generally make a pest of myself." She was eyeing him carefully.

"Look," she continued, "there's no ulterior motive. It happens that both our job descriptions are to find out and report what happened. We just report in different places. Can't you see that? Why do you have to make it so damn hard? We're both on the same side, Carter."

"It all sounds kind of naive."

"Naiveté is for back on Earth. As you and Philippe are fond of saying, this is a new world. I'm ready to invent new rules."

"And they are?"

She sighed. "Suppose I find myself actually one of the participants in an unfolding story, and write about that as honestly as I can. What's wrong with that?" She sighed again, a deep sigh, as if linked to her first sigh to form a pair of parentheses. "Besides, I *said* I'd like to talk to you as a friend."

"No, you didn't, actually."

"Well, I would. Okay, I'll sit on it until you've written your report, or you give me a go-ahead. One or the other. You satisfied now?"

"Where does that leave us . . . ?"

"You talk. I listen. I comment. I help. We're friends. We try to find out the truth. . . . Besides, I thought you bought into all this already when you invited me along with the search party."

"You invited yourself. I just agreed."

She ignored his barb. "I kind of like this idea of being involved," she added. "I don't like just regurgitating events, like a tape recorder. Especially what passes for news among the nets. 'Wars and carnage, craft and madness, lust and spite.' Life isn't just a tabloid. We can make people aware that this is an incredible age of discovery. . . ."

Carter had stopped listening. He had frozen at the echo of Philippe's phrase from Tennyson. Recycled conversations; the evidence of intimacy . . . He could see them together, Philippe reciting his favorite poems to her . . .

She saw it at once in his face. He could tell. Even in his distress he was amazed at her perception in picking up some silent language he had scarcely known existed. They both fell quiet. He wanted to accuse her of something. What? Spending time with Philippe without him being there? He felt caught up in childish jealousies.

"Anyway . . ." she said finally. "You know, I'm in a dilemma about you." She smiled.

"It's a good sign when the woman you're with feels she has a dilemma." He didn't know what he was saying. The anger was beginning to subside as fast as it appeared. "You want to tell me about this dilemma?"

"Mmmmm. Maybe later."

They walked on. Carter stuck his hands in his pockets. Mars turned overhead two, three, four times.

"Listen," she said. "Maybe we could go back to talking about Stafford."

Mars went around again and set beyond the branches of a bushy olive tree. Carter drew a deep breath. "I'll tell you two observations I made, and then I'll spin a theory around them. Okay?"

She nodded.

"First observation, you already know. If Stafford drove past that *Mars-2* site, he could have reached the crater—where we found his buggy—by February 43.

"Second observation. Sometime between February 39 and 44 an odd spot appeared southwest of that crater. A spot that was warmer than normal on the evening of February 44. I found it on the thermal images."

"And this spot: it's not warm, every night?"

"Not on the thirty-ninth."

"And after? Has it stayed warm?"

"I only looked at images up to the forty-fourth. I don't know if they have anything since then. Got kicked out of MRL too soon."

"But you can go back."

"Yeah. I need to check for more images after the forty-fourth."

"And your theory? You said you'd tell me a theory to explain it."

"Okay. Here's what happened on February 43."

"The grand reconstruction."

"The grand reconstruction. Mind you, it's part speculation." Carter walked with his head down. He had to look at the floor to keep concentrating. "Stafford learns about the *Mars-2* lander somehow—where it might be located. He doesn't tell anybody because, well, just because he's Stafford. He'd rather go check it out himself in his own lone-coyote way than blab about it. So he makes what looks like one of his usual solo trips and gets out there on the forty-third. We know it was the forty-third from the disk he left. Also, that date checks with a normal rate of dune buggy travel out there.

"Now, this is where the theory gets interesting. *Mars-2*, believe it or not, was only the first of two goals for Stafford. He had some other goal. I don't know what it was. Whatever it was, he never did plan to go back to Hellas Base. He had a plan to go on west from the *Mars-2* site. He had some other target in mind, and whatever it was, he wanted to keep it secret. So he tried to make it as hard as possible to track him. That's why he drove a lot of loops around *Mars-2*, tried to hide his tracks on rocky ground, and built the wall and put the tarp around the buggy when he finally parked it."

Annie was listening intently, as if hearing something beyond his words.

"It's the second goal we have to figure out. We don't know if the two goals of the trip came together by accident, or if the *Mars-2* trip was just an excuse for some other secret he had in mind all the time. Whatever the second goal was, it involved getting to that little cone. I think he really hoped his tracks would be so shallow they'd get wiped out by the wind before anybody could follow him. I don't think he expected anybody to find the *Mars-2* site for years, let alone follow him to the cinder cone. Maybe loners don't realize how much other people care. Maybe he really expected to be given up for lost. Conventional wisdom is that you can't see tracks from orbit."

"But Stafford put that idea into your head about Lowell's canals, that you could see fine lines. . . . He expected you to find them."

"Maybe he mentioned that to me just in case something happened someday, not with any focused idea in mind. I had to do a helluva lot of processing to pick anything up. Anyway, it doesn't make sense that he would hide his tracks *and* hint at how to find them."

"So when he got to the cone . . . ?"

"He hoped that if people did track him there, they'd theorize that he left the buggy on foot and got disabled by some freak accident out in the middle of nowhere. At each step he did what he could to hide what was going on."

"Carter, I know you don't like to think about this, but maybe . . . suicide? Could he have had some medical condition? Just wanted to be out there, somewhere?"

"He's not the type," Carter said brusquely. "Besides, he wouldn't take out a buggy. I . . . I did think about that."

They walked on in silence.

"Maybe he *did* get lost, for all we know," Annie said.

"For all we knew until this afternoon."

"When . . ."

"When I found the hot spot on those flats southwest of the cone."

"Which tells you . . ."

"That—this is the really speculative part—that somebody landed a hopper out there and picked him up."

Annie fell silent.

Carter continued. "Stafford was out there; he could check out a potential landing site and give coordinates. And Stafford was there first. He had time to check a landing site. The area southwest of the crater is smooth anyway. He probably picked it out from orbital photos before he even got there. All he had to do was check it out, find the best area. Let his rescue party know."

Annie was listening intently.

"So the hopper heated the soil and you picked up the hot spot on the thermal image?"

"No. I thought of that first, the heating effect, but I doubt the cameras caught the area so soon after takeoff that the spot was still warm. You don't transfer much heat into the deep soil during engine ignition. It just blows dust and hot gas around. What I think we're seeing is a spot where the loose surface dust was blown away during landing and takeoff, probably in the afternoon of the forty-third. Once you blow away the insulating dust, the sun heats up the rock, and the rock stores daytime heat. Then at night it radiates it. That's what I saw in the photo on the night of the forty-fourth. Any little spot cleared of its dust looks warm at night in the thermal IR."

"But there must be a lot of little bare spots."

"Not so many. There's at least a little dust on most surfaces. A little bit goes a long way as insulation. You blow it off, you have warm rock, or at least cemented soil that holds the heat. Anyhow, the main point is, this spot appeared between the thirty-ninth and the forty-fourth. Something happened in that interval. I'm saying the something was a hopper landing."

"But who would fly out there and meet him? You make it sound like Stafford was keeping a secret rendezvous. But who's flying around Mars on secret hopper flights?"

"That's what we want to know, isn't it? You want to help me figure that out?"

She smiled again, at last. An enigmatic smile. "Wait," she said suddenly. "Wait till afterward. There's something you want to do first. With me."

He hadn't told her everything.

It could wait.

———————————————————●———————————————————

Phobos University turned and the night went on and on in her room. The day/night/day/night of the wheel turning, and Phobos orbiting into Mars' shadow and out of Mars' shadow into sunlight, and Mars itself turning, and their bodies turning and twisting, day/night, one over another, cycles upon cycles, endless blending. "God!" she blasphemed when he stroked her long black hair, pushed it away from her face, and then gripped it tightly. But it was not blasphemy; it was a call to the universe, to a kindred spirit. It was as if she were surprised at her own body.

What was different about her? The thought flickered through Carter's mind. And he found the answer. When she made love, she withdrew into herself, into a hunger. She became something new: a creature of hunger, of need. He was playing her, sounding the depths of the need, following a trail blazed by her unspoken request. This was something different than with any other woman he had loved: he was making love not with an erotic body, but with a whole, erotic personality. The doing with and the doing to and the being done to were all mixed together. He was both master and servant of this creature's need. She was the extension of his fingers, and yet detached, another continent. With scarcely a word she invited him to be her master, and as he accepted, this made him at the same time her servant.

In the low gravity, he delighted in lifting her and turning her, letting her fall back to him. Slowly, slowly. When he held her, it was by her wrists, and sometimes she breathed his name again and again, like a heart-beat.

There was no night and no day and no morning to come because they were on Phobos and they were far away from Mars City. At last they were free and for this moment it was endless night and they could make love until they needed nothing more. There was only the wheel, turning, turning, and the creature of need.

Annie thought of something she had seen, far away, near the Phobos airlocks: a little girl, newly arrived on a ship from Earth, dancing in delight in a hotel lobby, jumping, floating, skipping, spinning with her arms out, embracing a new world. Annie, too, had become a little girl, dancing, floating, spinning, embracing.

They had slept and made love again and declared it to be their own morning. They talked—not just words of love and sensation, but exchange. To Carter, it was mystical, this talk: talking to this person as if conversation were normal; talking to this hungering personality as if sentences were a way to communicate. There was a new presence lurking—the third entity that was a new creation, their relationship. How could she just talk, Carter thought. How could she sit here and say sensible words, as if the third party did not even exist? It was lurking, looking over their shoulders. It was glowing with invisible light, hanging in the air between them. How could that mouth even pronounce ordinary words?

But they talked, they had to talk, about Stafford and the search. The search whose character had changed now, from a search to save a life to a search that might mean something stranger than death on Mars.

"I want to see the pictures," she said.

"We have to go to MRL."

Saturday morning, MRL. The sign out front said the lab would be open today only until noon.

The screen flickered to life when he punched up the image he had been studying the day before. The crater appeared. Now there was something new. The image was streaked and spotted with dropouts. Lines and clusters of pixels that made up the image were missing.

"What the hell?" he said. The little crater was mostly clear, but a speckled swath of missing pixels covered the hot spot. He fiddled with the contrast and stretch controls.

Nothing. There was no signal at all in the missing pixel positions. He called up adjacent frames. Same thing. "Shit," he said.

He stormed to the librarian's desk, leaving Annie studying the fine print on the disk they had slotted.

"I don't know," the young woman at the desk said when Carter brought her back to the booth. She stared at the screen with a mystified but uninvolved expression. Carter was angry. She was Saturday staff. What did she know? "It looks like electronic damage to the original data. Sometimes we see dropouts like that. We've had malfunctions in memory."

"That's crazy. I had them out just last afternoon. They were fine. The images I was studying, they were fine. Now it's shit."

"I really don't know. We do see dropouts like that sometimes. Some glitch in the system . . . If you'd like to talk to somebody in the technical . . ."

"Yeah, I'd like to talk to somebody. I'm up here on special assignment." He explained who he was. Explained about Mars Council. Pulled out his ID, noting with gratification that the young woman seemed cowed. "I've got to talk to somebody in authority. Not just anybody. Who's in charge of the satellite imagery?"

The librarian punched a number into her console, scowling at both of them. "Ms. Romero isn't going to like to be bothered on Saturday."

Ms. Romero was out shopping, God help her, but she was planning to stop by her office at one, according to her machine.

Before they left the library, they hardcopied the image still on the screen. Evidence from the scene of the crime.

"I had these images up yesterday and they were just fine and now they've all gone to hell. I can't get what I want from the image I've got on the screen. The area I want—the image is ruined."

Ms. Romero looked at Carter and Annie coolly from behind an imposing desk. She tapped unconsciously at the X key on her console. "As I said, there's not much we can do."

"Oh, come on. There's got to be some duplicate storage."

"Not at all. Satellite imagery is not that high a priority. Original images are kept in storage for ten years, and a sampling of images is kept permanently—you know, for geology studies and meteorology. But we don't have fail-safe backups for every image. We don't have infinite storage here, you know. There's a lot of demand for space.

"Some kinds of data, there's fail-safe backups. But not for routine images. They're used mostly for weather analysis and site-specific geologic analysis. Every once in a while we may get a glitch that takes out some bits. It's rare."

"You expect me to believe Phobos runs on a system where bits of data disappear inside the computer overnight?"

"Of course not," Ms. Romero said, sounding defensive. "But if a transient comes through the line when the data is being transferred, you stand a chance of losing some bits. If it's not high enough priority files to have a duplicate data set, you're out of luck, to put it bluntly. You can't expect Phobos to keep duplicate data sets on all the satellite imagery. Really."

Carter clenched the arm of his chair, angrily.

"I'm sorry if your project is hampered, Mr. Carter. Really I am. But this sort of thing happens sometimes. We try to trace each case to its origins, to learn how to prevent it. Those geophysicists, for instance. When they were experimenting with electromagnetic pulses—I mean we were losing data every time they pressed their button."

"But yesterday . . ."

"I don't know that what you saw yesterday was any better than what you have today. Maybe you were seeing what you wanted to see. . . . Anyway . . ."

"I had a goddamn contoured and processed image. . . ."

Annie put her hand on his arm.

"Anyway, as I was saying, I'd be glad to take you back and show you the system, but you understand there's no 'original image,' just a bunch of numbers floating in the computer somewhere. You tell me what you want, I'll be glad to go in there and call it up myself—it's just the same as you see downstairs in the lab." She was condescending now.

"No thanks."

"I doubt if the images will help with your project now, from what you say about the dropouts. Maybe some other images . . . By the way, what did you say your project was?"

"He didn't," Annie said.

They left Ms. Romero with a page of "X"s on the screen of her clean, white terminal.

"That was all bullshit," Carter said. They were walking home with a set of the damaged prints in an envelope under Carter's arm. A group of University students from Germany walked past them, singing. When did you ever see American students singing? they said to each other.

"There are too many obstacles here," Carter said.

"Keep talking," she said.

"Braddock never wanted to take us out there to that crater, you know. I'm convinced of it now. He held off for days. And why didn't I get these pictures you wanted at Hellas in the first place? Why the delays?"

"Bureaucracy's never perfect, that's what they'll say."

"This goes beyond imperfect."

"I tend to agree. They're stonewalling you."

"Are you ready for another piece of the puzzle?"

"What?"

"Think about where I said that hot spot was located—where someone landed to pick up Stafford. Think about how that relates to our departure from the site."

"Oh, my God," she said.

"Right. When Braddock brought in his people, he had them land directly on top of the same spot where Stafford had been picked up! They deliberately landed on top of the one spot that could have given them away."

"And Braddock was the one that called them in! When you were walking around the rim. I saw him. He just called them in on his own. He's in on it."

"I've been going round and round on this. We have a lot of people here, hiding something. And it means we're all pawns. Me, Philippe, you—most of the people at Mars City for all I know. You think about that, you begin to go crazy."

"You go where the story takes you," Annie said quietly, as if quoting some journalism professor. She paused, thinking. "You know, maybe I have one for you."

"What do you mean?"

"It's about Braddock. At the net I have access to our biographical files about public figures. There's something I didn't think about too much before, but maybe it's relevant. He was in charge of a big drilling project in Zaire a couple of years ago. It was supposed to be a pure geophysics project, but the African Federation threw him out. They claimed he was working on a secret project of the U.S. Security Agency to gain control of oil reserves in central Africa. It was a little flap, but now, in this context, well, maybe it's relevant. Maybe we're dealing with people that have an interesting past."

"What about Lena?"

"She's clean. Pure science type. And Stafford, of course; same thing."

"We have to figure out what to do next," he said.

"I'm getting an idea about that."

"Look. I'll play a game with you." He pulled two scraps out of a wastebasket. "You write down what you think we have to do next, and I'll do the same. Let's see if we're both so smart that we agree. At least, then, I can hold my head up and deny I told you everything."

". . . in my bedroom."

"It wasn't in your bedroom. It was along the goddamn promenade."

"Oh, yeah."

They wrote on their scraps. They turned them over. His said in a scrawl "Polar Station." Hers said in neat print "Elena Trevina."

"Are you afraid?" she said.

"Yeah," he said.

"So am I."

20

The shuttle to Mars City eased away from the Phobos docking port. Carter, with Annie webbed in beside him, watched Phobos slide away into the distance. He was musing to himself: Maybe this whole thing is simpler than I thought. You trust each other, not because you are lovers but because you are friends. Why shouldn't she be able to write about Stafford and share love with me at the same time? Maybe there don't have to be complications.

He had a dreamlike image of a stone bridge built across a river: once built, it was a permanent structure, easily merged into the nature of things, like old, moss-covered English bridges, part of the landscape. He did not know that his model for such things was too simple; he did not yet realize that even the strongest bridges built in the night are magical things, made of mist, able to disappear and reappear with the wave of an emotional wand, like bridges in a fairy kingdom.

Below, in Mars City, on the day Annie left, Philippe had felt inflamed. It had started with anger and confusion. Annie was gone. Cryptically, her machine said only that she was out and would return. It didn't say when.

Phobos? Was it Phobos? Carter had gone to Phobos.

Why should he care, Philippe told himself. Slowly the anger and confusion mutated into something else, some sort of manic energy that may not have been healthy. It started with a conscious decision to work. Anything to stop thinking about Annie and what might happen. The rest of the week stretched before him. He thought about Schrödinger's strange ideas: The past was particles, fixed. The future was waves, malleable. Our work alone creates the future, turns it into the fixed structures of the past.

Besides, he had not really wanted an exclusive relationship. Had he?

Life so far had taught him that he could stop caring through drugs, drinking or—what was harder—by starting work. He had been feeling stalled, as if all the wheels of his engine were jammed, welded together with molasses. It amused him that his metaphors for it were consciously Victorian: he felt that all the wheels were connected by a system of rods and gears, and if he could only grasp one wheel and turn it, he could force the rest of the machine to start. Curious, he thought, that in this age of liquid field devices we still use metaphors from the era of Watt. "Get those wheels turning." "Get up a head of steam."

Well, that is what he needed to do. He would return to a dormant project that he had almost finished before the Stonehenge opportunity came along. He closeted himself in his studio, a biology lab temporarily abandoned when funding was cut off by a Russian agency in some political debacle—probably traceable to the scandal over development rights in the Crimean resort peninsula. The Russian biologists had been called home and the lab was empty when he arrived.

Once he got started, Philippe worked feverishly during the weekend, as if completion of the long-dormant project would release him from something. Only final assembly was needed from the parts he had already cast. He tried to force himself to think of nothing but the emerging, glinting tree, twice as tall as he was. Why should he care what Annie did? Women and men were meant to be friends. Women were there to be loved when they were approachable. He did not want to own her. He did not want to own anybody.

Still, she could have called him.

The aluminum and crystal tree grew in front of him. It grew around him, really, because he had a cherry-picker that allowed him to move around it and into it. He worked on the tree like nature herself in the spring, frantically, bending branches, extending shoots. Most of the crystalline leaves already had been attached, but now the tree was sprouting new growth.

He did not even sleep on Saturday night, a night when, passing once directly over his head, within eyesight, Annie and Carter were spending their second night together, making unconditional love. In Philippe's eyes, the tree had ceased to be metal and glass; it had became something evanescent. Branching over him, it became a hovering female principle, the moon goddess of ancient Europe, the many-faceted Hindu goddess Kali, Durga, Devi, who was as ever-present and as active as time, who stirred the dormant male principle. Was he an artist in control of his craft, creating something for the pleasure and inspiration of future travelers to Mars, or was he merely the wombless male struggling in impotent frustration to create . . . some*thing*, any*thing*? The goddess loomed above him, many-branched and many-leaved, and he tried to put Annie's face on it—that would have been the fitting symbolic climax of his dreamy stupor. But he failed in this. There was no face. He fell asleep and woke up Sunday at noon on the studio floor.

After a few more hours' work, the main framework of the tree, the trunk and graceful branches, stood nearly complete. Aluminum, it gleamed under the spotlights he had rigged around the cluttered studio-storage room. A dull metal gleam with a hint of Earth's sky blue. Outside, in the thin Martian carbon dioxide, it would probably stay bright, not tarnish to dull oxide gray. Philippe was excited, for no reason that he could explain, by the idea of Martian skylight glinting off the branches, the idea that it would be pink light instead of blue. Who had ever seen aluminum picking up a pink sky glow?

Remaining was only the task of attaching the last of the myriad crystal leaves, each with its name inscribed. There were fifty new ones still to be included. Gravely, hurrying in a blind ferment of work, he hung them one at a time by their little wires. The tree began almost to give off a light of its own, a kaleidoscope of crystal refractions and reflections. The Martian tree blossomed, hour by hour as the day wore on. Martian spring. Monday he would erect it in the airlock plaza. At least he'd have something to show for this period, when everyone else had given themselves up to the hysteria over Stafford and when relationships had changed . . . .

_____

In the shuttle, on the way down, Annie sat next to Carter and feigned dozing. She thought about loving him. She changed the wording in her own mind; she thought about making love with him. Something had happened, some release. An unexplored space that had always been there had been touched by this man. It had come as a surprise. Looking back on it, she was not even sure she liked what had happened. That lovemaking could release something new in her, at this point in her life, was not what was supposed to have happened. What could she say of herself? She was a professional woman, whatever that silly phrase meant. No, she was a woman. A traveling woman, a woman of the world, who liked men. Who liked sex, if the truth be known. Well, what was wrong with that? There were lots of men, and Mars was particularly safe: all incoming arrivals were screened before departure from the Crystal City, a policy adopted after the AIDS III panic in Moscow and then Tycho. Vitality. An occasional man from Mars could not hurt her.

Whenever an inner voice nagged her about this, she managed to dismiss it with two thoughts: (a) her life was her own; (b) she was a student of human nature, a writer. Getting to know people and how they worked inside their own heads was what her life plan was all about. It had not been hard, taking occasional lovers. She prided herself that former lovers were still friends. Well, a few of them she hadn't heard from for ages. But certainly not enemies. Not one was an enemy.

Did she want to feel it again, what Carter had brought forth? Of course. But did she want it intruding into the framework of her life? Did she have any control over the answer? Now she recognized that the psychic space he had found had always been part of her. Simply, her body had exploded in his grasp. The way he held her, she had wanted him not just to make love with her, but to have her, to take her, which suddenly seemed the same as giving him the gift of herself. Not just sharing, which is what love had always been supposed to be . . . had always been for her, but giving everything as a gift, giving herself away to him completely, knowing that she could have herself back when it was over.

The real problem, she began to realize with horror, was that she was a twenty-first-century woman brought up on her mother's twentieth-century ideology. What she had inherited, a progressive credo of sexual niceties, turned out to be incomplete for her. Its ideologically pure equality was supposed to cover not only friendship and economics, but sex. This pleasant theory of sexual equivalence had seen her through numerous relationships, but now she discovered that it did not satisfy every corner of her psyche. Carter had revealed new corners, untouched by ideology, and full of mystery. The mystery involved an unexpected rawness in Carter. Somehow, mutual respect and desire had been blended with a new knowledge of surrender and re-creation.

And what of Tomas, kind and loving and cheerful Tomas, who was back on Earth? She had not felt this with him. Could she? Could he learn? Did she want him to learn?

By the time Carter and Annie arrived back at Mars City on Sunday afternoon, Philippe was nearly ready to install his sculpture. What he had in mind was a grand gesture. The tree would stand outside, in front of the main airlock entrance. The only tree to grow in the natural Martian soil would greet all visitors to the new world.

Philippe had visualized Annie being there, during the installation. She would look intrepid, and spend her time shooting holeos of the ceremony. There would be good angles from atop the airlock door. During her absence, these visions had taken a sad new cast: they no longer seemed an extension of love between them, but merely his own male posturing.

After Annie had left, he had gone ahead and scheduled the installation of the project for Monday afternoon, March 2. He tried to convince himself he did not care if she was back or not. But surely, by Monday, she would be.

Now the tree stood in his studio on a heavy platform on rollers. With a tractor, it could be hauled out through the equipment bay and then lifted into position with a crane.

After Carter and Annie landed, Annie suggested they go find Philippe. Philippe, whom she had left behind: she had to find out how he was doing. Carter followed unenthusiastically. They found Philippe in his studio, bleary-eyed, still tinkering with his tree.

The sculpture towered over them, sparkling and tinkling slightly in the quietly circulating air currents generated by unseen machines that were within the province of Carter's job description. Annie stood under the tree, listening to the shifting chords. "Nobody's going to hear it, once it's outside," Annie said. She studied Philippe's face.

"Maybe not for a century," Philippe said, poised over one of the branches with a pair of needle-nosed pliers. "Whenever they get the air pressure up enough for people to walk around without suits." He had not looked at her at all, except when she came in, when he looked at both of them and then looked away.

"But the light on it will be beautiful," Philippe continued. "It will refract and reflect . . . diffuse light differently at different times of day. I used the hardest glass I could make. I'm hoping it won't get sandblasted if it's in the courtyard between the airlock and the shed. I'm going to make a garden out of that spot. . . ."

Carter stood staring up at the huge structure, while Annie had Philippe take her for a walk around it. "It's wonderful," she said to Philippe quietly. She gave him a radiant smile, as if nothing were wrong.

When they completed their circuit, Carter said, "It's really good, Philippe. It's beautiful. A tie to Earth, but different."

"Different," Annie echoed.

"How many leaves are there?" Carter asked.

"Over four thousand. One for every person who has been on Mars, according to the registry. I've been assembling it all since Friday."

Carter glanced at Annie and suppressed a strained smile. "All that since Friday?"

"*Je suis très fatigué.* Of course, I made the branches and most of the leaves months ago. They were waiting for me."

Annie said, "We should get to put our names on them."

"There is one with your name on it. And one with Carter's, and mine, everyone's. If you look, you'll find one leaf that is different. Scarlet. That is Stafford's."

"Oh, where is my leaf?" Annie laughed.

"I don't know anymore."

The comment stung her. She knew Philippe was in pain. She should have handled it better, but damn it . . . Annie walked around the tree, closer to where Philippe was working, as if looking for her special leaf. "It must have taken forever," she said. She wanted to hug him, but couldn't with Carter there. He looked like a little boy, trying to be brave. . . .

Well, she had made this bed and now she was lying right in the middle of it.

"I thought about leaving room on the tree for new leaves," Philippe was saying. "Future arrivals. They could have a ceremony every six months. Attach leaves for new people, and the tree could grow. Then I thought, no, I will design it for today, so there will be no bare branches. It commemorates how far we have come. In the future, when people come to Mars City, they can look at this and say, 'It all started in '09. That is how far they got by '31.' I hope this will be a benchmark for them all to see a continued increase, a kind of progress." Philippe sighed. "Tomorrow I must get up very early. They move it out into position."

"We've got to tell you about what we found," Carter said. "Come on. Let's get you out of here. You look like you're going to drop. Let's go somewhere comfortable where we can talk." Carter started for the door exuberantly, trying too hard to be cheerful and to stand near Annie at the same time.

When Philippe went to turn out the lights on the far side of the studio, Annie trailed behind him, eyeing the tree judiciously from every angle.

"It's good to see you again, Philippe," she whispered to him. "Everything will be all right."

When they left, Philippe turned out the lights one by one and they all watched the tree fade into night-dormancy.

On the way to the restaurant, they passed a pregnant woman in the hallways.

"Are they still having babies?" Philippe said after she had passed. He waved his arms. "Here it is, March. Why don't they just have them all in January and get it over with?"

Carter: "What's that supposed to mean?"

Philippe shrugged. "I don't know. It just popped into my head. I have had no time to think about what it means. I think it is black humor, probably."

●

ARRIBA Y ADELANTE, said the sign over the door. FROM THE SONORAN DESERT: FOOD FOR THE GREATEST DESERT IN THE SOLAR SYSTEM! Someone had penciled an extra "S" in the second "desert." Inside, they made their plans over "cheese" enchiladas and beans from the greenhouses.

Philippe was full of his impending unveiling, trying to avoid the sense of triangle among them. Carter and Annie let him talk. Phobos was exploding in them, but it was as if they did not dare to verbalize it. Their own private story they were not ready to talk about, and the other half, the evidence, seemed as if it might evaporate if exposed to a hearing.

It wouldn't be an unveiling, really, Philippe continued, unaware of their urgency. The crane had already emplaced the huge basalt boulders and slabs he had brought in, making a pseudo-Japanese garden around the tree site—a Tharsis garden, he called it. It was a combination of a Zen garden and the English standing stones that had inspired his Martian Stonehenge. He loved stones that whispered of paleolithic mysteries. For new visitors, arriving at the Mars City gate, it would be a foreshadowing of the Stonehenge installation, which they might see later during their stay on Mars. Everyone would be invited to see the tree being emplaced into the center of the new garden.

"Look, Philippe, we've got something to tell you," Carter said finally, as Philippe ran down. "We've all got to go to the Polar Station. You should come. Something is going on there. We don't know what it is, but we need all of us, together." They told the story of Phobos—the impersonal part. The thermal image, the theory that a hopper had picked up Stafford, that Braddock had instructed his own hopper deliberately to obliterate the pickup site, that someone had tampered with the stored images that Carter had seen on Phobos, that the hopper that picked up Stafford must have come from the Polar Station.

"Couldn't the hopper have come from Hellas?" Philippe asked.

"I went through the whole manifest of hopper flights from Hellas as soon as I got there. I called down there again yesterday and talked to maintenance people. There were only two hoppers out on the forty-third and I talked to the two pilots; they were at the seismic installation the whole time. The seismic crew verifies it. Everything sounds kosher. And remember, you and Annie interviewed all the people who outfitted Stafford when he went out; you said there was nothing fishy there. I just don't believe you could start making secret flights out of Hellas without it getting around.

"The Polar Station is different. Small, tight, exclusive. And it's the only other place besides Hellas close enough to reach Stafford's crater in a hopper. . . ."

"Unless there's a station somewhere on Mars we don't know about," Philippe said.

"Come on. A conspiracy theory is bad enough. Let's not make it fantastic. It had to come from the Polar Station; that's the place to start. But we don't know what we're getting into. We may need all the help we can get. You're the only person I can trust. We don't know who all is trying to cover this up, or who is watching us, to see what we do next. We need to be fast and decisive, without advertising in advance. I'll requisition one of the shuttles that can get us there. I'll make it Tuesday morning, the day after your tree is unveiled. No one will expect us to descend on the pole the day after your tree goes up. Meanwhile, we've got to make it look like business as usual, like we're starting to put the Stafford thing behind us. Your tree is a great diversion."

"Oh, thank you very much."

"You know what I mean."

Philippe looked thoughtful. "How could this hopper be from the Polar Station? It makes no sense. Elena would know. . . ."

Annie responded, "Maybe she's in on it. She can do anything she wants down there. Nobody's looking over her shoulder. If she wants to send one of their hoppers out to pick up Stafford in secret, and if she's got a pilot who will keep his mouth shut, who's going to know?"

Philippe: "But she was helping in the search."

Annie: "Interesting lady, huh?"

Carter said nothing, but his mind was racing. He had been wrestling with that one in private for forty-eight hours.

Philippe finally headed back to his studio, leaving Carter and Annie at their table. He didn't look back.

"I've got to go work on my stories," Annie said.

Carter didn't want her to work on anything; he wanted her to be with him. He didn't examine this feeling; it just seemed natural, presupposed. He didn't wonder why sex creates possessiveness.

"I've got a lot to catch up on," she said. "I really ought to write a follow-up on Stafford and the *Mars-2*."

"But you said on Phobos, you'd sit on what we talked about. . . ."

"I said write, not file. I want to make a record as we go. I'm beginning to think my role is more than just reporting. Maybe I'm the chronicler of this thing. Maybe there's a book in it. . . ."

"But you still agree: everything so far that we've done together, it's off the record until we find out what goes on at the pole. You can wait till then?"

"Yeah. God, you're a worrier."

"I don't want to make it hard for you, Annie. You know that. We're helping each other. You said it yourself. Only, it's getting delicate, you know? Stafford's pulling something and I don't know what's going on, and I'd just like to find out before we go off half-cocked."

"I understand. You don't have to keep lecturing me."

"Come on. I'm not lecturing. I just . . ."

21

On Monday morning, Carter lay in bed alone, waking slowly, feeling a mounting pressure, like something pushing down on him. Tomorrow, sixteen days after Stafford had disappeared, they would board a requisitioned shuttle and fly to the Polar Station and . . . what?

He opened his eyes. For the first time, a room on Mars seemed claustrophobic. For the last week, he had been feeling the excitement of a search, but now he felt apprehension and desperation building again. His arrival at the Polar Station would blow the lid off whatever was going on.

Uncharacteristically, he lay in bed a long time, musing. What if Stafford was really alive at the pole . . . ? Maybe if he could find Stafford, the old guy could explain everything in his fatherly way: "Now, Carter, just shut up and listen a minute." But the hope was clouded. Were there really secret programs on Mars? Was he, himself, really a pawn in someone else's game? And how long had *that* been going on?

If Stafford had needed to go to the pole, why couldn't he just fly down there quietly? The question answered itself. Stafford could do nothing quietly; he was held too much in awe. People always thought he was "on to something." Maybe there were good reasons for what Stafford had done. Assuming Carter's theories were correct. This morning they were beginning to seem more like wild speculation.

Carter lost his internal struggle to remain detached and analytical. Part of him felt outraged. There weren't secret projects on Mars. There weren't games being played here. If there were, his whole world was a farce. Carter, of all people, should know what was going on. It was in his job description to know everything that was happening on Mars.

Carter had a growing, unfamiliar feeling that he had not only a professional assignment to figure out what had happened, but also an independent, moral imperative.

He struggled to accommodate his suspicion that Stafford was not dead. It bothered him that this belief was now so strong, because he had no solid evidence. Circumstantial evidence, maybe. What if the thermal signature, which now could not even be reproduced from the data, turned out to be a blemish, or worse yet a figment of his strained imagination? What if he proved nothing at the pole? "Maybe you've been on Mars a little too long, Carter." It was the voice of some kindly Council representative, goaded on by Braddock no doubt, who would show up one day at his office. "Maybe you need a change . . ."

There was a weak spot in the theory: If Stafford was hiding out at the pole, how could he ever plan to reappear? He couldn't return to his buggy and come driving out of the desert after a month as if nothing had happened! If he ever turned up alive, it would be obvious that he had used one of the public vehicles from Hellas to fabricate a hoax—a deed that could conceivably lead to dismissal from Mars. So there was a go-for-broke aspect to Stafford's actions. There had to be a clue in that.

Unless Stafford planned to disappear from sight permanently . . . But that made no sense. No, he had elected to take a colossal gamble. He would have to stay hidden until he had accomplished whatever he set out to do. What was worth risking his reputation for? Besides, if he had really been picked up and taken to the pole, who at the pole was in on it? Lena? So she had been deliberately lying to him in his own bed? Well, hiding the truth, he amended. And if Lena was not in on it, then who? Carter had a laughable picture of Stafford cowering in some room at the Polar Station, unbeknownst to the rest of the staff, fearing discovery.

Or being held prisoner?

None of the pictures made sense.

Then there was the Annie situation. And the question of how Philippe was feeling about it, which you could never tell about anything.

Late Sunday night Annie finally answered in her room, but she would not come out. Claimed she had disconnected her 'corder earlier to finish a report. "I'm going to file something on Philippe's tree. I've done a great interview with him." Well, at least it would make it look as if they had put the Stafford incident behind them.

———————————————●———————————————

Not wanting to think about Annie or his own backlog of staff reports, and not sure that he was capable of thinking about anything clearly, Carter got up, took a bath, shaved. This morning, he would devote to putting out fires in the office—the crap he had failed to deal with last night when he got in. This afternoon, the unveiling. Tomorrow, the blitzkrieg on the Polar Station.

Everything was normal in his office. People expressed sympathy about Stafford, and then screamed about the budget report from the financial office. The screens lit up as usual.

Why did he feel people were watching him? Jeez, he was getting paranoid. If there was a conspiracy, were there people in Mars City who were part of it? Or was it limited to Braddock and the polar cabal?

He felt like a general in a bunker, awaiting some climactic, distant battle. He could not avoid the feeling that fate had arranged some dread event for him, and was maintaining a facade. Over a solitary lunch, he struggled to concentrate on his reports. It was a pain to work on them in this mood, but he forced himself to finish, reasoning that he had to free his mind to deal with whatever fate might be preparing for him.

The unveiling of Philippe's tree proceeded according to plan. Carter watched from the sidelines. A suited crowd gathered in the little garden-like alcove outside the main airlock. Helmets gleamed in the sun. As Philippe had said, the alcove looked like a Zen garden. Oddly suggestive boulders, artlessly dotted at random, stood on manicured cinders and gravels of reds and grays. In the center rose the shining metal tree with its crystal leaves refracting the sunlight's blues and golds and reds. Annie had set up three holeo recorders on tripods. There were a few speeches, and Annie clambered from one recorder to another, spending most of her time shooting from a perch atop the airlock doors. The crowd bustled impatiently. To Carter, they seemed unaccountably anxious to be out of their suits.

The turrets and antennae of Mars City formed the backdrop to the garden and its new tree, with its shining leaves. To a thousand travelers of this future, this would be an introduction to the new culture that was growing on Mars, the twig, the new offshoot from Earth's ancient ways, budding now on a new world. Long-term Martians would come to treasure it: Philippe had placed it so that the tops of its sparkling branches were visible from the observation lounge on the upper level of the Nix Olympica Bar, across arching roof lines bristling with antennae, duct access ports, and domed skylight windows. It was a symbol of wistful tenderness in what many first-time visitors perceived as a sterile alien-industrial setting. Philippe had planned it that way. It said: This is our new home.

After the ceremony, the small crowd dwindled quickly. Carter and Philippe, bulky in their suits, said nothing to each other. They stood, staring at the leaves, which flashed occasionally in the listless air. Annie dismantled her camera setups. "Tomorrow's the big day," she whispered.

They followed her to the airlock and turned in their suits together.

They bustled, putting their suits in their lockers. It seemed to Carter that they were uncomfortable to be together but more uncomfortable to be apart.

Finally, Annie turned to them.

"Look," she said, "could we all go somewhere? We need to talk."

———————————————●———————————————

As Philippe was saying, "but we have a right to be angry," Annie finally lost her temper.

"No! Damn it, I just don't accept that," she said. "*I'm* the one who's pissed. You guys don't own me, you know. Either one of you. Why do you have to act that way and spoil everything?" Tears were welling in her eyes. She tried to hold them back. Her eyes flashed. Then she slumped almost imperceptibly and stared at the floor.

They had come to Carter's room, all three of them, out of desperation for a place to expose their feelings.

Carter sat at the end of the bed, away from Annie. He felt his own anger welling up. It was he who had wanted her in the first place, he believed. Philippe never really wanted anybody. He just played; played at women, played at life. No, that was unfair. Well, the hell with it. The thoughts that crowded in on him seemed too self-serving. So he said nothing.

Philippe stood leaning against the wall, almost laconically. His stance projected a detached air, but his thin face was grim. He sat down in the single chair, elbows on widespread knees, leaning toward her unflappably. He stared at her in silence, as if daring her to continue. Finally he said, "You are pissed?" "*You* are pissed?"

"This is crazy," she muttered, almost to herself. "And it isn't fair." She was still looking at the floor.

"What is it, that is not fair?" Philippe said.

"I just wanted friends. I like you both, that's all. I just wanted to be free and to do my job and to have friends. And, yes, lovers, too. In fact, we all love each other if we could just open our eyes to it. That should be good, not bad. I didn't want you to be jealous. I didn't want to make a mess."

Philippe: "But I have not acted jealous, or angry. I have just tried to do my work and to see you and . . ."

Carter: "Come on, Philippe, you know we've all been tense."

"Well, if you are feeling such love for me . . ." Philippe said sarcastically, "you might have come and talked to me about what you were doing next, where you were going. That you were going to Phobos to see him."

Annie: "Bullshit! How many women have you had, Philippe? Did you tell them all about the next one? About the one you were seeing tomorrow?"

"Sometimes . . ." With a Gallic gesture of exasperation, Philippe blew a burst of air from his pursed lips. It rustled his hair. "Well, it depends . . ."

"You and your supercilious attitude. There was some real affection here. You could have let it go at that, but now all of a sudden you are acting possessive and wrecking everything. Both of you."

Carter stirred. "You could have said something. You could have talked."

"You and all your talk about a new planet. Both of you. And then you want some sort of twentieth-century behavior. This isn't high school anymore, you know. Nobody's talking about going steady here. I'll bet every goddamn man on Mars feels free to take a lover when he wants. So how do you get off bitching at me?"

Carter: "Because you weren't open with us."

Philippe: "You were sincere, you just weren't honest."

Annie slammed her palm on the bed. "What the hell! It's only been a few days. A couple of sporadic, spontaneous incidents a few days apart! You act like I broke a contract. I hate to tell you, we didn't have a contract. Is that what you ask from your lovers, a contract? A daily log of comings and goings? Well, to hell with that!" Suddenly she shook her head at the floor and muttered again. "Crazy." Quietly, as if she were resigned. "Besides, don't I have any rights to form intimate bonds with friends? This isn't about starting families, you know. This is about having a full life. . . ."

Philippe: "A sailor in every port, in other words."

Annie: "A sexual life, yes."

There was an instant of silence, and Carter stood up, shoulders tense, legs like lead. "Sporadic incidents," he mimicked. It came out as a burst of icy sarcasm. Carter's voice didn't sound kind anymore, even to himself. "Anyway, you could have leveled with us."

Annie: "You want my life, is that it? You want to know my life? Well, there's more to it. You want me to be so damn honest? Let me tell you. I'm not looking to live in a nice little house with a man and a nice little contract. I had that, a long time ago, in my life. It didn't work. After a while he hated me and I hated him. We split. I like men though. You guys both know that. I like relationships and I like sex. They aren't always the same, either. You want the truth? So the truth is, there is another guy back on Earth. Tomas. Tom. He's my number one. You get the idea? I eat vegetables and meat for nourishment and candy for pleasure, you know? You guys are the candy."

She paused, only for a moment. "Wonderful candy. The best. The kind that adds something to your life, you know? At least that's what I thought. But don't give me that twentieth-century crap about how all my attention, all my sexual chemistry and admiration and friendship have to be focused on just one of you. 'Oh, there could only ever be one man for me.' Maybe you guys want to believe that stuff down inside, when it suits you, but you know it isn't true. I thought you were guys that understood something about that. You're both always going on about how this is a new world, a new society. New rules and new traditions. I can see that didn't mean anything!"

There was silence in the little room, and the air seemed thick, like syrup. Annie ran a finger along a rough brown stripe in the bedspread. Suddenly her voice grew quieter. "I happen to care for you guys. I like your freshness, both of you, and intelligence. You wouldn't believe most of the men I meet. . . . And I'm sexually attracted to you. You guys are real to me. I love you. We're doing something important together. I learn from you." She looked at Carter. "That's the way it should be with friends.

"But if you want to know everything, Tomas is my real love. He's the one I go back to. He's who I connect with. It's like psyche to psyche and family to family. He's who I really make love with; who I'll have children with. The fact is, if you're so damn curious, we're married. And we have our own apartment and our own arrangement." She stopped and looked at the floor. "We have our own lives, and I travel all over. We're free, but he's always the one I come back to."

She was still looking at the floor, as if her anger had taken something out of her.

"Oh, that's great, Annie," Carter stammered. "That's great. Nice going."

Philippe said, "And you'll do anything for a story, yes?" He turned and stormed out, slamming the door.

"Carter? . . ." she started.

"I can't deal with all this, Annie. On again, off again, off the record, on the record. What's your game, Annie? I've got enough to deal with at the south pole. I'm not sure I have time to deal with someone I can't . . .

I thought there was something between us. I mean, something, you know, that could last. Trust at least." He stared at her finger still tracing lines on the bedspread, back and forth.

"There *is* trust between us, Carter. Just be open to it."

"I think you better just get out of here, okay?" Carter said. Just go. Go and stay away."

Annie left. She closed the door quietly.

Carter thought to himself: What is she talking about? But he could not grasp his own thoughts. Had something been wrong in those moments when time had crystallized between them? And if so, would he forever be the prisoner of those moments? Was it simply that he was in love with her? Is this, finally, what it meant, being in love? Was it as simple and as biological and as terrible as this?

Carter needed to walk. He walked to his office. Evening was coming on. The hallways, usually bustling with people, were mostly quieting down. Tomorrow was his first trip to the pole, and suddenly he didn't care.

He wondered if he were undergoing some sea change. A new phase. He had been happy on Mars. It was enough, the job and the life around him. He had never felt alone on Mars. Never felt . . . empty, the way he felt now. The very idea of sculpting Mars City out of steel, soil, and people—the very idea had kept him company. He had been happy to fall asleep thinking about energy consumption and temperature control and traffic flow; happy to wake in the morning and take command of his piece of the human mosaic, implement his decisions, and see the people in the office working with him and making little jokes. He knew he had never been as close to them as he was with Philippe, but he had always been happy just to try to keep the rest of the staff—his staff—challenged and excited. And when a project was done, there was a new world full of diversions: going with one woman or another to see the new holeos from Earth; a weekend in one of the so-called Mars Hotel love suites. Or more prosaically, a ride outside to help the geologists in field trips to the vast hazy rim of Valles Marineris or the lava caves of Tharsis. Drinking in the Nix Olympica Bar with the guys from Engineering, or Philippe. Conducting tours for any of the extraordinary visitors who passed through Mars City and wanted to know how it all worked. Once he had spent an evening in the Nix Olympica with Jacqueline Forrest. Her agent had called him up; she was researching a role for a new Nicole Wolff production set on Mars. She said that when they came back to start shooting, she would see him again. That had kept him going for six months, but like most movie projects, it had never materialized. But there was always something new, and someone new.

Women. Mars City was swarming with them. Bright, aggressive, full of life, wanting to love, each in her own way. A hundred women; a hundred ways to love. And he had to pick Annie.

As Philippe had once joked, life was full of surprises, even if they came a year apart. . . .

His life had seemed complete. Now he questioned if he had ever been in charge of anything. People coming into his life on strange terms of their own . . . People staging disappearances . . . In charge? He laughed to himself bitterly. Whose pawn was he? In this skeptical mood, the specter returned of a connection between Annie's appearance and Stafford's disappearance. He tried to think of Annie as some kind of agent, sent to monitor his own progress with the investigation. Whose agent? What was behind Annie's smile? He recalled a line on one of his dad's old disks: Just because I'm paranoid doesn't mean they aren't really out to get me.

It was hard to focus on this line of thought. Annie had made him reassess everything. During the field trips, and more clearly when they had worked together during the weekend on Phobos, she had given a sense of complicity and partnership he hadn't experienced before. Annie had seemed a co-conspirator with him, not a conspirator with someone else. Con-spirator. A good word for a lover.

This was the picture of Annie that had grown in his mind. Reality continued to contradict it. She had been . . . He toyed with a new ego-salvaging fantasy of Annie torn between her impulses. In this desperate picture, Annie remained noble. But another interpreter of the same facts would argue that Annie had turned up in Nix-O to get a story, insinuated herself into the middle of it (first-person journalism, she called it!), and seduced them both, all in order to stay (he smiled coldly to himself) abreast of developments. If there had been a surveillance camera overhead all the time, isn't that what it would have shown? How do you judge purity and sincerity from the bare camera-eye record of facts and actions?

So, Carter thought, after all this, Lena was right. Annie had been using them. You never knew . . .

Which reminded him. The pole. He reached for the phone. He requisitioned a shuttle for the morning. He had purposely waited to the last minute. Give those bastards at the pole, whoever they were, as little warning as possible.

The call forced him to give up theorizing and face Annie's role. All right. Make it three passengers. If this was her game, make her play it.

Was that a reason or another rationalization?

He left the office, walking again just to walk. Into the metal heart of Mars City. As he cooled off, he began to imagine that two years in the future, it would be good to sit down with her and try to get at her thoughts on what had happened. Maybe they could have a friendly talk one day. He would no longer let her use him; but it might be interesting to listen to her try to justify herself. Maybe *he* could learn something for a change. . . .

He gravitated to the Nix Olympica. In the midst of the blue and the chrome, he found Philippe, huddled alone over a drink. He both did and didn't want to talk to Philippe. Through an effort of will he went over and sat down.

Philippe was staring into his blue drink.

Without looking up, Philippe said, "I don't know why the poem talks about Truth and Beauty. Beauty always comes before Truth. First Beauty. Then Truth."

Carter sat down beside him.

Seeing that Carter was making no response, Philippe rambled on. "I went walking. I walked around the construction area, where they're working on the new housing module. When you're inside you can hear all the vibration. All that drilling. I couldn't stand it. I went up to the observation deck. Nobody was there. I lay there on one of the couches and looked out through the dome. As it got dark, Phobos came up and sailed overhead. It was so quiet. Then it went away, and I thought: All this talking and building and organizing we do, it's just a wrinkle on time. Most of the universe's existence is just . . . nonexistence, you know? All that space out there, where nothing is happening." Philippe was staring fixedly into his drink, like a man obsessed. "All that history on Earth when there were no animals and no people, for example. Just wind. Like Mars before we came. And before the big bang, all that preexistence, or whatever it was . . . That's the natural state of things. We're just anomalies. All this shouting and fretting and organizing we do, worrying about things, those are just momentary aberrations, little transitory organizations of atoms, like a cluster of leaves floating in a stream, coming together and making a pretty little pattern for a moment, and then breaking up and going back to a natural random distribution. . . ."

Philippe took a long drink and continued. "You know how life started?"

Carter said, "No," expecting a joke.

"There were all these molecules floating around, and some could form special links with others. . . ."

"I think we ought to talk about Annie. . . ."

"That's what I'm doing," Philippe snapped. "There were certain molecules that had the ability to pick up other atoms arranged along their length, so that when they broke in half, they had created copies of themselves. Pretty soon there were molecules so big that they had structures and could absorb whole pieces of other molecules. . . . And eventually they grew big enough where one could ingest another. . . . But to keep it all going for three billion years, they all still had to send out their half molecules to link up with other half molecules. If they didn't do that, the whole thing would stop in a single generation."

"Annie."

"I *am* talking about Annie, damn it. The only way you get good sex with a woman is to happen to be there when she wants it. All the rest is just . . . posturing." Philippe was still staring at his drink, his second double blue.

Carter wanted to say don't talk to me about sex, but at the same time did not want to say it. "Ah, drinking to forget?"

"Just drinking, damn it. There's nothing to forget."

"Nothing to forget! . . . ?"

"We've been asses, Carter, my friend. We've been—what is the expression?—had. We've been had."

Carter ordered an expensive Martian beer. The people in the greenhouses were recently developing a pretty good home brew in limited supplies. Necessity, the mother of invention.

Philippe and Carter waited in silence for the beer to arrive. "To the friendship of asses," Philippe toasted when the beer came. He guzzled a heavy mouthful. "I really don't want to talk about it," he added.

They stared at their drinks.

"We need to talk about it," Carter said. "Besides, I've been thinking. We ought to patch it up with her. She's expecting to come with us. We can't just sit there in silence. I could exclude her, since it's my own requisition—part of my budget—but, hell. She'd show up anyway. Besides, she's been helpful."

"Helpful to herself. Hell, she has been using us. You don't see that? It's as plain as anything. She gets a good story. An exclusive source or two. A little sex on the side . . . It's a great career, journalism. She's got all her programs running. Talk about manipulation."

Carter stared glumly into his beer. What he was saying was not what he had expected to say. "Suppose it isn't true. I mean, the facts are true but your interpretation isn't. Suppose this doesn't have anything to do with manipulation or sex." My God, Carter thought, where is this coming from? "I mean, suppose it's like an Escher drawing and now you have to look at the fishes instead of the birds. The same set of images, but different pictures . . ."

"Whether it's two plus two or three plus one, it still adds up to four. Why do you make up excuses?"

"Our century's metaphor for reality is a jigsaw puzzle, where each piece is a fact, and once you have all the facts, they fit into one picture: reality. But suppose facts are like mosaic tiles; the same set of facts can fit into any picture you want."

"Philosophy, it is so helpful."

"Philippe, look. Suppose you're making a sculpture of a woman and you have this beautiful model who comes in and poses for you. You like her. You find her intriguing. You take her out to dinner and you end up spending the night and have great sex. Are you using her?"

"No, but . . ."

"And maybe she likes you and she makes a gift of posing for you for a whole Saturday without pay, because she knows she's planning to stay with you anyway, that weekend . . . She's thinking maybe she'll move in with you. Is she using you?"

Philippe shrugged. "There is no way to measure motivation; there are only actions. We have to judge the quality of the actions."

"You've conned her into giving you free time and free sex as well. She's conned you into a place to live. Manipulation, yes?"

"But you are leaving out . . . there is a set of standards. . . ."

"We all keep saying this is a new world. Annie's evolving her own rules as she goes, her own style. She's becoming less of a classic journalist and more of a writer-participant, helping to search for Stafford, and writing about it at the same time. What's wrong with that? She's a good writer. She's reported well and made a balance between reporting the news and keeping our trust about what we've found. I mean, in some detached sense, if you strip away all the old conventions, what's wrong with what she's done?"

"In a job like that, one must avoid even the appearance of conflict of interest."

"You say that because you're hurting and you want to accuse her of something."

He shrugged again. "As you like."

"Of course it hurts. I don't like it either. She should have leveled with us in the beginning, before she started these relationships with us. But human beings haven't figured out how to level about that in ten thousand years. How would you have felt if she said, 'Oh, tomorrow night I'll be sleeping with Carter. Have a good time while I'm away.' "

Philippe downed the rest of his glass.

"Well?"

Philippe snorted. "I think you are missing the point. Down below all the platitudes, human beings are programmed to want to get their DNA together with someone else's. That is what I was telling you. Love is mucous membranes wanting to get in contact with each other."

"All this bullshit of yours is just your defense mechanism, Philippe."

"Animals are just jolly big clumsy ambulatory mechanisms to carry genes around until they can get in contact with other genes. I mean, why do you think teenaged girls act the way they act? I have this niece in London, you would not believe her. Spends the whole day trying on different clothes and arranging her hair. Spends the nights looking for the loudest, most crowded spots. You think *people* are the grand high point of evolution? Wrong. Evolution produces big molecules that have the ability to interlock and split and make more molecules and store little molecular predispositions to make big casings around themselves. The molecules have the ability to make wonderfully complicated casings to carry them around. We're the casings. It's all perfectly . . . normal. None of it matters. I forget what I was saying. I'm drunk, my friend. At last."

"That's all very nice, but what are we going to do with her?"

Philippe ordered another beer. "We just go on. We go test your crazy theory about the pole. You want to take her along, obviously. Okay. Count me in. We let her get her story however she wants. The hell with her. Just watch her. Keep an eye on what she's doing. Better we have her where we can keep track of her than out of our sight writing God knows what. But you should not let her make a fool of you, or me either. Meanwhile, we adjust. New facts take a little getting used to. Flexibility is our middle name, *n'est-ce pas?*" He raised his glass and waved it around the room. "To flexibility."

Carter could get no more out of him.

By the time Carter got back to his room, he was convinced Philippe's version of it was right. Annie had not only insinuated herself into the investigation and wormed information out of them—out of Carter anyway—but by seducing them both, she had consciously tried to insure a maximum number of allies.

The beer helped him decide that he had weathered the worst of hurricane Annie, and that the storm was over. It was a glitch on the side of the larger issue of Stafford's disappearance, and he was lucky to get out of it as easily as he had. There were a dozen other outcomes that would have been disasters. . . . If she had used the information differently . . . If it had come out that they had been lovers while he was covering the investigation . . .

With her along, he would be able to watch her manipulations. . . . Maybe she would even level with him.

Anyway, he would talk to Lena. Without Annie. Lena had been approachable enough before, God knew. Maybe Lena would level with him. Maybe somebody would level with him.

As for Philippe, Carter would be glad to have him along, with his common sense and humor. They had both been conned by Annie; it was time to reconfirm their friendship. Liberté; égalité; fraternité! Philippe was a good right-hand man in any undertaking. Besides, he had been making noises about gathering information on the polar cap, and creating a final sculpture to be installed exactly at the pole. With his Stonehenge and Martian Tree projects in place, Philippe had begun carrying on about a new field he was inventing; planetary art, he had called it.

His 'corder pipped.

It was Annie. "Listen, Carter, I'm sorry. I'm really sorry. I didn't handle it well. I admit it. We've all got to talk. Philippe agreed. There isn't much time."

Of course, she had to ask Philippe first.

He hung up on her and turned off the unit.

All night he hated himself for it.

B O O K 5

The South Pole

Thou art Mars of malcontents.
—William Shakespeare,
The Merry Wives of Windsor, 1600

22

Outside Mars City, the sun came up cold and red in the southeast. Tuesday morning. The red glow crept across the soil-mounded tunnels and observation towers and began to burn the frost off the tiny windows in Carter's office as the sun gathered its heat.

Carter sat alone at his desk. Well, this is it. Funny how clocks and worlds keep turning at constant, uncaring rates, when momentous events are building. The sun rises with monumental unconcern, just as it rose on the day of the Magna Carta signing, or the first day of Gettysburg.

A fuzzy patch of sunlight began to slide down the wall opposite Carter's desk. Show time.

Certainly by now they would know he was coming. He had had to reserve the shuttle the night before. Word would have spread. They'd be getting ready for him, Lena and the rest of them.

It was almost time to head out to the shuttle. He walked over to the tiny window. Through the clearing frost, he could see the shuttle, sitting on the desert landing pad, crouched on its spidery legs, waiting. He looked around his office one last time, feeling like a character in a twentieth-century movie, who should be pulling a gun out of the drawer and sticking it in his belt, hidden by his heavy black sweater. Crazy thought.

It could be a wild goose chase. They could hide Stafford in some underground lab or out in a rover. They could deny everything if they wanted to. If there was anything to deny. Still, he had to have a look around. The pole was exerting some force on him. The magnetic pole.

Those were night thoughts. The rising sun, growing brighter by the minute, cut through the fog. For him, light had always made the night-shadowy shapes of things suddenly more definite. He hoped it would work this time.

Now, in the daylight, the real world was returning. He would have to force the mess with Annie back into its place, like stuffing a sleeping bag into a sack. She had said she wanted to talk. Would she even show up? He would pursue the mission and to hell with her if she thought she could . . . To hell with everything until he found out what had happened to Stafford.

Go down to the pole and see everything with your own eyes. The trick here is to keep those eyes open, be ready for anything.

He headed for the airlock.

He passed the little bistro down the hall from the airlock suiting room, catering to shuttle passengers and still-spacesuited field crews with their helmet collar rings shining around their necks. Coffee and doughnuts on the run. No sign of Annie or Philippe there. Truth was, he wanted to grab Annie and shake her, and find out the truth. He wanted to kick Philippe's ass back into gear, too—make them sit down and formulate a plan. If they showed up. Forget about all the psychological crap going on between them. Time heals, and all that.

All the while, a traitorous voice whispered in his ear: It wouldn't hurt to listen to whatever she might have to say.

More night thoughts. Remember, the sun is rising.

There they were, in the airlock. Philippe suiting up and Annie tinkering with her suit's fittings as if she had just arrived. She looked tense, as if on the verge of saying something, but stifling it.

No one else was in the airlock. They would have the shuttle to themselves. Annie and Philippe began suiting up on a semicircular bench in the corner, busying themselves with the bulky garments. Carter claimed a bench across from them. He wanted to prove he could keep his distance.

Carter kept his face blank but, he hoped, not unpleasant. At least Philippe wasn't smiling that goofy grin of his.

Philippe gave Annie a good-natured nudge. "I told her I was sorry I got angry," he said. "It's just that I was totally unprepared. Besides"—he made his self-deprecatory shrug—"you should never take my anger seriously."

"We should talk before we go to the pole," Annie said quickly, as if trying to wrest the initiative from Philippe. "There's no use being mad at each other down there. We don't know what we'll run into. It could be important to all of us. I'd just like to straighten this out ahead of time, if we can. I need to clear the air, I guess."

"So clear away." Carter hardly felt like being warm.

"This is hard . . ." Annie said.

Carter let himself study her face. No matter what maps he constructed with his mind-words when they were apart, something different happened when he could watch her face. She radiated a capacity for honesty and inner pain beyond anything that he had met before.

Philippe remained silent, as if he had already made his peace.

Annie hesitated, with a look pleading for him to give her an empathetic cue to continue, but terrified that she should lose her place in some carefully rehearsed speech. "Help me," she said.

"Jesus, Annie," Carter blurted. "I look at you, your warm-and-friendly act, I want to believe it, but I find myself thinking, what does she really want?"

"Like Freud," Philippe chimed in. "What do women . . ."

Carter ignored him. "Last night, I was thinking that if we had a magic camera recording us for the last two weeks, I could ask any jury to watch the tapes. You'd have no defense. They'd all say you were just using us any way you can to get your story. You can say what you want, but that's what the tapes would show. Right? Nothing wrong with it, I suppose. You get your story, a little love on the side. It's kind of a blow to see it that way, you know? There's such a thing as feeling used."

"Define 'used.' "

"I can't. I always had trouble with that word. Never really used it before. Now I get the idea what it feels like."

"I've known a lot of men who have trouble with that word."

"Okay. So I've learned something. You're a great teacher."

Philippe: "Don't get holy on us, Annie. You have to see how it seems to us. You have been using us all along to get your story. There's no way to distinguish that from the alternative."

Annie cocked her head to one side. "The alternative. And what is the alternative? You've made a very nice presentation of the Annie-is-a-bitch theory, thank you very much. Now can you also put an alternative into words? Go ahead."

Philippe picked up his fleur-de-lis helmet. "Maybe if I think about it."

"No! Don't lock yourself away in your helmet yet. You think if you get your feelings hurt you can just hide away. Well, it's not fair. Look. I could give you some BS about how you're just getting paid back for centuries of the double standard. But that's not the point. What I'm trying to say is something else. Suppose a woman meets men she likes, and she's attracted. Suppose she's trying to grope her way through life like anyone else. Suppose she's away from home for a long time and she has an arrangement."

"An arrangement."

"You know what Tomas and I do? He's a journalist, too. Wanted six months off from the network for a project he's doing. He's heavy with book. You try to hang around each other with your minds on projects like that, you get on each other's nerves. Maybe you guys don't know. You've never been married. Neither one of you. You don't know what it's like when it stops being just entertainment, and you're actually trying to build something. We want our life together, but we want our own lives, too. I wanted time to be a really good reporter. We decided we'd take our six months apart. We always want each other, thank God. IPN lets us send a message to each other on the network almost every day. I miss him and he misses me. But . . . marriage isn't just the bungalow in the burbs anymore, you know? We decided we were free to see other people. We're convinced we will keep loving each other, so we reached this decision: You can't shut yourself off from the other half of the professionals in the world, the other sex."

"Pretty words."

"It's hypocritical to work with people every day and pretend attractions don't exist. Love between human beings is a wonderful thing. At least it should be. Babies aren't a factor anymore; it's not two hundred years ago. Sexual taboos evolved in agrarian villages, to prevent disrupting society. That's not our problem anymore; lack of connection is our problem now. So why not an occasional human intimacy beyond dry work?

"And there's something else." She was hitting her stride in the speech she must have planned for the previous day. "Tomas and I, we never accepted the old idea that there are only two modes of male-female interaction: cold isolation or screwing. The idea that you're either doing it or not. There are a million levels of intimacy and attraction, a glance, a sharing of words, a thousand ways of touching . . . The three of us, we've shared what we wanted to share and there was no need for you guys to start acting possessive. . . ."

She looked at them despairingly. "Look, I *want* to pursue this story. I *want* to do it in your company. I want to help and I want to report what I see. I'm going to the Polar Station in any case, but I propose let's go as comrades. What do you say?"

"We can't keep you off the shuttle," Carter said. He forced a smile.

She turned to Philippe for confirmation.

"Comrades in arms, so to speak. One for all and all for one." Philippe saluted with a lanky flourish. He really does think everything is a game, Carter thought bitterly. Maybe that's what they have in common.

He was about to say something more, but the pilot came into the suiting room, a tall, wordless chocolate-skinned man who kept looking at his watch. The pilot finished suiting up as if not even thinking about it. He seemed not to notice them. His attitude seemed almost a pretense.

The pilot's presence wrenched Carter back to the reality of the moment. Carter studied him carefully. What did he know? Was he in on some plan? With Lena? With Braddock? With Annie herself? The pilot looked bored. Finally he gave them a nod with a friendly grunt and headed toward the airlock. "C'mon with those suits. Let's get this show on the road."

Philippe finished with his own suit in silent concentration. He adjusted his helmet and headed toward the airlock with the pilot, fumbling with his locking collar. "See you out there," he said as the door sealed behind him.

At least a pilot had showed up. Carter had half expected some delay. Some new excuse. Sorry, the shuttles had to be serviced. We'll take you tomorrow, or Wednesday. The arrival of a pilot meant that whoever was pulling the strings behind the scenes was letting them come. Or would there be some last-minute hold on the takeoff?

Play this by ear. Be ready for anything.

Carter watched Annie sealing up her suit closures. She looked like a ski queen in oversized down leggings. Carter tried to shake off the thought that he enjoyed seeing her in this puffy, cuddly cocoon, the thought of a cozy fireplace in a ski lodge. He had been thinking what he wanted to say to her, going over and over the half-formed questions.

She started past him toward the door, smiling briefly at him. He blocked her way with his arm, pushing her against the wall more roughly than he intended. He was surprised that she made no protest. "Do you just collect men?" When he had rehearsed the question over and over again in his mind, he had never used the word "just."

She closed her eyes and brushed her black hair away from her collar, breathing out a long sigh, almost as if he were not there. "I collect friends. I love Philippe because he loves everything. I love you because . . . you're serious. You're like a well that is very deep, but it's all below ground, and I can't see where it ends." Her eyes were still closed. She might as well have been somewhere else, alone, thinking out loud.

He kissed her briefly, and she opened her lips to him. It was a kiss there was no time for.

Annie noticed that the cargo shuttle smelled of dust and oil. Most of the cocoon seats had been removed and replaced with cubic cartons, snap-locked together three deep and strapped into place. Their three cocoon-like seats were one in front of another, on one side. Annie was in the middle with Carter behind her.

As she clambered into her cocoon in her bulky suit, she had a strange thought that the dust could have no odor until it was brought inside a human habitation. Odor, like sound, could hardly be conveyed through the thin Martian air. Like sound, it needed a richer environment than the Martian surface to come into being. Once liberated in the air and humidity of a shuttle or a bus or one of the bases the varieties of Martian soil took on their own personalities. In the lava regions of Mars, the dust that came inside seemed to take on a pleasant odor like very old wood. Like her grandmother's house overlooking the giant ruins of the deserted Kawasaka theme park in sprawling Kamuela.

Professionally, the last two weeks were the peak of her life. In personal terms, she had made a mess. And her great reconciliation speech had been barely adequate. She still felt the psychic pressure, as though the three of them were silent atomic piles, about to explode if they came too close. At least they were still together. And still on a path toward a solution to the puzzle.

The silence in the shuttle grew more oppressive. Would they never blast off? She glanced back at Carter, who gave her a grim smile. She could see his mind churning. Would he ever just . . . accept her? Would there ever be any sort of equilibrium between them? She could see him trying to formulate some sort of plan. And there was a touch of independence, as if their kiss had liberated him from his sense of loss. She could read it all in his serious, square face. She would have to give both of them this gift of independence before this was all done. This would not be hard for Philippe; but for Carter . . .

She could see that Carter was about to propose something or other when the pilot came on the intercom in a preoccupied sort of voice. "Stay webbed in," the pilot said over the intercom, "it's only a half hour till we're on the pad at the Polar Station." The pilot was above them, in his own pressurized cabin, a sort of bay window protruding from the side of the shuttle. "Okay, let's go," he continued, and the engines cut in, kicking them in the seats of their chairs as if a giant piston had hit the bottom of the ship.

She looked quickly out the window. She had expected to sense more dust spraying out from under the ship, but the concrete landing pad had been swept clean by the comings and goings of countless shuttles. Hellas Base dropped away below them, like a set of tin cans and towers buried in banked soil. Annie caught a glimpse of the tangled cobwebs of tire tracks spreading out from the base itself, and then the whole complex slid out of view behind them. The landscape itself dropped away and she could see the hills along the rim of Hellas, and the cratered desert beyond, where Stafford had disappeared. The ship seemed to rise faster than on the Phobos run. Presently they crossed the Hellas Rim and arced out across the highlands of eroded, empty craters.

Philippe started sketching out the window with his pen. "Always a pen," he had told Annie once. "Then you can't waste time erasing, trying to correct your mistakes. You have to capitalize on your mistakes. Once you have done it, you have learned a lesson. If you correct it, you learn nothing." Interesting philosophy. But now the jolt of acceleration made his tracings erratic. Philippe stared out the window grimly, as if trying to memorize the look of the landscape dropping away.

The raw thunder of the ascent engines was nerve-wracking. Poor Carter, Annie thought, always planning; and now he could say nothing until the engines cut off. She could feel her hair pulling down and straight, due to the heavy acceleration. With great effort she turned to give Carter a look and a smile. He started to say something, gave up in the noise, and touched her shoulder for a moment. The gesture pleased her, and she placed her gloved hand on his. The weight of takeoff pressed their hands together, and then, suddenly, there was only the whir of fans and pumps, and their hands jerked upward as they floated sickeningly upward against their seat belts.

They passed through the tenuous blue layer, and the blackening of the sky settled down on them from above, like Death's dark shadow reaching to take them away. The blue layer contracted into a thin band at the horizon. They coasted on their way to the polar ice fields.

Carter recovered immediately; Annie had still not lost the instinct to fight against weightlessness. Philippe fished for his pen, which had flown out of his hand when the engine cut off, and was drifting and bouncing under the seats.

"We've got to agree how we're going to handle things," Carter began. He was always funneling his strength into a plan. She had him pegged. "Lean your heads in here," he said, "I don't want that pilot listening to us on the intercom."

Philippe pulled his nose up from between the seats and leaned his lanky frame toward them. "Say on, *mon capitaine*. This is when—as you say in your charming phrase—the shit hits the fan."

Annie watched Carter with a mixture of warmth and sad pity, wondering if he were talking partly to fill in the space. Did he have to make an effort, talking so coolly? Perhaps not. Plans always saturated his mind. At least he had captured their attention and kept them from starting another roundtable of mutual sexual politics. "We've got twenty minutes to talk," he was saying. "We should agree on how we're going to handle this.

"They know we're coming, of course, ever since I requisitioned the shuttle yesterday. How they're going to react, we don't know. So I propose two phases. Sort of a good cop-bad cop routine.

"Phase one: we go in there all sweetness and sincerity and concern. Tell them how puzzled we are that the evidence we've turned up suggests the possibility of Stafford being picked up by a hopper, possibly from the Polar Station. We don't know how that could be, but we're checking it out. Want to interview hopper pilots, check the logs, that sort of thing. We don't accuse anybody of anything."

Annie interrupted, "Oh, come on, Carter. If it's a cover-up, we won't find anything."

"Of course. But we're playing for time. Get them off guard. Snoop around. Besides, how do you know some shuttle pilot didn't have a private deal with Stafford? Snuck out in the dead of night and brought him in and hid him away somewhere for some secret project? Who knows what kind of weird deals Stafford might have made down there? Maybe Lena and the rest really don't know anything. So we come in all innocent, like we're assuming nobody knows nuttin'. Act like we're on her side, you know? Let her make the first move. Let's just see how they react. Then, if we're not getting anywhere . . ."

"Phase two," Philippe said. "Lure them outside and cut their air hoses. We make them shit in their suits."

"Well, we turn up the heat. Start asking pointed questions. Annie, that's when you get aggressive. You could be cool in phase one, like you're just tagging along. But phase two, you turn investigative, come out swinging with embarrassing questions. We point out that you've agreed to hold the story while you're working with us on the investigation. But the more we emphasize this, the more we show our strong suit: You're the press, and you're free to start publicizing everything. Bring the networks down on them. In fact, we could even project that we're on their side and you are embarrassing us with our friends.

"While you turn up the heat, Philippe and I watch them squirm. Philippe sleuths around, pretending to sketch or something, but really figuring out what's happening behind the scenes." Carter smiled. "Well, what do you think?"

"You are a devious bastard," Philippe said, applauding. "Very good."

"Considering it's the last minute, not bad," Annie added. "Here I am, Annie Pohaku, your innocent reporter."

"Oh, yeah," Philippe said.

Carter seemed to be warming to his own plan. "We could have a phase three in our hip pockets as a last ploy, where all three of us come down hard on them. I point out that I've got to say something in my final report. If they don't play ball, I tell them I'll turn over all my unresolved questions to Mars Council, with the finger pointing at them. And Annie will be raising the same questions in public. My guess is, we won't have to be too blatant about it. They'd rather come up with some answers than have the Council drag it out of them."

Everyone agreed.

"One more thing. When we get there and we start in with them, let me do the talking, okay?"

"Right."

"Right."

Carter looked relieved.

————————————————————●————————————————————

During the rest of the flight, Annie tried to concentrate on how she would cover this story. Part of her said it would be a simple unfolding of events and she would report it. Another part of her guessed it was not that simple, and smiled inwardly about the ace she had up her sleeve; if things get messy, she said to herself, I can show Carter I'm not just tagging along stealing journalistic scraps from his table.

A hissing sound broke her reverie. Descent. Pumps churning; fluids flowing out of valves. The machine, preparing itself.

She craned to look out the little window. Below them, the polar fog was visible. The craters and stratified cliffs, and the endless polar dune fields, were misty behind a white haze that seemed to hug the ground.

In front of her, Philippe was glued to his window. She turned back toward Carter, with her knees out to one side and her chin on her shoulder. The mission they were on, and the coming confrontation, excited her. She was glad for the friendship of both of these men, but it was Carter who fascinated her, now.

He was looking at her, earnestly. He leaned forward. "Do you want something to exist between us?" he asked.

"Yes." She touched him. Too late to turn back.

"Then try not to hurt Philippe."

"Don't worry about Philippe," she said.

"How can you say that?" he asked.

How could she say that? Instinct. Something about having been close to him.

"I know."

Carter turned to the window. She turned and looked. Below, white flecks on the landscape. Patches of snow, on the south sides of hills and crater walls. White crescents. Snow made Mars look more forbidding, Annie thought. She remembered being afraid of snow as a child, when her parents took her to the top of Mauna Kea for the first time. All that bitterly cold material, burying soil that should be warm and fertile.

Below them, the landscape passed in silence. White patches spread to more contiguous deposits. The landscape was turning creamy white, the color of Martian snow tinged with dust.

Annie was surprised Philippe had said nothing about the snow. She studied him again. He was hunched against the window, the pink radiance making his face glow. He seemed lost, as if in a dream.

Ahead, along the distant horizon, slowly spread the amazing blackness, like a shadow spreading across the polar cap. It was the first time Annie had seen it. The Clarke Project's film of carbon deposits. The black soot that was shot down weekly from Phobos by the planetary engineers in bombs that colored the polar ice black, made it absorb the wan sunlight, changed it to gas, added it to the Martian air. The blackness that made Mars more livable. For better or worse, we're creating the future, she thought.

"Stand by." The pilot's voice on the monitor. "We're comin' in."

"I think that when we get there . . ." Carter started.

"Wait," she whispered. She felt a hundred different feelings twisting and shifting like a mass of kelp in the sea. Some of the strands were hers and some were not hers. She took off her thick suit glove. Of course the pilot wouldn't approve. She slid her arm behind the back of her chair, reaching toward him. "Here."

He took her hand.

"No. Like you did before. My wrist."

He held her wrist, tightly at first, then loosely, circling it and stroking it. She turned her arm back and forth in his grip, breathing heavily. He gripped her arm tightly, against the back of her seat. Insidious warmth spread through her. She threw her head back, closed her eyes, and then pulled her arm away. Maybe she was unbalanced, she thought. She leaned closer to him. "You drive me crazy, you know." Then she returned to the window.

The snow below them was streaked with gray and black, where the wind had carried outlying deposits of carbon. All of the horizon was black now.

Carter was leaning toward her ear. "Annie . . ."

She wanted to give him something more. "I want everything to work out," she said.

"The evil goddess cares about her friends?" he whispered in her ear.

She moved her hand back against his leg. To her own amazement, she seemed perfectly comfortable, cool and warm at the same time. She took her hand away again and put on her glove.

Striped cliffs curved below them, like a model contour map made out of sheets of thick cardboard. The polar sediment deposits. The contours were striped and defined by bands of orange and white, where layers of ice alternated with layers of soil. A billion years of Martian history, neatly ordered by seasonal and orbital cycles. At the base of the cliffs was a broad disturbed area, building modules mounded with dirt, roads leading off across the lowlands, parallel to the cliff faces. The South Polar Station looked lonely.

She cried out and then laughed when the shuttle engines roared to life, punching them down into their seats. The light in the cabin flickered as the shuttle descended through a bright, white fog layer. Below, they could now see a cluster of building modules partly obscured by ground fog and partly buried by fresh dirt. Beyond the buildings, the north-facing cliffs rose out of the haze and glowed rosily in the light of the low sun.

The shuttle balanced on its burning bush of flame for only an instant, and then dropped onto the scorched concrete pad with a heavy jolt, as if their pilot had done it too many times to care about the niceties of a soft touchdown.

Below her window, beyond the scorch zone of the landing pad, Annie could see snow on the ground, glittering in the low polar sun. The odd, slanting light outside was not so much white as glowing with the color of her own flesh. The fog was rising, and the stratified cliffs of ocher soil and pinkish ice were now hidden behind the mist, but the sunlight reflecting from them suffused the whole fog bank with a weird, peach-colored glow. Even the buildings were almost hidden. In the midst of the colored haze, the prefab buildings, protruding from their russet soil berms, were silver-gray cardboard outlines. Heavy construction vehicles were parked at random in the fog. The whole place looked crude compared to Mars City or even Hellas Base.

Movement in the fog. Emerging from the luminous mist in front of the buildings, shadowy at first, then taking gray-blue shape, suited figures moved toward them.

Annie could not identify the figures. No, wait, that had to be Elena's white helmet, marked by its black stripe. Elena and two others, walking out to meet them.

By the time Annie and the others climbed out of the shuttle, an enormous crane already towered overhead and a ground crew was already unclamping pallets of cargo. Annie looked around. She could make out the sun's tiny disk, hanging in the bright sky to the north.

"Hi, Lena." Carter's voice. He was waving.

"Welcome, welcome," Lena's voice said over the intercom. "Are you all tuned in?"

They all gave a high sign. Annie could recognize Braddock's dour face behind the plastic.

"Braddock's here," Elena continued, gesturing. "And this is Doug Sturgis, on our staff." Sturgis also looked grim, from what Annie could see of him.

"What's this?" Carter sounded cheerful. "No brass band? No bus to the airlock? We have to walk? What kind of cheap place is this?"

"Pretty cheap." Elena forced a laugh. "You want the expenses charged to your department?"

In a moment they were walking across the hoarfrost deposit. Annie was startled by the crunch of the ice crystals underfoot, audible through her suit. The crystals sparkled in spite of the diffuse light.

"The ground frost is really early this year." Elena's voice. "Usually it doesn't start forming for a few more weeks. We thought it would be forming later each year, on average, if the Clarke Project is working." She laughed. "There are people around here, they'll tell you the thing is back-firing."

"We were surprised to discover you were all heading down here." Braddock's voice.

"Well, we've got a problem." Carter.

"Let's talk when we get inside." Elena.

2 3

Carter let Lena lead the way from the shuttle toward the base.

Let her have her way at first, he thought.

Sturgis was new to him. A wild card? Sturgis, Sturgis; had he heard that name before?

As they headed away from the shuttle, he watched Annie maneuver into place in front of him, beside Lena. In her puffed suit, out here in the cold, open air, away from the shuttle's forced intimacy, she was inscrutable again. Well, he'd be watching her, too, one way or the other.

His mind raced with conspiracy theories. Now that he was here it was hard to believe in some sort of polar cabal. He glanced ahead at the Lilliputian base, tiny and vulnerable against the frozen wasteland. Oh, sure, a polar cabal.

He studied Annie's puffy figure, in front of him. Did she suddenly look different? A different shade of blue? A different shape?

And Lena. Another puzzle. He realized he'd been wanting to see her.

He felt like he wasn't getting enough oxygen.

———————————————— ● ————————————————

As they unsuited just inside the airlock, Carter was hit by the aroma of the air, so different from the dusty, antiseptic, synthesized air in the shuttle. Some chemical presence—wet paint?

Okay, he said to himself. Pull yourself together. This is it.

He sniffed the air conspicuously. "My diagnosis is that you need to check your air filtration," he said. Lighten the tension.

"We're behind on changing the carbon filters," Lena said defensively. "Carbon shipment was delayed."

She was taking him seriously, for chrissakes. "Delayed? Just call me. Hell, we'll just scrape a new batch off Phobos . . ." Keep joking with them. You've got them off guard.

"Well, actually, the last shipment was bumped for some other stuff. Lab stuff we needed. Urgent priority. But we'll take care of it."

Philippe faked a sneeze, but no one noticed his joke.

"Well, you didn't come all this way to talk about air filters."

"Actually, we did, in a sense. The problem we have, it's a question of clearing the air. . . ."

Lena gestured. "Come up to the conference room."

It turned out to be a utilitarian conference room on the second floor, next to Lena's office. The whole place was utilitarian. Boxes piled in hallways. Scientists never had enough room for their stuff. They passed through her office on the way. It wasn't the only access to the conference room, but Carter had the impression she wanted to show it off. It was cramped, smaller than his own. A spectacular Navajo rug covered most of the floor. Must have cost a bundle to ship that here, Carter thought.

She caught him looking at it. She laughed freely. "My one extravagance. Spent a summer at the USGS in Flagstaff just after your market crash. The ruble exchange rate was fantastic. I could have bought one twice as big. Used up a third of my weight allowance to bring it here. But then, I didn't have much else to bring in those days. I was starting over. Navajo rugs are about the same mass as husbands, but harder to throw away."

They were sizing each other up, Carter thought. A lot of fencing.

Several boxes of microdisks marked DATA and another marked AC-COUNTING sat on a wall shelf. The boxes looked dusty. The screen of Lena's terminal was glowing, but blank. The disk lying beside it was labeled ORGANIC ANALYSIS. Carter noticed Annie looking at it. She looked up. Their eyes met, firing question marks at each other.

In the conference room, Annie felt uncomfortable. The room was cramped. There was a Velasquez window on the wall opposite her, behind Elena—a narrow but spectacular vertical slit that rose from the floor and curved partway across the arch of the ceiling. They took seats around a scratched plastic table. Annie kept finding herself staring out the window, wishing she had surveyed the outside landscape before taking a seat. Looking outside from a warm room was different from being outside, vulnerable in your suit. She needed to get down every impression about this place. Lena, across from her, blocked the view of the surface. But she could see the pale sky, a veil of pink fog, somber but beautiful.

Elena forced a smile at Carter. "So?"

Under the pretext of fishing out a notepad and pen, Annie switched on the high-gain recorder she had clipped to the inner edge of her bag. She sat very still. There was something unseen passing through the room, like radiation of some undiscovered wavelength.

Carter looked tense. She knew that look so well now. His muscular body looked poised to spring from the chair. He was trying not to think about her. He hadn't looked at her since their eyes met a moment before, in Elena's office. Organic analysis.

"What did you say you do here, Sturgis?" Carter asked.

"Communications. It's Doug. Doug Sturgis." Sturgis was an interesting-looking sort. He had a rectangular face, strong but bland, and very short hair, hardly more than stubble. He wore pants with bright blue suspenders over his white shirt, a mode that had been popular in the twenties. On one finger was a heavy ring, probably from some university. He had tiny, bright eyes. His bland face and a peculiar indoor quality of his skin made it hard to guess his age; perhaps it was thirty-five. Maybe forty. He looked as if he was made of vinyl. "By the way, speaking of communications, you'll have to turn that off, Ms. Pohaku. That recorder you hid away."

Annie flushed and reached into her bag. Damn. She knew he had not seen her. He had sensors in here that could detect her equipment. This was going to be trickier than she had thought. "Sorry," she said. "Force of habit."

"And I'd prefer no one take any notes," Sturgis added, with an over-innocent smile. "For the moment, at least."

Who was this guy? Annie watched everything. She felt detached. Now she had to become a giant recorder herself.

Carter turned to Elena. "We have a sensitive problem here," he said. "Maybe we should discuss this with you privately."

Elena looked as tense as Carter. "It's okay." She gestured around the table. "Everybody here's involved. Administratively."

"Same among us," Carter said. "My friend Philippe's been helping me get material for my report . . ."

"Good chance to see Mars," Philippe chimed in.

". . . and you know Annie here has been helping us, trying to cover the story at the same time. Win-win and all that."

"Not much to report so far," Annie contributed.

As if to be helpful, Sturgis got up and returned a moment later with glasses of water for everybody. "We don't have a lot of luxuries to offer down here," he said apologetically.

Carter continued. "You understand, I'm under orders from the Council. I'm coming to a dead end, almost, trying to understand what happened to Stafford. Actually, it's not a dead end, but an unexpected end. We're hoping you can help us."

"Of course. If we can," Elena said, smiling.

If only I could describe that smile in words, Annie thought.

"The trail led us here. We think there may be some clues here, might shed light on what happened."

"Clues?" Lena said.

"Let me list some of my findings; see if you don't agree. For instance, we all remember Stafford's dune buggy out in the desert." He looked intensely at Sturgis. Annie observed that Sturgis was glaring back. A nice male turf battle. "Don't know if you heard about it, Doug, but Stafford had piled up a rock wall blocking the view of his buggy, as well as putting a cover over the thing. To my eye, he had planned to leave the buggy there, and he deliberately concealed it. That's fact number one."

"Hardly a fact," Braddock broke in. "An interpretation maybe. But even when we were standing there looking at it, there wasn't any proof of what Stafford intended. If he had already encountered strong winds, he would have tried to shield it when he went out on foot. That might explain why he drove into that cinder cone, too."

"Okay, let's call it an item. We have a chain of items here. The second item is that on the night after Stafford arrived at the crater somebody landed a hopper just outside the crater wall and then took off."

They were all silent. Lena fingered her glass of water and glanced at Sturgis, whose face was growing darker.

"Now that sounds like an interpretation if there ever was one." Braddock again. "You want to talk about how you drew that conclusion?"

"Sure. Orbital imagery."

"What kind of orbital imagery?"

"For the moment, let's just leave it that I've been looking through the data banks with special techniques."

"You don't have an image of a hopper sitting there."

"I don't think there's anything in my mandate from the Council that says I have to tell you what kind of image I have." Carter was smiling and cool; Annie had to hand it to him. "Look, Lena, this is a delicate situation. I don't . . ."

"Hell, Lena." Braddock looked as foul-humored as Sturgis. "He comes in here talking about hoppers and he's got no data to back him up . . . I've got other things to do than . . ."

"Calm down. Let's hear him out."

"But you've got no hard proof?" Sturgis asked. "Hard-copy images to lay in front of us?"

Carter shrugged noncommittally.

Philippe butted in. "Carter's analysis of the images led you to the buggy of Stafford. That was hard evidence."

Sturgis glared.

"And then there's item three," Carter continued. "Where's the only base on Mars that can reach Stafford's site with an unaccounted-for hopper?" He paused. They looked at each other. "Right. We're sitting in it."

"How do you know it was a hopper?" Braddock said. "If you've just got orbital imagery, how do you know it wasn't a cargo shuttle? If a shuttle was really out there, it could have come all the way from Mars City."

"Unlike the records up here, the records at Mars City are quite precise when it comes to shuttles. I've checked them. No large vehicles flew out in the time frame we're talking about." Carter sat for a moment with no expression. "Look, do you agree that *if* a vehicle landed out there near Stafford's buggy, and *if* it was a hopper or a bigger ship, we could go out there and distinguish which was which from the blast marks and the imprints?"

"You're saying you've got evidence that a hopper landed somewhere near that crater we visited?" Braddock paused. "I mean apart from where my crew landed?"

"Let's just say I can prove there was another landing."

She had to admire Carter's handling of it. He had Braddock just where he wanted him. Braddock couldn't really deny it without revealing that he recognized the one way the original landing marks could have been destroyed—by having his own ship land on top of them.

"Sounds kind of vague."

"Let me put it to you straight: Somebody flew a hopper out of this station and picked him up. I've chosen to come to you direct and get your help. Now we can resolve this together. Did somebody fly out of here without you knowing? Is that possible? Can we check the records? Can I interview your pilots? I want to find out what's going on. I'm sure you do, too. I know I'm taking up your time, but let's work together on this. What do you say?"

Elena stood up and gazed out the window with her back to them.

"Oh, my God, it's snowing."

They jumped up from the table and crowded around the window, pressing against each other like kids.

"It's never happened this early since we've been here," Elena continued. "And usually it only happens closer to the pole."

Outside, Annie could see myriads of tiny crystals wafting out of the sky. Suddenly, out of view, the sun must have come out from behind the fog. The crystals were transformed into a million sparkles, a parade of shiny confetti.

Carter moved to the window, followed by Philippe. Only one at a time could stand close to the heavy glass for a good look.

As they took turns, Annie joined them. The dry, crystalline snow lay on the soil in windblown swirls, making a magical landscape of vanilla ice cream and orange sherbet. Opponents, suddenly united by magic. She made a mental note.

Braddock and Sturgis went back to their seats, as if the snow were beneath their dignity. Finally, the group at the window turned back toward the table, self-consciously.

"I think we can work together," Elena said, finally. She had remained standing.

"So what can you tell us?"

"Look," she said, "you've brought us some disturbing news. Give me the rest of the day to make some inquiries while you see the station and settle into your rooms. Okay? We'll meet again in the morning. First thing."

"You know how important this is, don't you, Lena? You understand the gravity of the situation. Maybe we're past the stage where Stafford's life hangs in the balance, but we don't know that. And I need to wrap up my report. I want it to show your complete cooperation, of course."

"Don't worry. It's just that, well, I don't know how to react to your accu . . . your assertions. I can't really give you any answers now. I mean, I don't know what else to say. I can respond better when I get some more information." Seeing the look of anger settling on Carter's face, she added, "We'll get you some answers."

"Give us the run of the station, to do some interviews."

"We'll be happy to give you a tour. As soon as you settle in. You can ask questions as you go. Meanwhile, let me start right now to do my own digging. As director, I'd like to ask some questions around here myself. We can agree on that plan, can't we?" They were fencing again, Annie noted to herself.

"What about the run of the station?"

"Look, you're really putting me on the spot. Nobody has ever just arrived and been given the run of the station. There's a lot of sensitive equipment here. Everybody goes through a training period. You've got to grant me the courtesy of following our normal procedures." Touché.

Carter shrugged. "I might be able to get authority from the Council to do what I want. But for the time being, we're your guests. So we don't have much choice, do we?"

"No. You don't," said Sturgis quietly. He was smiling at them with his bland face. The smile looked out of place.

24

The meeting was breaking up. Carter seethed quietly as the snow continued to fall outside. Another delay. Finally, Lena ushered them from the conference room, through her office and down hallways past labs and storerooms with windows of various sizes. The windows offered glimpses of the polar world outside. The ground had turned entirely crystalline, a sparkling creamy white. The snow was not thick and lush, as during a winter storm on Earth. It did not drape the landscape with a fresh blanket. Rather, it was dry and spartan, the sort of snow that might blow through an open door into a deserted ballroom after a revolution, blending with crystal chandeliers and glinting silver candelabras. The snow frosted the rocks and sand drifts, and seemed to condense on the surfaces of the chartreuse tractors, camouflaging them into the grainy pale landscape. The sky was still white with fog, and the horizon vanished into the mist.

First, Lena showed them the cramped, colorless cafeteria, but it was still an hour before noon. "Come back up here for lunch," Lena told them. Then they headed toward their rooms. Carter was amazed when Lena asked, "You have a contract number we can charge the rooms to?"

It wasn't an unreasonable question, just out of place, like asking about casket expenses during a funeral. He swallowed his impatience and explained to her that the Council had set up a specific account for the investigation.

Down two flights of stairs they were given three tiny rooms in a row: Carter, Philippe, Annie. The rooms were hardly more than cubicles. Small table, mirror, closet, bed. Bare metal and Martian ceramics. Showers and toilets were at the end of the hall.

Lena left them. "I've got to talk about all this with my people." Carter stood at his door and watched her disappear down the hall. Cold. Professional. Not a private word to him.

After she disappeared up the steps at the end of the hall, Philippe and Annie popped out of their doors.

"What do you think?"

"She's stalling."

"Stonewalling. Who the hell is Sturgis?"

"Let's meet in half an hour for lunch. Talk about it."

The privacy of the room seemed to give Carter his first chance to think. No ideas came.

He tried to reach Lena by 'corder, but her machine said she was out. No return message arrived. When they started up the stairs to the cafeteria, a young man materialized to lead them. With a smile, he introduced himself as a research assistant.

"What sort of research you do?" Annie asked him.

"Sedimentology. Working on the ages of the sediments. The whole cap is layered, you know."

When they arrived at the cafeteria, the man left them.

"Obvious sheepdog," Annie said.

There was no sign of Elena, Braddock, or Sturgis.

"I tried to go out and look around after we went in our rooms," Philippe said. "But you can't leave the hall without picking up an escort. 'A guide,' he called himself. He said we should not go anywhere; he would take us around after lunch."

They dawdled over hearty soup, served by a cheerful cook.

"You know what impresses me . . . a lot of construction equipment outside the windows," Philippe said.

"Exactly what research are they supposed to be doing here?" Annie asked. "Run that by me again."

Carter explained. "The basic idea is that the geology and environment at the pole is very different from most of the planet. In the polar ice cap, you have this huge concentration of frozen water and in wintertime frozen CO_2. Under the seasonal cap, you also have layers and layers of stratified sediments, brought in by summer dust storms, deposited between the layers of frost. In fact, the winter snowflakes condense on the dust particles lofted into the atmosphere by the summer storms, so the dust particles get carried to the ground at the poles and packed into the sediment layers. They're really thick. The strata show ancient climate cycles, like tree rings. Periods of lighter or heavier depositions. People used to think the old sediment layers would be the best place to look for traces of ancient life. They were thinking about the water on the edge of the polar cap; some of it melts in the spring. Of course, they never found much, except for Stafford's layer of enhanced organics and microbes. But that was the original motivation for the Polar Research Station."

"So that's why she might have been doing organic analysis on samples? That disk, in her office . . . ?"

"I was surprised by that, too. I didn't think they were doing much of that anymore. But they still do a lot of excavating, to reconstruct the ancient climate cycles. That's why all the construction equipment. One of the headaches of my life, all the stuff they want shipped down to the pole."

The afternoon was taken up with a meaningless tour of the base, with an anonymous underling telling them pointless facts about the history and function of different labs. Lena was nowhere in sight. It was as if everything was on hold. At dinner they were given their own table; they could only agree that there was not much they could do.

When they got back to their rooms, Philippe put on a broad American accent to imitate the guide. " 'Chem lab's down that way, but I'm not authorized in there so I can't show it to you.' " He grimaced in disgust. "Right."

At nine there was a soft knock on Carter's door. Exhausted from frustration, Carter had been lying alone, trying to think what to do tomorrow; thinking of Annie. The knock startled him with guilty pleasure. I knew she'd come, he thought.

It was the smiling "guide" who had taken them to dinner. "The boss wants to talk to you."

Lena was waiting for him in her own room. The room was only a little bigger than the cubicle he had been given. On one wall, over a tiny couch, she had a giant orbital photo of the southern polar cap in summer—it was like an abstraction, white spiral on ocher rust. One wall was covered makeshift shelving. Among the oddments, he noticed a beautiful and ancient Russian icon, with its painted, bearded Jesus surveying the room. There was a data cube, labeled in Cyrillic print: Novels of Dostoevski. And a couple of old Korennova novels in thin-paper flight editions. She had time to read? A small black enameled Russian wooden vase with a design of flowers. It reminded him of his home, when he was a boy. Why did she bring all this stuff all the way to Mars? Fragments of a life. People bring what is important to them.

Lena smiled at him as he took in the details of the room. She wore a zippered jumpsuit, a favored garment of Martian field researchers. It was a striking black, open at the neck, and set off her auburn hair.

"I knew you'd come," she said. When the door was closed she reached out and gave him a little kiss on the mouth. "I've been wanting to see you again."

He returned the kiss but then held her by her upper arms.

"What's up, Lena? What's going on?"

She put her hands on his chest, as if to push him away, but still he held her by her upper arms. For a moment her expression seemed clouded by a flicker of exhausted defeat, but then she was smiling again.

"We've got your curiosity up . . . ?" It was a hollow attempt at teasing.

Her playfulness angered him. "Talk." He gave her a little shake.

"A tough guy, eh? Are you being Bogart? You should have said, 'Talk, sweetheart.' "

He didn't feel like joking. Philippe could have pulled off some wise-crack, reacting to that. In Carter, only anger rose. "Come on, Lena, stop bullshitting me."

She twisted from him and backed away. "Carter, I want to straighten everything out. I want to be your friend. But there are some big issues here. I'm not totally at liberty . . . It's hard to talk."

Like a wolf cornering prey, he pushed after her, stopping just short of violence. He backed her toward one end of the room.

"All right," she said firmly. "Don't make trouble. Sit down." She gestured to the little couch. He noticed that the huge orbiter photo of the polar cap had a tiny blue enameled pin stuck outside the white spiral, marked SOUTH POLAR RESEARCH STATION. She sat on the bed facing him. "Really, don't be angry. We've got to be allies."

"What d'ya mean you're 'not at liberty'? Mars is open. That's the whole concept of Mars City and Phobos University. 'Common scientific resource . . . ' Do you want me to call the Council into this?"

"Listen. I can explain it to you better if you tell me more of what you know. Then maybe I can fill in some pieces."

"What I know! I told you what I know. In your little conference. In front of everybody. Now you drag me down here and . . ."

"I thought you'd like seeing me again."

Carter waved his hands ineffectually. "Come on, Lena. This is serious. I was sent to get information from you. Instead, you're pumping me."

"You weren't sent. It was your idea to come."

"I have a mandate to figure out what's going on."

"Okay. Look. We're concerned about your . . . about Annie Pohaku. I didn't want to start going into some of the delicate issues in front of a reporter. That was a hell of a thing to do, bringing her here."

"Why not? You can't just go out and find idle hands in Mars City, you know. She and Philippe . . . they make a good team. And she gets a story out of it. Besides, for now she's sitting on it. So if it's a matter of timing . . ."

" 'She gets a story out of it.' You're still very naive."

"Why? What's she done that caused you any problem?"

"How am I supposed to make any decisions with a damn reporter hovering around." She looked vaguely off to one side. "It really makes me angry," she added, as if to herself.

"Why? You got something to hide? You know damn well, you get a reporter involved, everybody starts posturing to look good. Nothing is normal."

"That's the way it was on Earth, maybe. Not here. There's a different attitude on Mars, maybe because we're still so new and there're so few of us. It's like, we're all . . ."

". . . all in this together. I hear that all the time. What a bunch of romantic crap. We've got beyond that stage now. Look. I want to keep Annie Pohaku out of this. If we have a meeting tomorrow to talk about your report, she stays out."

"You can't do that. From the earliest days of Phobos University, the press has a right to attend all meetings here. The funding statutes—you know, open scientific research. There's no way you could keep her out. She'd have us over a barrel."

"There are some special considerations here. I'm getting conflicting advice. Look, I'm appealing to you. I'm really caught in the middle. There are circumstances here that you don't know about. They probably override the funding statutes."

"What are you talking about? How can you 'override' statutes?"

"Besides," she ignored his question, "you know how the press is."

"How is the press?"

"They'll twist anything you say. You're at the mercy of their personal slant. They can make you look like a leech. Especially when you have a delicate situation you're trying to keep quiet."

"Damn it, Elena! I don't have to listen to you insulting Annie. Are you going to talk to me or not?"

"Damn it yourself, Carter! You come swooping in here with your little reporter in tow, ready to accuse us of God knows what, and then you insult me for not being polite. It's you that owes me an explanation of what's going on."

The word "little" stuck in Carter's mind. The adjective that women apply to other women they view as competition. "Is it Annie you're upset about, or some secret you're trying to hide? Let's just forget it, Lena. Jeez." Carter got up to go.

Elena sprang to her feet. "Wait, Carter, I'm sorry." She put her hand on his arm, but he shook it off. He kept his other hand on the doorknob. "Maybe I am a little jealous. Who wouldn't be?" A pretty compliment. "But that's not the main thing here."

"What is the main thing here, Lena?"

She said nothing.

"At the beginning, this looked like a tragic accident. But now Stafford's gone and it's snowballing into something . . . I don't know what, and you're not helping me. I've got a commission from the Council to investigate it and make a report. What have you got?"

"I want to help you, Carter. Stay with me tonight. Talk to me."

There were tears welling up in her eyes. My God, Carter thought.

"Just tell me what's going on, Lena."

Philippe, sitting in his room after dinner, had felt useless during the whole trip. Carter had asked him for help; all he had done was tag along, saying "yes" and "no." Why had he really come? Was it just his private motivation: the chance to see the ice fields of the south pole for the first time, the chance to sketch out ideas while the others scurried around . . . ?

And what was the point of that? Once, he had invented a questionnaire for himself. The main purpose of my art is: (a) to show off, (b) to contribute something to society, (c) to earn a living, (d) to relieve a psychological compulsion, (e) I haven't the foggiest idea. He wondered why the answer was (e). What would Rodin have said, or Pericles? Had his heroes felt as ordinary and confused as he did?

Well, he was no more naive than Carter, with his American ideas of open societies and noble cities motivated by science. So here they were and now Carter was stuck, hitting dead ends as he explored his formal channels, probably with Annie at his side. No, he had promised himself not to obsess about Annie. At least he had his art to fall back on, to fill the vacuum she had created.

Philippe looked at his watch: 9:00 P.M. local time. So, now was the time for action. He was the only one who could dare to prowl about on his own, and dig up . . . something. As Carter said, if anyone stopped him, he could always play the innocent artist. That was one benefit of being a creative person. No one took you seriously.

His own suspicion was that everyone here had something to hide. He could see it in their eyes. Something about this place, it was not normal. He could imagine the whole place being bugged and monitored, like the hotels in Washington in the mid-twenties.

He was about to open the door of his room, when he heard Carter's voice in the hall. Opening his door a crack, he could see one of Elena's goons—the "guide" he had talked to earlier—taking Carter off down the hall. "The boss wants to talk to you," the goon said.

Philippe watched them through a crack in the door as they headed up the steps. Here was his chance. He was pretty sure he could find his way back to Elena's office. It was late; nobody was around. Maybe . . . Surely it wouldn't be open.

What would he need? He grabbed his sketch pad. Where was the mini-cam that he always carried on trips? He rummaged through the side pockets of his little bag. Where had he packed the damn thing?

Suddenly he again heard noises in the hall: a knock next door, and voices. Listening once again at his own door, he discovered that the goon had already returned, to escort Annie off to some meeting. ". . . wants to talk to you." He didn't catch the name. Through the cracked door he watched them disappear in the same direction that the goon had taken Carter.

Philippe figured he was next. He peeked out. This time another goon was far down the hall to the right, back to him, talking in hushed tones on an intercom. If he could slip out and up the steps before the man turned around . . . The hell with the camera.

Blindly, he slipped up the steps, back through the dim hallways, past the storerooms and labs, toward Elena's office and the conference room. Outside the windows the wan sun was riding low along the horizon, and the gloom of foggy polar late-summer twilight was settling in. There was still a thin snow in the air; snow falling had always been a staple of pretty Christmas-card scenes on Earth, but here, it took on an ominous quality, like the volcanic ash falling prettily on San Francisco. . . .

Ahead, he could hear voices. The conference room. Elena's door was open. Her office was dark, but flickers of light and conversation spilled into the hall, punctuated by restrained laughter.

Philippe edged closer, and stuck his head cautiously into Elena's door, trying to keep a nonchalant expression on his face in case he blundered into someone. I'll just tell them, he thought, "Sorry, didn't know I wasn't supposed to . . ." People would accept any bullshit from someone they classified as an artist. He opened the sketch pad and pulled out his pencil.

The voices in the conference room were growing heated. No one would be coming out soon; they were too involved. Philippe stepped into Elena's darkened office, and slipped into the darkest corner. The door into the conference room was ajar, but blocked his view. Light spilled into the far side of Elena's office, across the bright red and black of the Navaho rug. He had followed his nose, but he did not dare stick it around the door. He stood in the shadows to listen, Jim Hawkins in the apple barrel.

"We can't send them back to Mars City." It was Sturgis. "God, there's no telling what they'd say. Have everyone down here for sure."

"Well, you can't just shoot them." A second male voice. "Can you?" The speaker laughed.

"God damn it, this is serious. We need more time. They don't realize what they've blundered into. You know what I hate about people like them? They're so damn ignorant about the real world. Can you imagine him threatening us with the Council? As if a bunch of corporate contractors would back him up. We can get to their CEOs, you know. You don't have to worry on that score. But it's better to keep this from getting any messier than it is. Somehow we've got to make them give us more time."

"Annie Pohaku's the one you have to watch."

"Oh, hell, she's a zero. She's a starry-eyed cub. Real reporters in Washington, they send people like her out to get their lunches."

"She's plugged in. She's got a whole network behind her for chrissakes."

There was a pause. That seemed to stop Sturgis.

"Maybe Lena can talk some sense into them." A third male voice. Was it Braddock? No, not Braddock. One of Sturgis's underlings. "Lena ought to be able to wrap Carter around her little finger, he's such a little shit. When Lena gets done with him, he'll volunteer us more time, out of the goodness of his heart."

"It's all Romero's fault," Sturgis went on. His voice grew angrier and angrier. "If she hadn't botched her simple little assignment in the Phobos photo archive, Jahns wouldn't even be here. Not to mention Pohaku."

"Carter's not so bad." Still another male voice; was it familiar? "He's prudent. We may just have to level with them, you know. Don't get excited. Lena can put it to them, explain the situation."

"Oh, fuck the situation," Sturgis said angrily. "A good piece of the world order may be at stake here. I'm supposed to be responsible for security; first I get forced to depend on Romero, who screws up everything, and now you tell me I have to depend on Trevina. People like that will blow everything wide open if we're not careful."

"Oh, don't get so grandiose. Might be interesting to see how this all turns out." The other voice gave a sarcastic laugh. "Besides, you need to learn, even you can't control everything."

"God damn it, it's not funny, Stafford."

A message machine beeped. "Hey, Doug. We can't find Brach. He's not in his room."

"Oh, shit," Sturgis said.

In Elena's room, Carter sat as Elena paced back and forth, pulling herself together too easily. "Sorry, Carter. I can't tell you much yet." She stopped behind her little table, as if for protection, hands spread on its surface. She was cool now.

"Can't, or won't?"

"Won't. Not yet."

"What do you want me to say in Mars City?"

"Carter. You're a good person. Give us time. We're trying to decide how to handle this, now that you've blundered into it. We'll meet again tomorrow. I was hoping to talk some sense into you tonight."

"Handle what? For chrissakes, Elena."

Her shoulders slumped slightly. "Everything. I didn't know what this job was going to lead to when I took it. I think they're right, though, the people who say that some science is too important for scientists to handle. With you here, everything is more difficult. We don't want a lot of attention drawn to what's happening here. That's what I want to get across to you. Do you think you could just trust me on that?"

"Draw attention?"

"You're good, Carter, but you're naive. We're all naive, I guess. Anyway, you don't see the big picture. You don't see what's really important."

"Maybe I would if you'd talk some sense."

"I'm not going to talk anymore tonight. I've said enough already." She laughed, and her eyes burned into his. "Poor Carter. We've all got our problems. It isn't going to be easy for me, this mess you've made. Tomorrow we've got a meeting scheduled at ten. We'll try to work it out with you. But for now, come on. Stay with me tonight. Let me show you I'm not such a bad person."

Carter rarely turned down such an invitation. But tonight he felt tempted only by the chance to gain information. Who was exploiting whom? "Sorry. Maybe we'll make a date after you tell me what's going on."

She slumped perceptibly.

"Can I go now, or do I have to wait for my warden?"

She pressed a button on her terminal. "Your escort is on his way." Her face was harder now.

When he was leaving, she said, "Be careful, Carter, you could ruin everything."

What the hell was that supposed to mean? Carter decided he wasn't cut out for mysteries. Besides, he was sick of people telling him he was naive.

●

When Carter reached his room, he found that Annie and Philippe had left a message on his machine. COME TO ANNIE'S ROOM. NEWS. ANNIE & PHILIPPE.

Annie's room was just like Carter's. Philippe's gangly frame was sprawled on the bed. He jumped up when Carter came in. Annie sat in the chair by the desk.

"I have seen the holy ghost!" Philippe said. "He's here!"

"Who? What are you talking about."

Annie just sat there, grinning.

Philippe slid onto the table, pulling his feet up in front of him and wrapping his arms around his knees. He looked over the tops of his knees with a mischievous grin. "Stafford!"

"Here?" Carter found himself leaning against the wall in the corner by the door, as if he had been blown over. He was surprised at his own reaction; he had told himself that's what they would find.

"Here. Alive."

"You saw him? You're sure?"

"Well, I did not actually see him. But I heard him. I heard them talking to him. Finally they used his name. Certainly it was him." Philippe described how he had crept out for a reconnaissance. "I got out just in time. Almost got picked up in the hall on the way back here. I managed to hide in a men's room if you can believe that."

Carter turned to Annie. "You saw this, too?"

Annie explained that she had been invited out for a talk. "I had the dubious pleasure of chatting with Braddock," she said.

"Now, we are one step ahead of them," Philippe said.

"Unless they've got this place bugged," Annie said, looking around.

"Oh, I think we can count on it," Philippe said. "Of course, I do not know, but I make that assumption. But now, you see, it does not matter. We are getting at the truth. How do you say it, we have got the goods on them. The bastards." He looked up at the ceiling. "Did you hear that, Mr. Sturgis? Bastards."

"Oh, come on," Carter said. "This is just a little dump of a research station. They don't have bugs in . . . I mean, I'd know."

"Wake up, Carter," Annie said angrily. "Don't you know how easy it is to bug a whole complex?"

Philippe smiled, pleased with his discovery. "Annie's right. We have some ponderous fecal matter going down here. You can't keep pretending everything is normal. They can't either." He looked up at the ceiling again. "Right, Sturgis?"

"Talking to Braddock wasn't much fun," Annie said, more relaxed.

"Why? What'd he do?"

"Nothing. I just don't like his attitude. They divide us up and interrogate us one at a time, like suspects. It's the classic police ploy. The whole thing is incredible."

"What'd Braddock want to know?"

"What we knew."

"What'd you say?"

"That you had already told them what we knew, this afternoon."

"Did you say anything about the pic . . ." Carter stopped and looked around the room.

After an awkward pause, Philippe said, "Go on." He looked at the ceiling again. "We're not telling them anything they don't already know. Hey, Sturgis," he yelled at the ceiling, "we got lots of really interesting pictures, just waiting to be published." He whispered to Carter as an aside, "I don't really think it's bugged, but then you never know."

"Annie, did Braddock say anything about Stafford?"

"No."

Carter turned to Philippe. "What about you? Did you overhear anything to explain what's going on."

"No. They were pretty upset. They kept talking about needing more time, about keeping us here. Stafford said maybe they should come clean, but Sturgis didn't want to."

"Wait. Stop," Annie said, standing. "Stand up. Come here."

Blank stares. They got up.

Annie was smiling. She walked between them. "What's the matter with you guys? Stafford is alive! I want to see some smiles." She hugged them both in a wide embrace.

When they had finished talking, Annie made a show of ushering them both out at the same time.

Carter lay in his bed, pondering.

So. Was the story nearly over?

He had a sudden and depressing vision of his Mars City, which he thought he knew, as a hollow facade. The pioneers of Mars had been scripted into unknowing roles, storyboarded by people who understood "what was really important." He and his friends had been struggling ignorantly in the red dust while the puppet masters' laughter resonated all the way back to the spinning cabarets and green resorts of Earth.

Stafford, alive? He could close the book. Hand in his report. Be done with it. Settle things with Annie. Maybe go back to Earth. A real planet, crowds, decay, and all that. But what would he say about the polar plot to cover up Stafford's movements? Would they even allow him to hand in a report?

Why hadn't Elena and Sturgis come pounding on the doors, demanding to know where Philippe had been? They must be caucusing to figure out what to do next. And what about Annie's role? Would there be some new moment of revelation with her, when she told them her next secret? For the first time he was beginning to feel immune to her secrets, like a patient inoculated with small doses of a dangerous pathogen. Still, he could never believe that she was a complete fraud. Not after . . . what? Loving her? Being in love with her?

There were two shows going on here, simultaneously. He realized he didn't know which was the main show in his life. Annie? Or Stafford and his disappearance.

Annie's most outstanding characteristic was the level of concern she radiated. ("You were sincere, you just weren't honest." Philippe's words came back to him.) Anyway, Philippe's theory—that she was just using him to get at her story—still nagged at him whether he believed it or not. In fact, whether *she* believed it or not.

But the more important thing, as usual, was tomorrow. His mind kept toggling back and forth between his mission and his feelings. One thought would block out the other. He would have to live with his doubts about Annie for the time being, he told himself. He would have to focus his concentration on the problem of Alwyn Stafford and Elena Trevina and Doug Sturgis, and how they all fit together.

The image of Elena drove a new thought into his mind. So, Lena was the one who had used him, used sex to get close to him. What had she said during their night together? What had she asked him? He had to admit to himself that he couldn't remember much of it. That whole night, his heart hadn't been in it. A sorry admission.

What if . . . What if Elena's friendliness was all a ploy, and what if Annie had been sincere all along? What if he and Philippe had been wrong about her, in the heat of their jealousies? He tried to picture her as genuinely drawn to both of them, with her real lover a hundred million kilometers away. For that matter, what if Annie and Elena had both been sincere, had both been ordinary human beings coping with existence one day at a time. He drifted toward sleep with his mind in confusion, hoping dimly that the light of day would clear away the uncertainties.

25

Ten A.M. They gathered in Lena's conference room. Carter, Annie, Philippe, Elena, Braddock, and Sturgis. Forced pleasantries. The tension each of them brought had not yet begun to anneal. The room seemed brighter than yesterday, as if the light level had been turned up a notch.

Right, Carter thought to himself. Here goes nothing.

"There's somebody we want you to meet," Elena announced. She gestured toward the door.

Stafford stepped in quietly. He smiled guiltily, like a small boy returning for dinner after running away from home for only an afternoon. Carter had tried to prepare himself for a moment like this, but no preparation could be adequate. He was seeing a ghost.

Lena and her crew were silent. Passing up the chance to gloat or make some cute remark, Carter thought to himself. He wondered why she had even bothered to set up this grand entrance.

Stafford cut a commanding figure, standing as erect as his silvery crew cut, with his fists leaning firmly on the back of an empty chair at the end of the conference table. His eyes twinkled over his white mustache. "Resurrected. In the flesh. Don't all start cheering at once," he said. "Might disturb the scientists, if there're any left around here." He winked at Sturgis, who sat with a stony face.

Carter was glad he didn't react. He didn't want to give Lena and the others the satisfaction of thinking they had surprised him.

Annie and Philippe also failed to exclaim. The stoicism was nothing they had planned together. It was as if each took pride in rebuffing anything that the polar cabal could throw at them, even this seeming end of their quest. But Carter saw that Annie's eyes glistened with excitement.

Suddenly Carter realized he'd been running on adrenaline until this moment. Now everything was different. He managed an inadequate greeting. "Hi, Alwyn."

Stafford nodded, now with a profound smile. He looked as if he could read Carter's mind exactly. Philippe introduced Annie.

Lena's crew remained silent, almost respectful, as if letting them say a good-bye instead of hello.

Carter studied his old friend, his recent obsession. Stafford had a certain patrician quality about him, an aristocratic and self-reliant bearing, mixed with an air of loss. The twinkle in his eyes was a sad betrayal of secret knowledge, as if he realized he was one of the last of a generation that had ruled the world, a generation now caught up in some tragedy. Old American Anglos all had that sad, aristocratic air of having known the old days, and having no one around who could fully understand their surprise at how things were turning out. In Stafford's case, the feelings must have been intensified: he was the oldest Martian, the one who had known everything since the beginning of the world.

Carter saw their friendship flashing before him, as if he were a drowning man. Little things came back. Stafford was the only man Carter knew who still wore a tiny earring, in the old style. It was a bit of polished Martian hematite. Stafford had told him once, during their old bull sessions in Nix-O, like Zen master and student, that the earring had originally been a little diamond his wife had given him when they started their life together during his sabbatical year at Tycho. Then, when they came to Mars, his wife had decided the diamond was a needless echo of Earth. He needed something from the new world, one of the perfect hematite crystals he had found on an early field expedition. She took it to a tough young woman in the metal shop, and the two women had concocted what Stafford's wife called "Martian jewelry." Alwyn and his wife had sent the diamond in a small packet back to their daughter on Earth. They claimed it was the first diamond in the universe that had traveled from Earth to the moon and then to Mars and back—though there were stories that Nadya Peseka had been wearing her engagement ring during the fiery reentry disaster of '21. Carter remembered the wistful way that Stafford had fingered the jewel in his ear as he had told the story during one of their talks in Nix-O. His wife had died years before. "Thought about hitching up again," Stafford had said. "You see all these beautiful women around here. You think, that's what I want; you know? But finally I realized that any woman you get comes with a whole life of her own. Family. Plans. Habits. Furniture. Dreams of travel. Last thing I need . . . Naw. I've got enough to do."

The memories of Stafford came flashing back, even as Stafford stood there smiling expectantly in the flesh. Abruptly Carter was back in the present. He rose, walked to the end of the table, and gave Stafford a silent hug. He returned to his seat in silence. Philippe was studying Sturgis intently. Annie was fiddling with her bag.

Lena waited with a courtly air of deference till Carter sat down. He was still silent. There was nothing to say.

Lena nodded expectantly at Stafford, who turned to Carter. "Sorry to have caused a problem for you, my friend. I appreciate your coming to look for me."

"What's going on, Alwyn?"

Stafford glanced uncomfortably at Elena.

She turned to Carter. "This is hard for all of us. We've discussed it and we've agreed to try to explain it to you. All of you." She nodded at Annie. "It's a long story, but it's important. You need to understand what we're doing. We'll show you. There's one catch. It means you can't go back to Mars City or publicize this for two more weeks."

Annie started to speak. "Two weeks! Wait a minute. I never agreed . . ."

"You wait a minute," Sturgis said to her from across the table. His voice was strained, as if he had been waiting to be unleashed. "You barged in here, now you better hear what we've got to say. It won't do you any good to object, anyway."

Lena interrupted. "Wait. Let Stafford explain it to them."

Stafford stood at the head of the table. "I'll tell this in the order you experienced it." He began pacing the room, as if he needed to move in order to talk. "You were correct in your analysis, Carter. I compliment you. I drove out there into the desert. I found the *Mars-2* lander, of which I am inordinately proud. That may be the best thing I did in this whole affair." He glanced at Sturgis, who pursed his lips. So, Carter thought, Lena's been reporting my theories to them. Or was Philippe right about the rooms being bugged?

Stafford continued. "Following the plan of Mr. Sturgis, here, I made a confusion of tracks at the site. Then I drove on to an agreed-upon spot, that little crater, stashed my buggy in it, and let them pick me up in a hopper. We came back here. People were supposed to think I had been lost in the desert. Even if they did follow my tracks, they were supposed to find the buggy and think I had wandered off somewhere."

"But why . . . ?"

"It was a plan of Mr. Sturgis here to create a diversion and buy some time. It may have been a stupid plan in the first place"—Stafford was pacing and looking straight ahead, but Sturgis scowled—"but I bought into it."

"But why . . . ?"

"Don't repeat yourself, my boy." Stafford shot Carter a paternal look. Stafford had come to a window, where he paused, gazing seriously at the pale, apricot-tinged snowscape. There was no snow falling today. The horizon was clear and creamy, no longer shrouded in gray fog. But thin gray clouds muted the color of the sky, and the low sun was struggling to shine through.

"The *Mars-2* lander was my own idea. I'd been planning to go out there for months, long before I heard of Mr. Sturgis or the rest of it. I'd picked up various clues over the years. I researched it. I figured it out myself."

Annie fidgeted as if she wanted to talk. Carter hoped she'd stick to their agreement and keep a low profile.

"Then one day, eight or nine weeks ago, just when I was getting ready to go look for *Mars-2*, I got a call from Lena. Some of her people found something. Changed my plan."

"Something?"

"Don't worry. We're going to take you out and show you. It's in the category of artifacts. Artifacts that didn't come from Earth."

Now Carter reacted. He had been leaning elbows on the table, but he found himself back against his chair, tipping his head back and feeling the tingle in his spine. His breath came hard. He felt like the air had been knocked out of him. After all the searching and all the fantasizing about aliens . . .

Philippe grinned as if in some personal triumph. Annie was obviously struggling to restrain herself from bursting out in questions.

Sturgis broke in. "You begin to see our problem."

Annie, now staring at the table in an effort not to ask questions, was giving her head the slightest shake, no.

Philippe waved his pen in the air. "You're saying life really did get started on Mars? Intelligence . . . ? What kind of artifacts . . . ?"

"More like one big artifact. As for it, hold your questions. Better you should see it for yourself tomorrow. As for the interpretation, that's where we're still working. That's one of the reasons they called me in. But I swear, when you've got only one part per billion organics, and only microbial fossil, you're not going to convince me intelligence ever evolved on this planet. Nothing advanced enough to build what we've got, anyway. On Mars, there just wasn't enough time to get advanced life started. The interval between the end of the early intense cratering and the evaporation of the liquid water . . ."

"You're getting off the subject," Sturgis interrupted. "They've all heard your theories before."

"Most of us agree with him," Lena said. "What we've found didn't come from Mars."

The chill returned to Carter's spine.

"There's another factor," Stafford added. "We got an age on what we've found. It's in strata that test out at 3.2 billion years old. We got several sites. They all test the same. So it probably ties in with that layer of enhanced organics we found years ago. It looks like the microbial life may have gotten a start at that time. The climate was . . ."

"But did you date this artifact itself?" Philippe interrupted. "Or just the soil?" Philippe was always intrigued by archaeology. You had to hand it to Philippe, Carter thought; he was always intrigued by everything.

"Smart boy," Stafford said approvingly. "So far we can only date the soil."

"Then how do you know it wasn't just buried at that depth, more recently? Maybe somebody liked that particular kind of soil."

"There's no evidence at any of the sites that the soil was disturbed to emplace the artifact. The sediments settled on top. I'm sure of it. There's more evidence we'll explain tomorrow."

"But how can intelligence be that old? The solar system's only 4.5 billion years old. You're saying intelligence evolved in only, what, 1.3 billion years from the beginning?"

"You weren't listening, my boy. Did I say it was from this solar system?" Stafford paused to grip the back of his chair and face his audience. "It's not from Mars; there's no precursors in the earlier soil. And ever since that false alarm about creatures under the Europa ice, we've ruled out the rest of the solar system, as far as intelligence is concerned."

Stafford was warming to his lecture now. "And Gerault should have known better on that Titan business," he added, as if to himself.

"Anyway," he continued, watching Carter intently now, as if passing on his knowledge to the next generation, "my interpretation is that we're talking extra-solar. This stuff was left here by some nice folks from some other star. Probably some star older than the sun."

Philippe: "But then why haven't we picked up more signs of intelligent life among all the extra-solar planet systems? Beacons or something."

"Maybe intelligence—what we smugly call intelligence—is pretty rare after all. Suppose it takes a few billion years to get from organic molecules to a civilization. Maybe your typical civilization has, what, a hundred thousand years until an asteroid wipes it out? Interplanetary technology has to evolve in one of those hundred-thousand-year windows and start moving asteroids round to end that threat. Maybe only a few of them actually get out into interstellar space; the rest perish. You have a hundred-thousand-year window for a civilization out of a ten-billion-year-old history of the universe. So out of all the planet systems that ought to have civilization, only one in a hundred thousand actually does at any given moment."

Philippe continued, "But a habitable planet would regenerate intelligence from the surviving species in a hundred million years. . . ."

"It's all speculation. Anyway, interstellar civilizations are obviously rare. Maybe the galaxy's had several episodes of civilizations rising, then dying. We don't know what kind of interstellar flight technology they had, or how far they came to get here. Maybe they came through some loophole from the Virgo cluster or something. Hell, that's beyond anything I know about."

Sturgis broke in. "Look, you guys can go have your scientific argument later."

Stafford cleared his throat. "Yeah, well. Anyway, the people who built this . . . they themselves may be long extinct. All I can tell you is two basic facts: we've got one piece of alien technology on Mars, and it was put here 3.2 billion years ago."

Suddenly, Annie's resolve to listen evaporated. "What does all this have to do with secret trips to the pole? This is a fantastic discovery. Why was there no announcement . . . ?"

Lena and Stafford started to answer at once. For the first time, Carter had the impression they were genuinely trying to explain what had happened.

"He's coming to that," Sturgis interrupted. He smiled at Annie. The smile looked forced.

"If you have to blame somebody, you can blame me," Stafford said. "I went along with the plan."

"There's no question of blame," Lena said. "At first, when we began to get broken drill bits, we didn't know what we had. It took a few weeks to find out. When we began to realize it was weird, I had Stafford come down here for a little trip. That was still before we really knew what we had."

"But . . ." Annie started.

"Don't worry"—Lena glanced at her—"you'll get your story. The discovery, the early data—everything's documented. You're the first person from the media to get here. You'll have the greatest story in the world."

"Lena did call me," Stafford continued. "Maybe that was a mistake from your point of view, Ms. Pohaku. You probably feel she should have called you. Or one of your colleagues. Called in the press right away. Of course, science doesn't usually work that way. There's always a period of gathering data before you publish or put out your first press release. Even in the most routine research."

Now Annie was fully into the conversation. Her eyes darted from one person to another. "But this isn't routine. This is alien artifacts! And you said nothing? After everybody's been looking for something like this for two hundred years?"

Carter kept trying to send thought waves at her: Cool it, let them tell their story. Suddenly, watching Annie press her case, Carter felt detached from everything. This woman of all women, whose skin he knew, whose aroma he knew, in this room she was just another person, wearing clothes, focused on a task, focused away from him, like a different species from the one he had known. The whole world was full of surprise and paradox.

"The thing of it is," Stafford continued, "it wasn't clear from the start. At first, all we had was an unknown something, at depth. Something harder than our drill bits. You'll learn more about that tomorrow. As they began to map it and Lena made me realize how strange it was, I remembered something that not everybody knows anymore. For better or worse." He winked again at Sturgis, who was looking impatient. "Before I came to Mars, we were all given a heavy load of indoctrination, especially me. See, we were all looking for life on Mars in those days. The hope was to go beyond the fossil microbes that had been reported at the turn of the century—maybe find existing Martian life, or evidence of ancient advanced organisms; conceivably, even ancient intelligence. People started saying maybe the evidence for Martian life is buried, since the surface gets sterilized by solar UV. You look at the polar sedimentation rates from global dust storms—whole cities could be buried.

"Anyway, when the big franchises were let to build Mars City, one of the backroom justifications for government subsidies was that we might find something revolutionary—alien viruses or ancient technology. Your genetic engineering firms were big movers in this, because of the weird amino acids that were already turning up in comets. There was talk of alien viruses that could lead to nanoengineering breakthroughs. Anyway, Congress and the corporate CEOs were really pushing this project to keep the taxpayers' money flowing into their districts and companies." Stafford grinned. "Don't know if anybody believed in it, of course. But the selling point was that if anybody found ancient Martian technology or current Martian life, it might give the discoverers tremendous power to leapfrog over ordinary science.

"You have to remember, too, it was right after Sviridov's flight. There was the whole Russian-American thing. They wanted to get together and rule the world. They were terrified of Europe and China and Japan and Brazil. Russia had the untapped resources and the big boosters, and America had the industry and management. So they made a deal. Today you hear about the U.N. mandate over the Mars colony, but the Americans and Russians always regarded U.N. mandates as pretty words to be interpreted later. So they made this separate agreement, a secret protocol. They wrote it up as a condition of the first joint missions. Before we left, we got private briefings. Just like when the presidential candidate is elected and he gets his first secret briefing from the spooks, about all the state secrets, and how perilous everything actually is. They told us if we found any evidence of ancient technology, it had to be reported through certain channels. Not public. Then the U.S. and Russian governments would examine the data first. You understand: We had to agree as a condition of the flight. Nobody was wild about the idea, but nobody was going to turn down the chance to go to Mars. The vice president himself talked to us. Hell, none of us actually believed we would find anything at the level they were talking about." Stafford's eyes gave off their sad and secret twinkle. "You have to realize, too, the level of national paranoia about technological secrets. Culturally, the Japanese had already taken over Hawaii, as I'm sure you know, Ms. Pohaku. In terms of the cyber-economic grid, Europeans were busting out all over the world. Intercontinental missiles were still being built by one little fundamentalist country after another. Everybody tends to forget this stuff, today. . . .

"Anyhow, that's what we agreed: Report through channels if anybody found anything. I was under oath. That's what I remembered when I realized they had something odd at the pole. So that's what I advised Lena. For better or worse. Nobody outside the Polar Station knew about it. We reported it just the way I'd been told, not through the press or even the Mars Council, but directly to security back home. I thought it would be just a formality that would make everything legal. I figure paperwork never makes any difference, anyway. Just keeps up employment for lawyers and bureaucrats, so the authorities have something to get you for if they think they need to.

"But it turned out, they seized on it. Like kids with candy. Turns out they had a lot of their people already in place here, in case something like this happened."

"But that's outrageous," Annie burst in. "The press has a . . ."

"Hear us out," Sturgis interrupted.

"It may seem outrageous to you by standards of the present world—the period you grew up in. But the Central Security Agency"—Stafford snorted—"they're hooked into the old Russian/American way of looking at things. You wouldn't believe how governments can unearth old legalisms if it suits their purpose. None of us expected the protocol to be invoked. We gave up on the idea of discovering technology on Mars years ago. You know as well as I: my own work here had become a standing joke, an example of a dead end in science. You fly all the way to Mars to confirm a bunch of dead germs they already had detected in meteorites anyway. When people embark for Mars now, nobody even tells them about this stuff. But for better or worse I followed the rules I had agreed to. We sort of reactivated the system. It was terrifying to behold. All these people, like our friend Sturgis here, came out of the woodwork." He smiled disarmingly at Sturgis.

Carter: "What do you mean, you reactivated the system?"

"We were under orders to keep everything secret. The bottom line is, under the old protocol, we're supposed to keep the lid on this for ninety days to allow a preliminary investigation. That was the wording in the original agreement. Just ninety days. That figure was a compromise between scientists and the security people back in '10. The scientists were against secrecy but they already had a ninety-day deadline for publication after receipt of new data on space projects. Anyway, I had waited a lifetime to find something like this; by the time we knew what we had, it was already several weeks after the initial problem with the drills. Ten or eleven more weeks to investigate before going public didn't seem like such a bad thing. At least that's the way I rationalized it. Well, the good news for you guys is that we're past seventy days already. So it's really no big deal for you, Annie. Just two and a half weeks to go. If you just build your story for a couple weeks, you'll have a fantastic scoop; everything will be smooth and easy. For all of us. You don't have the frustration of waiting as long as Elena and I did."

Carter: "But why the crazy stunt of getting lost in the desert?"

Elena: "Once we had agreed to keep the whole thing secret, we had this problem. We couldn't just fly Alwyn down here for the remaining eleven weeks, it would attract too much attention. You know how everybody watches what Alwyn does. They always think he's on some magic quest that will bring back the Holy Grail. He was the guy we needed, but he was also the wrong guy in terms of public attention. We flew him back and forth for short trips a few times as things were coming to light. But more and more people started asking questions.

Sturgis piped up. "Even you were asking questions, Mr. Jahns, if you remember. And my job was to keep it secret. The first few weeks for me were hell. As we brought more equipment here, more people were involved, it looked like the cover was going to break wide open. Our people told us that rumors were starting to circulate in Mars City about massive excavation projects at the pole. The early workers in the tunneling didn't know what they were involved in, but once we began to expose the artifact, we had to quarantine the base, of course. None of the workers could transfer back to Hellas or Mars City. Our people were still worried. The psychodynamicists predicted the story would break out like a virus in another few days. We were running out of time, and I'll tell you frankly we were frustrated we couldn't crack this thing. We just kept saying, 'If we have a little more time . . . ' Then, on top of everything else, you show up on Mars, Ms. Pohaku. First major network reporter in a long time. Our people were tracking you. You weren't as experienced as some other reporters I've controlled in similar situations on Earth, but you were the most worrisome person on Mars. Our people had predicted you would arrive here at the pole days ago to ask questions about excavation if we didn't do something fast." He smiled, knowingly. "You're a little late. . . . Anyway, to make things still worse, around the time you were arriving in Mars City, the field team turned up higher-than-normal concentrations of organics in the soil layers around the machine. Ms. Trevina here went nuts. Everybody wanted Dr. Stafford down here full-time, in the lab, ASAP. Meanwhile, I'm sitting here, charged with orders from the highest level to keep a lid on this thing for the prescribed period. God, what a headache." Sturgis had a way of emphasizing "highest level," Carter noticed. He was enjoying himself, enjoying his tale of tribulation. "I had nightmares about what would have happened if we publicly transferred Mr. Stafford here. I could just see the stories you would have written: FAMED BIOLOGIST OF MARS SPENDS WEEKS AT POLE ON MYSTERY MISSION. Things were already too hot. So, the idea was to create a diversion, to divert attention away from the pole, just for that last month. That's where the disappearance came in."

"It only made sense," Stafford added, "after you bought into the philosophy of it all."

Sturgis interrupted, "The philosophy was sound. It was my idea. Remember, I was brought down from the foreign affairs office on Phobos as soon as Washington got Dr. Stafford's report. We were operating by the book. The discovery was to be kept as quiet as possible, and evaluated for possible consequences to the world balance of power. I can tell you since you're in the midst of it: We're gonna keep it covert. My job is to enforce the policy. It would be the same thing for UFOs. If something anomalous turns up, our side better know about it first. That's the whole idea behind it."

"Our side?" Philippe said.

Sturgis looked at him blankly.

"Who's the other side?"

"Why, everyone else. The people who aren't on our side. It changes from decade to decade of course. Democratic governments are unpredictable. That's the way the world is. I mean, can you imagine what will happen if we really break the technical codes embedded in this thing? Or to put it the other way, do you want this to burst on the world without any control? Do you want some third world corporation to dominate world technology just because they decipher it out first and get to the U.N. patent office first? Just imagine that for a while."

"But somebody has to figure it out first."

"It better be us. I'm sorry about your European background, Mr. Brach, if you see it differently. But the whole stability of the world for the last century has been because of our American policies. And it's up to us to keep it that way. Besides, we found it."

"But you're already sharing this with the Russians. You said . . ." Philippe sounded incredulous.

"That's a question of national policy. All above my head, Mr. Brach. I'm just supposed to enforce the security arrangement here. Right now, I represent the protocol for the good of both parties."

"And you put together this idea of having Stafford disappear?" Carter asked.

"Yes," Sturgis said proudly. "This was no ordinary operation. This is like the goddamn second coming. I mean, we've discovered alien technology here. You do whatever is necessary, it's a military operation." His eyes were gleaming. "So we put together this cover story of Stafford being lost in the desert. It was great. It worked. Everyone forgot about us. You should have heard our psychodynamics team. Our ratings dropped to zero. Zero! At least for a while. Bought us complete obscurity during the final weeks of the investigation. Like he says, sorry it caused you grief, but it was a routine cover operation."

Carter: "You can say what you like, but we've arrived on your doorstep. I wouldn't say it worked."

"Ah, but nobody knows you've found anything here."

"But I need to file my report. What are you going to do about that?"

Sturgis made an uneasy glance at Stafford. "Look, everybody's problems disappear if you just accept the pressure we're under, and the importance of keeping this news from getting out for just these final two weeks."

Annie: "Stafford said two and a half weeks."

Sturgis: "Whatever. By then, all the formalities will have been met. The highest authorities can decide what to do next. . . ."

Annie: "So what you're telling us, Mr. Sturgis, is that this whole thing is some plan of yours, justified by some secret policies that none of us ever heard of?"

"Not just a plan of mine. I can show you the papers and the authorization. It comes from the highest levels. It's been in place for years. If you knew who I work for. . . ."

"You can quit trying to impress us. I think we all know who you work for. . . ."

The meeting dragged on and on.

Annie walked down the claustrophobic hall toward Sturgis's office. After the meeting, she had asked Carter, "Why the hell don't you get mad?" He had said, "No need to, yet." She couldn't understand that. He was always too controlled.

She had told Carter and Philippe she had to go off to think. It wasn't quite true. Wasn't true at all, not to put too fine a point on it. Sturgis had asked her to meet him. She couldn't pass up the chance.

"I'd like to talk to you alone," he said. He would be on the make, of course. They were all on the make.

When she left her room, she looked up and down the hall. Seeing it empty, she pulled out one of her dark hairs, fixed it with a dab of gel between the bottom of the door and the floor. Then she put a piece of tape slightly more visibly between the door and the jamb; a red herring. She wanted to test Philippe's paranoia; if Sturgis's people really were spying on them, it would be good to know.

"Of course, you realize what a fantastic opportunity this is for you."

Sturgis had invited her, unimaginatively, to meet him in his own office, a lab that he had commandeered two doors down the hall from Elena Trevina's office and the conference room. It was after lunch. Carter and

Philippe had gone off with Stafford to his chem lab. She'd have liked to have gone with them. But Stafford, she could reach anytime; Sturgis . . . If she blew this chance she might not have another.

"Sorry," he said when they entered his office. "There's not much of any place nice to take you, here at the pole." Then he closed the door.

The office was as clean and sterile as an operating room. The screen in the corner had a sign taped onto it, printed in large type: PRIORITY SAFE. As she read it, he laughed. "I don't really know what it means, but it sounds good." So, he was going to ply her with his self-deprecatory mode. The desk was bare. A few notebooks thrown carelessly on one gray shelf. One said PROTOCOL. "It doesn't mean I don't do anything, the empty shelves," he said.

"You seem to do quite a lot."

"I know you don't think much of me. We represent opposite needs of society, in a way, but peaceful coexistence between us is possible."

"I'm sure."

"You created quite a problem for us, but there are ways we could handle this that would be to the advantage of both of us. There's no need to compromise your principles."

"As long as I don't report what I know."

"Two lousy weeks. All right, two and a half. Look, there's no question about your right to this story. Your job may be to report, but my job is to keep you from reporting temporarily, and I'm running things here, so that relieves you of the responsibility. Nothing goes out until our deadline on March 22. That's a given."

"Eighteen days."

"After March 22 . . . you can do whatever you want."

"As long as still higher authorities don't veto it."

"I doubt if that will happen."

"So . . ."

"Things can either be pleasant or unpleasant."

"What's your idea of pleasant?"

"We work together. You agree not to make trouble for us. I feed information to you. When the time is up, you have a tremendous story. It's win-win. Furthermore, it will encourage trust between the media and the researchers who will be coming in."

"You realize, of course, we reporters get unhappy being 'fed information . . . ' That's not a nice phrase."

"I mean I'll help you get the information."

"What if my concept of the story includes the word 'cover-up'?"

"It's national policy. You can't embarrass us, much as you might like to. Of course, I might appreciate a positive slant on it—how we upheld the law, gave the country a head start."

"The law? An old, secret agreement nobody's ever seen, to suppress the truth? You call that the law?"

"Yes. It's a safeguard our country put into effect. Your country. You know, I never figured out why you guys in the press have to look at everything in the worst possible way. And run down the leadership. Is it some kind of psychological compulsion?"

"Mmmm." She paced around the room, wondering when to change tactics. She wanted to break through his posturing, to get at the real man. She paused at the long thin window. Outside, through the thick glass and the thin air, the sun was screened by haze and some spacesuited figures were walking across the landing field, small and lonely in the dim light. "It seems to me I already have the basic information. You guys are running the usual sort of good old boys' secret game, and you cloak it with high-flying rhetoric. And you're keeping us prisoners so that your game isn't spoiled. I don't buy it."

Sturgis, who had been happy, grew red. "Don't you feel like a parasite, Annie Pohaku? How do you live with yourself? You can be as cynical as you like, because you don't have to keep things working. We are the ones who have to keep things working, while you chip away. . . . Anyway, I assure you I have the authority. I can show you the papers."

"Mr. Sturgis, I think your plan and your papers can go to hell."

Sturgis turned even redder with anger. "What you people don't realize is that to have a democracy, the political system has to have a backbone. A lot of squeamish people like you don't want to look at the backbone. But let me tell you, all through history, it's people like us who preserve the system, keep things peaceful and happy, the way everyone wants. Sometimes we have to deal behind the scenes. Look at North's early career. A lot of people now call him a great president, but it was people like you tried to bring him down for his work behind the scenes. All through history people like us have had to be there, but we always have to work in the background because of people like you. We're the ones who deal with all the problems ordinary people don't want to talk about. We're the ones who weed out terrorists and despots so you don't have to think about them."

"But we don't have terrorists."

"Yeah? What about when they blew up LAX in '13? I call that terrorism."

"But that was nearly twenty years ago. You don't hear about terrorism now."

"You think the world changes so fast? The reason you've grown up with so few incidents is 'cause you've got us on the job. Cut us out of the picture and see what happens."

"I guess we're really lucky to have you guys."

"Sarcastic b . . . No, I'm sorry." He paused to regain his composure. "Listen, did you ever hear of the Riphah conspiracy to blow the pressure seals all over Tycho?"

"No."

"Exactly. That's just the point. We got them just in the nick of time. And not with all the legal niceties that you guys are always crying about. So nobody ever heard about it. You included. All these scientists and academics at this base—they just go along with their happy little lives as if . . ."

"I'm not a scientist. I'm . . ."

"Listen, the last time we had a period of calm like this was under Eisenhower. You go back and look at it. The historians, all the intellectuals, said he was a lousy president because you had status quo. But that's the point. That's when we had real operators on the job, taking out terrorists before they could stir up trouble. Quietly, behind the scenes, you know, so that ordinary citizens could go on with their lives. You have to have people like us on the job, looking out for the interests of democracy so you people can enjoy it."

"That's what you *believe?*"

"That's not just what I believe, that's the way it *is*." A flicker of uncertainty passed across his face as if he were mystified by the difference, but it was not a mystery worth thinking about. "One thing I don't like about you and your friends, you think you are such philosophers."

"Look, Sturgis," Annie exploded. "I grew up hearing schoolteachers and presidents tell me that Mars was an international human adventure for everybody's good, a role model for other international programs like the CO_2 projects, et cetera et cetera. Maybe it was all bullshit, but that's what I learned in school. That's what my elected government told me."

Sturgis had resumed grinning genially, as if secretly enjoying her discomfort. "Well, I don't have to defend . . ."

"Listen to me! You pass yourself off as an official of some agency. You smile while you say you lied to us all, and we have to follow your secret rules. Well, most of us never agreed to your damn rules, you hear? Maybe that's why the system works as well as it does. If you guys didn't play straight with me, why do I have to accept your word when you announce rules to me? Oh, no. I've got a story to file."

Sturgis became very calm. "I don't think you'll be doing that. All the terminals are secure. Have been for months. But in another few weeks . . . Imagine what you'll have when we finally do lift the press restrictions. You'll be worth a million! The lone captive reporter, released from the heart of the story. The nets will love it."

"Meanwhile, I suppose you'll lock me away."

Sturgis smiled, as if to dazzle her with his white teeth. "No, no. I told you I'd take you all out to see the artifact. I won't renege on my promise. Maybe it will change your mind. Meanwhile . . . Hey, let's not argue. I think when you see what we've found, the magnitude of what we're doing here, you'll come to agree with the extraordinary measures."

Annie gritted her teeth. She had forced enough out of Sturgis; now she could calibrate him. He was typical of so many self-perceived important young officials in the government: a little boy playing with big guns for the first time. She had met a lot of them during her assignments, and the worst were always the ideological purists from either side. She decided not to provoke any more argument.

The important thing now was to put the story together and get it out. She knew Sturgis and Elena and probably even Stafford—maybe even Carter himself?—would try to stop her, but by God, she wouldn't let them.

"Anyway, look," Sturgis said, "I'm not trying to make things miserable for you. It's just a job. We've all got a job to do." He was affecting weary patience, as if being reasonable.

Annie stared icily at Sturgis's empty desk. "Look, my people will be asking about what's going on. I don't know about Carter's people, but my people'll certainly start calling if I don't report in within a few days. What're you going to do about that?"

"We'll cross that bridge when we come to it. The fact is, Ms. Pohaku, according to our background checks, your people aren't calling in every few days. The word I get is that your boss sent you here to research a documentary—they don't expect anything on that for weeks. As for your stringer reports on Dr. Stafford, no one expects anything from you if there's nothing new to report. The suspense is over. As far as the outside world is concerned, Dr. Stafford is extinct and therefore you are, too."

"They'll start checking up on me, sooner or later."

"There are a dozen cover stories we can put out to get us through that period. I can tell them you're out in the field on the cap, and we can't patch through; I can tell them you're ill; or that we've got equipment malfunctions. I can send out all kinds of disinformation. That's what I do." He laughed. "It's just a different kind of disinformation than you guys put out."

He studied her intently, as if analyzing the effect of his words. "Remember, no one will pay attention to how we managed this situation, once the discovery is announced. Any big scandals you try to start about government secrecy, they'll be lost in the shuffle once people realize we're talking alien artifacts."

Annie had a feeling he was right. She said nothing.

She walked to the window. The meeting was over. She stood at the window for a long time with Sturgis waiting for her. The sun was still at the same height. She felt that it should be rising, starting a new day. Or at least setting, ending something. But it seemed frozen in place, and, unbelievably, the scene outside seemed entirely normal. She had had this feeling once before, the morning she woke in Hilo and heard that the stock market had crashed in New York and Moscow, hours before. That morning, too, she had stepped to a window. She had felt surprise, to watch the rain falling gently on the huge leaves, dripping from the petals of the plumeria. The world economic order had gone into convulsion, yet the rain had fallen normally, and the distant green mountains had been swathed in low morning clouds, as if nothing had happened.

Outside, on the Martian landing field, some men were using a forklift to move a huge crate. They were waving their arms at each other and laughing at some joke, as if it were just another day.

When she returned to her room, neither the tape nor the hair that she had put on the door had been disturbed.

B O O K 6

The Ancient of Days

Change [in human history] no longer means a new stage of coherent development, but a shift from one side to another . . . as understood by designers dreaming up the fashion for the next season. . . .

—Milan Kundera,
Immortality, 1990

26

At dawn, as the lights slowly came up in her room, Annie lay half-awake. Today they would see the ancient . . . thing . . . that had been found.

Philippe's tree came into her mind, branching and branching. The future was like that. Branch points. She was an ant, climbing the tree. Each branch, once followed, led to a different future. Perhaps, even though each branch was unique, there was not really so much difference between them. Perhaps it did not matter which branch she chose at any fork. This direction might lead to one life; that other direction might lead to another. This direction led to one future of the world; that to another. But from a distance, all branches of the tree looked the same.

She was determined to break this story wide open, which might be a climb up a branch leading to a different world. But she wondered about her own motivation. Why was she so anxious to violate what seemed to be a vast and tidy legal machinery? She had to be careful not merely to be paying back Sturgis for his arrogance. The story was more important than that. Was she defending a free press? Was she just after a career-making story? Was it a crusade for truth? There had been famous editors who had held back news for the good of the country; but those cases usually involved lives at risk, or unspoken agreements to suppress scurrilous personal stories that had no bearing on performance in office. Here, it seemed to be only knee-jerk secrecy; the desire for power to control events.

And after all, it was only two weeks. Was it the duration of the charade, or the principle of the thing? She tried to ask herself: What if the ban had been for one day? Or two months? Was there a time limit when her answer would have been different?

At some point you have to stop asking questions and go with instinct. Let the pieces fall where they may. Something new and cleaner would emerge from that.

●

Later in the morning, the blue buses churned down a well-used road west of the Polar Station, spewing clouds of dust around them.

The south polar country was unlike any Carter had ever seen on Mars.

Instead of a blistered landscape of ancient craters and broken lava flows, laced with aborted river channels, it evoked old, odd familiarity of sedimentary hills. There were rounded slopes and steeper cliff sides scored with blocky red strata, which projected raggedly like rows of old, disintegrating bricks. Now the bus crawled along the foot of a terraced hillside that rose on their left like giant pieces of thinly layered cake. The top of the cake disappeared into a tenuous mist that hung above them, almost invisible against the pale sky. The aroma of dust seemed to hang in the air of the bus, as if it came in through the vents. That was impossible; but he couldn't get the sensation out of his head.

Stafford sat close to Carter. "Those red cliffs always remind me of the red-rock country of the Southwest. I can imagine Navajo shepherds on the hill crests."

Lena was standing at the front of the bus like a tour guide, hanging on with one hand and waving toward the hills with the other, and holding forth over an intercom. ". . . the strata. You've got a billion years of snows, seasonal dumping of dust grains at the poles, and orbital cycles thrown in to complicate things. And an occasional volcanic outburst adding a layer of ash. It's all there." She couldn't help adopting the role of teacher. "The whole history of the planet, including the most amazing part, as you'll soon see."

The bus rolled on into thicker polar fog. Gloomy light filtered through the low clouds onto the frost deposits, turning Mars an uncharacteristic gray instead of red.

Through the haze, they could see the fresh creamy white of the recent snow, draping down from the plateaulike surfaces atop the cliffs. On the lower sun-facing elevations along the road, it was already evaporating. Pockets of thicker white frost lurked in the shadows of the brown boulders that dotted the bases of the slopes.

Lena lectured them on the passing landscape, as if understanding the geology would make them forgive the conspiracy. How many people has she brought here in the last ten weeks? Carter wondered. What had she wanted from *them*? He tried to shake the thought. Is she really just an ordinary person caught up in great machineries? Sure, she had pumped him for information. Wouldn't he have done the same? Wouldn't Annie have done the same? Hell, Annie *had* done the same. Were questions asked in bed automatically less honest than questions asked in the conference room?

He leaned against the bus window, feeling strangely relaxed and sardonic. He thought of the missionaries and priests and now the agency operatives who had come to Mars. Must be nice to have a value system that lets you see things in black and white. But black and white, as humans had proved again and again, were the most dangerous colors in history.

Ah, well, in this bus, for once, all he had to do was sit back, observe, judge perhaps, be ready in case one of those right moments came along. . . . He pictured himself as a lion in the veldt, half-relaxed, half-ready to spring . . .

For now, he didn't have to judge Lena. He knew he was not attracted to her in any long-term way. He would return to Mars City and rarely see her again—perhaps at a meeting now and then. They would act friendly and professionally. With luck, his final report—if he had to write a report—would not have to say anything about her. Funny, Carter thought. This had started off to be *his* assignment, but it was splintering into a thousand shards. There was something in it for everyone but him. He was just along for the ride, now, literally. He would finish his report; a little fragment of the whole, it would be forgotten. In the hubbub, he would return to work.

He turned to watch Annie. Annie would face a different problem with Lena. If Annie were to write the whole story, she would have to judge Lena. She would sit in judgment of them all. They would all become her characters, assembled from the parts she collected. It would be Annie who made all the moral judgments. He himself would record only facts and recommendations. Philippe might make sketches and paintings and sculptures; but no matter what "feeling" he put into them, they were morally neutral objects in the end. It was Annie who would be forced by her medium to make judgments.

Did the judgments matter, in the long run? Professors would argue about the reports. Whichever way Annie wrote it, someone else would come along and write the opposite, just to make a buck. You had to live by your own judgments, not the ephemeral judgments of historians.

The sheen of Annie's black hair caught reddish highlights from the landscape outside. He realized with a tinge of despair that he measured his time in intervals from the times he could be alone with her. Yet, at least, now he knew the framework of her life; that was better than operating under the false assumptions he had carried with him earlier.

Suddenly they broke out of the fog, revealing the sunlit cliff in sharp and stark outline, as if to say there might be only one fixed reality, in spite of the historians and writers.

"See that drill rig up there?" Lena was saying.

They all peered to the left, where a tower rose atop one of the plateaus, silhouetted against a sky the color of a New Yorker's flesh in winter. The base of its legs was hidden in a faint ground mist hovering at the top of the cliff. The tower seemed to hang in the sky.

"Keep it in mind. You'll be seeing more of them."

Later, ten kilometers down the road, they dropped into a wide, shallow valley mouth, seemingly eroded through the polar hills by some defunct drainage. An array of drill towers stretched up the valley floor, spaced half a kilometer apart. They labored up the valley's ramplike far side onto a broad *bajada* apron skirting along the foot of the layered hills, and bounced onward. Every ten kilometers or so they passed another single tower, perched on a slope or a hill crest to their left. On one low hill, there was an array of drill rigs, arranged in a geometric grid.

Coming into sight now was the mouth of another broad valley. The valley's far side was a steeply rising cliff, more imposing than any they had seen yet. The cliff's foggy summit was surmounted by yet more drill towers. Clustered around the base of the cliff were vehicles, stacks of crates, and temporary inflatables with winking lights on their airlock doors. In the base of the cliff, shored up by Martian concrete, was the wide mouth of an enormous cemented tunnel, from which vehicles came and went like ants around their hole.

Elena Trevina explained everything to them. Her crew had been drilling all over the cap, to get core samples that would let them map the strata sequence that recorded ancient climate variations. They were trying to deduce the unique Martian history of that rarest of solar system commodities, liquid water. The terraced cliffs that encircled the pole offered cross sections of strata that simplified the mapping of the older deposits, while the drills offered access to pristine buried deposits.

The drill data, they hoped, would shed light on conditions during the long-lost Martian springtimes of three or four billion years ago, when— according to most researchers—polar ponds and seas sparkled in the once-thicker Martian air. Perhaps there would be answers as to why life had never gotten much of a tentacle-hold on Mars, had never gone much beyond the now-fossilized microbial forms scattered in buried rocks and sediments.

The drills labored year round, but the favorite time for fieldwork was in the "warm" southern summer, when the sun wheeled all day above the horizon, eating away the snowy veneer of carbon dioxide frost and revealing the permanent, dirty-white layer of frozen water trapped underneath—the sun, like a bright vulture.

Success of a poor sort had come in '25 when the drills hit a meter-thick stratum of grayish soil that had a higher-than-average content of organic materials, averaging just in the range of a few parts per billion—an extension of the layer Stafford had studied a decade before. Barely out of the noise. Hardly evidence of ancient, teeming life, but enough to make scientists twitch. Stafford had spent a year studying materials from the site. The layer was 3.2 billion years old. Since the microbes were rarer below that layer, and more abundant above, Stafford had concluded that the layer might mark the climax of the fluvial period, when life got its start, but after which life died out because of the declining conditions.

Polar research had continued unabated, Lena recounted. The main efforts were to answer why, except for sporadic local anomalies, most rivers had stopped running and the water had frozen three billion years ago. There were efforts, both by drilling and by finding the oldest outcrops, to concentrate on the strata laid down around that time.

Results of a different sort had come about ten weeks back, when two successive drill bits shattered at a depth of five hundred meters. Initial speculations of the geology team centered around massive nickel-iron meteorite fragments, or some mysterious ore body. The splintering of two successively stronger drill bits capable of penetrating such materials ended that speculation. Eventually, imaging in the drill hole seemed to show a smooth, rounded surface, unmarred by the drill bits. Chemical probes showed a metalloid structure rich in titanium, silicon, and carbon, but failed to identify the precise composition or molecular structure. This is when Stafford had been called by Lena, and the secrecy lid had clamped down. Eventual enlargement of the drill hole allowed more complete imaging, and precarious human inspection revealed a horizontal-lying tube, a pipe about the thickness of a man's body. It ran east-west. In every test they could devise, the tubing proved impenetrable.

The next step had been to make another drill hole one hundred meters to the east. It uncovered what appeared to be an eastward extension of the same tubing. They couldn't keep drilling all over the pole to trace the extension of the thing. Geophysical measurements from the surface were attempted, in hopes of mapping the extent of the metal mass, but with no success.

By that time, still in early February, with the protocols in place, it was a crash program with unlimited budget, to learn as much as possible within ninety days. Sturgis and his security team had seized control of the operation and ordered the most sensitive geophysical equipment sent from Mars City and Phobos, piggybacked on other freight shipments so as not to attract attention. The science team had gone along with it, choosing to interpret the ninety days not as imposed secrecy but as the normal data development period before publication.

Renewed attempts to detect the buried tubing with the new geophysical equipment from Earth gave marginal results. But the drilling went quickly in the soft-rock polar sediments. New holes sunk one, two, ten, twenty, fifty kilometers to the east always hit the tubing. Where the tube crossed under the eroded valleys, it was shallower and easier to reach. When the drill holes had tracked a hundred kilometers of tubing, a curiosity was discovered as cartographers fit the positional data points onto ever-refined maps. The tubing, which at first had appeared to run straight as an arrow, did not follow a great circle on the globe, nor did it run truly east-west along a latitude line around the south pole. Instead, curve-fitting programs confirmed that the actual positions of the tube fit a spiral, and the center of the spiral lay close to the pole. The whole thing looked like a giant burner on an old-fashioned electric stove.

If the tube truly followed a spiral, it would wrap around the pole many times. Still more precise curve-fitting procedures were performed. Projection of the calculated spiral pattern indicated that the coils would be spaced roughly six hundred meters apart at this distance from the pole.

The geophysical probes were pressed back into service, surveying six hundred meters south of the line of the tube. A possible signal was buried in the noise, at 623 meters. A new drill hole probing the 3.2-billion-year stratum uncovered another tube segment running east-west. Or rather, it was not really *another* tube segment, but what came to be viewed as the next coil of the same tubing as it wrapped around the pole.

What would be found *at* the pole itself?

Geophysical probing around the true pole found nothing. Drilling found nothing.

Meanwhile, the cartographers refined their curves. The new solution put the center of the spiral not at the south pole, but offset about twenty-five kilometers from it, generally in the direction of Hellas basin.

They moved the geophysical probing efforts to that site and found evidence for a massive metal-rich complex beneath the surface. The polar sediments were deeper here. The complex was buried at the 3.2-billion-year stratum at a depth of thirty-two kilometers, out of reach of any excavations.

"At that point a different kind of information came into the picture," Elena was telling them. The bus had rolled to a stop in the valley mouth and they were suiting up. "In the late twenties they had begun mapping a paleomagnetic field of Mars. There's not much of a field now, of course, but three billion years ago the magnetic dipole field was pretty healthy around here. Way above the solar wind background. Of course, it showed a certain amount of wander. Fluctuated in strength and went through polarity reversals. The geophysicists developed some preliminary mapping of the pole positions as a function of time. Guess what? Our metallic complex was buried at the position where the magnetic pole was, 3.2 billion years ago. Near as they could tell anyway. This whole thing was somehow designed around the magnetic field of the planet at that time."

"Planetary engineering!"

"At least planetary-scale engineering."

"But what did it *do*? What was it for?"

"Nobody's got the foggiest." Lena was smiling and obviously enjoying herself for the first time in days.

Stafford explained, "That's how we can be so firm on the date, we've got two independent lines of evidence, like we mentioned yesterday. The pole position and the date of the strata both say this thing was emplaced 3.2 billion years ago. The error bars are pretty sloppy, maybe plus or minus 0.05 billion, but it's somewhere around 3.0, 3.2, 3.3."

"One thing bothers me," Philippe said. He had a very serious expression. "If this thing is less than a meter wide, and spaced six hundred meters apart, weren't you incredibly lucky to hit a piece of it with a drill? Do you expect us to believe that?"

Stafford: "We musta had two hundred drill holes out there by the time we hit it. If you figure the tube is nearly a meter across and lines of tube are six hundred meters apart, we were getting a fair chance of hitting it. Woulda hit it sooner or later."

"C'mon," Elena called to them from the front of the bus. "Get your helmets on. We're going out there."

After they were out on the surface, Carter discovered he had been so excited that he put on his helmet too fast. The inner fitting that held the microphone had slipped and was scratching his neck. He had to speak loudly to be heard.

The bus was parked near a cluster of instrument boxes and vehicles in the center of the broad valley mouth. Carter and the others walked across the frosty soil to a fencelike barrier, erected from pipe lengths that were diagonally striped with yellow and black. The barrier surrounded a pit that had been widened and reinforced to form a broad shaft, as much as ten meters across, which disappeared vertically into the valley floor. Out of the shaft came an array of cables and tubes, like a mass of giant black worms slithering out of a hole. The cables ran to various instrumented wagons parked around the hole. A brilliant yellow bulldozer brooded nearby.

Peering as far as they could over the barrier, they could see that the inside of the shaft was lined and illuminated, and that it descended about forty meters.

"This is one of the shallowest exposures," Lena was intoning over the intercom. "We're in a pretty deeply cut valley."

An elevator cage ran down one side of the hole. There were two suited figures working in the claustrophobic space at the bottom of the hole.

"Look. At the bottom," Lena prompted.

Peering downward, Carter could dimly see a strangely innocent tube crossing the bottom of the hole. It was smooth and had a greenish metallic luster. Here, at last, was what humanity had awaited since the days of Herschel and Welles and Bradbury and Clarke, the fantastic discovery of an artifact from another civilization. In that dully gleaming curved surface, the four-century attempt to confirm "the plurality of worlds" had become reality. Here was the first stop on humanity's long road of search for companionship, or at least non-uniqueness, in the cosmos. No matter that it was three billion years old and that its builders were not only nowhere to be seen, but perhaps long vanished. Whatever the caveats, this little tube proved that humanity was neither some unique mistake of Nature, nor necessarily had dominion over field and fowl.

"Shouldn't we have music swelling up in the background?" Philippe said.

The tube might as well have been a deep sewer line attended by city engineers. The patchy greenish patina reminded Carter of aged bronze. They stood around the railing, Annie panning downward with a minicam. Eventually, there was nothing new to see. The city engineers bustled around the surface, in the spotlights, as if repairing a broken water main.

Carter tried to fix the moment in his mind for the rest of his life. Gusts of wind off the polar hills blew the bus-and-tractor-disturbed dust into little eddies around the mouth of the drill hole. Even the wind was special: it blew across the polar wastes where *They* had been.

"There's one more thing." Lena's voice jarred Carter out of his reverie. "Remember how I told you about the big buried complex at the far end of the tube? Well, this is the *other* end." She gestured toward the cavelike aperture in the hill.

Led by Elena, the group started walking toward the foot of the hill on one side of the valley, where the dark maw of the tunnel loomed, surrounded by the flashing turquoise lights that designated an emergency shelter. It looked like the entrance to a carnival ride.

Suddenly Sturgis's voice on the radio broke Carter's reverie. "Give it up, Annie Pohaku. All the satellite communications channels on your suits are closed. Did you really think we'd leave you a comsat channel open to the outside world?"

Annie's voice came on, angrily. "Shit."

"We wanted to see if you'd try that." Sturgis again. "Suspicion confirmed." Carter could almost imagine a smirk on his face. "But you see, we hold no grudges here. Come on; there're things to see."

Annie made no reply.

Carter immediately realized what had happened. With the distraction of the drill hole, and with its alien contents finally confirmed by their own eyes, Annie had attempted to raise one of the Marsnet satellites on an emergency channel. And failed, thanks to Sturgis.

So they were truly cut off.

"It's important that we stick close together," Sturgis was saying, "since you have no outside links if you wander off and get into trouble." He sounded sincere now that he was speaking to the group as a whole. His sarcasm always seemed reserved for Annie. "I apologize to you. . . . It's crazy to cut off the emergency channels, I know, but this whole situation is an emergency of a unique sort. Really, we can't afford to have anyone wandering off. Anyway, we won't be outside very long."

They approached the cavern. Carter caught up to Annie and touched her puffy arm, catching her by surprise. She swung her shoulders toward him aggressively, to see who it was. Her arms fluttered upward, an ineffectual gesture of defeat, and then she touched his shoulder in return.

It was not truly a cave, but a long tunnel, cut into the hill by Trevina's crew. The tunnel slanted down. A long catwalk led down its center, flanked on either side by rails for carts that had hauled equipment in and dirt out.

Partway down the tunnel, in a zone constricted by massive dark rock, was a tripartite airlock. They squeezed into its narrow central chamber, flanked on either side by larger chambers for the rail cars and machinery.

As the airlock door opened, Sturgis took his helmet off and gestured for them to do the same. It took an effort of will, breaking the seal, with the bare Martian rock around them. But Carter was relieved to get his helmet off. With the back of his hand he soothed his chin where the misplaced mike had rubbed his skin raw. The humid air was bitterly cold and their breath hung in front of them in ragged clouds of gray vapor.

Elena waved them on. "You should see the pumps we've got for keeping up the air pressure in here. Course, we lose some through the rock porosity, but we manage to keep ahead of that."

Stafford nudged Carter and pointed clumsily ahead of them, where the tunnel seemed to open into a larger room. "Wait'll you see this."

They had been saying that to him since yesterday.

Lights blazed from scaffolding, making a latticework of starlike beacons around them. A vast room the size of a stadium had been hollowed out of the strata. The cavern looked as if it should have been dank and dripping, but it was as dry as chalk and bright as day. The solid rock walls had been neatly pared away, to expose surfaces banded in red and brown like stacks of old books. Some of the horizontal strata were delicately thin; another was ten meters thick, a single band the color of mahogany.

The vast underground room was dominated by a single, unprecedented structure looming in the center. Elena waved toward it in a cheerful, sweeping gesture. "Well, there it is."

Towering above them, in the cleared space at the end of the cavern, was a huge, organ-pipe mass of vertical cylinders, with the same greenish metallic sheen that they had seen outside, but this time rising vertically.

The cylinders had different diameters, tiny ones clustered among the big ones. The whole complex had a fractal quality. There were large tubes, smaller tubes touching them, still smaller tubes of shorter or longer length nestled among those. The outer surface was an impenetrable complex of small tubes studded with still smaller tubes. The diameter of the complex was perhaps forty meters. On the left side of the room they could see the only horizontal tube in the room, the same as the one in the pit outside, entering the cavern from the left at eye level and piercing the cluster of tubes in a baroque collar of fittings that gleamed faintly of gold.

Surreal organ pipes gone mad, erected in some deserted cathedral. Organ pipes left by . . . whom? Giants? Dwarfs? Strangely, nothing in the installation gave a clue as to the size or shape of the unknown beings who had left this . . . thing.

A deep, broad shaft had been excavated around the vertical tubes to a depth of thirty meters. Down, down the tubes plunged, and disappeared into the soil at the bottom of this excavation.

"We think that all the horizontal tubing was laid on the surface that existed 3.2 billion years ago, and then covered during later centuries by younger sediments." Lena patted the horizontal tube, as if it were the most normal thing in the world. "What you see here is the end of the horizontal spiral, where it joins this"—she looked toward the towering complex—"we call it a node. The interesting thing is that the pipes in the node run vertically down with no sign of disturbance, as if they were sunk in carefully bored drill holes or magically pushed directly through the soil. We don't understand that."

Carter was developing an odd feeling about the room. The upward and downward thrusting of the strange tubes was clean and direct, and yet something was uncanny about it—about the very air in the room. Carter was surprised to feel the hair rise on the back of his neck. It was as if there were some presence, some unseen purpose, hidden in the room with them. It was the feeling you have when you waken at midnight and sense that something unseen and unfamiliar is in the dark bedroom with you. Yet the presence did not seem evil. The more he examined the feeling, the more it seemed neutral. Or was it positive?

Stafford, holding his helmet under his arm, beamed proudly. "As Lena said, the horizontal tube is an extension of the same tube we saw outside, in the drill hole. But it doesn't extend any farther west. This is the end of the line. It's the outermost end of the spiral around the old magnetic pole. The vertical node was big enough for us to locate with geophysical detectors on the surface, and the goal of our tunneling was to get in to where we could see it. You see, we've exposed the top of it. We don't know how far down it goes." He pointed toward the top of the cold room, where the ceiling was shored with carbonal cross beams.

The tubes ended at different levels, each terminating in a rounded, solid cap. Not quite hemispherical, Carter noticed, more like ellipses or egg-shaped curves. There were no seams; it was as if the rounded caps

were turned out smoothly from solid masses of metal. The caps gleamed
uniformly with the now familiar, subtle greenish hue.

"The interesting thing," Lena added, "is that we think there's another
node at the other end, at the site of the old magnetic pole. From the
surface measurements we made before we started excavating, this node
and the one at the magnetic pole have the same signature in the mag/
grav surveys. So the whole artifact, it's a long spiral with one of these at
each end. We don't know what they are. Look. It goes down and down."

They were still standing where they had entered, on a wide ledge inside
the airlock door, dwarfed by the scale of the cavern. In front of them was
another railing, the edge of the excavation, which was even wider and
deeper than the one outside. Workers in the bottom looked like small
beetles. They walked forward to the edge. The tubes disappeared into the
flat soil at the bottom of the excavation.

"We tried to get as much vertical exposure as we could, but finally we
gave up. Nothing seems to change as you go downward. The geophysical
measurements say it probably goes down for kilometers. God knows how
far. Hard to get a reading on it. May go all the way into the core for all
we know."

They had gazed for many minutes in silence, as if the unseen presence
had robbed them of the power of speech. Finally, Philippe reached for a
sketch pad, which seemed to bring all of them back to reality, and the
questions poured forth.

"But what does it do?"

"Did you take any readings on the soil they cleaned out of there?"

"Of course."

"Did they strain the soil? Don't archaeologists strain the soil with filters? I mean, there might have been artifacts."

"Naw, nothing. No ray guns, no credit cards with photo ID, Rosetta
stones, nothing."

The room seemed to ring with questions as they clustered around Elena
and Sturgis and Stafford. Annie had her minicam out. Carter walked off
along the fence, gazing alone up and down at the green organ pipes,
tuning in and out of the conversation, which seemed almost irrelevant
to the majesty of the construction.

"What tests have you done on the composition?"

"You said nothing can penetrate this material?"

"That's always the way it was in the old movies. Nothing could cut
through UFO metal."

"I've told you as much as we know."

"We decided the thing to do was to level with you guys. Now you know as much as we do. You can see for yourselves: This whole situation is unprecedented. You see why we have to take certain steps."

Now Carter heard Stafford's voice, clearer than the rest. "You're in it with us now. You have to decide if we did the right thing."

Funny phrase, coming from Stafford. Stafford had been in on it. Agreed to ditch his buggy and send them out on a wild goose chase to buy time for Sturgis. Or rather to buy time for himself. Sold out, even? Sold out to Sturgis or to ego? Carter wondered if he would have done the same thing if the call had come to him. You had to allow for the fact that Stafford was taking his last shot at his lifetime dream. You couldn't blame him. Maybe he thought it was all a big joke. Stafford was like that sometimes. A curmudgeon to the end.

"You can go down and touch it if you want to," Lena was saying. "Two at a time. In the elevator. Go ahead. Take off your gloves."

While the first two parties went down, Stafford took Carter off to the side. "Well, what do you think? Aren't you glad I brought you here?"

"You brought me here?"

"Shhhh."

"You brought me?" Carter repeated in a lower voice.

"Sure. I recommended you as the person to contact, in the unlikely case that something happened to me."

"You didn't know I'd find you."

"Didn't I?" Stafford's inscrutable smile. "C'mere." He gestured before Carter could argue. "I want to show you something." Stafford dragged him over to a corner where the horizontal tube emerged from the wall of soil. "Look. It's the darndest thing. You've got this seamless mass of tubing joined to tubing, and then there's this." Stafford pointed.

There was a bulb swelling out of the side of the tube, the shape of half an egg. But there, in the middle of it, as plain as anything, was the flush head of a screw. It was not an ordinary screw. Instead of a straight slot or Phillips head cross, there was a three-branched star indented into the surface. "I discovered it myself. It was only exposed by the digging on Tuesday. Look, can I tell you something that is secret—you won't even tell Annie?"

"All right."

"I don't want anybody to know, but I went back to the lab and made the appropriate screwdriver. Pulled the little sucker out of there. Guess what I found."

"What?"

"Nothing. That little bulb-shaped dingus came off. That's all. Nice little solid piece of very dense metal, felt like. No apparent function at all. Like a piece of chrome on an old Cadillac."

"That's crazy. How did you know it wouldn't cause some disaster, like opening a valve or something?"

"Aw, you don't put a dangerous cap on something with just one screw. Besides, at my age I didn't want to wait for some committee to debate it. Now that I know, I'll report it and wait in great suspense for some official grand unscrewing."

"Jeez, Alwyn. You could've . . . It's not good, having you running around loose."

Stafford winked.

"I'm serious."

"Go ahead, touch it."

Carter reached toward the metal, but felt almost a physical repugnance against touching it. He could not explain it to himself, and so he forced himself to touch the surface. Smooth, the sensual feel of well-formed metal, like a clean knife blade that has just cut fresh bread. And he had the most subtle sense that some kind of mild current passed up his arm.

"Funny feeling, ain't it?" He winked again and led Carter back to the elevator, where they rode down into the pit.

At the bottom of the pit, the rest of them stood at the edge of the tube assembly, where it disappeared into the soil, like a corrugated wall of curved surfaces.

Carter joined Annie and Philippe, trying to sense their emotions. Annie was running her hand along the surface. She wore a strange smile, half full of joy, half full of fear. As if answering his question, she whispered, "I don't know what to say. I feel like a moth near a flame. . . . I can't explain it."

"It is inscrutable," Philippe said quietly, almost to himself, jotting in his book beside his sketch of the tubework.

Annie rode the tiny elevator with Carter, back up to the main level. She stood against him, closer than necessary in the elevator's tight, open platform, pressing against his shoulder. "I . . . this is crazy." She stood looking up at the top of the node, as if she had said nothing.

"What."

"Tonight when we get back. Come to me. I want you." The elevator reached the main level. She squeezed his hand and walked away from him.

MARCH 5–6

So it was done, Annie thought to herself.

Buried beneath the polar cap of Mars was this . . . thing . . . and what were they going to do about it?

Outside the tunnel, they were climbing back into the bus for the evening ride back to the Polar Station, Philippe swearing softly as he bumped his helmet on the bus's low padded door.

The whole thing had been overwhelming, and she realized she wanted to share it with Carter by holding him in her arms, but she purposely avoided boarding the bus with him. Philippe came and sat across the aisle from her, but she said little to him. There was little conversation anywhere on the bus, at first. It was as if they had all been stunned into a confrontation with their own souls. Finally, Philippe began sketching and jotting in his anachronistic notebook as they waited to start.

Inside that hollowed cave, with the artificial Martian air cold in her face, Annie had felt something, a beginning of something new. The very existence of this vast, ancient machine marked a new reality for humans. It was like the Renaissance, when the discoveries of Copernicus and Columbus had forced everyone from poets to popes to recognize that the real world was much wider than they had thought. Proof at last of aliens' existence marked a birth date for a new humanity.

That was how she felt when she had first seen the alien machine.

But now, waiting for the bus to drive them away, she felt a different reality. The story was not a beginning; it was an ending. Everyone else would focus on the future impact of the knowledge and the mystery of the machine's function, but the real story was the end of the age of uncertainty, the end of innocence. For a long time it had been known that life was not unique to Earth, but now we knew, by God, once and for all, that neither was technology unique to Earth. And if there had been two intelligent species in the universe, there had been millions. It was a form of disillusionment.

Suddenly she felt a wave of anger wash over her. Sturgis and his people were treating this miracle like some corporate secret, like a new gadget. Treating it like it belonged to them. Ending or new beginning, she reaffirmed silently, it belonged to everybody.

Carter maneuvered cautiously into the bus. His legs felt strangely heavy, as if he had been plodding through molasses. Philippe was already sitting with Annie. Carter took a seat in the back with Stafford, and waited for them to seal and pressurize.

Stafford nodded to him paternally, as if waiting for him to speak. Instead, Carter studied the rest of them in their seats, as if searching for some clue as to what would happen next.

Annie seemed to be in her own world. Elena and Sturgis had paired off in the front two seats. The odd couple, Carter thought. What did they have to say to each other? Not much, apparently. Lena stared out the window most of the way home. He was beginning to understand her: the scientist, trying to do her work, who had gotten in over her head. He realized he had stopped thinking about her as a piece of this puzzle.

The bus began chugging along. He turned to Stafford.

"Alwyn . . ." he began quietly.

"Interesting situation, ain't it?"

"What is that thing?"

"Nobody knows. That's the whole point." Stafford turned and studied Carter's eyes, as if looking for some medical symptom. "You know that strange feeling when you were near it? I noticed it right away, the first time. Later, after I had been around the thing a lot, I got used to it. But it doesn't go away. Can you imagine a machine that interacts somehow with living material? Maybe through some sort of field at a close distance? Hell, I don't know . . . I'm just drifting. But I keep thinking, whoever built it might have seen linkages in nature that we can't even think of, and built them into machines whose purposes we can't even imagine."

"But there must be some way to start looking at the design, the purpose . . ."

Stafford tapped Carter on the shoulder in a fatherly gesture. "Look. Sometimes you run up against a brick wall. You're frantic to find out what's on the other side. You know it's something wonderful. You and Annie and Philippe are going to knock yourselves out for the next few days trying to figure out what's on the other side. I know. That's what I did myself when I got here. But sooner or later, you'll realize that it truly is a brick wall. You beat on the wall, but the only thing you come to know is the brick wall itself. Would Neanderthals have been able to make sense of a radio?" He sighed. "What I'm saying is, I've come around to thinking we'll never know what the machine was, what it did."

Carter was annoyed by the gleam in Stafford's eyes. "This thing on the other side of the wall, are you sure it isn't just another secret you and Sturgis and Elena are keeping for yourselves?"

Stafford grew defensive. "Don't put Lena in the same boat with Sturgis. She didn't know she was going to get caught up in this."

"I know. I finally figured that out. But what about you? You're telling me you're just gonna sit around in your base here with your friends and spin secret theories. . . ."

Stafford's face turned red against his white hair. "God damn it, Carter, don't lecture me. You know as much as we do now. If you're so damned smart, you go figure out what it is."

"But you could've brought in all this help from Earth. So much equipment . . . All you had to do was make this public. Experts would flock . . ."

"To hell with the experts from Earth. God never wrote any rule that said you have to publish a new discovery on the first day, before you've had a chance to study anything. Show me where it says that in the Ten Commandments." Stafford stared at the lifeless gloves he had placed on the little shelf in front of their seats. "Sorry. Christ, Carter, you know I'm defensive on this, in spite of my bluster. Anyhow, it was only for a few weeks. . . . I didn't know how it would turn out. I suppose now I'll turn into the scientific villain of the piece when Annie puts out her story. It was a dumb thing, you bringing her. I thought you had more sense."

"Don't you start in on Annie. I get enough of that from Lena."

"She's just jealous."

"Oh, sure."

"It's normal."

"Let's change the subject."

"Even if I did know any big secrets, how could I tell you? Way I got it figured, anything I tell you goes in Annie's ear." He elbowed Carter in the ribs. "I can't take that chance, can I? I probably shouldn't have showed you that little screw."

"I thought we were going to change the subject."

Stafford smiled enigmatically.

"I can never figure you, Alwyn. Sometimes I think I know you. Other times . . . Here you are, part of some underground government conspiracy. It doesn't fit. You always seemed, well, irreverent."

"Remember the hobgoblin of small minds? I may be inconsistent, but it got me in on the biggest discovery of the age, didn't it?" He was still smiling mischievously. "Devious little game I got to play with my buggy back there, I admit it. But it gave me the chance of a lifetime here, not to mention my chance to go after *Mars-2*. You gotta admit I played my cards pretty well."

"But Sturgis . . ."

"Forget Sturgis." They were whispering now, conspiratorially.

"How can I forget Sturgis? He's the one that caused all the trouble. He's the one enforcing secrecy, not to mention holding us prisoner! Won't ever say so, of course, but that's what it amounts to."

"Sturgis is small potatoes."

Carter said nothing.

"Look, Carter . . ." Stafford paused. "You need educating. Sturgis is just a cog in society's engine. What societies do is, they organize their little value systems and then they build huge engines to keep the system chugging along without changing. Inside the engine they put little cogwheels like Sturgis to keep it running. People like us come along and discover new things that threaten to change some assumptions, make whole assemblies useless. The engine doesn't like that. You should worry more about which way the engine is heading, and less about the little oily cogwheels." Stafford turned away to the window again, to watch as the bus approached a whitish, house-sized boulder that had eroded out of the cliff face and rolled almost to the road.

"What do you mean?"

"Bureaucracies get ingrown. These security guys are a classic case. Do you know that last week they torpedoed four years of preparation for the joint Existence Field experiments with the French, because they were afraid EuroTech would get ahead of Nanosoft? You let those guys have their way, the basic search for human knowledge about the universe will be controlled behind the scenes by midlevel functionaries. Subconsciously, that's why Sturgis and his friends are afraid of people like you and Annie. If Annie breaks this story before their deadline, it will dramatize the sterility of their ideas about keeping the public and international scientists from knowing what's going on. But, you see, if it comes out after their deadline, then the truth-suppression aspects of the story are lost. The big news will be the discovery itself, and to the public it will look like a nice orderly process."

"You saying she can get this story out of here? Look, if you wanted to help get it out, you could . . ."

"Certainly not. I would never hint at such a thing." Stafford gazed out the window with a bemused look. "Nice day out there, isn't it?"

"Jeez, Alwyn."

"Hey, what's the matter? The worst is over. As for me, I'm happy. We'll get several nice little papers in *Science* outta this—if *Science* can spare enough page space from their fruit fly research and gossip columns." He began studying Carter again.

"Who the hell's side are you on, anyway, Alwyn?"

"I'm on their side, according to you." He had a pious smile. "Besides, if I publicly hinted at sympathizing with you, I'd lose what control I do have over the situation. So I'm not saying anything. We'll have to wait till Annie writes the story to find out her version of whose side I was on. And when the revisionists get done, we may never know whose side I'm on."

"Stop bullshitting me."

"You could say I have certain ideas of my own, in my own little way." He looked out the window as the hills passed by, holding their secrets. "For example," he said, suddenly raising his voice above their previous conspiratorial whisper, "a lot of people are missing the most exciting aspect of this."

Annie and Philippe turned to listen.

"The Martian microbial and organic materials seem to be associated mainly with the artifact layer," Stafford continued. "From the evidence I have, any of the stuff below that layer exists only where water has percolated down through porous soils and cracks in rocks. The data are still noisy, but the general soil concentrations seem to peak near the 3.2-billion-year-old layer, and then decline slowly after that. You see what I'm driving at? The bacterial life-forms that had us so puzzled when we called them Martian were not originally Martian at all! They were just residues left on Mars by accident when the aliens were active here emplacing their machine. Mars was more clement; the bacterial hung on for a while and then died out. They were never suited for Mars, and Mars turned pretty hostile. It explains why they are most abundant at 3.2, but less abundant in older and younger rocks and soils, and why life never evolved beyond that stage.

"So if I'm right, Mars never did form life of its own. The only way life got there was to be delivered by older aliens. Other planets may have been accidentally seeded, too, when they were in periods of attractive climate. And remember, the racemes are different from terrestrial organisms, so we did not grow from the same event that seeded Mars. Terrestrial life either originated on its own as in classic theory, or it was seeded during another alien visit to the solar system." Stafford beamed proudly. "What d'ya think a' them apples?"

———————————————————●———————————————————

When they were filing out of the airlock into the Polar Station, Carter wanted to catch up to Annie in the hall, but Philippe drew him aside and waited for the others to leave. He pointed with his chin at Annie's receding figure. "She is a beautiful woman, but the relationship is over for me. I thought you would want to know, yes?"

"What are you saying, Philippe?"

"She has her own private world. She lets no one into it. I am tired of it, you know? We will see what she does with all this. She will have to make something of it. Then, perhaps, at last we will understand her. She . . . I am tired of her mystery, I think. Maybe you are not. It may be a problem for you." He gave Carter a gentle slap on the back.

"I've got enough problems."

"Yes, and I am still here to help you; I have done very little, but I want to do what I can if you need me."

"You're our eyes and ears. You found Stafford the other night. You're our philosopher as well."

Philippe grew more expansive. "I've been thinking about that, the philosophy as you put it. We all know this is a philosophic milestone: the fundamentalists, for example, will have to recognize that we humans are not necessarily the unique lords of the galaxy, as they would like to believe. Earth is no longer the imperial capital of the universe. But on another level, a political level, as long as Sturgis gets to manage the story, there will be no real effect. Sturgis and his friends, they will arrange things so that they come out heroes, the defenders of liberty. Lena and Stafford will be great discoverers. Annie will get her sensational story. I will come out a noble onlooker. Nobody will care about your report, so you will be safe. In short, nothing changes. Maybe that is okay. You have to decide for yourself.

"But as Stafford says, if the story breaks before Sturgis is ready, that is different. It would ratchet humanity one notch forward. Sturgis and his pals will look like fools defending your archaic American desire to rule the world. His whole house of cards comes crashing down. Such a collapse, it is something humanity needs, every generation or so. It is curious, you know, inbred bureaucracies always become obsolete when science moves forward. Look what happened with Galileo and his trial. . . ."

Carter said nothing.

"And I will tell you something else. Nobody will deduce any state secrets from this machine for a long time. This is truly alien technology. Alien to our way of thinking. It's not like looking at the hardware in a Japanese sensie unit, trying to figure out how they did it and how we can make a better one. When you look at something from Japan, even if it is far ahead of what we've got, you share a common technology base, a common structure of physical insights into nature. Here, we're dealing with something else. Somebody was here 3.2 billion years ago and built something. That is all we can say. We don't know how far ahead of us they were, technically or biologically. We don't know if they had the same way of organizing physics."

Carter felt frustrated. "Stafford says the same thing. But I think, if they study it enough, they will have some breakthrough. . . ."

"I've been thinking. We like to claim that science is the process of discovering the absolute reality of the universe. But, you know, Newtonian physics was invented by people who believed in clockwork machines. Later, wave mechanics was invented by Schrödinger after he got interested in Hindu principles—Brahma extending continuously through the universe, organizing itself temporarily in little packets of karma. So there is a question. What if our images of the universe simply mirror our cultural conventions? Maybe each race re-creates the universe in the mathematical image of their own belief systems. Of course, the underlying reality is the same, but the way you organize it may lead you to discover different aspects, and to build different kinds of technology. You understand? We may not have the philosophic paradigms to understand this alien machine, or whatever it is. Maybe we're like the archaeologists who assign the label 'ceremonial object' on everything they do not understand." He turned to the window again. "We keep calling this thing a machine, probably because it looks complex and seems involved with magnetic fields. But maybe we should just label it a giant ceremonial object and let it go at that. Maybe it is an *objet d'art*. What if some future archaeologists dug up your Washington Monument and assumed it was a machine, and then kept trying to analyze its function?"

He banged his long arm wildly against one wall of the hallway, then the other, and then the ceiling. "Anyway, I think it's time to think ahead to something new. Now we know what they have here. It is wonderful. I want to make something wonderful out of this experience. I don't know what. But"—he slapped Carter on the back, harder this time—"I think

Annie wants you. It shows I was right, of course. Her desires are beyond comprehension. It is your problem now."

In Carter's room, the terminal showed a message. It was from Annie. "Hurry. I want you."

━━━━━━━━━━━━━━━━━━━━━━●━━━━━━━━━━━━━━━━━━━━━━

Annie was sitting on the bed. Everything except her posture spoke of openness, of offering, of her own sensuality. Her hair flowed onto her shoulder like a waterfall in a black river. She wore a blouse with buttons, half of them undone. She had put on a full skirt, also with a row of buttons. They were open halfway up one side, revealing her brown, smooth leg. She stared intensely at him when he came in, as if she had been sitting for an hour watching the door. Only her posture . . . She was rubbing her arms as if she were cold.

He locked the door and turned toward her. She whispered to him, "Shhhhhh." She had put music on. Slack key guitar from Hawaii, fluid as a breeze. In the midst of Earth's popular music of violence, this was music of pleasure. "If they are there, I don't want them to hear," she whispered. She glanced meaningfully at the walls, the ceiling. The music filled the room.

"Here." She gestured for him to sit beside her.

He began to unbutton her blouse. She wore nothing under it. He caressed her breast, her shoulder.

"I've got to go back, you know."

"Back."

"Home. To Earth. You know that, don't you?"

His hand did not stop moving.

"Wait," she whispered again. She took his hand. "It's nothing to do with you. It's my life. . . ." She was looking at him with an intensity he hadn't seen before. As if she were trying to get inside his brain. As if he were a patient. "So I want to give you two gifts."

Carter said nothing. His hand was under her skirt now, where she wore nothing. Whatever she was giving him, he would take. He ran his hand along her thigh, and played with the buttons. One at a time. . . .

"This time here on Mars, it has been an adventure," she was whispering. "Some different universe. I'm sorry we have so little time. . . . Make love to me. Do what you want. Punish me if you want. . . . Maybe this is the last time for us. I want you to see what you do to me. I want you to know that it's real, it's not just pretend. . . ."

Their playing went on for hours, and the third time he made her come, she screamed.

"Third time's charmed," she told him.

Still later, they were quiet, lying across her bed. "And now there's that second gift I wanted to give you." She was still whispering, holding his hand and running her fingers across his chest and his face. She had become serious. "I'm going to break this story, one way or another. After that, there'll be a million journalists here. They'll think they have the hottest story in history, but once the story has broken—I see it now—it will become routine. They'll come here and stick cameras in people's faces and do what they are trained to do, and pontificate on the evening news, live, from Mars. Or almost live, when you think of the transmission time." She smiled, wistfully. "After that, it will just unfold, like an origami puzzle."

"I don't understand what you are talking about."

"I'm beginning to see the whole pattern. In a way . . . I'm tired of it. Can you understand that, Carter? I'm tired of all these games people play. Little boys and girls, trying to exercise their power over each other. Sturgis and his secret missions. Lena trying to stay on top of it all. The reporters who will come and jockey for the inside story. Even Stafford, with his discovery, trying to milk it for all it's worth. I love him, but . . . Can you understand this, Carter? These are little games that are just triggered by events, like clockwork. People are immersed in them and can't see the pattern of it all. What's important is what happens between human beings on a personal level: not who wins these little impersonal games with their little rulebooks and their little tally cards. Robots can do that. We are imperfect, and therefore precious, like flowers."

She sighed. "Don't you understand? It was you who helped me see that." She was still holding his hand. She had stopped moving her fingers. They lay motionless, side by side. "For now, I'm right in the middle of this. And I'm going to finish it. I'm the only journalist who will have been in on it since the beginning. With you. You and Stafford, and Philippe. I'm going to finish it and then I'm going to go home. Then, I have to write about it. This discovery was a momentous event in history, and it shouldn't be debased by the clockwork games, media one-upmanship, and all that. The real story has to be described in human terms. I owe that to my future children. Maybe a book. I'll live by the sea, which I love; I'll live with Tomas, whom I love. I'll have those children. I'll live somewhere where it's wet and green, and watch the flowers and listen to the rain on the leaves of the plants. I'll remember you and I'll tell the story of what really happened here.

"I do love you, too, in my own way. And I don't think you believe it. And I want to prove it to you." Her fingers were moving again. "I want you to know you are part of me now. I want to give you a gift so you'll know. The only gift that will prove it to you.

"You see, what happens next depends on us. I've kept my promise to you." She was whispering. "I haven't published the story of your investigation, except for the stories about Stafford's disappearance in the first place. But I've done one thing." Her whisper grew still quieter. "I've written up everything you found on Phobos, all the evidence pointing to the Polar Station, and I've locked it away. So it's already logged in my file under my security code with the network. There's no way Sturgis and his people can get it back. It's got a routine time lock. If I don't send new reports and update the file within a week, the net will take a look at what's in there. It will lead them right here, and they'll find the biggest story of the century. They'll break it, and they'll find stringers to send down here from Phobos, to find out what's going on. So even if we do nothing, the story comes out."

Carter looked around the room again and whispered, "So that's the end of Sturgis and his lies."

"You don't understand him. You're too . . . pure. To people like that . . . what he's doing is not lying. It's creating a cover—routine business. You have to realize, this guy expects a promotion when it all comes out— just for keeping it quiet this long. Exactly for lying, as you put it. If the lie is uncovered, the next step is to lie some more, confuse things, so no one knows what to believe. Create villains, for instance. Innocent bystanders like us. Remember, he's expecting praise from all his friends. A pat on the back from the White House. Lying is a sign of manhood to people like that."

"I can't figure why Stafford goes along with him."

"You're unhappy 'cause your hero has feet of clay?" Annie laughed. "I talked to Stafford out there. I don't think he sides with Sturgis."

"Is he playing both sides?"

"He said he has to work around Sturgis. I think he sees Sturgis as an impediment. Sturgis wants to believe he is saving the world, that he carries its weight on his shoulders. Stafford says people like that leave a wake of chaos behind, and that his attitude is to stay out of the wake."

"He gives Sturgis too much credit. Sturgis just gets off on wielding power."

"I think Stafford is looking beyond Sturgis, at some larger game." She smiled. "But I can't figure what his game plan is."

"So . . ."

"I've decided I want to have my own game plan, too, not just wait for the clock to run out. I think that's my job and I think it's the right thing to do. I don't think these people have the right to take over this discovery for themselves. We're supposed to have an open world. History doesn't just hand it down to us, we have to keep re-creating it. The evil here is not just that people like Sturgis are running everything, it's that they think they're supposed to run everything."

"That's all very nice but there's not a hell of a lot we can do about it."

"There is something we can do. That's why I'm talking to you. I want you to understand. You and Philippe have this idea I'm just trying to manipulate you, that I've just been using sex to . . ."

"And here we are again, aren't we?" Carter commented. He pulled her toward him.

"Things are all mixed up together. I love you, Carter. I think about you all the time. You do something to me that is . . . I've never felt it before."

"Thought you loved Tom the ape, or whatever his name is." Carter's hand was still.

"I do. I can love many people at once, in their own way, but I can only live with one person at a time."

"A cute line."

"It's true about everybody. People just don't admit it."

"Carter." She was pleading. "I'm giving you a gift. Listen to me." She curled against him and whispered in his ear even more quietly than before. "We mustn't let them hear. I could just let the clock run out without telling you, and my story would appear. But I want to prove to you that I haven't been using you. When I set up my file, I also set up a code that would alert the net to open the file sooner. I don't have to tell you any of this, but I want you to know. I'm offering you power over what happens. After all, if you tell this to Sturgis, he could send fake updates to my net and keep them out of my files, and that would prevent the story from coming out until he releases it. I'm putting at least part of the fate of this story in your hands."

Carter sat up and searched her face.

"But here is the important part," she added. "My code. It will trigger their computers and get them to open the file immediately and release the story. All I've got to do is get a message back to the network with three code words in it." She snuggled even closer, whispering so that he could hardly hear. "I figured that if Stafford really was here, they obviously had some secret operation going on, and they might be trying to hold us here incommunicado. I figured they'd have to let me send a message out, sooner or later, just to keep up appearances. Sturgis will have to send something out for each of us—that we're off on a trip or something. If I can get him to let me send some seemingly innocuous message . . . All I have to do is insert the words 'satisfactory,' 'series,' and 'situation' in my message. I picked three S words: S A, S E, and S I. Easy to remember. Doesn't matter what order. If they get something with those three words, red lights will go on everywhere."

She pressed against him, giving herself to him again. "This is crazy, but I'm giving you everything, just to prove myself to you. I'm putting it in your hands. I wanted you to know you can stop me now, if you choose to. Now you know. Sooner or later, Sturgis is going to have to put out something about why we are down here so long. He'll want our cooperation. You'll have to talk to him. Tell him about my plan if you want, I dare you. But if you talk him into putting out a message to the net with our code in it—even your own press release about *Mars-2* or the search for Stafford or whatever—you'd be the one to break the story. This way, at least you know I'm leveling with you." She paused. "I'm being as open to you as I possibly can. I'm putting it in your hands."

During the slow polar dawn that extended the polar half night, they were lying together, quietly and sweetly, when they felt a sudden jolt, like someone hitting the bed, and an alarm bell began ringing in the distance, down the hall.

2 8

The 4:00 A.M. tremor had shaken the whole building. Annie, throwing on a robe, rushed to her door. There was a moment when people stood frozen in their doorways, staring disbelievingly down the halls toward the alarm bell, and then across the hall at each other until they realized that something serious was happening. Carter came up behind her, struggling to put on his pants.

Moments later, an apprehensive crowd was racing through the halls toward the labs. Annie, Carter, and Philippe joined the melee. The power was still on, but the nighttime lighting in the station was set at a dim level. The polar night-sun gleamed dully from the horizon through the small windows in the hallway, creating a copper glow, like some vision of purgatory. A crowd of scientists and staff had backed up, elbow to elbow, outside the lab doors. The claustrophobia of the tiny station, which she had been able to ignore until now, suddenly pressed on her in full force. She struggled to ignore the feeling. Concentrate on what's happening.

The doors of the lab opened onto the end of the hall, and one of the aides was barring access to the lab itself, pleading with the crowd. "C'mon. Keep back. Let them find out what's going on. We'll get the info out to you as soon as we can."

Standing in the crowd, peering past the heads of the other onlookers, Annie could see banks of electronics with flashing readouts, and a large holographic globe, set out in the room's center, with red pulses glowing deep in its interior. Stafford was nowhere to be seen.

Slowly the message was passed back to them, through the jostling crowd. The single large tremor had occurred at 3:54. Although it shook the whole station, the air pressure seals had not been breached. The tremor had been detected by seismometers in the seismic net that extended all over Mars, but it had been felt by humans only at the station, not at Hellas Base or Mars City. It was deep, triangulated at a depth of around eleven hundred kilometers, somewhere beneath the polar ice. Tiny tremors were continuing, around the same depth, too small to be felt and too small to be picked up anywhere but by the polar seismic net.

"What does it mean?"

Nobody knew.

"Are earthquakes common at high latitudes?"

"Minor tremors, yes. Adjustments to the increasing weight of polar sediments. But nothing like this."

Little groups began breaking off, heading for breakfast, looking grim but beginning to relax. As Carter, Annie, and Philippe followed them, Philippe joked, "So it wasn't you guys who set off the seismic network."

"What?"

"The walls are thin. You guys were kind of noisy, last night." He said it as an acceptance.

"Sorry, Philippe." They both said it at once. Philippe shrugged, with a faint grimace.

It turned into a day of awaiting seismic news, interspersed with abortive planning. "After all, we can't just commandeer a hopper and escape," Philippe kept telling them at breakfast. "We can't do anything."

"If we could just send a message . . ." Annie looked at Carter meaningfully. Word from the seismic lab came that aftershocks were now occurring one hundred kilometers above the original tremor.

"Do you think it has something to do with the machine? Maybe they built some kind of machine that drew energy from the planet's magnetic field and . . ."

They felt no more shocks.

Annie decided to give up unproductive fantasizing about causes, as she called it, and work on the larger story that was all around her. Then she saw her chance. Her first step was to send Elena a formal request to send out a story on the earthquake, including interviews with seismic researchers and a damage report on the building. If she had a chance to choose the wording . . .

To send out her code words would preempt her offer to put the choice in Carter's hands. She had been serious about the offer. But it couldn't be helped. The quake had dropped the opportunity into her lap. Maybe *making* the offer was gesture enough. Besides, he still had the option of spilling the beans to Sturgis.

Elena sent her a preapproved press release.

There was still a chance. She asked for permission to add a paragraph about lack of damage to the buildings. Elena agreed. She submitted her own innocent addendum:

> In spite of a series of minor tremors, detected only with seis-
> mometers at the South Polar Research Station, the condition
> of the facility itself appears to be satisfactory. The seismic staff
> continues to evaluate the situation here. Otherwise, conditions
> here, five hours after the quake, are normal.

Twenty minutes later, her 'corder confirmed that the bulletin was out on the net. All but the last paragraph. The story amounted to only the original press release, over her byline.

She stormed up to Sturgis's office.

"I was expecting a visit from you."

"Damn it, they cut my story. I suggested it in the first place."

"That's right. Think of this as a war zone. There's a certain amount of editing that must go on."

"Censoring. . . ."

"It happens. Besides, you don't trust me, and I don't trust you. Think of it as a sign of mutual respect."

She could not afford to show too much anger. It would make him suspicious. "I don't do press releases," she muttered. With this display of righteous indignation, she left. Sturgis had won another round.

She would bide her time and strike again, she swore to herself.

She swung through the cafeteria at lunchtime, but it resulted only in a pointless philosophic argument with Philippe, which put her in a darker mood and sent her off on her own to process the story on her own terms.

She decided to hit the halls with her 'corder and minicam, recording impressions all over the station.

Her real fear was that Sturgis would pretend to give her free rein, but at the last minute destroy all her video material and supporting notes before he let her out. So she made her own plans. In public, she projected acceptance of Sturgis's offer to let her collect notes and break the story, implying she would suffer through these few weeks with subservient grace. She made a show of her camera work and took 'corder notes in public, even requesting—with no response—a taped interview with Sturgis. Privately, she decided to work in two mediums, electronic and written. She pulled out a set of small, red, Japanese notebooks Takemitsu had sent her as a going-away present. "Emergency backup . . ." his little card had said. If he only knew.

The writing surprised her. Transcribing her 'corder notes onto paper, she discovered that they had the advantage of immediacy, of recording personalities on the spot. She came to enjoy the writing. It was somehow longer term than the electronic records: it had the advantage of not just recording, but of synthesizing after reflection. But she wrote in secret, by hand. Takemitsu had sent a little pencil, too, but she preferred using a little sketching pen Philippe had given her, only days earlier—now so long ago. Curly, nineteenth-century letters, ragged and barely legible, from lack of practice; cryptic abbreviations, and her own pseudo-shorthand.

Writing had a physical and even sensual feel that was unfamiliar. She was surprised at her reaction to it, this trying to get things down on the little pages. Ideas became part of her. She pictured herself two centuries back in time, with the Brontë sisters. She began to realize what sketching must be like for Philippe, who had talked of impressions entering his eyes, mixing in his brain, and traveling down his arm onto the paper.

At the same time, she made preparations to prevent Sturgis from destroying the work. She tried to visualize how they might come after her. "Give us all those videos you shot." "Is this everything?" "Now we're going to search your room." The first line of defense was to back up her videos with duplicate chips that she hid in various parts of the station as the opportunity appeared, coding these locations into her written notes.

But the electronic copies weren't safe; she knew Sturgis's people had detectors that could pick up electronic data storage. Even a hundred buttons would be no guarantee. They could sweep her luggage, her body, even the whole station. But they were powerless against simple little notebooks as long as no one knew about them. She would have to hide them, too, one at a time, as she filled them.

Should she tell Carter about the notebooks? The question nagged at her. Finally she decided against it. Demonstrations of trust and love were fine, but you had to have your own life.

Later, she knew, she would have another problem: the organization of facts was different from the facts themselves. There was the question of how to cover Elena, Stafford, even Sturgis himself. Could she depict any of them as, somehow, "good" or "evil"? Or were those merely labels we assigned from our own biases? No one, even Sturgis, thought himself to be evil. . . . Especially Sturgis. They all thought they were on the side of the angels, carrying out their professional duties.

Later that night she was on a roll. She told Carter she needed to be alone. She wrote as much as she could: the arrival at the station, their first meeting with Stafford, Sturgis and his rules.

When she filled the first notebook on Saturday morning, there was the question of where to hide it. Scientific facilities, she had noted, were always full of clutter. She wandered artlessly around the station, with her equipment, recording impressions. When she came to Stafford's lab, she saw an open door. She peeked in. Stafford had apparently stepped out. She found a dusty recess behind shelving that had not been moved in ages. Checking the room for surveillance monitors, she stood against the shelving as if to take an image, and behind her back, slipped the first notebook there, to pick up after the story broke. After all these centuries, the high-tech warriors could still be defeated by the simplest sword—the written word.

She returned to her room and started filling the second notebook: how the artifact had looked in the cave, how it had felt being there, her talk with Sturgis, how the tremor felt.

She did not write what she had been doing when the tremor struck.

———————————————————●———————————————————

Carter spent Friday in amazement. Annie, the night before, the night that would not leave his mind, had placed a bomb in his hands. Would he really play a role in getting the story out before Sturgis's deadline? Probably the question was academic; there was no way to get a message out. But if the chips were down, what would he do? No doubt Sturgis had the law on his side. When do you break the laws of your country? Were "break" and "laws" words that he really believed applied here?

And what of the tremor? Entries posted on the net, including a spare account with Annie's byline, indicated that minor seismic disturbances were still being detected at a depth of 950 kilometers under the pole, triangulated by the polar seismic grid. Now and then he would stop and try to feel them—some vibration in the building or under his feet. But he felt nothing. Everyone wanted to believe that it was Mother Nature, hidden, working at her own schemes somewhere in the mantle of the planet. But, said some, what if it was the machine? Worse yet, what if the machine and Mother N. were working in some unholy alliance?

There was nothing he could do about it. He tried to return to his immediate duties. First he put in a request to Lena for a formal review of possible damage to the station by the jolt. By midday, he was putting the finishing touches on the first draft of his report of Stafford's disappearance—the disappearance that had suddenly become a nondisappearance. The others were right: In the big picture, his report would be moot. He needed to supply some written record to keep the bureaucracy off his back, but his official role had been reduced to irrelevance. Except that now, Annie had put this bomb in his hands and thrust him back onto center stage.

Throughout this mess, he reflected, Annie always had her goals laid out, while he was always improvising. But her determination seemed too simple. It was as if she could avoid uncertainty merely by announcing a reporting objective. She was ever the journalist, with a one-track mind. It must be nice, he thought, just to hop around the solar system asking questions, cavalierly making friends and enemies, taking responsibility for no one. Having no planet depending on you.

And Stafford had a point: The scientists would, in any case, soon report the discovery anyway. Even without Sturgis's spooks, they would have kept the discovery quiet for months, getting the bugs out, getting it just so, putting together their just-so stories. This whole crisis about beating Sturgis's deadline was the kind of issue he hated, manufactured by those looking for some moralistic point to outrage themselves.

Why not stop whining and let them release their report in a few weeks, by the end of March. Maybe he should go talk to Stafford. Get a commitment that they would put it out on time. . . .

There was even the chance that Annie was bluffing. A small voice urged him to consider that while her code might be real, she might not have any automatically timed message in files. It was another one of her ploys to sucker him in, use him to get the story out. He put away the thought. He didn't want to think about her this way.

By late morning, the seismic triangulations had been refined. The original tremor and the continuing tremors originated directly below the far node of the alien device.

"You know what I'm going to do when this is all over?" Philippe was being his expansive self, at lunch with Carter. "I sketched plans last night while you were, um, occupied." He smiled. "I would like to make a monument at the present day pole. *They* left *their* monument. We should leave ours. A real pole. Big, aluminum, right at the true pole of rotation, homage to their tubes, or whatever they are."

This was when Annie came by. She listened for a moment. "What's the point, Philippe?" she challenged him. "Right now, we've got . . ."

"The point? It will be there for all time, just as their monument is. Two species' monuments. Besides, it will confuse the hell out of the next species to visit Mars, a billion years from now. Figuring out the relationship between the two installations." Philippe's eyes sparkled. "I don't want it to be too phallic. Still . . . it ought to be a pole. The pole that marks the south pole. In the long term . . ."

"For me," Annie interrupted, jokingly, "I don't care about the philosophy anymore; I just want to get Sturgis where I want him."

Carter glanced around the room. He had seen some of Sturgis's crew sitting at a table, dressed slightly too neatly. No one seemed to be hearing them.

Philippe stared at her, hard. "Look, this discovery will come out, one way or another. Four hundred years from now, what will people remember about this year? The pitiful political issues surrounding the discovery? No. The discovery itself, and what we do with it. That is why I do what I do. I sit here at this table, trying to look into the future, trying to turn this experience into something, and you just laugh at me. It's what I was telling Carter. What makes me feel isolated is that I don't understand why everyone here acts as if only their problem-of-the-week has any importance."

Annie grimaced.

"You Americans," Philippe continued, "you are a nation of problem-solvers, as you are fond of saying. But you don't seem to know that solutions are never solutions. Solutions are only the birthing pains of problems for the next generation. That's what we have learned in Europe. Life is bigger than solving your current problem. It goes on, of its own accord. Do we remember the political intrigues in the court of Elizabeth? No, we remember that guy who was writing plays—Shakespeare. Of course, there must have been courtiers, and political reporters. They dealt with the short term. Others have to speak for the long term. It is not so dishonorable, but if you do it, you are doomed to laughter and neglect. A generation later, they may adopt your ideas, when they turn back and call you a hero. Well, that is life. You know what my favorite writer said? 'Those who create deserve more respect than those who rule.' Kundera. I am sick of short-term crises—the games of people who want to feel involved with power."

Annie smiled, but was red-faced. "Well, I'm sick of your Kundera." She pushed her chair back roughly and stomped off, out of the cafeteria.

Philippe and Carter looked at each other in blank amazement.

"I never wanted her to come between us," Carter said. "She's going away anyway, you know. Back to Tomas."

Philippe made a show of ignoring what Carter was saying. He paused, staring down the hall, toward infinity. "Do you really think it made any difference who won the Second World War, a hundred years ago?"

"Jesus, Philippe."

"All right then. What about your Russian ancestors? They and the Americans almost destroyed the world over the issue of their communism. But now they are the rich capitalists exploiting the resources of Asia, and you Americans have a muddled social democracy." He made a few idle lines with his pencil, and smudged a gray area with his finger. "I don't know. People raise families, pursue their careers. That is what is important. The only thing that happens when they get excited about ideological issues is that people get killed. Usually in the name of justice and humanity."

"Did you hear what I said? She's going back to Tomas. She's leaving as soon as this is over. She is important to me, you know."

Philippe looked up at last, with a lame smile. "It is all right, my friend. She was never the only one for us. There are a thousand more, eh? Think of the number of women we will never know. . . . Man's relationship to women is the great sadness of life." He was launched into one of his monologues. "The two great burdens of our time are singleness and marriage."

Carter smiled. "Go fuck yourself, Philippe."

They both laughed. "Yes. It is a good idea."

Annie came running back in, and stood before them, breathless. Philippe smiled wryly. "Do you remember, this is how it all started. You came to us with news. What news do you have this time?"

"The epicenters are moving upward. The tremors are occurring now at 850 kilometers."

Philippe: "What does it mean?"

"No one knows. They say they've never seen anything like it."

Philippe: "Did you see Stafford?"

"No. He's locked away in his lab. Working on samples."

Carter: "Did anybody project a time of arrival at the surface?"

"I didn't hear anybody talk about that."

"If you have maybe three hundred kilometers in a day, and—what?—eight hundred kilometers to go, that would be . . . less than three days!"

It was the next day, Saturday, when Annie came to the same table again. "Sturgis wants us in the conference room. Now."

They met in Elena's conference room. Sturgis paced up and down as he talked. One of his aides sat at the head of the conference table, saying nothing. Carter felt his heart pounding. Would this be a showdown? He was ready.

Annie took the initiative when they came in. "When do we get to go home, Sturgis?"

He smiled enigmatically. "I've been thinking about what you said."

"Or are you going to put us on bread and water to save food for your troops?"

"And about your attitude."

"What attitude is that?" Philippe said.

"Especially your attitude, Ms. Pohaku." He turned an icy gaze on her. "Rather . . . what shall we say, disloyal? I think you have the idea that this discovery belongs to the whole world." He chuckled unconvincingly. "Not to the people who made it."

"So . . . ?" Annie challenged.

"You're wrong, you know." He looked from Annie to Carter without changing his expression. "Your government is very interested in this apparatus. That's what you should remember."

"During the long cold nights in our cells?" Annie returned his icy smile.

Sturgis took no notice. "I say 'your government' advisedly. Remember, it was the American and Russian people who paid to set all this up. That should interest you, Carter. American mostly. Taxpayers. We have a right to get a return on the investment."

"You mean, *you* have the right? You and your friends? A right to control truth, dribble it out to the masses as you see fit. . . ."

"You're becoming tiresome, Ms. Pohaku. I'm not a chief. I just try to be a good Indian."

"But, of course, that isn't why you called us here," Carter egged him on.

"In my role of a good Indian, I have been monitoring communications from the outside. I have to say, you were right. I'm beginning to get queries from your various people about your whereabouts. Not you, Mr. Brach;

from the dossier we've got on you, I'd say you're an oddball lone cuss, anyway. Nobody seems to care if you're down here at the pole or out in the field for a few weeks. By the way, that Stonehenge thing you did—craziest bunch of shit I ever heard of. I just wanted to tell you."

Philippe said nothing, but watched Sturgis expressionlessly.

"Course, you artists are used to hearing that all the time," Sturgis continued. "Right? I understand that the more the public complains, the happier you are. I just wanted to cheer you up." He was smiling cheerily again, but it was the face of a true believer. He looked pleased with himself.

"As for you two"—he turned to Annie and Carter—"you're a different story. We've been into your e-mail files. A few messages accumulating, but nothing significant. Still, we can't have you just dropping out of sight with no explanation. But these earthquakes give us a perfect card to play, and we're going to play it. We'll explain to them. Ms. Pohaku naturally wants to stay here and cover the unfolding seismic story. And Mr. Jahns is concerned about structural integrity of the station. We're already responding to your request for an assessment of the buildings. The pressure seals are now being studied, one at a time, and Elena will give you a more specific report later today.

"On top of all that, we're going to say we've rigged up a field trip to the pole to improve the seismic detectors, and you guys elected to go along. Two weeks. Ms. Annie Pohaku will be getting her story and Carter Jahns will be getting emergency information about the seismic risks down here." He chuckled again. "There's enough gossip about you two already, according to our people in Mars City. When you say you're going off into the field together, everybody will wink and shut up for a while.

"Course, I don't really care what you do. You can really go out in the field if you want, long as people back in Mars City think you're doing your, um, duty. *Comprende?* I've got a cover letter from Elena, authorizing your presence on the field trip.

"What I want from each of you, now, is some sort of personal message we can send from you back to your people, telling them to be cool. 'Stafford not here. Unable to confirm story about hopper from Polar Base, but am following leads. Have signed onto polar field trip to get more info on seismic activity. Will report when I get back. Hello to everybody. Wish you were here.' That sort of thing. If they call in, we'll tell them you're out there. We'll stall 'em, make up some communications glitch if we have to. Like I've been telling you, if you'll work with us on this, then everyone will come out ahead: the Mars research facilities, Ms. Pohaku and her network, the public, everyone. In a couple short weeks, everything's over with. You can all go home. We announce our discovery. Stafford returns from the dead. Everybody has a smile over our successful security operation. Annie Pohaku writes her story and wins a Pulitzer prize. Jahns submits his report, wraps up all the little formalities. Everybody's happy."

Sturgis placed reusable pads in front of Carter and Annie. "So, if you'd just write out what to send and where to send it, and let me look at it . . . Oh, and, Ms. Pohaku, if you could just indicate that there is nothing new on the Stafford story, just to downplay it while you work on it."

He looked mildly surprised when they started writing without protest. "No cross-table talking, please. Just write. A few lines should be enough. By the way, my people know enough to detect whether you are playing straight with us. So don't try to get cute."

"Hands on your desk. Eyes on your paper," Annie mimicked.

Carter began writing inanities about his own reporting, how he was still gathering info on Stafford, how a report was being prepared regarding effects of the earthquakes. He wondered what Annie was writing. Annie's message was the critical one. Annie, working across from him, face glowing with concentration.

When they had each written for a minute, Sturgis stopped them. "Okay. One more thing." He picked up their half-finished pads. "I wanted to take a quick look at what you're saying." He read each half-finished letter carefully.

Carter glanced at Annie. Her face was grim. She was watching Sturgis intently. Sturgis seemed still to be enjoying himself.

"Well, they look okay, but what do I know? Right? Shall I just finish them off and send them?" Annie glanced at Carter. "I'm sure—with your journalistic scruples, you would feel that censorship was rearing its ugly head. Government censorship. No, we wouldn't want even a hint of that." He smiled, as if sharing his joke with them. "It should be your own writing. You each know the other's style better than I do, the way I figure it. So why don't you just take each other's pad"—he put the pads down in front of them—"and rephrase them for me. Go ahead. Change the words and finish them off."

Carter stared at the pad in front of him. Annie's printing was bold.

ARRIVED AT SOUTH POLAR RESEARCH STATION. GOOD LUCK: EXPERIENCED THE SEISMIC TREMOR HERE. EXCLUSIVE STORY SENT EARLIER; I WILL STAY ON IT. CONDI-

TION OF STATION REMAINS SATISFACTORY BUT WITH NO DAMAGE REPORT. SITUATION REGARDING STAF-FORD DISAPPEARANCE UNRESOLVED. I PLAN STAY AT POLAR STATION FOR TWO MORE WEEKS TO PARTICI-PATE IN FIELD TRIP AND WORK ON BOTH STORIES. SUG-GEST YOU HOLD FURTHER REPORTING OF STAFFORD INCIDENT UNTIL I CAN GET MORE INFO. I'M WORKING ON A SERIES OF

He started rewriting her message.

I AM CONTINUING WORK AT THE SOUTH POLAR RE-SEARCH STATION. IT WAS GOOD LUCK TO BE HERE DUR-ING SEISMIC TREMOR AND GET EXCLUSIVE STORY, SENT EARLIER.

Carter paused. His mind was whirling. His legs began to have the heavy molasses feeling that he had felt when they left the artifact. Some deeper voice, beyond rational thought, was talking to him. Intuition, he thought, the buried summation of everything you've experienced, piled haphaz-ardly into some deep chambers of the brain, telling you things you didn't know you knew. If you had enough time, you might assemble them in some logical order, and be able to tell someone why you acted as you did. But sometimes you did not have enough time . . . He felt he could not get up from the table if he tried, and he could feel the sweat in his armpits. Sturgis was pacing up and down. Carter looked up at Annie. She was watching him. Her face was somehow both expressionless and pleading.

"Come on," Sturgis said, from the other end of the room. Carter con-tinued printing.

A SERIES OF MINOR TREMORS HAS CONTINUED. NO DAMAGE REPORTED TO POLAR STATION. ON STAFFORD SITUATION, NO FIRM NEWS, BUT WILL DO INTERVIEWS AND TRY TO GET SOMETHING. HOLD FURTHER REPORTS ON STAFFORD UNTIL I COMPLETE SATISFACTORY STORY. I WILL REMAIN HERE FOR TWO MORE WEEKS AND WILL PARTICIPATE IN FIELD TRIP TO GATHER MORE INFO ON SEISMIC NET STORY AND ON THE RESULTS OF THE EX-

TENSIVE POLAR STRATA EXCAVATIONS. WILL BE IN
TOUCH.
   ANNIE

"How's that?" Carter said in an offhand way as Sturgis picked up their
papers.

   Sturgis perused Annie's paper first, then read what Carter had written.
"Cute, Carter. Nice try." He struck out the phrase about the excavations.
"We don't need that little bit about digging. Otherwise, they're perfect.
I congratulate you." He handed the papers to the aide at the head of the
table. "Okay. Run the semantic tests and then send them. Send them."

------------------------------ ● ------------------------------

"Somebody told me once," Carter whispered later in Annie's ear, "when
you're writing a report for a bureaucrat, you put in something so stupid
even the bureaucrat can spot it. He takes it out. Then it becomes *his*
report. I figured it would work for Sturgis. When he took that line out
about excavations, he'd love the rest and feel he had done his bit for
truth, justice, and the American way."

------------------------------ ● ------------------------------

Sturgis was outraged when IPN broke the story late that afternoon. Sturgis
denied everything, but IPN had opened Annie's file of notes. The Newsnet headline ran STAFFORD DISAPPEARANCE ON MARS: NEW CLUES POINT
TO SOUTH POLAR RESEARCH STATION. The story cited rumors from
highly placed sources suggesting Stafford might have been picked up by
a hopper from the Polar Station. Then the calls came in from all four of
the major global nets. None of them knew about the artifact; they did
not know what questions to ask, but they wanted answers.

   Sturgis drafted evasive replies, in a doomed effort to preserve the secret.
The nets replied that their people were already on the way.

29

Carter, Annie, and Philippe were feeling a heady glow of victory as they headed the next morning toward the "tower," a room atop the South Polar Station, surmounted by a clear dome that gave a commanding view of the sky and the bleak polar hills, swept by bone-colored snow.

Sturgis and his crew were bustling around when they came in. Stafford, silent in the background, nodded to them.

When they arrived, Carter recognized the odd mixture of exhilaration and apprehension he felt in these domes: being under the sky without a suit. The pink light filtered everywhere. High clouds scudded overhead. He wondered if such clouds had existed in the initial years, before the pressure went up.

The story was out and the networks' reporter-stringers were on the way. The die had been cast and the world would never be the same. Make that two worlds, he thought—both Mars and Earth. He could not identify a specific moment when he had decided to accept Annie's plan. He felt as if it had been something growing inside him, not a decision he had arrived at consciously. When the opportunity caught him by surprise, he had acted by instinct.

Last night, when Annie curled indivisibly against him, she had whispered, "You will go down in history, you know. You figured out where Stafford was, and you wrote the words that broke this thing wide open. I'll write it that way, because it's true." True? How many heroes, described in the books as clear-eyed visionaries, had really thought anything out? How many had merely reacted to some spur-of-the-moment poll of conflicting inner voices?

"So I rate a page in your book?"

She nudged against him. "I'd say you definitely rate a page in my book."

Carter noted with guilty satisfaction that Sturgis was livid; he looked like a man harassed on all sides. Within an hour of the messages going out, yesterday afternoon, Sturgis had been besieged by questions from the nets and headlines about strange doings at the pole. This morning, the message had come that stringers from IPN and the other nets had chartered a shuttle flight from Phobos direct to the Polar Station. It was due in minutes.

"So," Annie said impudently to Sturgis as they came into the dome. "Your role here is over?"

Sturgis turned on them angrily. "What's she doing here? Out! I want her out. We don't have the press here during an operation. And the artist, too. This is no sideshow. Get them the hell out of here. Jahns, you stay. You're supposed to report on this to Mars Council. Just be damn sure you get it right."

Annie and Philippe were gripped by their elbows and hustled out by Sturgis's men. Philippe called out to them with a grin as he was being herded down the hall. "What do you call security agents at the south polar ice cap? Martian Polar Cops."

Carter winked at Annie as she disappeared. He felt confident; everything was only a matter of time now.

Sturgis scowled. He had turned to an open intercom with the seismic lab. "Sir," a voice was saying from the intercom, "something's happening with the seismic activity, under the machine. It's still getting closer to the surface."

"Any danger?"

"Not that anybody knows. None of the science staff seems to know what to make of it."

"Just make sure they keep monitoring it. Get a record of what's happening. And evacuate the cave at the excavation site, just in case something happens."

"Yes, sir."

Wild-eyed, scanning the sky, Sturgis contacted the pilot of the incoming ship. "This is Douglas Sturgis. I'm an authorized representative of the U.S. Security Agency. A temporary classified operation is under way here. We also have a seismic emergency. Be advised that we refuse you permission to land here."

Carter finally saw it, the ship materializing as a moving point of light in the bright sky.

"That's all very well, sir," the voice came back, "but I'm ballistic. There's only fuel for braking. I'm coming in. Sir."

In the sky above the dome, the ship curved beautifully out of the sky and landed on the pad outside the station, raising thin clouds of dust.

Sturgis was still on the mike. "I know you're ballistic, but you have no permission to enter the station. You will refuel and depart." Sturgis turned to his staff. "How long to refuel? Minimum."

"With both Sabatier pumps . . . three hours. It's a drain on the batteries, but . . ."

Into the mike, he barked, "You have three hours on the ground."

The shuttle sat on the pad, looking self-satisfied, as the dust clouds dissipated.

"Acknowledge. Do you understand?"

The voice returned. "I've got reporters here who say they are coming out to look around. They want access to the station."

"Denied."

"Uh . . . they say you can't do that. They say . . . hold on . . . they're talking about freedom of the press and they say they'll camp outside your door until their air runs out."

"Access denied. We're posting armed guards at the airlocks. You copy?"

"Armed guards?" Carter cried out. Sturgis ignored him.

The voice from the shuttle continued. "Right. Access denied. Um, they say they're coming out anyway."

"Well, stop them."

"Um, there're more of them than there are of me. Sir."

Sturgis turned to one of his omnipresent aides. "Break out the rifles. They aren't coming in here. We'll go out and meet them. Set up a security line outside the airlock."

"Rifles?" Carter confronted Sturgis. "You have rifles on Mars?"

"Out of the way, Jahns."

Carter noticed Stafford slipping out, as if avoiding the confrontation. He wished he had Stafford's moral support. He plowed ahead with the argument.

"There aren't supposed to be weapons here. This falls under my jurisdiction, Sturgis. You can't . . ."

"As long as you didn't know about them, that's how we could be there protecting you."

"What's that supposed to mean?"

"Get this guy out of my way."

"They won't work anyway, outside. Will they?"

"Don't worry. These will. Don't worry, Jahns. The orders are just to arrest anyone who tries to cross the line."

"You can't . . ." Sturgis's aides were moving toward him. "Sturgis! Damn it." But Sturgis had turned to the radio and Carter found himself grasped on both sides, being hustled down the hall. The goons acted like it was part of a normal day's work. Jeez, Carter thought to himself, maybe for these guys it is a normal day's work.

Moments later, Carter found himself deposited by Sturgis's aides in the cafeteria with Annie and Philippe.

"What's happened?" Annie exclaimed.

Carter still felt in a state of shock. "We've got to find Stafford," he told them. "I've already called him on the 'corder," Annie said.

As if on cue, Stafford showed up in the cafeteria a moment later.

Carter was explaining Sturgis's plan. Stafford sat quietly as the others' reactions swirled around them. "They can't do this." "Guns . . . ?" "Sturgis must be crazy." The white mustache and twinkling eyes gave away no secrets. Stafford must have been a hell of a poker player.

Stafford glanced around the cafeteria cautiously. "Let's get out of here," he said, as if answering the questions.

Stafford led them to his lab.

Stafford gestured at the door as they entered the instrument-jammed room. "They wouldn't let me put 'Exobiology' on it. Story of my life. We can talk here." Annie took a position in front of the shelves arranged with rows of drill core samples. She put her 'corder on the table. "For God's sake, Stafford," she said. "What's going on here?"

"First, I want to tell you guys," Stafford continued, "I have to admire the way you handled this. Of course, you turned our little project into a helluva big mess. Still, I was kind of proud of you for that. You know, I told them it was a stupid idea, faking my disappearance. But Sturgis and his people thought anything was worth it to gain a few more weeks. Anyway, you did a good job."

"You heard him, Alwyn!" Carter exclaimed. "Sturgis is refusing entry to a ship of reporters. He has guns."

Philippe: "He must be crazy. How do you know he is stable? He could kill us all."

Stafford: "He won't kill us all. People like him are always stable. Their problem is that they are too stable. They follow whatever set of rules they've gotten locked into. That makes them predictable. I've been doing some thinking about this. I think it's getting out of hand."

Carter: "Out of hand? It's a damn crisis!"

Stafford: "Calm down. There won't be guns used on Mars, not on my watch."

Carter: "How do you know?"

Stafford smiled inscrutably. "It's interesting to watch him in action," Stafford said. "He wants to believe he is saving the world. Crisis isn't a bad word with him, it's his element."

"You give him too much credit," Annie snarled. "As Carter says, he just gets off on wielding power."

"What are you going to do to stop him?" Carter said.

"Me?" Stafford waved his arm around the room, with a guilty shrug. "Do my work. Of course, to do that, I have to get along with him. No choice. He needs me, too. Comes around and asks me if I'm okay. A technocrat's version of sensitivity. You can see he congratulates himself for being so aware of feelings. . . ."

"But what does that have to do . . . ?"

"He's always willing to raise the ante to get what he wants. But he doesn't want violence. He just wants to come out the hero. And he does have a certain legal authority. We just have to prevent him from getting himself in a situation where things get out of control."

"What can we do?"

Stafford frowned at Annie's 'corder. "Annie, turn that damn thing off."

She turned it off.

"Look, you've got to understand, officially I'm not involved. Right? That gives me a certain freedom of action. I haven't said anything about subverting Sturgis's authority. I've said nothing, and you've understood everything. Right? Now, you've got to clear out. There's something I have to do and I've only got a few minutes. . . ."

———————————————————— ● ————————————————————

An hour later Sturgis's men, Stafford, and Elena Trevina were suiting up at the airlock when Annie, Carter, and Philippe joined them.

Outside, the hatch had opened on the shuttle, which still sat quietly on the pad. Figures had come forth, like animals from the arc. They were armed with cameras and holeo units.

Sturgis caught sight of Annie and Philippe, and repeated the scene in the tower. "You're not going out there. See they're confined to the base."

"You don't have any police powers."

"The hell I don't."

"Oh, come on, Sturgis." It was Stafford. "Let them come. They can't hurt anything. Let Annie cover her story for God's sake. You know your people back home won't want to face questions about freedom of the press. You've got her where you want her."

Sturgis shrugged. "Bring Jahns out with us. He represents the Council. Let the rest of them watch from the tower." Suddenly Sturgis paused, looking at the reflections glinting off his white helmet, as if surveying some panorama of history, invisible to anyone else. "You know," he said, as if giving his troops a pep talk, "I finally figured it out. People like our guests here are always talking about the so-called judgment of history. They're concerned with whether 'history' "—he pronounced it sarcastically—"will write down in its golden book that they did the right thing. They think the right thing is to challenge authority. Well, today, the authorities are going to make sure that the laws get upheld."

He put on his helmet.

Outside, in the frozen stillness, the reporters from Phobos had assembled with their equipment, and two groups squared off, the reporters in front of the shuttle and Sturgis's crew in front of the airlock door. The reporters, Carter could see, were not seasoned video crews. They were part-time stringers. Earth-based nets, dedicated to the proposition that the people must be entertained, had decided years ago that nothing exciting happened among scientists in sterile labs on Mars; but they had enlisted part-time stringers on Phobos, just in case. Now the stringers saw their chance for glory. Tripods had sprouted. Cameras were up and running, and dishes pointed toward distant comsats. Whatever happened, the scene was going out live to their nets. Still, Carter noticed, they seemed nervous and amateurish compared to Annie, who outranked them in terms of experience and clout.

Annie. He turned, and could see Annie and Philippe in the glass-domed tower behind them. He could see that Philippe had a large notepad and was sketching the scene.

Sturgis's voice in his helmet: "As I told you already, this station is temporarily closed. You'll have to move back to your shuttle."

"We're not moving."

"Move these people back to their shuttle."

"We're not going back. We want to come inside." They edged forward, cautiously.

"Move these people back. If they keep coming forward, shoot their airpacs. They'll have a few minutes to get into their shuttle."

"There's no authorization from Mars Council . . ." Carter's voice rang in his own ears. He turned to Sturgis's sidekicks. "Do you guys want to be the first to go down in history using guns on Mars? Illegally? Firearms on Mars are illegal."

"Shut up, Jahns. This is a security operation. Certain procedures have been authorized."

Carter saw the rest as if from Annie and Philippe's point of view. The face-off. The reporters, pushing forward more aggressively. A shoving match. Stafford moving forward into the fray. Sturgis's men raising their rifles, uncertainly. Stafford behind Sturgis. Crowding.

"Ohhhhhh." Sturgis's cry blasted through their helmets. "Something's . . . I'm losing air!" Sturgis was spinning around. He began lurching drunkenly for the airlock door.

Sturgis's men's guns drooped, as if in a unified moment of indecision. The reporters pressed after Sturgis. The whole unruly mob moved into the cargo bay airlock, like ants flowing into their hole.

Inside the airlock, events continued in rapid succession. The fight had gone out of Sturgis's party. It was far too late to salvage the secrecy that Sturgis had so carefully maintained. Already, the live coverage of the standoff and the rifle-wielding security force had made the ten-minute journey to Earth and was beginning to appear in minute-long sound bites on the evening news programs, at one longitude after another. Sturgis's and Elena Trevina's 'corders were beeping furiously.

When they ran the holeos later, it was impossible to read individual actions in the melee of shoving figures. Body language was hidden by suits; facial expressions, by helmets. It was like watching plastic dolls collide; you could not read emotional content. No one could determine how Sturgis's airpac had been pierced.

Inside it, they had found a fragment of meteoritic iron.

Annie's priority was clear as soon as the shuttle had touched down. She had to get a message out to her own network about the artifact. The stringers had their links to the outside. The key was to reach the one from IPN before that link could be shut down.

As soon as she and Philippe saw the confused throng surge into the station, she raced from the tower to the airlock with Philippe at her heels.

When they arrived, the airlock entry hall was still in tumult. A shouting match had ensued between Sturgis's men and the reporters about their rights. A camera was smashed. Sturgis was discovering the pea-sized hole in one side of his airpac. He was shouting obscenities as the chaotic argument spilled into the hallways. Cameras were pointed in various directions as the stringers tried to decide between bleating questions at Sturgis's crew and filming the inside of the Polar Station.

Annie knew that none of the stringers had grasped, in the chaos, what was really going on, but that disclosure of the artifact would come spilling out within minutes. Desperately peering over shoulders, she spotted the man with the gold logo of IPN. She went after him.

"I'm Annie Pohaku."

"I recognize you. What the hell is going on here . . . ?"

"There's no time. I know everything. The whole story. You're still patched through to the outside?" He nodded. "Give me your mike. Quick. We've got to get this out before they shut us down."

Moments later she was on the air. "This is Annie Pohaku at the South Polar Research Station on Mars. What is probably the greatest discovery in the history of science was made here just weeks ago. . . ."

The story was out.

As she finished, Sturgis was throwing down his suit in disgust and was heading down the hall with Carter and a dozen others in hot pursuit. "Been nice working with you, Sturgis," she called after him.

She spotted Stafford in the chaos. "And now I see perhaps the leading authority . . ." she was saying, to set up an interview; but he was already brushing by her.

She caught up with Stafford in the crowded hallway. "What was that about?" she said, struggling to keep the camera going in the jostle. "They found a meteorite in his airpac. That couldn't have been natural. The chances . . ."

"Maybe it *was* natural. Did you see the pac? There was only a slight downward trajectory. Might have been secondary debris from an impact on the surface."

"Oh, come on."

He aimed his voice toward the camera mike, "I'd say it was natural, a fluke event at a critical moment. Here on Mars we've learned to expect the unexpected. . . ."

"You can't really believe that. . . ." But he was gone into the crowd.

And before she could chase after him, the alarm sirens went off for a second time.

As the new arrivals glanced around apprehensively, word spread through the packed halls: the seismic tremors were increasing. Triangulation showed that they were now moving very rapidly toward the surface. It was near the pole, under the polar node of the artifact. At this rate, something would be happening on the surface near the other node of the machine, within two hours.

No, new triangulations showed a rapid acceleration in the ascent. Make that one hour.

Sturgis, still in command of the base, had the presence of mind to order all satellite monitoring systems to be focused on the site. "Get the Phobos systems tracking on the other node. If anything does happen . . ."

"You can't see the pole from Phobos."

"Well have them point as close as they can. And the polar orbiters."

"Polar orbiters aren't always over the pole. We'll do what we can."

Carter, Annie, and Philippe had tracked Stafford to the tower, where he was attempting to cobble together a spur-of-the-moment analysis as reports streamed in from the seismic lab.

In the tower, technicians were frantically relaying messages from the seismic researchers, trying to establish what was happening. The seismic disturbances, they said, were rapidly nearing the surface. Outside the tower dome, Carter noticed, the landscape looked as still and sullen as usual. As reconstructed later from the satellite data, a multimegaton explosion shook the south pole fifteen minutes later.

Suddenly one of the voices patched through from Phobos cried, "Oh, my God!"

"What? What?"

"It exploded! A huge area, toward the pole. I can see . . ."

"What? Describe what's happening!"

"There was a flash. A huge cloud is rising. It's several kilometers wide. It's spreading. . . ."

They all stared out the tower window toward the south, scanning the horizon for some sign of the distant violence.

Seconds later, the southern horizon dissolved in a white mist, racing toward them. It was an evil unsettling, like a sandstorm without any wind. They could only stand and stare, as the wall of white fog raced across the landscape enveloping everything. The mist enveloped the glass dome and everyone in the room was knocked to the floor.

The reconstructions showed that the subsurface explosion had blasted a crater above the polar node, and satellite images revealed the shock wave racing across the polar cap surface, kicking up the powdery, dusty snow. The explosion was initiated when the seismic activity reached the thirty-two-kilometer-deep node at the other end of the artifact coil, and the outburst accelerated to the surface in less than a second. It blew thousands of tons of debris outward, creating a crater two kilometers wide, which filled with slumped-in rubble, cemented with ice. Whatever structures of alien tubing might have been in place in the upper kilometer of soil, whatever traces of alien activity, all had been destroyed.

Reports came in, also, that at the excavation site where the nearer node had been uncovered, a transient thermal pulse had heated the exposed tubing to incandescence, killing a man and a woman who were unfortunate enough to have been standing near the tubes in the cave during the final stages of the evacuation.

The eventual analysis from the images obtained at Phobos revealed that something luminous, with a radiant temperature approaching four thousand Kelvins, and a size estimated at not more than a meter, had been ejected from the center of the blast, embedded in a mass of ionized gas. Satellite images showed the brilliant, blurred mass rising several hundred kilometers and disappearing out of the frame in a hundredth of a second. Combined with the framing rates, this gave an indisputable velocity of a tenth the speed of light. By the time this analysis was complete, the object was crossing the asteroid belt, and beyond the range of any possible tracking.

Among all the available data, the mysterious ejected object appeared on only six images, obtained by three satellites in the fraction of a second following the explosion.

———————————————————●———————————————————

Later, Carter and Stafford were sitting in *Arriba*. "What do you mean, 'What was it for?'" Stafford exclaimed, when Carter asked him his theory of the machine's purpose. "I told you, that question may not make any sense. It may be less answerable than it was before."

"Don't you care? Why are you just giving up?"

"Ever hear of cargo cults? When ships and planes delivered equipment on Pacific islands a century ago, the natives thought the stuff was supernatural. Would it have made sense to ask them what it was for? Radios, and stuff like that? Could they have answered?"

"But you can guess. . . ."

"But you can guess," Stafford mimicked with sarcasm. "That reminds me of the way we were educated in high school. They thought it was better to feel good about yourself than to be proven wrong. So we had lab lessons like 'Make up a hypothesis to explain the data,' before they even had told us what was going on in the experiment. Then they'd pat you on the back when you came up with nonsense." He snorted.

"But you have to be able to come up with some hypothesis," Carter said, "just to guide your thinking. . . ."

"All right. You want me to say it was a big machine built by the aliens for some noble purpose and it was lying in wait to be activated by us, and then it launched a little ship back to home base. Is that what you want? Then what?"

"Jeez, Alwyn. Maybe when you fooled with that screw . . . You think you 'activated' it?"

"Naw; nothing happened. It was just a screw. Anyway, the point is, I don't think anything. Speculating is a waste of time. That's what I'm telling you. We don't even have any observations of the projectile after it left Mars, it was going so fast. So there's no way to *test* any hypothesis. You can hypothesize it melted the polar ice for them. Or that it was a game for their Fourth of July. Or that God put the whole thing there to puzzle us. He's laughing at the joke. So far, there's no way to test any of those ideas. Better not to verbalize them at all." He smiled at Carter in a paternal way. "I know it's frustrating."

Philippe came in. Stafford turned to him. "I was just explaining to Carter, here, that the first step on the road to wisdom is to admit that there are things we don't know. We don't know if there's a Jehovah-like god. We just do the best we can. In the same way, we don't know what this thing was built for."

Stafford glanced around the café and made a little, self-conscious laugh. "Of course, maybe we can find out. That's my job. That's enough to keep me happy here for a while. I tell you what. When I learn something, I'll let you know. Tell that to Annie. I'll let her know, too."

As Stafford left, Philippe remarked, "He is the one I cannot figure out."

———————————————————— ● ————————————————————

Sturgis disappeared without a good-bye, a few days later. The discovery of the artifact was now common knowledge on Earth. Whole teams of reporters and additional researchers would arrive within months on the next flight from Earth. Sturgis, as it turned out, had been recalled to Tycho with all the security personnel. Annie announced confidently that it was a political decision to withdraw from an embarrassing situation, before the hard-core reporters arrived from Earth. Pull them back into the shadows, rather than allow a confrontation.

Annie was due back at Mars City, and Stafford had announced he

would go to the excavation site to study the post-explosion state of the
object. On the last night, they sat around a table with Stafford in his
lab. Stafford was in a more expansive mood. Now there was an air of fi-
nality.

"You know," Stafford mused, "I had no idea all the social machinery
that would start operating when we reported the find. Suddenly all these
people like Sturgis came crawling out of the woodwork."

"Cockroaches," Philippe said.

"Turns out they had a small network of sleepers in place here, just like
the networks. Mars was full of people on secret retainers. They never
would have been called in if I hadn't followed my instructions and reported the find. I felt like I was stabbing Lena in the back."

"She didn't know about you filing that report?"

"Not at first. I thought it was routine. We fulfill any requirements from
our own sponsoring agencies . . ." Stafford's voice trailed off uncharacteristically. "If I had it to do over again, well, I don't know. . . . By the way,
the nearer node is still intact. They say the rock is fused for a few centi-
meters where it was in contact with the tubes themselves, but you can
still see the tube surfaces, just as before."

"What did it . . . ?"

"I'll admit now that 'machine' is the right word. Our presence activated
it." He glared at Carter. "But as to its purpose . . ."

"You still say we'll never know?" Philippe asked him.

"If I had to bet, that'd be my bet, now. But I don't just accept it. After
all, I'm on my way out there to see what else I can learn."

"What will you do?"

"Spend the rest of my life trying to get more info about this thing. But
some things are beyond our level of knowledge. You have to be realistic
about your place in the universe."

"What I don't understand," Philippe said, "is how could you accept
your role in this. You let Sturgis remain in control—a little dictator."

Stafford looked carefully at each one of them. He had a quizzical look
on his face. He stared at Carter last. "You think Sturgis was in control?"

They stared dumbly back at him.

"Think about it."

"What do you mean?"

"If I had stood up to Sturgis's plan at any point, I would have been
shipped off to some safe corner. He would have found somebody else for
his team. They would have known less, of course, all modesty aside. But
people like Sturgis don't care about how much we learn. All he wanted

was for scientists to study the machine, and his job was to keep the story from leaking out, and prevent outside interference."

"But you . . ."

"My dream has always been to get some understanding of alien life. Just because I followed my dream doesn't mean I bought into all the constraints Sturgis put on it."

Philippe: "One might say that, morally, you sold out. Unless, of course, you are prepared to confess that you shot that bit of iron into Sturgis's airpac. Which is what I believe. You were standing near him. I ran Annie's film again."

"Why, that's crazy." Stafford was unperturbed. "Anyway, even if I did, do you think I'd be prepared to admit it? The source of that meteorite will go down as one of those unprovable things. If someone took credit for it, some hotshot in the attorney general's office might . . . Well, anyway, you don't go around 'shooting' meteorites into things. Although—and this is off the record, Annie"—he smiled curiously—"I did do some experiments once along those lines to study how fast the rock would erode from small meteorites that got through the old atmosphere.

"And as for morality," Stafford sighed wearily, "why is it that when 'morality' comes into the discussion, people suddenly have such prehistoric attitudes. Like, if I didn't publicly attack Sturgis physically, I was selling out." He sighed. "Selling out means taking no action against him."

"Oh, right, and you were a whirlwind of action against him?"

"I told you, anyone who subverted the agency rules could be in serious trouble legally, or at least in terms of research funding. And what would that accomplish? For instance, if I were in that position, I'd just lose my chance to contribute to this investigation." He looked at Annie, wistfully. "I'm not going to sit in front of Annie, here, and give a listing of everything I, ummm, let's say, set in motion. Still, you might want to think about it. Why did you end up here? Did Sturgis succeed after all? And then there is the pleasure of seeing my friends, um, growing up. But what do I know? I'm just an old duffer doing my research.

"I'm going to have to be getting my stuff ready to go out in the field." Stafford rose. He clasped Philippe by the arm, then Carter. "You guys, well, I'll see you the next time you're down here at the station. And, Annie, the best thing about this was meeting you. You're a remarkable person. If you go on back to Earth, well, I hope you'll return and I'll see you again. Anyway, you're in my memory.

"Oh, you guys might want to look around the lab." As he left, he nodded toward the shelves where Annie had hidden her backup note-books.

"What did he mean by that?" Philippe asked. "Looking around the lab."

"Probably nothing," Annie said.

Annie had long ago removed her notebooks. Certainly this had nothing to do with that, she thought. Hours later, she crept back. In the place where her notebooks had been stashed, she found what Stafford had left. It was a fist-sized tool, homemade. Taped to the side of a little tube was an iron pellet. A powerful spring could fire the pellet with enough force to penetrate an airpac. . . . So there were many things he had set in motion. And not all of them, she decided, could go into what would become her book—at least not until some later edition, years from now, when it could hurt no one.

Epilogue

There comes a point in love that later on the soul seeks to surpass. Happiness wears out in the effort to recapture it. Nothing is more fatal to happiness than the remembrance of happiness.

—André Gide,
The Immoralist, 1902

On Mars, dust takes a long time to settle.

Carter returned to work in his office. He handed in his report, with a colorless retelling of the circumstances of Stafford's disappearance, his work at the pole, and the eventual recovery of his dune buggy. As everyone from Philippe to Sturgis predicted, no one cared about the report; it was eclipsed by the public announcement of the artifact's discovery and the explosive destruction of its southern node. During the following months he made several trips to the Polar Station where he spent long hours in the cavern, staring at the emerging fractal network of cylinders from another world, immeasurably separated from him in time and culture. When he was close to it, he could feel its presence in his bones, yet it taught him little except that he had to teach himself what to think about it. What he thought about everything. Annie had gone home to Earth.

He spent long evenings with Alwyn Stafford and with Philippe Brach talking about the latest news, and evenings alone thinking about Annie. Always the question was with him, whether to try to contact her or let go. Once, he saw her on the holeo news. He found himself wanting to touch her.

Finally, late one night, he knew that the constellations affecting him were beginning to change; it was time to write her, and he sat down in front of his screen.

Dear Annie,
How long ago it all seems. Do you remember?
And do you remember that you told me the best way to talk at a distance was not to talk but to write, so you could take time to say what you meant?

The sad thing I have to tell you is that Stafford died. Maybe you heard through the nets. It was peaceful, a stroke, in the cave at the excavation site. He was doing what he loved. The last time I saw him, he told me these were the happiest days he'd had on Mars. A good way to go. He still didn't know what the machine was for, but he said it was something "humanity could gnaw on."

Sometimes I sit in the observation room of Mars City, looking out across the red desert. It is the season of wind, and I can see the top of Philippe's tree, with the wind shaking the leaves so that they sparkle.

Philippe is building a piece of "human art," he says, to go at the pole, to complement what was put there long ago by the creatures we can't imagine. He says our adventure makes him think about what art is; he calls it the production of things that are pleasing to the senses of our species. He had planned to put it at the south pole—a literal new south pole. But they won't let him because they are afraid it may interfere with the machine, or what's left of the south end of the machine. No evidence has been found of a similar installation at the north pole (that's a mystery); there's lots of research there now, and they may let him put it there.

I think Stafford was right: no one is closer to understanding what the artifact is. Crowds of new people come and go. They've been digging in the crater the explosion made, and analyzing soil samples there, but they find nothing instructive. They've started new housing and lab modules at the Polar Station, to staff a huge colony of scientists. Shouldn't they rename it? "South Polar Research Station" is pretty bland! It should be named for you, since you broke the story. Did you tell me the Hawaiian for "house" is *hale*? They can build with sandstone from the hills and name it Hale Pohaku—House of Stone. There must be a thousand new scientists at the pole already, and they have expanded the excavations. The cavern is twice as big, but still you can see only the mass of tubes. As mysterious as ever. I keep thinking I *feel* different when I'm there, and I think Stafford said something about that, but it's something nobody can measure.

Mars City's population has grown fifty percent and a new module is under way. Horrible crowding since the new construction isn't done, and that doesn't make my life any easier! We are still the main port because Mars City is in the equatorial plane directly under Phobos's orbit. But the population is leveling off, and, amazingly, we are struggling for existence. The budget went up after the discovery, but now they are cutting it again, right in the middle of the construction! Why is there apathy in government circles on Earth? They seem to have lost interest in the artifact. Fewer ships arrive now. What is wrong with the people on Earth? Are they jaded to the point of exhaustion?

I complained to Philippe and he gave me this quote from one of his old books, *Mosquito Coast*, by Paul Theroux:

> *Ain't that always the way? You get on to a really serious subject, like the end of civilization as we know it, and people say, "Aw, forget it—have a drink." It's a funny world.*

It is a funny world. Funnier than I knew.

Philippe is the same as ever. He is working on his polar monument. Happy as a clam.

There! I am giving you direct eyewitness news from Mars— or is it nonnews—for your next story! And will you write back to me? Will you tell me about your life now?

I think of you often. No, it is more than that. I wonder how two people can be drawn together and then lose contact, especially in an age of easy communication, even across astronomical units. Friends come and go, but if we become lovers with someone, I think we become part of them, like brothers and sisters. Brothers and sisters do not lose love or affection just because of distance. Sweet sister, can we maintain some connection? I would like to be a tiny piece of your life. And always, I remember . . .

We were a star that was about to become a supernova. Our love could have lit up the galaxy and the lives of our friends.

He read the letter. It was going too far; he hit DELETE.

Later, after a night in Nix-O, he typed it out again, more or less the same, and posted it to the e-mail code she had given him. He did it fast, completely, all in one grand motion, before he lost his resolve.

He watched his screen for days. Nothing came back.

—————————————————————●—————————————————————

Four E-months later, he got a letter in an envelope with an orchid drawn by hand in one corner. It had cost her ten New Dollars, half a day's wages, to send it. He took it to the observation room in Mars City, so that he could see across the brick-red plains to Earth, which was the evening star. The Phobos shuttle was coming in on a column of pale light as he slit the envelope, carefully.

> *Sweet Man,*
>
> Always we will be part of each other's lives. The adventures we shared were unique.
>
> Now I am living in Hawaii with Tomas. We are both doing writing and tapes, and sometimes we take short assignments from the Japanese networks. I have a good contract to do a book about the discovery. I'm going to ask Philippe if I can use some of his sketches made during the actual events. It would be beautiful. I'm actually nearly done with the second draft, but I can tell that my publisher is interested only because they hope it will reveal some scandal, not because it would be an eyewitness record of a historic event. If somebody found an original diary by a sailor on Columbus's first voyage, the companies here would publish it only if it detailed a murder or gay sex among the crew.
>
> I am writing to you from Liliokalani Garden in Hilo. It is an old Japanese garden on the bay, and I can see the sailboats, and smell the water. I come here to be alone sometimes, when I am in town for shopping. The old Japanese bridge curves over the dark pond, and beyond I can see palms, and plants with huge flowers you wouldn't believe. Beyond that rise the skyscrapers overlooking the bay. I want to tell you that Hawaii is absolutely the best place in the solar system for sleeping. The air cools just a few degrees and wafts through the open windows of your room, and when it rains you can hear the drops splat-splatting on the big leaves of the tropical plants outside your window. And sometimes, when I fall asleep at night, I remember everything with you and Mars.

I just got your message yesterday. When I said write, I meant, write by hand. Then there is something personal. Something that touched your body as well as your mind.

I am happy with my life just now. I am happy to be back home, among the plants and the smells and the water. I had a baby boy. Did you know? I suppose there was no way for you to learn. Of course, he is Tomas's. He is named Tomas, Jr. But his full name is Tomas Carter. You know why. Tomas doesn't know why. I said I liked the name.

I want to give you a gift. Probably it is something I shouldn't say. The gift is that you are the one in my fantasies. You understand that there was not enough between us for me to give up my life here. There was an incredible intensity. It frightened me. It was different from the more comfortable feelings I have with Tomas. It had more to do with me than with you. I was afraid of what we had, what you did to me. It's a feeling I don't have with Tomas, but I'm not sure I (or anyone?) could build a life around it. Remember, you can love many people but you can only share your life with one at a time.

Enough of that. Understand that my life is pleasant and I am moving into the future.

Life on Earth is strange, especially after Mars. I don't know if you can sense what is happening here. You've been on Mars, how long? Four years? After Mars, where you are constantly thinking about the life you are building, and the basic elements for survival, everything seems superficial on Earth. There is such complacency here, people's lives are concerned with frivolity. On Mars, we were living on the edge. On the frontier. It was us talking directly to God and the Universe. You knew that if you went outside you could die. Still, I'm glad to be in Hawaii, which is still (at least in part) a quiet backwater, except for the Japanese and Russian resorts.

You asked about the funding cuts and loss of interest in Mars. There is an ironic twist to "our" story. The discovery of the artifact will go down as the greatest discovery in the history of human life, I'm firmly convinced. I know you believe that, too. And yet, you are right, no one is interested anymore!

There was an initial flurry of headlines. Front page headlines in the New York Timesnet, the London Timesnet, and Novii

Era! My byline. (I know, I checked out the tapes in the library.) How's that for a story! Coverage for the first weeks, as long as it was a mystery and a political thriller. But it was just another orgasm of the media. How long can you keep the public titillated with pictures of a tube, once they've seen it; especially if it just lies there and doesn't do anything?

After Sturgis was called home, there was no freedom-of-the-press story or suppression-of-science story. Washington was very clever, to nip that story in the bud.

Oh, by the way, Sturgis was on the net the other day. He had done some assignment at Tycho, and just came back from the moon. There was a ceremony in the gardens of the Old White House, just above the president's offices, honoring him for his "part in the historic Martian discovery," and reassigning him as head of New White House Security. Stafford was right. People like Sturgis never go away.

Anyway, the media have been left with the story of an ancient, giant, and dead machine on Mars. After a few weeks it became yesterday's news. They aren't interested in secrets that take years to pry loose by careful research. I know. If I try to do a news story or a tape on it today—as opposed to my "I was there" book—my editors tell me to forget it. Did you know that everybody lost interest in the moon for thirty years after the first landings? It must be like that.

There is another aspect, which may explain it. Here's my pop-sociology theory: For a hundred years, the mythic idea of alien civilizations was built up so strongly in people's minds that from the point of view of The Great Earth Public, the aliens already existed. There was the whole trend line from Percival Lowell through science fiction to the charting of planets around other stars, and we had seen all the old movies from Spielberg to Kovaleva, and UFOs are a fixture of the media for most of a century even though no one ever brings one back . . . Subliminally, everyone on Earth was so convinced of rampant alien civilizations that the actual proof was an anticlimax. Especially when the proof turned out to look like some Japanese scrap metal. Now if it had been a walking, talking robot, preferably with tits . . .

I realize now that the main emotional driver for me was not

just to release the information a few days earlier than would have happened otherwise. The main thing was to shine a light on people like Sturgis, who hide behind their shell of dogma and assume the right to manipulate what happens to everybody else, because they are sure they know best. I was never sure that you understood that.

You sent me a quote. I have a quote back for you that explains it. I've been doing a lot of reading and I'm taking a philosophy course here at UH-Hilo. I needed this chance to read because it helps my own writing. My quote's from an obscure book by Goethe, a romantic novel from 1774:

> *Those people [are not] unhappy who, giving pompous names to their shabby occupations or even to their passions, pretend that these are gigantic achievements for the happiness and welfare of mankind.*

1774! Can you imagine? It has Sturgis written all over it. Maybe we all have to apply it to ourselves. Your grand mission on Mars? For me, I am happy with my Tomas and my Carter. And I've given up on the crazy world outside.

Say hello to Philippe. I was sorry when I heard about Alwyn's death through the nets, here. I was glad to get more details from you. I know it must hurt you; you were his best friend. You are a bit of a stoic, you know. Do you let yourself feel the pain? Don't hide from it. It is a natural and good thing.

I've thought a lot about Alwyn and things he said. I'm not sure how to say this, but it seems to me he was controlling the unfolding of everything much more than we realized. Even you. Do you remember, when he disappeared, his notes specified that you would be the person who would be able to find him. And you didn't understand why he said that. But he had carefully planted a *lot* of ideas in your head! I think he had somehow chosen you and was giving you a sort of Zen test. He would agree to Sturgis's scheme, and research the artifact, but would rely on you—if you passed the test—to defeat Sturgis. Does that make sense?

Everybody's interested in the new sensies. They've got all this fantasy universe you can plug into. You see kids walking around in a daze. Trying to get anybody interested in the real environment, like Mars, is impossible. I know, I've talked to IPN about coming back to do a Mars Today special. Neg-a-tor-ee. But someday it may happen. If I came back, what would I do about you?

All our adventures with the Machine—that was only one reason why being with you was special. Together, we touched the cold, hard, crisp, red, dusty wonder of the real universe. You can't feel that on Earth anymore. Thoreau (another book I read in my course) said, "To be awake is to be alive. I have never yet met a man who is quite awake." On Mars we were awake together. And I hope I can transmit some of what we experienced together to Tomas Carter, the way your mother transmitted to you some kind of richness that I sensed in you. It wasn't just the adventure of chasing down that story, but the feeling of looking God in the face. I look at Tomas Carter in his crib and he looks ready to receive that wisdom. Maybe that's how you looked to Alwyn.

I fear that in another fifteen years Tomas Carter won't have that look anymore . . . He'll be like everyone else. Carter, what happens to us when we grow up?

Do you realize that scientific and political revolutions may look important in history books, but more important than revolutions is love between individuals? All the kinds of love? Did you ever read Pasternak? Maybe your ancestors and my ancestors understood this better than most Americans.

Wait. Let me say it better. Love between unilluminated people, people with ignorant ideas of the universe, can seem ugly, almost obscene, like a painting that glorifies war. But after we have learned something about the universe, after we have comprehended our little place in it, after we have learned in our hearts that we humans are only one of a million intelligent species that have come and gone, then love becomes something brave and noble. That is what I have with you.

Carter kept the letter on the little desk in his room, always intending to answer it. But he knew it represented the kind of friendship that would feed on communication not daily or weekly, but at some slower rate.

And far below the ageless polar snows of the south pole of Mars, the alien coil with the nodes at each end lay buried, caked with dust and ice. Its chambers (chambers was a better word than the researchers' original term, "tubes")—its chambers were filled with 3.2 billion years of silence. Mighty in the simplicity of its lost engineering, it was not waiting, or remembering, or dreaming; it was only a castoff, left behind. Forgotten, in fact. Its builders were long gone, converted back into ionic star stuff shedding photons into the permanent darkness. The release of its relativistic entity, triggered by human approach, was no more important, in a sense, than the last tick that a long lost watch might make, when its discoverer picks it up and turns it over.

The machine had more meaning than a footprint petrified in mud or frozen in lava, because it was purposefully designed. Yet it had less meaning, in its way, than the Rosetta Stone. It had the same meaning as an arrowhead in an Illinois cornfield, a stone axe lost in a French cave, a fragment of a painted pot, staring into the sun every day from a cobbly desert in Iraq or Peru or China or Arizona.

It was a leftover, an accident, something once crafted, for the purposes of its builders. Something They needed when They came to Mars. So it was something used and appreciated, something left behind after They had passed by the solar system, stopping briefly on a brown but clement aqueous planet, on Their way from somewhere to somewhere, doing Their own business as creatures do, fighting Their fights, loving Their loves as Their chemistry dictated, wishing Their wishes, feeding on Their food, arguing Their arguments, playing Their play, dying Their deaths, smiling Their smiles, and laughing Their laughs, before passing on into distance and time, and knowingly or unknowingly leaving their descendants in one way or another on one planet or another, to become part of the time-lacing network of fertile molecules, and all their bizarre and myriad organic constructions that can be called Life in the Universe.

Washington, D.C., Moscow,
Paris, Tucson, Punalu'u
1988–1996

About the Author

William K. Hartmann is known internationally as a scientist, writer, and painter. His scientific research involves the origin and evolution of planets and planetary surfaces, and the small bodies of the solar system. He is the lead author of what has become the most widely accepted theory of the origin of the moon. Asteroid 3341 is named after him in recognition of his planetary research.

Hartmann has been involved in several space missions. He was a Co-Investigator on the NASA *Mariner 9* mission, which was first to map Mars in detail with an orbiting spacecraft, and on NASA's Mars Observer mission. He is currently a Participating Scientist in the U.S. *Mars Global Surveyor* mission.

In 1981, he was nominated for the Hugo Award for his collaboration with Ron Miller, *The Grand Tour*.

Hartmann holds a Ph.D. in Astronomy and an M.S. in Geology from the University of Arizona, and a B.S. in Physics from Pennsylvania State University. He lives in Tucson, Arizona.